Tawnie K. Bailey

She Smiles

ISBN: 1-4810-7540-3
ISBN-13: 9781481075404

To my knights of long ago (Duane, Ron, Eric, and Chad)
for giving my world so much color.
To my mom for all of her selfless love.
And to Jeff, for my happily ever after.

Chapter 1—Angelina

September 1, 1991

Dear Charlie,

I was told in the ninth grade that I'd be a disappointment for a blind date as I had a beautiful name and was, at best, cute, but not beautiful. And if my date heard he was going out with an "Angelina" he'd have unfulfilled expectations when he saw me. So, I apologize now.

Yep, that is me. I am Angelina. People always say I have a beautiful name as if I had anything to do with it. My parents picked out horrible names and my aunt encouraged them to choose Angelina, after some romance novel super-girl. Think of the pressure. I was a whopping 4 pound, 11 ounce baby girl my mom and dad tried VERY hard to not create. My mom took the super-mondo doses of birth control pills doctors doled out in the 1970s and still I arrived. My dad wanted to name me Hazel or Irene. Mom's choice was Teara, as in crying tears-a. So, I got lucky with Angelina.

I have brown hair and eyes but nothing exotic or amazing (I do wear violet contacts, which are rather striking, but are nonetheless false). I've been called beautiful by more than one gentleman, and my brothers' friends have paid them money (or rather traded old porn) to find out my bra size. I am 5' 8", so my ability to eat large quantities of chocolate is masked by long legs.

Ah, but all blind dates are described based on personality, as in "she has a great personality." Well, I wouldn't go that far. In addition to working two jobs, I'm very active in school clubs, had a short stint in the band, and I've been known to play basketball in high heels and a strapless dress.

My classmates would probably say I'm the pretty girl who talks to everyone, but they really don't have a clue. My brother Aaron tells me I inherited my grandmother's nose (and a lard ass). God help me if that's true. I stare at my profile a fair amount, HOPING a cartilaginous monstrosity isn't growing while I sleep. I've been picked for the "less than wholesome" (aka slutty) roles in our high school plays, so I don't think anyone else has caught on that my granny's nose is coming, but I do wonder. And as for the "ass thing," it's hugged by my size 4 jeans, so no Mix A Lot songs for me.

Tawnie K. Bailey

I'm a senior in high school with a 3.82 GPA and have worked at a veterinary clinic since I was 12. Last year I decided to try a job where I didn't have to use my brain so much, something like flipping hamburgers or scooping ice cream. I ended up at the law offices of Mark Sullivan, where despite my best efforts, another "family" was born. At times I consider becoming both a veterinarian and an attorney, but building a career from others' tragedy seems dismal.

Have I scared you off yet? Bianca described you as tall, attractive and intelligent. I hope you are kind as well. My oldest brother had an invisible friend when he was little that made him hit his head against the wall. Is that what you will be to me?

Very Truly Yours,
Angelina

The clock looms next to my bed, ticking away my hope for a normal night.

Yoyo stands up, his pom-pom tail erect. I hear something slam up against the wall in the hallway, rattling my door, then slide down the wall outside my room. The vice around my chest tightens. Please, oh please, just go to bed.

"Angie, come out here!" he barks.

Oh crap.

"What Dad?" I ask, approaching the hallway. He's leaning against the wall, his trademark Jack Nicholson widow's peak absent as black hairs stray from their slicked back position.

"Do you know why I'm drunk?" he sneers, supporting my belief that Grandma had an affair with Archie Bunker.

He belches before I can answer. "It's because I'm proud of you." He staggers closer to me, his chest inches from my face. "You go to your little jobs and get good grades. You're not like your God damned older brothers. They're losers." He's hovering over me, hanging onto the wall, his sour breath branding my forehead. As one eye droops, his swaying falters and vomit spews out of his mouth down the wall and onto the carpet just inches from my feet, barely missing me. He tries to wipe it off with his hand then tumbles into his room a few feet away.

2

I look down, realizing my hand's been splattered. I walk into the bathroom, my whole body trembling, unable to control the tears. Who in the hell gets puked on by their Dad? I scrub my hand, creating marks with my nails, the scalding water intensifying the redness.

Ok, buck up. I handle dog diarrhea and vomit all the time at the clinic; I can do this. I stare into the mirror, my eyes resting on my latest volcanic creation. God! What did I do to myself? I lean closer to the mirror, my finger retracing its path of destruction on my forehead to the little bright red and bloodied bump. I splash my face with cool water and return to my bedroom. I close the door that doesn't really close and try to concentrate on my English assignment while my heart and eye spasms beat a bad duet.

My pulsing eye stares at the pink walls adorned with a few posters of studly men, the eye twitches making the boys do a little dance for me. The walls used to be covered in 65 Dog Fancy and Cat Fancy posters but a few years ago I replaced the wall pets, worried that my image as a teenage girl wouldn't survive if anyone saw the décor. Although they're still riddled with the tack marks, nobody's seen my grown up walls.

I sit back on my bed in my too-pink room when the phone rings.

"Did your dad come home stinko?" Mom asks, the traffic roaring in the background.

"What do you think?" I don't mean to be sarcastic, but I can't help it.

"Are the boys home?"

"Just me. Dad puked on the wall and the floor," I say, my voice deadpan.

She sighs. "Did he clean it up?"

"Does he ever?"

"Will you please clean it up?" I can hear the disappointment in her voice.

Are you kidding me? "He did it, he can clean it." I will not turn into his little wifey!

"He won't remember, will blame it on your dog, and it'll stain the carpet," Mom pleas.

"My dog weighs six pounds and produces pop-can sized messes. Dad made a brown pond in the hallway."

"Would you set a towel on it and I'll take care of it when I come home?" she asks.

"Fine." Yoyo *has* done his share of damage to our house.

I hang up the phone and walk toward the kitchen, stepping over Aaron's carburetor and Todd's baseball mitt in the living room. I reach under the sink behind the overflowing garbage can and grab some paper towels and Pine-sol. I don't know if this is an appropriate choice, but it's all we have. Maybe someone should advertise for vomit removal on their cleaning products. I can picture it now, Annette Funicello holding up a bottle, smiling while kids and hubbies puke, "Great wives know Vomit Begone is the best throw up remover out there."

Returning to the hall, I see my white poodle's mustache is splattered with brown as his tongue laps at the puddle. "Yoyo, stop it! Dummie." I move him back into my room and kneel down. The acidic smell burns my throat, making me gag. The fluids soak through the towels and a few of the chunks drop back onto the floor when I try to scoop it up. I can't believe I'm doing this.

After washing my hands I walk back into my room, my chest tight and my mind winning its own Kentucky Derby. I straighten out my underwear drawer, pick up some stray papers off the carpet and feel the tightness ebb away. I still feel disoriented and "off" and notice the closet door ajar. I start to close the door, but what if it's messy in there? I need to study, but I should clean up the carpet better. Mom shouldn't have to clean up all of the time. I open the closet to rearrange my clothes: black shirts next to other black shirts, then dark colors, jeans next to jeans. The hippo rolls off my chest and I take a deep breath.

I wonder what this Charlie guy would say if I wrote to him about this. I can't believe I sent that letter. I wrote it after one of those bizarre moments when I wanted to let the crows fly, release them to the wind and see what would happen. But now it's out there and I'm probably going to get stood up on a blind date. How pathetic.

Ok, Angelina. You need to study. They don't let dummies into vet school.

I stare at the book, but my brain doesn't register the words. Screw it. I deserve a break. I grab Yoyo, his white curls caressing my hand. We head outside, where the wind blows through my clothes as our journey takes us up the hill. Yoyo likes to take his time smelling before he lifts his rear leg on the neighbor's roses. My arms are wrapped around each other; I jump and run in place, trying to ward off icicles. When Yoyo finishes watering the flowers, we walk up the hill. It's moments like this that make me grateful my parents fell in love in Seattle, not Alaska. My nerves are crying out for a Coca-Cola Slurpee and a Kit Kat, but I don't want to give Aaron any more ammunition; next thing you know, my brother will say I have thunder thighs and Jell-O hips.

"Angie, I'm sorry you had to deal with your dad. Have you eaten dinner?" Mom asks, working on the hallway carpet as I walk through the door.

"I ate some cottage cheese earlier." I say, returning Yoyo's leash to the hook next to the door.

"Let's order pizza."

This is a *huge* treat.

She stands up, wiping her forehead with her arm. "I'm sorry I asked you to clean this. I shouldn't have." Mom's brown and yellow Metro uniform is a good carpet-scrubbing disguise.

"He shouldn't have," I say, leaning against the wall.

"Let me clean up a bit and then I'll phone in the order. Where are your brothers?" she asks, walking to the bathroom to wash her hands.

"I haven't seen Aaron or Todd since I got home from the clinic."

"Any cool cases?" She yells over the sound of running water.

"Just a lot of ear infections, a few vaccines, and an old kitty for blood work." Mom returns to the hall, arching her back and moving her shoulders.

"Does your back hurt again?" I ask.

"Oh, a little. I'm just tired."

I walk into the kitchen and move papers, wrappers, pieces of pencils, and matches looking for something that resembles a coupon. I find some, but they're expired. Full price pizza it is.

I turn around, nearly bumping into Mom.

Tawnie K. Bailey

"You've been picking your face again," she says examining my destruction. "You have a beautiful face. I don't know why you always do this to yourself. I bought you thimbles, use them."

My eyes roll. Do you *have to* point out my flaws? Don't you think I'd stop if I could?

I go back to my room and call Morgan, the only person who's seen my face covered in OXY aside from my family.

"Have you finished physics, yet?" I ask, my fingertips trying to smooth a minute bump near my watch. "I wish I could get into this junk. It's not like I'm going to need this as a vet."

"Maybe it's to weed out the students who want a life," she says. "When's your next blind date?"

"This weekend. He's taking a ferry over from Bremerton."

"Did you tell him where to send the roses and mixed tapes?"

"Don't make fun of me. That weird Honda-dude freaked me out."

"Then don't go," Morgan says.

"My 'pool of potentials' is too small."

"And Friday night?"

"My usual." I sigh.

"Are you whining because I'm going out with Michael? You could come with," Morgan offers even though she knows I'd rather pluck out my eyeballs than be around her boyfriend.

"I'm whining because I have nowhere to go. If I had a boyfriend, maybe it'd be different," I say.

"You've had a lot of boyfriends, Ange."

"A lot of first dates. Not so many boyfriends, and I never stay late. You'd think I have cooties or something."

Morgan giggles. "I'm not going to feel sorry for you. You could go out if you wanted to."

"Not with *whom* I want." Who knew I'd want him so much?

"Beggars."

I've never dated anyone who made the first move and I'm not outgoing in that department. I haven't had any boy even try to 'feel-me-up.' Ever. Maybe all boys know my chest size is pathetic? All my dates have been gentlemen, even the ones with reputations of being 'players.'

6

I want to be in love before I add sex to the mix—I don't have to be married, look where it got my mom. But I need to love him. And, I don't mean what some of my classmates do, where they date some guy for a minute and are saying those three little words. At the end of the day, I don't want to be a locker room joke. Besides, what if I'm not any good at it?

Morgan's call-waiting clicks just as our doorbell rings out, announcing the arrival of my pizza treat.

I grab one carb-filled slice and head back to my room to finish homework and watch TV. If I had a port-a-potty in my closet, a locking door (okay, even one that closed) and a vending machine, I'd never see my family again. I'd crawl through the window and see the world without the garbage. I'd have to buy another backpack to sneak Yoyo into, but that's easy enough. I do have two jobs.

I turn on Love Connection, where I have "two minutes and two seconds" of commercials for sit ups. I used to run or do jumping jacks, but Mom kept opening my door and asking if I was okay. When she turned on the light, I was running wearing a nightgown and sweat. Then she said her therapist wanted to see me. Give me a break, I'm not anorexic. And, I'm not going to regress into a calorie obsession; a few years ago Morgan and I tried to limit our calorie intake to less than 500 calories each day, but we got crabby and tired and decided "skinny" wasn't worth torturing ourselves.

I'm trying to counteract my addiction to chocolate, that's all. Sit ups are quieter than running and I figure that if I can do 50 sit ups during every break it'll add up and maybe I won't be able to pinch an inch when I bend. Sometimes I get stuck on the four-thing and do a lot more than 50, but my goal is 50. The first few sets aren't too bad, but my stomach burns before I find out if the two contestants go on another date together. Sometimes I place Yoyo on my stomach and kiss his head during crunches. He doesn't enjoy it much, but it keeps him from licking the sweat off my face. He's sleeping on my chest right now, looking like a little boat rising and falling with the ocean swells. I rub his silky curls between my fingers, loving the contact. I turn on my fan

Tawnie K. Bailey

and lie back, letting it wash out some of the noises I'd rather not hear. I'm sure therapists everywhere would like a crack at me, but they'll just have to wait their turn.

Chapter 2–Aaron

September, 1991

My mouth tastes like barf. I puked down the outside of my bedroom window last night. I hope Mom doesn't see it, but it wouldn't be the first time. My head feels like it got smashed by a bowling ball. I should just go back to sleep. My eyes are heavy and they hurt, too. Man, I had a bad ass time last night. The light is too bright. It hurts my whole body to smile, so I won't. I've gotta piss. And I'm thirsty.

I fall back asleep, I think. Sometimes I just float through the moment into the sleep. But that depends on what drug I've taken. I like alcohol, my friend since junior high. I prefer Old English 800. I buy it from the Arab dude who works at the Lincoln Park Deli. He never cards me, so I don't even have a fake ID. I once bought twenty 40 ouncers, and his comment was "Oh, you goin' to a big party?" Yeah, me and me and me, all having a great big party.

Yeah, alcohol is great. I get a rush from it at first. As long as I don't get too wasted, then it's a downer. But crack. It is wicked. And it's cheap. And, I can make it and sell it and make thousands of dollars. I know I'm smiling because the vise on my head tightens down. I don't have to piss anymore. I wonder if I peed on myself. I don't remember. Maybe it made me warm for a while. I don't have any covers on me. Maybe I'm cold. I don't really know. My body and my head are in a disconnect. It would be great if it stayed like that forever.

My body hurts all the time. They don't tell you about that when they say you have diabetes. Doctors, I mean. They don't tell you how your toes hurt before you lose sensation. Or your dick—that it hurts and aches for a while, then you don't feel it very much. So, you have to do some deep rubbing to get off.

The worst is the stomach cramps. When I was diagnosed, I gave myself insulin injections just so they'd let me leave the hospital. After my hospital release, I didn't give myself insulin for at least three months. I hate needles. You can get Hepatitis and HIV and shit from needles.

Mom'll do it sometimes. She'll ask if I'm monitoring my glucose, and I lie. I don't know how high my glucose got during those months, but my stomach started killing me. I shit motor oil all week long and didn't have any control over it. Angelina would say something all prissy like "melena," the word for shitting black blood, but that's her. Mom just poked me with the glucose meter one day when I couldn't move. She got all panicky and ran upstairs to the fridge and got the insulin and gave me an injection. She took me to the hospital and forced me to take the insulin again. The stomach pain made me start giving myself insulin injections, though, and I am feeling better. Not great, but I know I drink and 'use' too much to feel great.

Shit. I've done far worse than last night. I fall back into my cloud. I ride it.

***

If you added every moment in class, I've attended maybe nine hours of high school. I showed up at school only if I was drunk or high on acid and couldn't deal with Mom nagging at me. I'd walk to school and go to class and rest my head down and sleep. The doctors said I had narcolepsy. Yeah, whatever.

Drug dealers swarm to Seattle High like flies to garbage. All kinds of people brought me "stuff" there. Mostly I liked the alcohol, and for a little while, pot, then speed and acid. Acid is pretty sweet. A dollar bill, cut in half is the size of 100 hits of the magic. You drop the little paper on your tongue and you are transformed to a world of heightened sensations. Everything is brighter and louder and just fuckin' crazy. After school I'd go home and sleep until just before Mom came home and I'd head up to the reservoir and drink. Jimmie, Frankie, and I'd have bonfires and drink Old English. Having a gas station across the street from the reservoir entrance is like having an open fridge for a foodie. The dumbfucks at the gas station placed the cash register away from the door, and the building is shaped like an "L," so we'd tuck the booze in our coats and walk on out.

Just before morning I'd head on home, eat some food and crash. Mom thinks it's my diabetes and narcolepsy. I used to try to hide the smell of alcohol since she can smell it from a hundred feet away, but hiding it takes too much work. She worries we'll end up like dad. Funny thing is, ketones smell like alcohol. Instead of getting mad at me, she gets worried thinking my diabetes is out of control. Maybe it is.

I wanted to be president. Mom said I could be anything. I know I'm smart enough for it. Too much of a smart ass, but smart enough for sure. Mom wanted me to go to college, but I'm 18 now and have less high school credits than a ninth grader. Mom wants me to at least get my GED. She keeps nagging me and driving me to South Seattle Community College for these stupid GED classes. Mom says "education opens doors." I say why open a door when you can crawl through a window?

I've gotta piss. I lift up my head. The whole room spins and my head rings. Benji, my dog, lifts his head. I walk into the bathroom, unzip my pants and pee. That is the best feeling in the world. Right up there with sex.

I was 12 years old when I first had sex with a hot little 15 year old blonde stuck in the foster care system. I met her right after the first time I got drunk. Fuck, I gotta stop smiling cuz my head is still screaming.

I crawl back into bed. Benji moves his head again. He's a good dog. I got him in the third grade; he's a black and tan terrier cross with long hair. He doesn't mind my drug-sniffing ferret and keeps my bed warm when I'm out. Benji's blind now and drinks and pisses as much as I do and he sleeps all day. Angie's boss tested him for diabetes, he's negative. But Benji isn't doing very well. He has no hair and the skin on his ass is black from chewing at it all the time. He understands me. I wish someone else did.

Chapter 3–Angelina

September, 1991

I cross the street, jogging toward the blue and white building which houses my dreams. Walking through the door of the vet clinic, I emerge from my chrysalis, no longer a measly caterpillar. The clinic's mixture of bleach and Parvocide is like a jock wearing Obsession. I greet Steven, veterinary assistant and my partner in crime. A former gigolo and flirt extraordinaire, he dropped his dirty boy ways when his brother died during Steven's first year in college. He's no longer an item on the Health Department's "uh-oh" list and is now a dedicated family man.

"You haven't bought your chariot yet?" he asks while typing a chart label.

"Unless you can turn a green pumpkin into a coach, it's still the good ole Metro for me," I say, pulling my scrub top over my head.

"You wanna a ride home?" he asks.

"Yes, please." I notice some of my favorite clients in the lobby. "Do you mind if I take the Gentrys in?"

"No, be my guest, but Dr. Mike is in a mood." My eyebrows rise.

Dr. Mike's French accent is harder to understand than Elmer Fudd on novocaine. He's normally a patient soul, but when he's had to re-peat "fecal" more than twice, his Napoleonic side emerges and steam rises out of his nostrils. When he's in a mood, I'd rather remain in my cocoon while the clinic's firebombed by a series of French expletives.

"Mr. and Mrs. Gentry, are you saving all of Seattle's sick kittens again?" I ask, walking past the floor scale towards the lobby.

"We found a kitten dumped in the vacant lot near our house. She's been whispering that she wants to come and live with you," says Mr. Gentry, a portly gentleman with gray hair and smile lines.

I laugh. "I'm off to college next fall and can't have both a kitten and my Yoyo sick from heartache while I'm gone." The Gentrys follow me towards the exam room.

Tawnie K. Bailey

"Are you going to come back and work here once you're a doctor?"

"If I'm admitted into the WSU's Honor's Pre-vet program, I could get into vet school after just two years of undergrad, but then I'll have another four years of vet school itself. Otherwise, it'll be eight years of college before I have to worry about where I'm practicing. "

"We'll just have to stop collecting cats after you leave," Mrs. Gentry adds, patting my hand.

"How long have you had this one?"

"We caught her two nights ago. She couldn't resist the canned kitten food." He pushes the spring-loaded latch of the once cream carrier and pulls out a short haired tortoiseshell kitten. I weigh the tortie and insert the mercury stick into her rectum. She rubs against my hand after I remove the thermometer. Not the usual 'tortie-tude.'

"If she's negative for leukemia, do you want her vaccinated?"

"We'd just like the usual combo vaccine. Unless she goes with you, she won't be going outside."

I smile. "Let me borrow her, then I'll have Dr. Mike come in and take a peak." I pick up the kitten and take her to the back and draw blood.

"We'll have the results in 15 minutes or so," I say as I run my hands against her fur and see a smattering of pepper-like debris all over—flea poop. I *hate* fleas. I know someday I'm going to have one crawling across my face while I'm talking to a client, probably a hot guy client.

"We have good news," Dr. Mike says walking into the exam room. "Your latest addition is clean and clear for leukemia. Let's look her over and see if she's healthy enough for shots." Dr. Mike places the stethoscope on the kitten's chest while I hold her. In addition to the fleas, Dr. Mike also finds earmites. Gentry kittens often enter their household with green eye and nose discharge, so this little girl is healthier than most of their clan.

I look up and see that ugly mole on Dr. Mike's neck, the long hairs waving at me. Dr. Mike pours mineral oil into the kitten's ears and massages the base of her ear. The kitten yowls and tries to get away while he wipes dark crumbly debris from her ears. She growls and shakes her

14

head, freeing black mineral-oil-laden debris to fly across the table and hit the wall. The kitten's ears lie flat against her head; I pull up the vaccines and hold on while Dr. Mike injects this little kitten-turned-tigress. "She needs to return in three to four weeks for boosters on her vaccines," Dr. Mike says as the Gentrys leave the room.

Dr. Mike is scribbling in the kitty's chart. Like his accent, his writing requires some interpretation.

"Pretty gross, huh?" He asks as I'm scratching at my head and arms, trying to eliminate the invisible creepy-crawlies.

"Fleas makes me itchy."

Dr. Mike lowers his eyelids and says in a weird voice, "Would you like me to give you a bath?"

"What?"

He repeats the question, Elvis eyes and all, his index finger tracing little circles on my wrist, scalding it. A tidal wave crashes into me, throwing me off balance.

"No, I feel itchy when animals have that many fleas, poor babies," I say and escape to the reception area. Maybe Dr. Mike mixed up his English again and meant to ask if I wanted to go home and take a shower? I've been here since junior high, when my legs were gangly and my chest flatter; I'm just being stupid to think he meant anything else.

My face is still sizzling and my heart thundering as I see Steven checking in another patient. "Angie, would you bring the next patient in?"

"I'll grab the next one," I say, not wanting to see Dr. Mike.

The rest of the afternoon is a blur and is filled with answering phones, checking patients out, preparing vaccinations, and cleaning the clinic. We all participate in every aspect of cleaning, allowing us to leave the clinic at a more reasonable time.

Thankful Steven offered to drive me home, I grab my purse and backpack. Steven and I say goodbye to Dr. Mike who's closing out the till.

Steven unlocks my side before climbing in and starting his truck. "I have to tell you a funny story."

Did he hear Dr. Mike's comments? He reverses the truck and waits for a VW Beetle to go by before pulling into the street.

Tawnie K. Bailey

"Carrie called me at work yesterday. Furious." I watch his brown eyes in the rear view mirror before he signals to turn.

"About what?" Carrie is Steven's wife.

"She found your panties in the laundry."

Chapter 4–Angelina

September, 1991

My cheeks are on fire; everything I know has been sucked up and blasted into the universe like a chainsaw on a carcass, leaving little splatters of me sticking to the dashboard. Does Carrie know I had a crush on Steven?

"When I got home, she showed me your 200 pound granny underwear and I started laughing. There's no way you'd fit them. I also told her a 16-year-old would never wear brown polyester control-tops."

Carrie thought they were mine? "Where'd they come from?"

"Dad walked through the door with his new girlfriend who's shaped like a refrigerator. She blushed and said they were hers. Dad's doing his laundry at our place again." Steven's Dad lives next door, but his house is in the process of a remodel.

"Maybe you shouldn't drive me home." Carrie is worried about something and I don't want her to feel insecure because of *me*.

"My stomach hurt from laughing after I saw how huge they were. I just couldn't picture you wearing anything like that."

"I don't want you picturing me wearing any underwear!" Steven lifts his eyebrows and I hit his arm. "You know what I mean!"

Steven laughs. "I'm sorry. I couldn't help it." He's still smiling when I leave.

I walk into the warm house and hear Clint Eastwood booming from the TV. Aaron's lying on top of the heater with a blanket around him, creating a tent of hot air.

Yoyo runs to me and tilts his head back howling. Oh buddy. I pick him up, cuddling his furry body while his tongue races against my cheek. I put him down, his nose burrowing into my clothing, hunting down the identity of all the other animals I dared to caress. Our other dogs will wag and sniff if I'm close by, but they're getting old and have a difficult time rising.

Tawnie K. Bailey

"Some guy called for you," Todd, my younger brother says, sitting on the recliner.

That's helpful. "Do you remember his name?"

"Nope, sorry." He doesn't have his I'm-joking smirk on his face.

"Todd, why do you answer the phone?" Ok, don't piss him off. He won't tell you if he's mad. "Was it Charlie? William? Troy?"

Nothing.

"How about Caleb?"

My baby brother gives me a sheepish grin. "Maybe."

Really? Caleb called? For me? Maybe he's broken up with Lyndsey again. Calm down. He stood you up and didn't think enough of you to be honest. And you've always liked him more than he's liked you. And that sucks. "Did he leave a phone number or say he'd call back?"

Aaron turns around, looks at me and smirks, "It sounds like our little Angel still likes Caleb!"

Oh crap. When Aaron knows something's important to me, he finds a way to exploit it. He once wanted me to go and buy him a soda and when I refused, he picked Yoyo up and dangled him over the deck until I agreed.

"I'm just curious," I say trying to downplay the situation.

"You just want his dick," Aaron berates.

"So would you, if you saw it," I say to shock him. He can be such an ass. He always uses words like dick and pussy and cunt—just to make me uncomfortable. Brothers and sisters shouldn't share details of their sex lives. And if Aaron finds out I don't have a sex life, he'll make my life hell.

I whistle for Yoyo and escape to my room. Should I call Morgan? No, we don't have call waiting and I should leave the line open in case Caleb calls back.

I start plugging away at calculus, my fingers like heat-seeking missiles finding little bumps on my arms and destroying them. When Dad's bedroom door opens, Yoyo jumps off the bed and runs out of my cave.

Dad knocks at the door, pushing it open with the first knock (good 'ole broken hinges). "I'm getting Chinese. You want any?"

"Chow Mein with the crunchy noodles for me, please."

"Again?"

I smile. I like to eat the same food for weeks. In elementary school I'd eat an entire bag of raw, hard spaghetti noodles. I'd suck on the tips until they were soft and eat them until my gums hurt from the tips poking into the tissue.

These days water is all-consuming. My aerobics teacher once said to drink one extra glass of water for every five pounds we wanted to lose. I wanted to be a size two so I drank over a gallon of water every day. My doctor warned me about brain swelling from kidney washout after Mom freaked when I missed too many cycles. And now I'm closing in on a size six. I still love water and microwave a cup every 30 minutes or so, trying to keep the frost away. Hot water tastes especially yummy in a cracked mug. Perhaps the mug has lead in it and I like the taste of lead? Or, maybe I'll get lead poisoning and my brain cells will drop off one by one until I'm stuck at home cleaning up my family's messes for the rest of my life.

"Could you wash a load of jeans for me?" Jeans are Dad's work and play dress code.

I add two pair of jeans to the pile Dad wants cleaned and trudge to the laundry room and start the washer just as the phone rings. Hoping it's *the* boy, I grab the phone.

"This is Caleb." The deep timbre of his voice makes the horse hooves gallop in my chest.

"Could you wait a second while I grab the other phone?" I run to my room, pick up the phone, then run back into the kitchen, replace the receiver and run back to my room. Now I'm out of breath and almost panting—not the impression I'd like to make. "Alright, now you have my undivided attention," I say.

"Most men would weep to hear that," he says while I try and control my breathing.

"But not you?" I can't believe that came out of my mouth.

"I didn't say that."

Oh the voice … "I'm generous with attention. I think that's why so many nerdy guys think I like them," I say.

"Do you?" He has a flirtatious tone. I think I hear him smiling through the phone.

"Sure I like them, I find intelligence very sexy."

"As do I."

Then what are you doing with Lyndsey? Or maybe you aren't with her anymore? "Unfortunately I haven't found the rest of the package as appealing."

"Poor bastards," he says.

"Poor me. Think of the difficulty of entrancing these future engineers. And I barely know how to use a T square."

"Mmmm, quite the dilemma," he says with an amused tone.

"I don't want to hurt their feelings, so they go on thinking there's hope."

He's quiet. "That's why I called. I wanted to apologize for standing you up last spring while I worked some things out. Now that Lyndsey and I are doing so well, I realize what a jerk I was to you."

What am I supposed to say?

"I never wanted to hurt you. I was just buggin'. I enjoy our conversations and being with you and I just wanted to let you know I'm sorry."

"I've never been stood up before, so I suppose I'll chalk it up to a learning experience."

"What did you learn?"

"Nobody compares to my dog and he still pees on the floor."

Caleb laughs. "You have high standards."

"Not high enough; I guess I need to either increase my standards or decrease my expectations."

"Touché," he adds. "I really am sorry."

"Me too." I am so stupid for getting my hopes up.

"Don't change your expectations. You should be treated better."

Agreed. Now what? I don't want to get off of the phone with him, but don't know what to say. "Hey, are you going to the Homecoming game next Friday night?" I ask.

"I did my time at Seattle High. I don't have any desire to repeat those experiences."

"Oh." I'm one of those experiences.

"Take care of yourself."

I sigh. "I always do." I hang up absolutely defeated. I haven't talked to him in six months, think of him daily, then he finally calls because he's guilty?

I hear the front door open and bags scooting across the counter. When I have my own house I want the bedroom doors to be solid, not this stupid hollowed out junk that allows every little noise to reach all corners of the house, including my pink cave.

Aaron and Todd are grabbing at the boxes on the table. Have you ever noticed how romantic Chinese food is in movies? The gorgeous hunky man and the beautiful one eat a few bites with chop sticks? Yeah, I eat with a fork.

Chapter 5–Aaron

September, 1991

I'm floating. Or maybe I'm swimming. My heart is beating faster and faster. And it's fucking amazing. I can hear things. Little things like the leaves landing on the ground. It's loud and heavy and real.

This morning has been fucking awesome. I'm with Frankie and Jimmy. Frankie is one crazy mother fucker. We just walked up to this house near Seattle High. Frankie knocks on the door and waits for a while to see if anyone is home. Nobody answers and he breaks into the house. I leave that shit to him while we wait in the backyard for him to signal us. It's such a rush, almost like sneaking into a girlfriend's house while her dad is awake in the next room. Yeah, almost.

"House cleaners are here!" Frankie yells. I can see him with the back door open. That's his code for 'I'm waiting with the door un-locked.' We used to try and hide behind bushes, but what's the point? If Frankie gets "made" I need to be able to run fast.

I walk up the concrete steps, my Nikes leaving little wet marks on the top of the porch. I should have worn a heavier jacket. I haven't been jacking houses for long, so I don't know if it's better during the spring or summer—I suppose people leave their windows and doors unlocked when it's warmer, but more people are out in their yards watching and shit.

Frankie's already gone back into the house. I go straight for the bathroom. I don't see any doilies or curvy furniture, and it doesn't smell like musty old carpet, so probably no senior people live here. Old people have a lot of pain killers, constipation and geritol stuff, but I'm after the prescriptions. We just scoop em up and go through them later. Sometimes, if we don't know what the medication is, we just swallow pills to see what'll happen. Ah, lots of hair spray is sitting on the counter, a girl must live here. There's a medicine cabinet, with a couple of bottles of drugs. I drop them in my backpack. I have to piss like crazy. My blood sugar must be off. I piss in the toilet, making some cool foam, and flush.

I move on to the bedroom. Frankie is looking in a drawer.

"Haha, I found the little bitty bikini!" he says with a big smile on his pock-marked face. He pulls a pair of dark purple panties out and stashes them in his backpack, then he puts one pair in his mouth and licks the crotch and drops it back in the drawer. I've seen the dude piss in someone's lemonade container and replace it in the fridge.

He once said my little sister looked like a hot brunette Elisabeth Shue. I laughed and told Frankie that Angie would never date a dumb ass like him. When he said he didn't want to date her, that he just wanted to fuck her, I ran up to him and slammed him against the wall and drew my knife across his throat, making it bleed. Frankie cried. I told him if he even dreamed about touching her I'd cut off his dick and shove it down his throat. He has a little scar on his neck now and whenever he gets out of line I point to his throat and smile. I am a Hulgey. Randy would've killed him already. You don't mess with my sister. She may be all prissy and shit, but she's fam.

"Stop pussy farting and let's get going," Jimmy says. We've been friends for the last five years but I think he'll be a serial killer someday. He'll start with his stepdad who tried to molest him when he playing with Legos. Jimmy's older brother walked in on him, then beat up the stepdad and gave Jimmy a gun—yep, an eight year old with a gun and an attitude. We've used it a few times and shot at cans and once pistol whipped a dude that walked in on us trying to steal his car a year ago. Grand theft is a felony, and it's harder to unload a car than it is to unload drugs around here. Jimmy's lived in our backyard camp for about two months now and nobody has figured it out. I built the camp in the woods about four years ago, but when construction crews invaded our stomping ground last year, me and some buddies carried our log-camp down to my backyard. When Jimmy isn't in it, I store a lot of shit that Officer Lim would love to find within its walls.

I move on to the VCR. They aren't hard to move, and, my older brother Randy doesn't have one. Randy is into drugs, but won't supply me anything but alcohol.

Jimmy has already got the jewels, he sticks them in his under-wear; he thinks if we ever get caught no "lady" would ever want them back, especially when he tells them he has crabs. I don't think he does, but that's a pretty funny threat.

We've been in the house for six minutes, which is the max we let ourselves hunt. We've talked about staying and watching porn at one house, but took it with us instead.

"It's time to head." I say as I walk through the kitchen and into the backyard. "Ah, fuck, I forgot to get the cigs I saw on the counter."

"Got 'em" says Frankie.

"I got the booze," says Jimmy. We close the door. We wear gloves, but I think it's stupid. When our own house got jacked in 1988, the thief left his big mitt of a hand print on top of the TV next to the dust-free shape of our missing VCR. The police didn't dust for prints or anything. I have to laugh. I punched the walls and wanted to go thief-hunting when some predator robbed our house and stole our VCR and here I am taking somebody else's VCR. Turnabout, man.

We walk out to the backyard and into the alleyway. We're only a few blocks from Seattle High, where we used to unload our shit. We walk across the street from Seattle High to their practice field where the graffiti meets the grey bleachers of the stadium.

"This is awesome shit, man!" Frankie says, all hyped up and giddy like a girl.

"You can keep your sissy drawers," I say when I see the panties. I don't take lady stuff without permission. That's like raping a girl in my opinion.

There's a bottle of Captain Morgan's, a half bottle of Tequila, a couple of cans of Rainier (who can stand that shit except my dad, man?), the VCR, which barely fit into the pack, and a bunch of jewelry.

"What's your fancy?" Jimmy asks me.

I see a little black box and open it. Small opal earrings stare back at me. "These are perfect," I say.

"Who are you trying to lay?" Frankie asks.

"Fuck, they're for my sister's birthday. She'd never take anything stolen. Since it came in a box, all I have to do is stick a price tag on it and she'll think I got them just for her."

"Ahhh, isn't that sweet?" Jimmy says. Frankie knows not to say anything about my sister.

"How about you?" I ask Frankie.

"I'll take the VCR," Frankie replies. Randy will have to wait, I forgot about Angie's birthday.

"Jimmy?"

"I'll take the gold ring, the silver necklace, and I'll share the rest."

We divvy up the drugs. Not too great, a couple of hydrocodone, a couple of valium tablets and that's about all.

Sometimes we'll go up to the reservoir during the day and smoke whatever we have, but I don't feel especially good today. I feel like an elephant stuck in the desert, super-ass-thirsty and have to piss. I don't remember if I took my insulin today or yesterday. Fuck I should get home and check my blood sugar.

"I'm going to head." I say and stand up. My head is pounding. Maybe I won't make it home. Maybe I'll die on the way home. I wonder who would go to my funeral. At my grandma's funeral, my cousin showed up in shackles and handcuffs. Yeah, this shit runs in our family. Mom would be crushed. She bitches and nags and drives me fucking crazy, but I love her the most. She'd die if I died.

I walk up the hill. Jimmy comes with, but my head's swirling around. I don't usually feel like this without taking something first.

"Hey dude, what's up?" Jimmy asks.

"I don't fucking know. I gotta get home."

"Alright, man."

I walk up Thistle. I've almost reached the highest point of the hill. My face is all clammy and damp. I buckle over and fall on my knees. My head is swimming and I puke on the grass, barely able to keep my head up off it.

"Hey dude. Are you all right?" I can't tell what Jimmy is saying. I can't even think right now. It sounds like a "wahh wahh" noise. My vision is going, everything is turning a muted color and tunneling into nothingness.

Chapter 6–Angelina

September 10, 1991

Dear Charlie,

I'm amazed you showed up at the coffee shop. I thought for sure my letter would have dissuaded anyone with a bit of intelligence from meeting me. Perhaps you have a tremendous sense of humor and wanted to see what kind of disaster you were set up with? I'm still surprised Bianca and Travis left us for two hours but as I explained, I don't know her that well.

I'm glad you didn't miss your ride home. Living several hours away from Seattle would have made missing your ride a disaster. I wish you lived closer. Bianca mentioned going on a double date again with her and Travis. I'm not sure I'd enjoy their company, but would entertain the thought of meeting you in downtown Seattle again, if you're up for it or could find transportation over.

Speaking of transportation (do you like my slick transition, there?),I just looked at my first car! Yahoo! It is a beautiful little British convertible, called an MGB. It's red and white and hopefully will be all mine. The man selling it's asking $3000, but the clutch has problems and my neighbor convinced me to only offer $2000. If he agrees, I'll have to save money for a European car mechanic to look at it. My neighbor is more of a "grease monkey" like my brothers—I know they fiddle with cars, I just don't know if they actually ever fix anything. No worries, I don't know how to drive a stick yet. Metro bus, it is!

Take care,

Angelina

I met Charlie this morning. I walked into the Bean Brewer and saw two guys, about my age facing the barista. I wanted them to turn around and make my panties drop to the floor while my notions about needing love evaporated. But no such luck for me. After they finished paying for their drinks, our eyes met. I hope my smile didn't falter or my eyes cloud over. Charlie, not one to need a pocket protector or be featured on GQ, had short curly hair and Tony Curtis lips, overall more of a Tom Hanks, less of a Jean-Claude van Damme. I wish I wasn't so vain, but I dismissed the possibility of losing my drawers.

"I'm Charlie," he said, his voice a drink of cocoa after playing in the snow.

Before I could respond, Bianca arrived. "It's been a long time!" She hugged Travis, looked him boldly up and down and said "I expected more. You still look like a little boy." Then she laughed and hugged him again.

Bianca is a brunette Marilyn Monroe—voluptuous top (damn it), long legs and neck and delicate features. The beauty sleeps through classes, doesn't study and yet when pitted against any MIT student would win their future earnings if based on sheer brain power alone. But she's a little volatile, and almost crazy, I think. She once told me that as a "wedding gift" she performed oral sex on her friend's groom-to-be the night before the wedding.

"So, Charlie, have you ever gone on a blind date before?"

"Nope, you?"

I smiled. "A few."

Bianca decided it would be cooler if she and Travis went to Pike Place Market by themselves. Charlie and I decided to hang out. I jumped out of my boys-aren't- allowed-to-see-me-eat-zone and suggested Mc-Donald's, my favorite restaurant. How sad.

"How do you know Bianca?" Charlie asked when we sat down.

"From AP classes last year."

"I took AP classes as well," Charlie said as he opened his Big Mac box, releasing the smell of yummy fried beef dancing with that oh-so-special-sauce.

"A date with a smartie."

"None other. It has to make up for my personality," he said.

"I'm pretty embarrassed by my letter."

"I wanted to see what the girl would be like in person," he said.

"I'm a train wreck trying to pass for a Mercedes."

He raised his eyebrows and took a drink.

"What's a typical day in the life of Charlie like?" I asked, removing the bun of my cheeseburger and adding ketchup to the dry side.

"Let me give you some background info first so you can appreciate me for more than just the nerd I appear to be." He sounded like Superman and his green-gray eyes were laughing at me. I wondered if his shirt hid an amazing superhero body....

"My official name is Charles M. Sullivan, the third, but I go by Charlie. I don't know my real Dad; my grandpa and grandma raised me. I have three older 'sisters' and one younger, or rather aunts I live with."

"I'm the second youngest, too." So far, he's said more words than Bad Date UpChuck.

"Do you think it's fate?" he joked.

"I should believe in something; fate sounds good," I said, covering my mouth and taking a bite. "I hope I didn't just offend you. You aren't going into the seminary or anything are you?"

"I'm not the religious type. The closest thing to a seminary has gotta be my public speaking for Students Against Drunk Driving."

Maybe he's a Boy Scout?

"My family has a lot of drug and alcohol dependency issues."

Okay, fate seemed a bit more plausible now.

I changed the subject. "Do you have a job, or are you still a tender, sheltered teen with rich parents?"

He laughed, his eyes crinkling at the corners. "My parents are far from rich and I'm not sheltered. I work as a caddy at a golf course."

"I tried to golf once."

"It isn't for everyone. There are people with a great deal of money out there who tip fairly well, especially older women who enjoy having teenage boys carry their clubs around."

Like Patrick Swayze in 'Dirty Dancing?'

"I'm a dance skater myself," I said. "My brothers were on the speed team and I did all the pretty stuff. It's the closest that I can imagine to flying."

"We should skate sometime."

"Are you implying we should go on another date?"

"I'd never do that." His eyes sparkled.

"Good, I wouldn't want Travis and Bianca to know we had fun without them. I can't believe they left us." He doesn't physically wow me, but my heart is still pretty fractured, and I compare everyone I see

29

to Caleb. So Brad Pitt or Tom Cruise could've been sitting across from me and I may not have noticed.

"I don't mind. I don't like the way she treats him," Charlie added.

"I didn't know about Travis until last weekend. She's been trying to get over her ex and let go of some of her psycho-stalkerish behaviors. I've been trying to get over my ex as well and thought I'd take a chance."

"How long has it been since you broke up with the fool?"

"We didn't really break up since we weren't officially dating. I found out he was seeing another girl," I said.

"And you're still trying to get over him?"

"Crazy, huh? She has more bragging rights about her bra size, but other than that, I don't think she's attractive and she isn't the sharpest person I've ever met." I took another drink. "Maybe she's great in bed. And maybe I could be great in bed."

Charlie's eyes widen. "But he thinks it's okay to hurt you?"

"Picture a girl who's incredible to look at, let's say Nikki Taylor. You assume she's stuck up or ditzy and then you have a conversation with her. She asks about your favorite novel, and you discover she has a brain. She asks about your dreams, and you discover this whole new world with color."

"I prefer brunettes, but could grow to like Nikki Taylor."

"The Big-Man-On-Campus at our high school chose me. He has a great body, is super-intelligent, well read, and comes from garbage, like I do."

"And here we are."

"I didn't mean to say those things. But I suppose you should know my family sucks and that I am perhaps not as emotionally available as I'd like to be. My older brothers are alcoholics and drug addicts and have no self-esteem. Dad is an alchy and regularly makes a point of letting them know how unimportant they are. And I'm trying to get over a guy that doesn't like me as much as I like him."

"I'd still rather be with you than Bianca."

"If you knew what she gives out for wedding presents, you'd change your mind!" I say.

"I too, have a 'crappy' as you call it, family. My mom used to burn me with cigarettes and leave me in motel rooms. She left me with her parents and never came back and my grandma, who makes me call her Mom, hates that I'm here to remind her that her daughter isn't perfect." He sighs. "She assumes the worst about me, my grades are never good enough, my friends are just waiting to lure me into a life of thievery, and she's an alcoholic. When she gets drunk she tells me I shouldn't have been born, and that she wishes I'd been aborted. Dad loves me but doesn't know how to stick up for me."

"And here we are."

"And here we are," he said.

"It's stunning how parents hold so much power and can destroy your whole world with a few words." I looked up at him, noticing his eye laugh lines, then down at the booth, the bright Ronald McDonald colors swirling together like a bad kaleidoscope.

"Would you like to see a little bit more of Seattle? We could walk around Westlake Mall, or I could show you where I work?"

He shrugged. "Sure. I'd hate to say I spent our first date at McDonald's."

"Tell me something crazy about yourself you wouldn't admit to many people," I said, feeling playful as we walked towards the mall.

He frowned. "Like what?"

"Well, I have a weird hang up with numbers—I like the number four and sometimes will just do a series of four sit ups over and over again until I remember I wanted to do fifty. Then, no matter how many I've done, I have to do an additional fifty."

His eyebrows raised.

"I'm loony-bin-bound."

"I just want to see your abs."

I laughed, a little embarrassed, the thought of him wanting to see my abs surprising. "Your turn, tell me something that you wouldn't tell most people."

"My mom dressed me in gowns and pretended I was her daughter and not her grandson."

"That's twisted and wrong."

"That's why I still like to wear dresses."

My eyes popped out before he laughed.

"I'm kidding, just trying to bring humor to a pathetic statement."

"Pathetic for her, not for you. She has some serious issues." I smiled, not knowing what to say, so I changed the subject. "Would you mind if we went to the bookstore? I just finished this great book and wanted to see if the author has any other books out."

"Sure, as long as you don't read it in front of me."

"On my worst day I'm not that rude. The bus ride home takes longer than usual on Sundays." We walked out into the rundown streets of Downtown Seattle. Walking onto Westlake Mall's escalator, I turned to face him.

That's when I realized I liked Charlie. He isn't Caleb, but that's okay. We entered Brentanno's Bookstore where we found *Presumed Innocent*.

"The author is an attorney and his main character is an attorney as well—and that's all I'll tell you. It isn't as great as the *Count of Monte Cristo*, my all-time-favorite-book, but it is suspenseful."

"The Count of Monte Cristo?"

"It's like chocolate, roller skating, and dogs all rolled into one for me." I described the best fiction book ever written. "The rest of the book is about the intimate details of revenge. I know I'm not doing this justice, you just need to read it."

"I never refuse a book recommendation, but I've already read it."

"You dork! You shouldn't have let me keep talking!" We lingered in the bookstore pointing out our favorites and giving advice. I purchased the Scott Turrow book before we left to meet Bianca and Travis back at McDonald's.

They didn't show up for another hour. When they returned, Bianca apologized with a smirk.

"I need to boogie," I said. "The buses run only every hour and a half on Sundays. And I have homework." Bianca snorted. I don't know if she does homework often, she just doesn't seem to care.

I motioned to Charlie. "I'll walk you most of the way to the ferry, if you'd like, my bus stop is on the way." He agreed telling Travis he'd meet him there.

I wasn't sure how to end it. I barely knew him and yet my palms were sweaty like a fifth grader. I leaned in, hugged him and thanked him for spending the day with me.

"For the record, this Caleb guy doesn't have to be all that special to see you're beautiful," he said, making the sun shine.

And now I'm sitting on my bed, my date with Chuck Woolery and the Love Connection long over. I want a guy who makes my heart speed up when I see him, who makes my friends jealous when they meet him; I want a guy who thinks I am the most amazing person he's ever met. I want to have mind blowing conversations with him, while wanting to tear off his clothes. Is that too much to ask?

Chapter 7–Aaron

September, 1991

Once again, I'm here in the hospital with the smell of piss and chemicals and all of the beeping and hospital noises. I guess Jimmy called my mom from some lady's house then called for an ambulance. Mom drove down just as the ambulance arrived. Jimmy left with the stuff before anyone got there. I can't believe we jacked that house just yesterday. It feels like ten years have passed.

Mom says my blood sugars were over a thousand. All I know is that I feel better now.

I've been hospitalized at least a dozen times since the building fell on me. My doc said if I didn't start taking care of myself I wouldn't make it six months. He said every time I go into a coma my brain cells die and my kidneys won't put up with the shit I do to them. Ok so he didn't swear, and I have out lived that time-line. My toes have gotten all red and thick and shit with quarter-sized ulcers, but Mom buys me these gay socks to improve my circulation. She buys this sugar- free pop too. Dad freaked when mom replaced his Pepsi with Diet Rite (Diet Rite White Grape and Diet Sprite are pretty awesome). She told him she wasn't going to allow sugar drinks in the house ever again, and if he didn't like it he could move out. I have to laugh about that—Mom pulling the "get out" card because of sugar. Dad shut up though, and she hasn't bought any sugared soda since.

I don't know why this shit always happens to me. I never asked for the broken bones or the house caving in on me. I certainly didn't ask for some disease where your feet rot off and your stomach hurts most of the time. I know other people live with diabetes, but I don't know how other people live with it and not take drugs. Sometimes, I can only live through the pain by knowing my little hit will calm down the piranhas that chew at my insides.

I can feel spit running down my chin. My arms are mountains I can't move enough to wipe away the slime. Some dumbass spit on me when I rode the school bus and I slugged him. Dad said if I hadn't hit him he would've nailed me for letting the little shit get away with it. The principal made me sit in the front seat on the bus with the little pansy-asses for the rest of the year. She told me she'd pay me for every book I read if I could tell her about the stories. I made a killing and I liked making her proud of me.

The next year I met freedom. Junior high. Walking through the halls, nobody knowing what room you're supposed to be heading to. A school counselor escorted me to each class for a while; then my mom walked me to class every day to make sure I attended. Then Dad offered the carrot—a motorcycle. I proved to everyone that Angelina isn't the only brainiac in this family. I've got the goods, just not the desire. Maybe I should've hung out with my friends from sixth grade— they've all graduated from high school—one was even the quarterback on the football team. I wanted to live, not just exist. I wanted life to go fast—to feel that stomach gush when you're about to hit the peak of a roller coaster and down you go, without ever crashing.

Mom's next to me, her snores crashing into my thoughts like a canon. She'll cry for a while then get mad at me. I'm fucking tired of feeling like this. Maybe I should just die? Or maybe start living.

Chapter 8–Angelina

September, 1991

"Charlie, I bought my MGB," I say, sitting on the floor with a bowl of Pine-sol and a rag, the phone propped against my ear and shoulder.

"That's awesome!"

"Almost awesome. When I try to shift it out of first gear, it grinds like crazy and the brakes scream. My neighbor thinks I need a new clutch and new brakes." I squeeze out the wall-cleaning solution and wash.

"I'd say congrats, but that sounds like a lot of cash," he says.

"Just another paycheck or two and I should have enough to fix it." I think the Brits are pretty upset about the whole tea spill because the cost of their auto parts is crazy high.

"What are you doing?" he asks.

"I'm in the bathroom…"

"Really?"

"No, I'm not "in" the bathroom, I'm wiping down the walls. And I'm procrastinating instead of writing an essay," I say.

"I usually just play Nintendo when I'm supposed to be studying."

Go ahead Charlie, call me a freak. "I'm supposed to write about somebody who's super important to me," I say as sudsy water drips onto my jeans.

"I called at a good time, then. What would you like to know?" he asks.

I chuckle. "I'm going to write about the most dedicated, amazing little bundle of urine-producing fuzz anyone could ever have."

"All it takes is urine production to impress you? I produce it too, you know. Why don't you tell me about him and I'll tell you what you should write."

"Charlie, have you forgotten this is long distance?"

"But you sound so close." His voice softens. "Almost close enough to touch."

"I've got Pine-sol and bathroom wall goo on my hands, you wouldn't want to touch me right now, believe me!"

"Tell me anyways."

"I always wanted a big, grand German shepherd who'd keep me safe and help me feel protected and ended up with a toy poodle."

"Definitely a change in plans," Charlie says.

"A few months after I started volunteering at the clinic, someone abandoned a shepherd pup at the hospital. Dr. Mike treated it for a deadly disease that causes the worst smelling bloody diarrhea and vomit. Somebody who didn't bother vaccinating their pup let my boss cover the bill (as if he didn't have bills to pay himself), and let us clean up all the mess."

"Stand up guy, huh?"

"Yeah. We already had two family dogs but I wanted one of my own. Since we lived in the city, my parents wouldn't let a monster-sized dog live with us and said I could adopt a poodle."

"That's not a real dog."

"My dad believes any money he earns is his alone."

"Is that why you have two jobs?" Charlie asks.

"No, I can't stand to have my brain idle; I start thinking bad things." And I produce red mounds on my face and arms. "I began my quest to clean and tidy anything with dirt, including neighborhood cars, dishes, and horse stalls to earn money for a puppy."

"And bathroom walls?"

"I developed my freaky OCD junk a little bit later. I found Yoyo and fell in love."

"My crazy mom just came home."

"Allright, I'll think of you with every soap bubble."

After Mom and I arrived home, Dad agreed to front me the $86 if I'd clean up the kitchen every night for six months. We were going to buy my little guy after school the next day. But Dad's truck wasn't there and wouldn't show for another three hours.

"Are you ready to go and get your dog?" Dad slurred as he closed the front door. I'd been waiting all day and even called the pet store. Somebody took my pup out of his cage into the adoption room. I didn't want to lose this puppy. "We can make it," he said, his eyes half closed.

"Dad, it's in Burien and they close in five minutes."

"Call them and tell them we're on our way."

"You shouldn't be driving," I said, stopping the eggshell cake walk. I didn't want my life to end *and* I didn't want Dad to hurt anyone else.

"What did you say?" I could see him teetering between an explosion and placidness.

"I said you shouldn't be driving and they're closed."

He looked at me, swayed and corrected himself with the wall. "Suit yourself. I thought you wanted that puppy."

"I do."

"We'll get him tomorrow."

I knew he'd be sold. I wanted to have something of my own to love. I walked to my room and cried. I don't cry often—a sign of weakness around here and something my family will pounce upon.

When I arrived home from school the next day, Dad's truck sat in the driveway parked at a normal angle. I listened at Dad's bedroom door, his nose-baying dominant over the fan. I called the pet store; the lady who looked at my puppy returned and took him out of his cage and played with him. She couldn't make a decision between the cream pup with the brown ears (my puppy, I hoped) and the red pup in the next cage.

The clock ticked slowly. We were never supposed to wake up Dad—ever. That's a crime tantamount to setting the house afire. As it approached 5 o'clock, I decided to do it. I knocked lightly on the door. No answer. I knocked louder, and still nothing, I opened the door. "Dad?"

Nothing.

"Dad?" I asked louder, his nose howls making any Basset Hound jealous. "Dad," I walked to his side of the bed and shook him a bit. "Can we go and get my puppy?"

"Hmm? What?"

"The pet store closes soon."

"Can we go tomorrow?" he asked.

"No," I said, my hopes about to be thrown into a junk heap for another life compactor to squish. "Somebody looked at him today."

He sighed. "Okay, I'll get up."

That night, Dad bought me Yoyo. When I earned the additional $86, Dad declined the payment saying I deserved to keep the money. For my toilet-paper-sparing father, that was *huge*.

I spell out Charlie and Yoyo's names with bubbles. I whistle for Yoyo, who's been sleeping behind the toilet during my cleaning frenzy. He shakes his skin out before running up to me and launching his body into my arms and sliming my face. I wanted something so different and fell for this little dog completely. Yoyo's the best thing that's ever happened to me and he wasn't my first choice.

Charlie's not my first choice either.

Chapter 9–Angelina

September, 1991

"Ange, do you have plans for Friday night?" Such an ugly question, and from a friend too. "Cause I met this guy, Jake, who attends O'Dea and has a friend …"

"Oh, Vanessa, I just went on a blind date. I don't think I'm allowed to go on too many of those and live to tell about it," I say smooshing up a piece of bread, the phone cradled between my ear and shoulder.

"Maybe next time. I thought I'd give you an opportunity to meet someone worthy of you."

"How do you know if this guy is worthy?" I ask, adding mustard to the dough.

"I met him; he seems cool."

I laugh. "Do you want me to remind you of the people you've set me up with?"

"No."

"The guy with so much hair sticking out of his shirt collar that he looked like George 'The Animal' Steele (a WWF wrestler), Chuck, (as in Upchuck), Mr. 'I-Have-Nothing-to-Say', then-"

"I know, I know. I am sooorrry, but that doesn't mean William will be like them."

I sigh and nibble at the rolled up bread and mustard creation. "If you have fun and like this guy, tell him I'll meet his friend next time." What if I don't meet this William guy and he turns out to be incredible, and I miss out on *the* opportunity? I mean, timing is everything. What if I met Charlie before I met Caleb? Would I be with Charlie? Would I have ever dated Caleb? The potential for happiness is everywhere. What if Mom dated somebody else?

"No good," says a male voice on the other line.

"What's no good?" I ask.

"You should agree to meet me. I promise you won't regret it."

"Is this William?" I ask, sitting up on the counter, my feet propped against the opposite cupboard.

"It is."

"And what makes you think I wouldn't regret it?" I ask, taking another bite of bread.

He chuckles. "Nobody regrets dating me."

"Are you always so cocky? I don't date egos."

"I'm trying to persuade you with my confidence," he says.

"Ah. Well try again," I say, a big glob of dough sticking to the roof of my mouth while I try to keep the smile out of my voice.

"I'm a good guy," he says, his voice becoming richer.

"If you say so...."

"I promise. I want to see if you're as beautiful in person as Vanessa says."

"What if I'm not?" I ask, my foot falling off of the counter and throwing my balance off. "What if I have green skin and a dime-sized wart on my nose?"

"We can always be friends."

I laugh. "I'll think about it and let you know."

"You should come out with us on Friday night. Then, maybe we could all go camping before the weather gets too cold."

"Who camps in September? The grass will be wet and we'll freeze," I say. Vanessa camping? Not in this lifetime.

"Haven't you ever heard of body heat?"

"Calm down, Mr. Horndog, I haven't even met you."

"I thought it sounded sexy," he says. "Come on out and play with us, Angelina."

"Tempting, but I have to work," I say.

"I won't beg, but think about it."

"I will." When I still wore Mary Janes, Dad promised us a camping trip but it never happened. Just as we were getting ready to leave, Dad told my second-oldest brother, Randy, to grab his sleeping bag; Randy muttered something under his breath as he ran down the stairs and my big brute of a Dad ran down those stairs with lightning speed. I crept downstairs and saw Dad straddling Randy with his hands around his neck pounding Randy's head into the hardwood floor. Deep purple marks covered his neck from the pressure of Dad's fingers. I'm sure his head hurt worse than his neck, but he never told me.

Vanessa gets back on the phone, "So what do you think?"

"He's a charmer," I say, taking a larger bite.

"And a looker," Vanny adds.

"Are you seriously considering camping with them?"

"I don't know. I've never camped before, unless you consider hotel rooms," Vanessa says.

Dad never took us camping after straddling Randy, but he did take us to his friend's house where our trailer sat rusting.

"Maybe next time," I say, hanging up as Aaron pushes through the front door.

"What's up, Sis?" Aaron says, opening the freezer and grabbing a Lean Cuisine.

"Is our trailer in Redmond or Renton?"

"You mean at Dick's?"

"Yeah." Dick, the dude who Frenched Mom at their wedding.

"Redmond. Why, you wanna go play in the mud?" Aaron asks, while listening to the hum of the microwave. Dick has acres of vintage and rusted out vehicles hiding behind brush and debris. There are tractors and old cranes, big rigs, numerous dogs, cats, and creatures. Every kiddos' dream, especially for my brothers and me. "I can stock up on Cheeze Its, Pepsi and grape soda," Aaron offers.

"Vanessa is talking about going camping with some guys."

"So you want to go and look at Dad's porn and grab some pointers."

I look at Aaron, this person who came out of our sweet mother and shake my head. "Do you have to be so disgusting?"

"You know that's what he hid under the bed, don't you?"

I look at my brother, and realize my naivete. "I prefer to think of our trailer as the place where you learned to drive a tractor, where we caught frogs and tried to befriend feral kittens that lived under Dick's single wide."

Aaron takes his lasagna out of the microwave, tears open the top and plops onto the adjacent chair. "Shit, Sis. There were bags and bags of porn; I never looked at the dates, so maybe Dad refreshed his stash or had favorites he couldn't part with, but why do you think we liked going out there so much?"

I think of playing in the various 'mobiles' that came to die on the property, of running wild and the rare times we'd spend the night at paradise. We'd unlock the little trailer and let the musty air escape, borrow cleaning supplies from Dick's wife and removing the dead flies from the sink, counters and cupboards.

"For someone who's supposed to be so smart, you sure can be dumb," he says, the pasta painting his teeth red.

Chapter 10–Angelina

October, 1991

The dishwasher is full of dirty dishes. Ever since Aaron got sick he inhales food continuously and never cleans up after himself. The counters are sticky with jelly and (?) Is that marinara sauce? I think it's the innards of a burnt TV dinner. I chip it off with my thumbnail.

As I'm retreating to my room, I hear the phone ring. "Hi Angelina?"

I recognize his voice instantly. For as much as Caleb's voice is burned into my memory, the timbre of Charlie's voice hits my brain right next to the smile center I think. "Hey, Charlie! First Caleb calls and then you."

"Oh yeah? What did that moron want?" he asks.

I laugh. "You're so subtle."

"Did he call just to stir up your affections?"

"He apologized for last spring," I say.

"Are you going out with him?"

"Geez, give me some credit. I'd at least make him grovel a bit. But no, he and Lyndsey are doing well right now, so I'm not sure what sparked the apology. What are you doing?"

"I'm stalling. I need to write a paper and thought I'd call my favorite city girl."

"Ahh, I'm your favorite? You know how to make a girl feel good, don't you?"

"And I don't even have to try."

"I'm glad you called. I have a paper to write, too. What's the subject?" Charlie and I are both in year-long writing classes that give college credits.

"It's pretty hokey—'The man I'd like to be.' I'd rather write about the creepy crawlies Travis contracted from Bianca."

"Are you kidding?"

"He went to the school nurse and she sent him to a clinic."

"Will he have this memento for the rest of his life?" I ask.

"Apparently he'll have just the memories of critters."

"That's gross! Although, it could be worse—he could have Herpes and then he'd remember Bianca forever. And I only know that thanks to health class," I add.

Charlie laughs. "You mean you didn't teach Bianca how to properly give away cooties?"

"No, I'm pathetically far behind her in bed notches."

"You should write about bed notches."

"It's supposed to be 'Who are you as a writer?' I think I'll integrate a couple of our letters into the mix."

"Oh great, so now Seattle High will know a nerdy white dude in Bremerton has nothing better to do than to try and woo one of their own. Then they'll come over and beat me up."

"Oh, are you trying to woo me?" I joke.

"You mean you can't even tell? I suck at that too? I'm so socially awkward. Maybe I'll write my paper on becoming a man who can talk to the ladies."

"You're such a dork." I pause, not sure how to bring this up, "Hey, can I ask you something?"

"Anything." Charlie is now serious.

"Well, some weird things happened at work the other day, and I don't know what to make of it. I'm not sure if I'm over analyzing."

"If it involved a man, think the worst."

"That's a great endorsement for your gender."

"I don't make any apologies for us. We're animals."

I laugh.

"No, seriously, what's going on?"

I relay the conversation about the flea bath to Charlie. "He was a veterinarian in France before immigrating to the U.S. He's married and has two daughters who are a few years younger than me. He invites the staff, numerous friends, and a large extended family over to his house whenever his kids have birthday parties or anything else to celebrate. I'm one of the family. And, maybe he chose his words wrong, or I didn't understand his accent?"

"Do you think he was joking?"

"I played it off that way, but it freaked me out. He's been asking for a hug at work for the last few months. Then again, he stood above me and petted my head for about 30 minutes in front of his wife and friends at a party, so it's probably just a cultural thing. About a year ago he hired this twenty-something girl then asked for hugs and touched her leg. She looked super uncomfortable and one day she just never showed up for work and he never said a word about it."

"Go with your instincts, girl. You're not stupid."

"It doesn't make any sense."

Charlie laughs. "You're assuming he's thinking with his head."

"I could've lived a long time without that visual."

"Hey, I didn't want to talk about some pervert with you. What else is going on in your life?"

"The usual. I wish you lived closer. Maybe then you and your car could come and save me."

"My car's on the fritz, but I would do whatever I could to rescue you. I'd even learn how to ride the buses."

"Ahh, my hero."

"Just say the word. I'm not kidding."

"Thanks. Unless you write my paper for me, as it stands I won't be receiving any credit for it."

"Okay, but just think about what kind of man you'd like me to become."

"Are you implying I don't adore you just as you are?"

"Adore sounds like I'm a puppy."

"I love puppies."

"Just what I thought." Charlie sighs before hanging up the phone.

I open up my notebook and read through the instructions for this paper. Who am I as a writer? I write to amuse people, I write to impress. I write so I don't have to see rejection in the reader's eyes. I write to invent other places for me. Safer ones. The ideas flow off the pen.

Okay, so it's pretty convoluted, but it's done. My teacher can work her magic with the red pen and edit it away. I've never talked about my family like this and don't know what she'll think. I should have written a "fluffy" paper—I'm good at those.

It's getting late, but I dial Charlie's number. It rings once. "Charlie? It's the one who adores you."

"I get the pleasure of talking with you twice in one day, huh."

"Does it feel like you won the lottery or something?"

"Are you gloating?" he asks.

"Yep, and from one over achiever to another, I thought I'd see how you faired."

"I'm having a hard time separating what I want my life to be like from the man I want to be."

"What's the difference?"

"I don't want to bitter about my family. I want to be married to a fascinating woman, but that isn't really about me."

"So, what would you have to be like to 'capture' the woman of your dreams?"

"You tell me."

I can feel myself blush. "You're funny. I think the Charlie I know is pretty awesome, but if you want to marry a self-possessed woman, you'll need to heal some wounds first."

"My mom's giving me the look of death. I'd better get off of the phone."

"Have a great night imagining your life without me when you become the Perfected Charlie."

"Why wouldn't you be in my life?" he asks.

"Oh come on, you only like me because I'm broken."

"Don't say things like that. Scratch that. Don't even think those things." He doesn't sound amused anymore.

"Good luck on your paper, Charlie."

"'Night."

I run downstairs into No Man's Land (aka the laundry room) and start the washer. We have piles upon piles of clothes that could be retired into some hall of shame. There are polyester shirts my oldest brother, Lee, wore ten years ago (like the cops on CHIPS wore at the disco) that end up being washed and rewashed since he doesn't live here and because nobody in this family throws out anything. So the clothes fall onto the floor and get mixed with a mound of dirty clothes.

I walk by the bathroom, looking to tackle a room that only needs a bit of cleaning when I notice new pick marks next to my ear. Maybe I should pore acid on my fingertips, eliminate the possibility of fingerprint identification (which may come in handy with my last name), and maybe I won't feel the uneven surfaces that force me to destroy them, leaving red shrapnel in their wake.

It's almost ten o'clock. I change into my skimpy babydoll pajamas (a joke from Morgan in return for the butt-less panties she opened in front of her parents), turn off the light, close the shades and turn on Love Connection.

Yoyo snuggles into the down pillow next to my head while I prepare for my two minutes and two seconds of sit ups. I can't wait for the show to return—my stomach muscles burn! Ah, to hear the tale of the clueless guy trying to schmooze the slut who is disappointed in the audiences' previous pick. She must have just wanted a free date, or she enjoys the attention of dating on TV.

I hear the music of the show echoing in my ear when Chuck Woolery introduces ME!

"America, this is Angelina, a veterinary wannabe with fake purple eyes, a thin and flat body and a dull personality!" The audience claps and woops. "She had the option of choosing her own date, but since she is admittedly AWFUL at that, she elected to have the audience choose for her. Her previous date, Caleb, left her for a voluptuous bimbo with a stable family. Did the audience choose the singing choir boy? Did they choose the married boss or the mystery man behind door number three?"

What do you mean behind door number three? I don't remember the Love Connection having doors. The clapping fades as Yoyo stirs and wakes me up.

Geez. I'd better go check on the laundry otherwise Dad will be mad and I won't have anything to wear tomorrow. I prefer jeans to anything else, but will wear a dress if I have to. Walking in heels is not so much fun, and pushing my broken down MG in heels would *really* stink.

I head downstairs and turn the dryer back on. On my way up I see the front door open and Mom walk in.

"What are you doing up?"

"I needed to turn the dryer back on."

She hugs me. She leaves the house smelling like White Shoulders and comes home smelling like diesel. "Did you have a good day?" she asks, looking exhausted.

"Alright. How about you?"

"I looked in the bus mirror and some kids were stomping on another kid's head."

"Oh my God! Is he okay?"

"I don't think so."

"I'm sorry." I hug her and go to bed.

Paper Shields

Writers are generally average people who shed pretense for vulnerability and truth. This truth is often long-sought and painful to discover. My excavations are nothing short of this pain as confusion, loneliness and desperation surface as the main revelations.

Because I read, I know another world lies beyond the paper; one where a definite pattern and order can be established. A world where a little girl knows her father will always be home—a world where people who supposedly love you, actually do, and always will. Writing acts as a tool to give definition and truth to the unimaginable—to give substance to my thoughts and feelings, a whirlwind of hopes and fears. Writing helps me analyze situations so surprises are kept at bay.

Loneliness has long been my companion and competitor. Her hand took mine in elementary school when my father and rescuer turned into my foe and disappointment. Escape and release of these feelings was found only through writing. I wrote of princes and kings, and of happily-ever-afters. I wrote of stories my brother told me while he comforted me under the bed, trying his hardest to drown out the sounds of my father beating my mother. Writing was impersonal; I didn't need to look into the reader's face and see the immediate and feared disapproval. I could tear down a wall and rebuild it before giving the opportunity for pain. This construction gave me courage to write and let my anger out at those that hurt me. I asked my paper father the questions I longed to ask my real, more destroying, intimidating father.

Don't you know how much it hurts to want your father dead? Don't you know how much it hurts to know you come last in his life? Don't you know how much it hurts to hate someone you're supposed to love? Don't you know how much I miss you?

Questions were asked, and my paper father couldn't hurt me. The answers were varied, and relatively unimportant, but I asked them, and that made writing irresistible as I embraced vulnerability only on paper.

Writing allows me to face things that are dangerous to me in the real world—to face questions of a little girl looking for a friend, but finding only coldness. Writing calms her fears and allows her to express herself without fear of disappointment. Writing gives me courage to watch my eighteen-year-old brother, with whom I used to crawl into bed when thunder roared, slowly die from diabetes—knowing he's been given seven months to live and knowing he doesn't want to live that long, knowing my brave little knight of long ago will know no happily-ever-afters. Writing gives me hope to override the walls of reality and bring contentment and trust for the future.

I'm sad that my mom's place of solace has frightened her. I know what it feels like.

Chapter 11–Aaron

October, 1991

"How's it going?" a booming voice bounces off the walls and breaks into my sleep.

I crack open my eyes, my lashes sticking with green shit. Nothing like having cedar shavings in your eyes to start your day. Doc said I need fake tears, but who keeps that around? "What's up?" I ask, slowly moving the wet sack of sand that has filled my body to roll towards my visitor.

"I heard you almost died the other day," he says, his body dwarfing the chair.

"Fuck. It's just bad eggs." I lift my left hand for the bed remote and find another IV in it. Well, that explains the ticking.

Doc Shawn leans in, his Old Spice more obvious and adjusts the remote so I can touch the buttons better. "Bad eggs with traces of cocaine and alcohol?"

"Somethin like that," I say, the bed whirling up so my head's almost eye level.

"The medic's glucometer couldn't even read it, the glucose higher than the hospital's ever seen."

"I'm their shining star."

"Aaron, your mom buys you insulin. Why don't you check your sugars and give your body what it needs?"

"Why do you show up here? Is my mom payin' you?" I don't need my shrink nagging, too. "You wearin my old man's cologne to make me feel bad, too?" Mom nags and drags me to go see him twice a month. I think he would make an awesome dad, but he gets paid to *not* be an asshole and listen to me. He says I should get my GED and go to college. Maybe I should be a psychiatrist? It'd be funny to listen to people as fucked up as I am.

"No, Aaron. Your mom cancelled your appointment yesterday and I saw you were here."

"Checkin up on other crazies?" I ask, my tongue exploring the cracks on my lower lip.

"You're not in the psychiatric ward," he says, smiling.

Fuck. I know. It's not the noisy chatter of the crazy house, it's the beeping, whirling shit of the your-body's-still-sicker-than-your-fucked-up-mind-floor. "You convince them I'm not tryin to off myself?"

"They didn't consult me before they stuck you in the ICU."

"You think I tried to kill myself?" I notice my arms aren't in restraints.

"Slowly. Don't you deserve to live?"

"Fuck. Why should I?" I ask.

"You tell me."

I chuckle, "You're a smart man, Doc. Turnin the tables and shit."

"Why haven't you been taking care of yourself?" he asks, his baritone voice softening.

"I just want the high too much and forget about the sugars. When my sugars soar, I think people have been messing with my insulin, so I don't take it."

"Your endocrinologist said super high sugars make people feel like they're on LSD."

"You mean I could sell my disease and make money?" I ask and then laugh, knowing that wasn't his point.

"I know you can do this. You're one of the smartest people I've ever met, and your potential is boundless." He's leaning forward, less than a foot from my bed.

"Did Mom slip you an extra twenty?"

"This isn't on the clock. I've been talking with you for almost four years, now. You're killing yourself, Aaron. Your scans show ulcers on your brain, liver, spleen and lungs."

That fits. I hurt everywhere.

"You can do anything, you just have to want it."

"I want drugs."

"Then you'll end up here, if you're lucky, or with a toe tag. Do you want your mom to have to identify her son in a morgue?"

"No."

"Then choose something better." He stands up, touches my hand, and walks out, his wing-tips clicking the sterile floor as he leaves.

Chapter 12–Angelina

October 5, 1991
Dear Charlie,

I just got off of the phone with you, so don't be surprised if the amount of "new material" is lacking. I only have so much entertainment left in me before the rewind button should be hit.

I just wanted to make sure you know that I don't regularly hang out with unknown men inside of McDonald's for hours. It was a one-time thing, and I hope you don't think I am "easy" because of it. I rarely eat food in front of boys. I'm sure everyone just assumes girls survive on air alone. Sorry to taint that image for you. I hope it isn't like learning the Easter Bunny isn't real.

I'm stalling and don't want to buckle down and finish my homework. If I were a great student, I wouldn't have waited until Sunday night to complete this task. So, you see, in addition to my aforementioned physical struggles, my ambition waivers a bit, too. Yeah, there goes my chance for a second date with you. I realize there are other fast food chains we have not yet explored together, but I think we should slow this down.

Thank you for spending the day with me,
Angelina

I'm studying in my room, drinking a cup of steaming water and deciding whether to throw away yet another letter to Charlie. I like him but my stomach doesn't flutter or tighten, and let's face it, if my friends saw me with him, they wouldn't throw down their panties either.

The front door slams and thunder rolls down the stairs. It's a weeknight, Dad is sleeping, and Mom isn't due home for an hour. The door slams again and more running. This time, Yoyo is up, standing and barking. Okay, that's weird. I get out of the covers, pick up my mighty defender, open the door (which falls off the hinge), and head down the hallway as the doorbell rings and Yoyo barks. I wish we had a peephole or some other security device, especially since our entryway lights catch fire when a bulb's screwed in.

I open the door and peer outside. A police officer is standing on the porch, his radio crackling. My hand encircles Yoyo's muzzle to quiet him. "I am Officer Lim of the Seattle Police Department. May I come in?"

"Why?" I ask. If I say yes, and let Officer Lim in, then he doesn't need a warrant. The sister in me kicks in and I don't want my brother (or brothers) going to jail again. Last Thanksgiving the Hulgey men (minus Todd) had a holiday reunion at the local jails. Mom, Todd, and I had a quiet dinner.

"I'm looking for Aaron Hulgey. Is he here?"

"I don't know. I've been in my room studying." Aaron just got home from the hospital yesterday. I hope he isn't in trouble.

He sighs, his mouth contorting into an expression of pure annoyance. "If you don't tell me where your brother is, I can charge you with obstruction of justice." He's angry and I'm a goodie-two-shoes.

"I don't know where he is. Do you want me to give him a message if I see him?"

"Are you kidding me? You tell him Officer Lim is finished playing games. If Aaron wants to play with the big boys, he can go to jail like the big boys." Officer Lim turns and walks away.

I "close" the door to my room and turn my music back on. It's playing Mint Condition's "Breakin' My Heart." Yoyo growls and I become worried. Shit, I should have let the police come in. I don't know who's here. What if it isn't one of my brothers?

I stand up, worried there's some creepy dude hanging out in my basement. Aside from Yoyo, I don't have anything that would even gross out a scary man. I look for any weapon and see my high heels and notice my cat's vomited up a hairball. I lean down to scoop up the cat vomit with a piece of paper then grab my heel with the other hand. Maybe I'll fling the vomit and then hit him in the eye.

"Angelina, thanks for saving my ass!" Aaron says, bursting in and almost hitting me with the door handle. "Officer Lim is *so pissed* at me!"

"Dammit, Aaron! You almost made me pee!"

"I made him look like a fool in front of the big boss man." Aaron, not one to deplete the family soap supply, is tall and thin. He wears his hair long, shaggy, and unwashed most of the time. It goes well with his overall Charles Manson look.

I shake my head but say nothing. Aaron has always been trouble to himself and others. He broke both of his wrists within a month of each other and his nose less than a year later jumping his bicycle. One of his friends threw a board up in front of him, and he landed face-first into a fire hydrant. The loudest person I know, the first to break a silence (and often with an inappropriate comment) was bleeding and quiet. He turned over and said he saw Jesus.

Last summer, Aaron decided he needed cash and heard that Lee's friend needed help removing appliances and anything of value from houses slated for demo.

I waited outside of the ICU doors for several hours until he recovered from surgery. Even though Morgan and I were candy stripers for three summers, the smell and sound of a hospital deteriorates when your family's inside.

When I finally saw him, his voice sounded like a hollow night wind with scratchy undertones. A huge laceration covered most of his face.

"Do you feel as bad as you look?" I asked.

"It hurts to breathe. Look at this." He lifted up his gown, showing a swelling in the shape of a two by four. "Nurse says my back has a matching imprint," he said, his eyes partially shut.

"What happened?"

"I wanted to make some money." His chest wheezed with each breath and dry skin stuck off his lips. "Lee's friend wouldn't let me work because of my tank top and shorts, but asked if I'd hand him a hammer." He took several breaths before he continued, "I heard a sound like thunder and the building collapsed around us."

"The doctors think Aaron's only alive because when he screamed he filled his lungs with oxygen. He has a concussion, eight broken ribs bruised lungs, crushed pancreas, and a tear in his liver that they've already repaired," Mom said.

"Sis, I saw an angel," Aaron said quietly. His eyes were closed, but tears spilled down his face. He opened his eyes and looked a little embarrassed, which made me believe him.

I thought of a flippant response such as 'Did he tell you to go back and take a shower first?' but decided against it.

After a nurse advised Aaron needed more chest films, Mom decided to take me home. "Aaron, I'll drive Angelina back home and see Todd for a little while. Then I'll come back here, do you need anything?"

"Just my Metallica tapes."

"What?"

"It's death metal," I responded for him. "Shouldn't you be listening to Crystal Gale or some other Christian music?"

"Yeah, maybe." He closed his eyes.

"I love you."

"Love you too, Sis."

And now Aaron is thrilled to have pulled one over on a police officer who actually tries to keep Aaron out of jail.

Chapter 13–Angelina

October, 1991

Morgan opened a murderer's file this week and let me read correspondence from the infamous serious killer, known for his intelligence and physical attributes. Her attorneys have been contacting clients to see if they want to keep their decade-old files or have them destroyed. Typos riddled the killer's page, but word processors weren't utilized by inmates back then. In a post script, an eerie notation read "I'm sorry for the errors. I typed this with my nose to leave my hands free to correct all of God's mistakes."

My family's crazy but at least they aren't sociopaths. My boss, Mark Sullivan, practices family and criminal law. His clients are not as infamous as Morgan's attorneys, but we have several who make monthly appearances for exposing themselves to women. I've been well versed in confidentiality and know not to even acknowledge a client in or out of the office.

"Hey, Angelina," Morgan says. "Michael's taking me to his church, so I have to head home early."

"No Keg tonight?" Morgan and I celebrate paydays once every few months and either boogie to the Keg or Red Robin and order a piece of mud pie. Morgan has a body boys would kill to look at (or touch) and she doesn't have to try. She has a metabolism that's just revved up and ready to burn any extra calories she gives it. Some people get all the luck.

After depositing the weekly banking for the law firm, I head to the bus stop, the leaves skittering off the ground while my hair plays facial peak-a-boo.

It's Friday night. Vanessa is going on a date with a new guy and I can't wait to hear the details. Morgan is going out with Michael. Poor me, I'll sit at home and... I don't know. I could bathe Yoyo. He's getting smelly. His hair is cute and soft and all, but it definitely attracts all smoke and smut.

Tawnie K. Bailey

As I'm walking home from the bus stop, I hear a car honk. I turn to look, expecting to see Little-Sportscar-Man who used to honk when I walked home from school. Once he rolled down his window and I actually approached the car just like a call girl. Later (stupid me), Yoyo and I met him at a park. His looks took a nose dive once he climbed out of the hot little car and his personality made anyone driving a Vega look good. He claimed to be nineteen, a Boeing employee and a student at UW. I don't remember how or why but he flashed his driver's license, showing a full frontal view of his face. Only people twenty-one and over have a full view of the face, all of us too-young-to-drink people have profiles displayed on our licenses. I don't care for liars; they have a tendency to want to marry you.

No Little-Sportscar-Man. I turn and see Caleb with Morgan's brother—just another reminder that everyone else in the world has a fun life to go to on a Friday night. The jeep pulls over just ahead.

"What are you guys doing?" I ask, approaching the jeep.

"Off to the gym, then to a comedy club later," Caleb says from the passenger's seat, his blue dew rag highlighted by the street light. "You want a ride home?"

"It isn't very far," I say, wanting to be in the vicinity of Caleb but not sure Morgan's brother wants me hanging around.

"Get in," Caleb whispers, "I don't bite."

"That's not the way I remember it," I say. What the hell. I'm with Caleb, who cares if he has a girlfriend. Caleb's cologne seduces me as soon as I climb in the jeep.

"What are your plans?" Morgan's brother asks. "Are you hanging out with my sister tonight?"

"She's going to Michael's church. So, beyond getting picked up by two of the nicest guys around, I don't have any plans."

"You mean two of the sexiest guys around?" he asks.

"I wouldn't go that far," I say as we turn up the hill. Our house is dark without a porch light to greet me.

"We'll wait here until you get in," Caleb says.

"I'm a big girl, Caleb," I say, climbing over his seat while he stands outside holding it down.

"Your personality, maybe. The rest of you, not so large."

"What does that mean?" I ask, thinking of my little A cups.

"It means I want you to be safe, and not think you could whip on anything out in the night."

"I *did* take Tae Kwan Do in third grade," I say, smiling up at Caleb, wishing he'd invite me anywhere. How am I supposed to get over this guy when he keeps popping up?

Strangely, the front door is locked. Our locks work, but the boys seem to believe in an "open-door-policy" meaning one of them leaves the door unlocked on their quick exodus from the house. I dig in my purse for my keys and unlock the door.

Yoyo bounces like a deer and wiggles all around. I grab his leash and take him outside. Sitting on the edge of the embankment, on a ladder, is my neighbor. What the hell? The street light creates a spotlight of sorts while he twangs on a *saw*, like cutting-down-trees-saw, singing "Moon River." Oh my God, he's serenading the moon. Is everyone crazy around here?

Yoyo looks at our neighbor then walks towards his favorite bush and sprinkles it with nature's water. We sneak back inside.

I grab a blanket and watch a few minutes of the news. Yoyo jumps into my lap, his eyes softening as I run my hand through his silky curls. What would Yoyo say if he could talk? He's been there for my first kiss, my first break up and the first time Dad hit Aaron. This little delicate creature is my rock.

I wonder what next year will be like. I'll be at Washington State University. Will I be restless? Dateless? Knee deep in studies?

The phone blares.

"Where the fuck is Lee?" Randy asks.

"Why would I know?"

"Goddamn him! You're gonna to have one less brother. The next time you see him he'll be in a fuckin body bag!" He clicks off the phone.

Did Lee wrap his car around another telephone pole? Did Randy just threaten to kill Lee? I don't have Randy or Lee's phone numbers. We have an address book, but their contact numbers change so frequently that the book's useless. Scraps of paper with phone numbers sit all over the telephone counter, but no names accompany the numbers. Really?

The phone rings again.

"Randy, why'd you have to be such an ass?" I ask, annoyed.

"Remind me not to get on your bad side," a familiar voice says.

"Charlie?"

"I called to say I finished my paper. What did this Randy do? And do you want me to beat him up?"

"Randy's my brother. He called a few minutes ago saying my oldest brother's going to be a in a body bag. He hung up before I could find out what's going on."

"Are they on drugs?" he asks.

"Randy might be, but my oldest brother, Lee, doesn't usually get into trouble unless it's alcohol or girl-related."

"He make somebody's boyfriend mad?"

"No, Lee's pretty easy-going. He's the one whose invisible friend 'made' him hit his head against the wall." A gentle spirit doesn't fare well in my family.

"Are you two close?"

"Not anymore. We used to go hiking through the woods up the block and he'd invent all kind of stories for us; we dug up medicine bottles and trinkets looking for a legendary miniature Noah's Ark."

"My older sisters used to paint me with make-up and roll me around in their wagons. Sometimes they said I was their evil step brother sent to ruin their lives," Charlie says.

"Lee's best friend received food stamps which he cashed in for junk food and gambled. I remember buckets of Hubba Bubba and Bubblicious with Slurpees and Chic-O-Sticks and, of course, candy cigarettes. Lee even let us win sometimes," I say. "When he purchased a 1967 Oldsmobile Cutlass Convertible, we'd sit in the car and dream about driving away to Hazard County."

Charlie laughs.

"I had quite the crush on Luke Duke, I had a thing for boys with blonde hair back then. We were going to drive there and I'd live with Daisy Duke while the boys played in the General Lee."

"Hazard County, huh. Who knew you were into dumb blondes."

"On Friday nights I'd wait under the kitchen table for the minutes to creep by until Dukes of Hazard started. We were hypnotized by the orange muscle car. When we were supposed to be in bed, Lee's friends and band mates would arrive and practice their music. Since my dad worked extra hours on Fridays to pay off the mortgage, we'd ride our tricycles and run all around the rec-room, build forts out of the sofa cushions and act like we lived in the wild."

"I'd trade make-up any day."

I laugh. "Me too. Lee built an insulated camp and tapped into the power pole for electricity. He tolerated Aaron running around the house, placing his dirty underwear on Lee's head and having water fights in the house. He even tolerated me barking at him and pretending to bite his leg."

"My friend, Angelina, an ankle biter."

"I was a German shepherd, Charlie. I just showed restraint," I say.

Charlie laughs. "Oh. What else should I know about you?"

"Nothing. You already know more than you should."

"Are you going to kill me, now?"

"No, I don't leave people in body bags. Lee probably didn't buy Randy beer or something stupid. I was all freaked and now I'm just annoyed with them." I catch my breath, realizing I'm not scared anymore. "How's your paper?"

"Stupid, but I wrote about the man I thought you'd want."

"Well, I'm glad I didn't tell you about Luke Duke before your paper."

"I would've gone out and bleached my hair."

"That would've been a tragedy."

"Like Death of a Salesman?"

"Exactly."

"What happened to your brother?"

"Too many disappointments."

Lee worked at McDonald's when boys feathered their hair then worked at a little deli half a mile away from our house (where I sold Blue Bird cookies and mints during second and third grades). He chopped off the tip of his finger on the meat slicer and was robbed at gunpoint during his employment. The finger incident caused Lee to faint on the floor and ended his brief consideration of veterinary medicine as a career choice. The robbery caused Lee to reconsider working at all.

Nonetheless, the allure of the American muscle car pulled him back from time to time. During my elementary years, Lee owned a 1967 Olds, then a 1977 Ford Mustang, followed by a series of Chargers, Pintos, and Vegas. It's sad to see the progression from muscle car to American reject mobiles, but so was the descent of his ambitions. "Lee graduated and was required to either attend college or pay rent, but he met a girl and fell in love."

"Let me guess, all good things came to an end," Charlie says.

"All other things disappeared when Lee crushed on a girl. When she dumped him, Lee stormed out of the house with a baseball bat and smashed his blue Mustang's windshield, lights and then the body."

"Wow. Do all of the Hulgeys take rejection so badly?"

"I don't know. I've never been rejected," I say, but then laugh. "Now a brown Pinto is all he hopes for."

"And you?" Charlie asks.

"I want a Jaguar."

Chapter 14–Angelina

October, 1991

My alarm screams at me. Yoyo jumps up as if it's his personal mission to make sure the alarm never sounds again. He runs up to my face, his tongue racing against my skin. Even though I clean his teeth regularly, his breath smells like the inside of a garbage can. We don't have a fenced yard, and I have no intention of walking Yoyo in my PJs, so I open the sundeck door and out he goes. He urinates on a wee wee pad and hurries back into the house.

I walk into my parents' room and into their shower, the only one of three that works. It's sad, but in the back of my mind I think if I weigh myself after I urinate the scale will show a number I like better. I'm 134 pounds—ten pounds heavier than when I dated Caleb. It's stupid to be so consumed by the scale, but I'm an American teenage girl and my brother thinks I have child bearing hips.

After my shower, contacts are inserted. Now dull brown turns to a dazzling violet. Angela, the prettiest girl in our school, has dark brown hair and blue eyes. Before Caleb asked me out a few years ago, a friend of his approached me to see if I knew of Caleb. He was our school's James Dean—everyone knew Caleb. His buddy told me Caleb thought I was a looker and naturally I thought Caleb meant Angela and *not* Angelina.

After Yoyo is walked and fed, I spray a little puddle of hairspray onto the counter, place my fingertip into the chemicals, and apply it directly to the hair in the curling iron to lock the curl in without the frizz. I'm frying my hair (yes, it does sizzle), and the risk of electrocution is there, but it works and looks good.

"The mechanic is supposed to be here at eleven. Here's $400 and the key," I say, pulling out a wad of twenties and handing them to Mom, who's waiting by the front door.

"Did you hear Randy punched Lee for not picking him up dinner last night?" Mom asks.

Tawnie K. Bailey

"He threatened a body bag over *dinner?*"

"I'm sorry, Ange. I know they don't always show it, but the boys love each other," Mom says.

We drive to the clinic where Dr. Mike greets me in the back office with his arms outstretched, asking for an embrace.

I smile as I drop my purse and then lean down to adjust the contents, ignoring his request.

"Do you have plans for next week?" His voice is casual, not creepy.

"I'm busy Friday night." I'm meeting William on Friday.

"We need to have a staff meeting and I thought we'd go skating afterwards. How about Saturday night?"

Ugh. A prime date night. I don't have any prospects, what do I care? "Sounds good to me." At least it isn't bowling like our last staff meeting.

I walk into the front office as our first patient enters, her yowl vibrating sheet metal. "Steven, is everything okay with you and Carrie?"

"Yeah. She felt bad for suggesting we've been snuggle buddies."

"Snuggle buddies? *Really?*" I say, swatting him with a file. "My car's getting fixed today; Dad's going to drive it here and your duties as chauffeur will be over." I can't wait to finally have freedom!

The day progresses normally until the clinic closes and Steven leaves.

Dr. Mike walks up front where I'm wiping off the reception counter and stands behind me, his breath scalding my skin. I feel his arms wrap around the front of me like a boa constrictor. "Do you want to play around?" he asks as his hand snakes up my chest and cups my breast.

My heart slides to the ground in a puddle, leaving my rigid body to fend for itself, my mind catatonic.

Dad's rusted Chevy pulls into the parking lot. Dr. Mike whips his hand away and jumps back.

My face scorched with an A, my heart collides against my ribs pounding my soul. Oh my God. That has to be an accident. "No, my dad's here. I'd rather work than be out playing." Please, please, please do not let this be real.

My brothers have versed me well, but nothing like this has ever happened to me. I *need* to believe our cultures are colliding and that Dr. Mike doesn't mean "play around" in an intimate sense.

He hands me cash and walks back to his office. I've been paid "under the table" for years, my wage varying between five and eleven dollars an hour.

I escape through the door and hope Dad can't see my scarlet face boiling or hear my heart screaming out its secrets.

When I was tiny, I'd sit on Dad's lap and rub his beer belly. He cuddled me and made me feel so safe. When Aaron would take away a toy or hit me, Dad would roar downstairs. "Aaron, get up here!" The Lazy Boy leg rest would slam down and Dad's eyes would become beady and small as he thundered at my brother. I wish I could tell on Dr. Mike; Dad would freak and beat his French ass. But then all of my hard work would be for nothing.

"Where's my car?" I ask, trying to ignore the unraveling of my dreams.

"The mechanic is still working on it." Oh crap.

Mr. Eli is wiping his hands on a rag when we pull up. "I had to redo the master cylinder and the entire clutch. I towed it to my shop then drove it here. When you purchase brake fluid for an MG you need to purchase British brake fluid."

Is there such a thing? "Okay."

"Whoever worked on this car installed the last clutch in upside down, that's why it made a grinding sound." He hands me the keys. "Why don't you try it out?"

I open the door, it's shrill scream just asking to be put out of its misery. I sit down deep into the racing seats. MGs are meant for people with long legs as the petals sit far away from the seat, I have the seat moved as far forward as possible and have the seat bolts at the under-side of the car at the most forward position. I turn the key. Not only does the car start, but when I depress the clutch, there is no grinding sound.

"Do you want to take it for a spin?"

"I don't know how to drive this stick yet." The Europeans place the reverse in a different location, and well, I haven't pulled a car out of our driveway since I crashed the rental car. It's true, the day I went to test for my driver's license I crashed the rental car into the side fence, left the entire right front wheel suspended in the air over the embankment, smashed in the rocker panel, and freaked my mom out.

"Let me take you for a drive then, if it's okay with your parents."

After we arrive back home, Mr. Eli parks the car presents a bill for $1,400.

"I don't have that much money. You quoted $372 for the brakes."

Mr. Eli just looks at me.

"I have $400." Then look in my pocket to see how much Dr. Mike paid me. There's an additional $250.

I give the money to Mr. Eli. "What do you want me to do about the rest? Can I make payments?"

"You called and asked me to perform a service. I'm a European car specialist. You pay a specialty fee." He cusses under his breath. "This is the last time I work with a minor. There are very few European car mechanics, in case you haven't noticed."

What am I going to do? "I'll talk to my mom." Crap! I'm shaking for the second time today. I promised when I bought the car I'd be responsible for all repairs, insurance, everything. I try to prove I'm mature, independent, and don't need them to rescue me.

I walk into the house and explain the situation.

"Let me see what I can do." Mom walks outside. "Mr. Eli, I don't know if you've heard or not, but your actions are illegal. You quoted $372 and the bill's over $1,400. When there is a written quote, you are required to inform the owner if the cost will be more than ten percent above the written quote. I am sure the attorney Angelina works for would be happy to go over this with you in greater detail. I do not appreciate you treating my daughter like she's trying to defraud you. I understand you've worked hard on her car and will give you the initial $372 and an extra $278. Unless you want me to call the police, you will sign a receipt 'paid in full' and you will leave without another word."

Wow, Mommy. I don't know if they are required to adhere to their quote, but I'm impressed.

Mr. Eli cusses. He then accepts the $650, writes the receipt for "paid in full" and leaves.

"I'm sorry I dropped this on you, but thank you."

Mom hugs me. "He's wrong, Angelina, not you." She's been a mediator all her life—she's the third child of eight. Her dad, a dynamite blaster, built their two bedroom, one bath house by hand for his bride. The poorly insulated house didn't have a foundation and felt like a strong wind would knock it over. She helped to care for her younger siblings and learned to make do with far less than she deserved.

Walking to school with holes in her shoes, young suitors sang to her as she looked like Elizabeth Taylor without the violet eyes. She also gave me her brains; in high school, she was the only girl in her class to take an advanced math course. After graduating, she met Dad, fell in love, and here we are. She's still making do with far less than she deserves.

**

I look across the street in time to see my neighbor drag out his ladder. It hasn't reached dusk yet. What will the new saw tune be tonight?

"Vanessa, my car is fixed! Are you doing anything tonight?" I ask, my head leaning against the phone while I try and file down my face-destroying fingernails.

"You wanna come over? I thought we could rent the Faces of Death movie and invite some friends."

"I don't know if I'll be able to drive over."

"What do you mean?"

"I haven't driven a stick since Caleb took me in his car. I might get stuck at an intersection and have cars honking at me like crazy. If I go the short route, I'll end up in the ghetto."

Vanessa giggles. "I'll come and get you. Then tomorrow we'll go and practice driving."

We arrive back at her house as some of our friends arrive. They're not the "usual suspects" but people we've known for years. Vanessa makes popcorn. She usually tries to feed me and anyone else who walks through her door. I'm not complaining, she's a great cook.

After the first stupid movie, and yes, gross too, Vanessa's new man calls. Vanessa smiles big as she climbs off of the floor and heads out of the room.

"Who is that?" Troy asks.

"Vanessa's dating a football player from the all boys' high school."

"Is he gay?"

"I think his family is wealthy."

"Ahhhh." Troy gives me a look.

"What?"

"All you white girls are looking for money."

"Troy, everyone is looking for money. When you add brains and brawn it makes Vanessa giddy." Troy smiles. "What are you cool chocolate men looking for?" I ask with a grin.

"Just love baby, just love."

I laugh. "What are you doing here watching movies with dateless old me?"

"Just hoping."

I laugh again. I've known Troy since the fourth grade. He told me once that when he thinks of me, he remembers my long socks and Mary Jane's playing hopscotch. I told him that when I think of him, I think of him bouncing dodge balls off of my head.

"Back at ya."

Vanessa comes back into the room with a big glow on her face.

"What did your Prince Charming have to say?"

"He's not visiting his grandma tomorrow, and wants to see a movie. After we go driving."

"Oh, that's cool."

"Hey Angelina, did you get your car rolling, then?" Troy asks.

"Yeah, but it cost more than the guy quoted and now I don't have money for insurance." Thinking about working more hours makes me uneasy.

"All work and no play, girl." Troy stands up and puts his coat on. It's almost eleven thirty.

"You too." Troy works at a grocery store to help his mom with bills. Troy wants to be a ball player, but is planning on going to college "as a backup plan."

"When I actually figure out how to drive the thing, I'll give you a ride." I stand up, rewind the movies and give Troy a hug as Vanessa searches for her car keys.

Vanessa drops me off and I close the door to her Honda. The last Honda Vanessa drove was crunched by a baby-poop green Pinto when Vanessa ran a yellow light. Despite Lee's recent affinity for Pintos and his poor driving record, he wasn't driving this one.

I get ready for bed and climb in between my sheets. I love the feeling of having the cold, silky pillow case under my head. I'm exhausted but can't sleep. What's Dr. Mike trying to do? The boa constricts around my chest with every thought. Now I'm just a dumb girl who lets boys do things to her.

Yoyo rises from my feet and lies down next to my head. I cuddle up to him. He senses when I'm sad and right now I'm crushed.

Chapter 15–Angelina

October, 1991

Dr. Mike approaches as I'm locking the front door. Is he going to apologize? Maybe he didn't realize his hand rubbed against my chest?

"Thank you for your help today," he says, his voice changing from business to slime. The hair on my neck moves and my chest constricts with every breath. Please don't try and hug me. I turn and smile, trying to diffuse the situation. He stands there. I smile a little as I walk by him, every arm hair standing at attention. I see his mole staring at me and try not to shudder.

"Of course," I say and leave by the side door as Vanessa pulls up.

When we arrive at my house, I take the top down off of the MG. Why would anyone make these tops so difficult? I need to fold the plastic triangle windows, unlatch the top from the front window and scoot the bars down off of the roof. Next the leather is rolled up and buried under the tonneau cover. What a lot of work to be cute.

Vanessa parked up the street. Our driveway and sidewalks are full of cars and we live at the steepest part of the hill. Why did I think I could master driving?

I'm scared to take my car out of the evil, taunting driveway.

"I didn't bring a helmet, so don't roll the car," Vanessa says.

"How did you know I thought of buying a helmet?" I don't have a roll bar on my car and worry about my car becoming a bowling ball. How stupid would I look riding around in a convertible with a helmet on? How classic? Imagine Chevy Chase vacation movies with Christie Brinkley and a Ferrari. What sex appeal would've been lost if Christie wore a helmet? I suppose she could've taken off her helmet and shook out her beautiful hair when Clark met her in the park … .

"Hey, Ness, will you get my car out of the driveway?" Vanessa giggles, but doesn't say a word. Instead she grabs the keys out of my hands and gives me a hug. My fingers are already looking for a bump to smooth next to my ear.

Tawnie K. Bailey

"I know, Angelina. We all have our issues." Vanessa gives me a sly look. She opens the driver's side door and climbs in. She tries to pull the seat forward, but it's as far forward as it goes.

"My legs aren't long enough to reach the pedals!" she laughs.

"Oh, geez. Let me see if Aaron can get this out of the driveway for me."

I open the front door and Aaron is sitting on the couch. "Aaron, would you pull my car out?"

"Why can't you?"

"I'm scared."

Aaron laughs his smirky laugh. "My little sis is scared of the driveway. What's going to happen when you have to drive up a steep hill?"

"I'll figure it out. I'll give you a dollar if you pull it out of the driveway."

"What's a dollar going to get me? You have two jobs, give me five dollars."

"No, never mind. I guess I don't get any of the benefits of having older brothers."

"Give me your dollar. You're fucking cheap, you know."

I give him the car keys and a dollar. He opens the front door and sees Vanessa.

"Oh, the two of you couldn't figure out how to drive a car backwards up a slight incline? And you guys are supposed to be smart?"

Aaron parks my MG on the street.

I laugh as I climb in the driver's seat. "Now I need to start it on the hill and not roll into anything!"

Vanessa climbs in, closes the door and tries to lean back in the broken passenger seat, facing forward an additional 20 degrees. "This is interesting."

"Nothing but the best for you Vanny," I say and smile. I turn the key and depress the clutch. It starts! I look for cars and move the car into gear, my foot easing off the clutch as I compress the accelerator. The engine revs and the tires scream forward. Then it lurches and dies. Vanessa, sitting too close to the glove box already, looks like she is about to take a header into the dashboard.

"Oh, boy." Vanessa usually has more to say than this.

74

I'm feeling overwhelmed. You can do this, Angelina. There are so many people who are shy more than one brain cell and can drive a stick.

I place the emergency brake on. Let's try this again. I compress the clutch, turn the key, other foot compresses the accelerator, release the emergency brake and slowly let up on the clutch. Away we go!

We drive up the top of our hill and around several blocks and Vanessa makes me actually stop at the uncontrolled intersections. I don't have any panic attacks, and I don't hit anything. We drive around for approximately thirty minutes and eventually I feel confident enough to stick my Boys II Men tape in and turn on the music. We're next to my elementary school: not exactly "cruising Alki beach" or any other cool place to be, but I still revel in the moment. My little car can actually be pretty fun.

I'm getting a little cocky with driving. I see a muscle car up ahead at an intersection. The "muscle men" are not anyone I'd be attracted to. They look like every male ever featured as the geek in a teen movie. Dark, greasy, unkempt hair meets pock marked pimpled face. But I'm sure they're nice.

"Hi," the passenger calls out as I wait for an oncoming car to cross the intersection.

"Hi," I give my polite smile. Vanessa looks ahead, but I can hear her trying hard not to giggle. It's our turn. I engage the clutch, compress the accelerator, and let the car go. This time, it lurches forward and dies. Vanessa breaks out laughing. I feel like I've been caught wearing diapers. I restart the car.

"Do you need any help?" one of the muscle car men calls out.

"Nope, thanks," I call out. I again try and pull away from the intersection and instead kill it half way through. The car lurches forward, Vanessa is thrown forward and caught by the seat belt and pulled back.

"I have to pee!" Vanessa cries out; she's laughing in her high pitched giggle where she can't control herself, tears running down her cheeks as the muscle car slowly inches by and the unattractive men with red blotches on their cheeks wave.

As the car continues down the road, leaving us in the intersection, I start laughing too. "You have to stop! I need to get this out of the road."

"You know they're going to circle around!" Vanessa is hysterical as I notice the muscle car's brake lights are on. They stopped half a block ahead of us.

"Be nice, Vanessa. Didn't you read The Red Dragon? The guy thinks he's hot and stops at a corner next to girls in a little convertible. They're rude to him so he shoots a loogie out of his mouth and it lands on the girl's stomach."

Vanessa looks at me for a moment before laughter peels out of her mouth.

"You better stop making me laugh or I'll make sure you lick the glove box!" I threaten and look over at her as the broken seat forces her to lean toward the glove box. I can't stop laughing. I wipe the tears away, start the car and pull out of the intersection.

She laughs. "I'm so glad I didn't pee myself!"

After Vanessa escapes, I can't contain my excitement. I have a car that works! What to do? I walk into my room and sit on the bed. I could walk Yoyo to the park—it's a pretty nice day out. Or, I could bathe him. I decide to make a call to Charlie.

The line rings three times before it's answered.

"Is Charlie available?"

"Who is this? Is this that slut from Seattle?" says an older female voice.

"Nope. Definitely not the slut." Oh my God!

"Good because Charlie doesn't need any extra strikes against him."

"Would you tell him that Angelina called for him?"

"No, I don't think I will."

Weird. But you can't catch me, I'm the Gingerbread man today. I'm on top of the world. Soon, I'll be able to leave this house whenever I want. Yoyo needs a seatbelt, then he can be copilot.

"Come on Yoyo, let's go for a run." I am not a runner. In fact, I generally can't stand it, but I have so much excitement spilling out of me that I need to do something.

I change into my Seattle High flop-of-a-fundraiser sweat pants. They're not the most attractive sweats, but I'm going running, so they'll have to do. Once Yoyo's harness is on, we head out. He investigates most bushes on our block then we pick up our pace to a slow jog. I call him and urge him forward and boy can those little legs move. We run towards 7-Eleven and the Community College.

We're about a mile and a half from home when I see Caleb's car stop in front of me. Oh great. I look like a buffalo in these clothes! No makeup, just sweat. Yummy.

He reverses the car as I slow to a walk.

"I thought that was you," he says.

I notice Yoyo smelling around the curb. "Hi, Caleb." Great, I'm panting. I look down and see Yoyo lifting his leg on Caleb's tire. I pick Yoyo up, hoping Caleb didn't notice. "I'm trying to get rid of some pent up energy."

"I can think of better ways," he says.

You're such a flirt and so out of my league in that arena.

"Why don't you come with me over to Troy's house?"

"I'm all gross and sweaty," I say, once again the dumb girl who sucked on cough drops just to make sure her breath didn't smell bad.

"So? You look cute."

"Ha ha."

"Come on, you can tell me about what great books you've read lately."

I'm tempted. You're everything I want. But you chose Lyndsey and I won't be a little fling, or lapse of judgment or whatever. "Maybe next time. I don't want to interfere with your male bonding time."

"My loss."

"No kidding. Maybe next time I'll smell like Dove soap and not Seattle sweat."

"If you insist. Sexy sweats, by the way."

"You like them? Seattle High has about 100 pair left from my reign as a class rep."

"They must not have had pictures of you wearing them."

"You know all the lines, don't you?" I'm still leaning into his car window.

Tawnie K. Bailey

"Angelina, I don't give out compliments easily. You'll just have to believe me."

I'm quiet for a while. "It's lovely, as always, to see you. Have fun with Troy. Oh hey, tell him I drove my car for the first time."

"You bought a car?"

"Yeah, it's a little British sports car. Cute but temperamental. Everything's finally fixed on it."

"Maybe you can take me for a spin sometime?"

"If you're lucky," I say and smile. I place Yoyo back on the ground, wave and start jogging back towards home. I hope my bottom doesn't jiggle too much in these! I jog back home with my little man. Maybe I should have gone over to Troy's … . No, I'm gross.

"What would you like for your birthday, Angelina?" my mom asks.

"I don't know. Maybe you and I can go to dinner or something?"

"We could go tonight since I work on Tuesday, if you'd like. You can tell me about work, your boyfriends, you know, what all moms talk to their daughters about."

"Maybe," I say needing to take a shower. I'd love to tell her about work, but she'd make me quit. People are impressed I work at a veterinary clinic and I need to have recommendations for veterinary school. I have been there so long that it would look bizarre on my vet school application to not have a recommendation from Dr. Mike. Besides, she doesn't need to add me to her long list of worries.

I think back on the day; I had a fairly "normal" teenage day. I spent time with one of my closest friends and saw The-Boy-That-I-Wish-Would-Love-Me. I wish I made memories every day that were just as extraordinary.

Chapter 16–Aaron

October, 1991

I've been clean for four days. Four fuckin long-ass days. I've been clean before, so it shouldn't be a big deal, but it is. Officially, it's been clean for six days, but the hospital kept me for the first two. I don't know what to do with my time. I sleep a lot, and when I wake up, I eat a lot. I'm having a hard time right now. I'm being sucked back to the reservoir. Everything I do, walking into the kitchen, grabbing some juice, all I can think is 'I could feel perfect'. All I have to do is walk out of the door. All this crap can just go away.

My little sister's birthday is this week. I have her earrings wrapped in my bedroom. Four years ago Mom sent me off to live with her sister in Vermont for a summer to try and get me away from my friends. My aunt and uncle took me all along the East Coast that summer; we went to the White House, all kinds of historical sites, museums, fancy restaurants and shit. They would take away my blankets in the morning and douse me with water if I didn't get up when they wanted me to. I wanted to hit my aunt one day, but my uncle came down on me; she is a crazy bitch, but I love her.

Overall, the summer was pretty awesome, but I'd never admit it to my aunt or my mom. When I returned home, Mom sent me to a private school. She'd just kicked Dad out again. Mom couldn't afford the new school, but sent me anyway. As part of the 'tuition reduction plan', I needed to sell fucking candy bars. I didn't ask to go to the nun school and wasn't going to beg people for cash. So I ate the evidence. Angelina stood in front of stores and went door-to-door on her birthday so my mom could pay for school (and the chocolate I ate). I think she peddled around two hundred bars. She's a good kid. A little stuck up, but I love her.

Last week Randy made a killing at a car auction. He bought fifty cars for $1500—thirty bucks a piece. We could make ten times that on each car in scrap metal alone. I have to laugh. Last month people piled shit all over the sidewalks for community cleanup day. Being a great business man, I went around with my little truck and picked up the metal junk that could be scrapped then turned it in and made like $400. One garbage collector thanked me for making his work easier.

I'm feeling better. Mom is watching me like a hawk. She checks my blood even when I'm sleeping, now. She's obsessed with this diabetes thing.

Benji seems to be feeling better, too. He's spunkier and awake more. I took him for a walk this morning. I can't even remember the last time I walked him. I usually open the front door and hope the dogs will poop next door and not in our yard.

It's hard to stay clean; the thought of how I feel right after I take a hit is so incredible. I have to try to stay focused on how I felt in the hospital, or how it feels to make my mom cry. I need to do this thing for me. This staying clean thing.

Chapter 17–Angelina

October, 1991

I'm seventeen years old today. Borracchini chocolate cake with rum filling, here I come! I'm meeting up with Vanessa, her boyfriend Jacob, and his buddy, William, at the football field later this Friday night for Homecoming. Yeah, I caved in; I'm going on yet another blind date, this time it's William.

The phone rings just before I leave for school.

"Happy Birthday, Angelina." Ahh, my smile-center friend.

"Thanks, Charlie."

"I'm sure you'd rather it be Mr. Muscles, Caleb."

"Come and see me, and I'll prove I'd rather it be you."

"Oh yeah, how would you prove it?"

"Use your imagination."

"Has the big 'one-seven' turned you into somebody else?"

I laugh. "No, I'm trying to be flirtatious, but you're not even biting."

"I've told you before, I'm a lover, not a biter."

"Oh, that's bad."

"Yeah, I tried. What are you doing this weekend, birthday girl?"

"I have a blind date on Friday night and a staff meeting on Saturday night after work."

"Another blind date? How could you cheat on me?"

"I didn't know we were blind-date-exclusive."

"But what if he takes you to Burger King, where will that leave me?"

"Don't worry. I prefer fried burgers over burnt ones."

"Are you seriously going on another blind date?" His tone has changed.

"Is that bad?"

"I thought what we had was special."

"I'll never date again."

Tawnie K. Bailey

"Ok, good. But I have a date this weekend, too. Happy Birthday, Angelina."

"Thank you, Charlie. You made my day."

***

I walk into the house and see Yoyo covered in blood. His feet, mustache, and chest are congealed into red matts. Oh shit! What happened? He runs to me, yodeling. When I pick him up, my fingers stick to his fuzz like a flytrap, his cologne sugar sweet. A raspberry jelly massacre.

I look in the kitchen and see no condiment disasters. Then, my eyes are drawn to the trash strewn across the dingy brown carpet, the Smuckers container the masterpiece of garbage art.

Ugh. I can think of so many other things I'd rather be doing on my birthday. The tub fills as my boy shakes. I place Yoyo in the water and pour dog shampoo on him like chocolate syrup on a sundae. Yoyo lathers easily, but the jelly seems to solidify instead of wash out. I grab Dawn, the detergent of choice for tar-covered kittens. Ah, goodbye jam.

I rub Yoyo dry and then move him to the living room to brush out his fuzz, the worst form of Yoyo abuse.

"So, baby sister, how's your birthday?" Aaron asks, slamming the front door. He saunters into the living room and hands me a Slurpee.

"How'd you know?" I ask, while Aaron walks over to the trash heap.

"Your dog snuck into my room when my eyes were closed, stood on my neck with his teeth bared and told me I'd better get you a present or he'd piss on my head. He said you've had too much cola Slurpee and to get you the banana." He kneels down and removes empty TV dinner trays, the offending jelly and unknown wrappers.

"Did he tell you about his plan to get into the trash, too?"

"Nah. He wasn't the mastermind. I already bathed Benji downstairs."

"But didn't clean up the floor?"

"I ran out of time. I wanted to have my sister's surprise ready when she arrived."

82

Ah, how sweet! "Well, thank you again for the Slurpee. Yoyo knew the right flavor."

"What are you doing for your birthday?" he asks from the kitchen, where the garbage can usually lives.

"I don't know. My car wouldn't start yesterday, so Dr. Mike told me to take the day off."

"I can go and look at it," Aaron says, kneeling down on the living room floor and scrubbing the goo.

"I got it working this morning after wiggling some wire in the steering column."

"You had to go European didn't you?" he says. Then, in Julia Child's voice, "Did you at least have an awesome day?"

"During my calculus class I received a Honeycomb watch—dug out of the cereal box just for me."

"Oh! Man this garbage smells like moldy underwear !"

"I brought my teacher a bouquet of long stemmed moldy roses as a joke, saved from some very bad dates with a card that said, 'It's either this or a toilet paper party at your house. Happy Teacher Appreciation Day. We love you.' So I think the watch is payback. I wished I'd left the bouquet at Lyndsey's house instead." Yoyo gets up and flops onto his other side, burying his head into the couch, exposing his tight ringlets.

"Ooh, girl, there is some Hulgey in you after all," Aaron says.

"I didn't say I'm going to spray-paint her house, just leave a gift."

"Who are the balloons from?"

During my writing class, a 23-balloon-bouquet arrived for me. "My honors classmates collected money for it last week." I feel so liked! I'd say loved, but I try not to overuse that word. "As I was walking down the hall with the balloons all around me, a large black gal said, 'Merry Fucking Christmas, Bitch' which pissed me off. I didn't recognize her and gave her a dirty look. She asked if I looked at her, I said yes."

"Did you punch her?"

"No, I thought my Happy Birthday was going to disintegrate since she looked a lot tougher than me. Then your buddy, Jerome, cut in and said 'Shit Keisha, you're just jealous. Angelina is nicer than you'll ever be.' And I walked away without peeing myself." I've brushed Yoyo out pretty well, and am now working on his toenails.

Tawnie K. Bailey

"Jerome's just trying to get in your pants."

"I've known him since you guys played baseball together in the fourth grade."

"So, I bet I could still sell him your lingerie," Aaron says.

I hit him on the shoulder

"Must have been a bitch to drive home looking like a hot air balloon."

"They wouldn't fit in my car so I had to take the top down and tie them in. Did you ever meet the health class teacher?"

"Nope."

"She's overweight, plays health videos then sits at her desk eating candy bars. She's trying to teach us about the consequences of sex. Abstinence first, safe sex later." Yeah, and our high school has the highest pregnancy rate in the entire state. "So, there's this box for anonymous health-related questions, today's question was 'If fructose is found in sperm, then why does it taste so bad?' She never regained control of the class after that," I say giggling when I think about the look on our teacher's face. Yep, I can tell you all about yeast infections and STDs (and boy are there a lot of them), but if I had to draw a cell, good luck! I *have* learned a great deal, though. Who knows about dental dams? They're a slick device used to prevent the transmission of an STD during oral sex.

"So, baby sister, what's the answer?"

"Shut up, Aaron!"

"What, you've never tasted any man juice?"

"No, but my classmates were shaving their legs during history class today. Because you told me how babies are made in Kindergarten, Mom must've thought I was well versed in all aspects of maturation and never told me about shaving cream." I first borrowed Mom's used razor blades in the 7th grade and I've shaved my legs dry since. Yep, not even in the shower. You'd think common sense would've picked up somewhere along the line, but it didn't and I've endured the wrath of dull razors on dry skin. Thanks Seattle Public School System, for without your help, I'd have perpetual razor burn—and more stubble.

"So, are you telling me I should have bought you shaving cream for your birthday?"

"I bought some as soon as I found out about the stuff," I say.

"Good, because there is no way you'll know about man juice if you have gorilla hair."

"I shaved, just not with shaving cream. And, stop with all that man juice stuff, I'm your little sister," I say.

"Oh, sorry. Mom picked up your cake early today so you could go out and eat with your friends or something and still have your cake afterwards."

"Morgan and Vanessa are picking me up in an hour."

"Why aren't you driving?"

"It's a two-seater, remember."

"Sis, I've gotta roll. Have a great birthday. Go get into trouble. It's the last year it'll stay off your record," he says, walking over, ruffing up my hair, then kissing my head.

"Thanks Aaron, I love you too." I get up and stretch my legs. Aaron did a pretty good job on the carpet.

Walking into my room, my wet clothes stick from Yoyo's grooming session. I notice a little wrapped box on my nightstand. The wrapping-paper-card says "Sissy Pooh Pooh." A smile creeps across my face as I open it and see opal earrings. It's unlike Aaron to not take credit for a generous act, but I think they're from him. Aaron receives a check from the government every month (Social Security? Disability?) and he spent his money on *me*.

The phone sings out.

"Are you sure you're not mad at me?" a French accent asks. Oh my God! Dr. Mike's touch wasn't an accident.

"Should I be?" I ask, my mind scrambling for a non-committal response.

"Steven reminded me it's your birthday and we didn't do anything for you. I thought you and I could celebrate it privately."

And there went my happy birthday.

Chapter 18–Aaron

October, 1991

"Mom!" I yell, loud enough for the Young and the Relentless to listen. "Do we have some flea spray?" I've been scratching all morning, waiting for Pops to pick me up for the auction and I can't live like this anymore. Pretty soon some Dune-like creature is going come out of me and take over the world.

"Aaron, come upstairs! Don't yell at me," Mom says, weariness squeezing the love away from her voice.

Fucking cunt! I was out partying last night when some douche gave me bugs. I should've known. She had that 'rode hard' look about her. "I asked if we have any flea spray," I repeat, my sock sticking to the carpet at the bottom of the stairs.

"If we do it's above the fridge. Angie may have brought some more carpet spray home. She says we have to spray it every two weeks."

I trudge upstairs while Army knives stab the bottom of my feet. The fire extends up to meet some badass charlee horse in my calves. That's what I get for not drinking enough water. My body's mad at me for not thinking last night. Mom's planted in the recliner, the brown and yellow afghan her aunt made ten years ago is draped over her.

I monkey climb onto the counter, avoiding the rusted paint can Mom refuses to move until Dad finishes painting the fence, and look into the cupboard where old Mr. Yuk stickers look me in the eyes. "This shit is old!" Todd's in high school, we don't need little green faces staring us down anymore.

"Aaron, don't use that kind of language," Mom says, the fatigue like a Mack truck running her down. "Does Benji need a bath? You could bathe your dog sometimes," she says from the living room.

"Fuck. You should see some of this stuff, up here. Do they even make it anymore?" My arms are stretched above the fridge while my legs teeter on the counter's edge. Angie's antibiotics from 1987! This is toxic waste! Go and be a parent. "I don't have money for flea spray, and something's been eating me up like I'm Gainesburgers or something." I have to get this shit out of my arms and my pits. It's driving me crazy. They're probably all reproducing and smoking cigarettes under my skin right now just because I gave some chic a ride. I'm still searching behind unlabeled bottles and broken lamp pieces. I know there is some liquid magic in here somewhere. I grab some oven cleaner, probably put up here before the Mr. Yuk stickers, and hop down. I shake the freaky bottle, wondering if maybe this old shit will just explode.

"Have you checked your sugars? You were super itchy before your diagnosis, maybe you need to increase your insulin."

"I don't need to take my insulin. You need to clean this house!"

Oh fuck. Mom's leg rest drops down and I hear her stomp into the room. I must've hit her button.

"Did you really just say that to me? I'm your mother. I have been there for every dirty diaper, scraped knee and broken bone. I work all day and worry all night. I'm not feeling good and there you go. Acting just like your father." Mom's looking up at me, her hair a mini-Medusa. She must be pretty tired.

"I'm sorry. I'm going to look like Benji's ass if I can't stop itching."

She sighs. "Let me see."

I show her my arm. It should look like a mine field of little bumps.

"All I see is your scratch marks. Go and put some calamine lotion on and check your sugars."

I spray one arm with the oven cleaner, leaving the other for some pink soothing liquid. The nozzle still works and the clear fluid bubbles up and burns both my nose and the skin. Die! Mother Fuckers!

I climb back up, moving the 1970's toaster I broke when I inserted a Sesame Street stop sign into the bread slot, but don't see any calamine lotion. There's Pepto. Same difference. I jump off the counter and carry the pink bottle to the shower, hoping I can wash away the feeling. The warm water makes me want to scrape and dry hump anything in site. Fuck. I turn the dial to cold. Let those fuckers freeze! Now I can finally think. Maybe I've got some weed seed stuck under my skin and it's sprouting and mutating and shit.

I finish the ice tour and pour the pink Pepto on me. I know it isn't calamine lotion, but he color is right and all I have to do is suffocate the little fuckers. Lewis and Clark used to kill syphilis with mercury. I guess a couple of hours at Seattle High is about to pay off.

My "control" arm where I sprayed the oven cleaner has turned a little bit green/black, kind of like slick motor oil. The burn left once I hopped in the shower.

***

Dad starts the truck, the low rumble shaking my ass. He says nothing but pushes Patsy Cline into the tape deck. He passes me a death stick, his own cigarette sticks to his lower lip. The truck smells like heaven…nicotine and car parts.

"We can't forget this, Sissy would be pissed if something happened," he says, holding up the doggie seatbelt that Angie insists Yoyo wears.

Dad pats his lap making the sissy dog wiggle and crawl over to him. Dad puts Yoyo's feet through the straps and the fluffy sheepskin hugs his chest. The click sounds as Dad mutters, "Stupid thing, it's more than we had when we brought you home from the hospital." He lights his cig and holds it out to bring me fire.

"What's with the dog?" I ask, curious why Yoyo's coming with us.

"Posterity."

"Trying to negotiate a cheaper fare by showing your pansy-ass side?" I ask.

"Shit," Dad says, pulling onto the street and turning towards me. "Can't a guy do something nice without his kids thinking he's a jerk?"

I laugh.

"Just thought we could take a picture of Angie's pup in her new ride."

"You brought your camera?"

Dad nods to toward the dashboard where months of pizza advertisements and T-oilers magazines have multiplied into paper towers.

"What kind of mobile do you have in mind?"

"Randy's friend said there's a little British number and a Porche. I thought maybe we could get your sister a nicer ride," Dad grumbles and pulls his Teamster hat down a bit farther still showing off his crop of old man ear hair.

Tawnie K. Bailey

Randy's buddy has been working the car auctions in Kent for a couple of years. He hooks Randy up with the shitty cars that nobody wants and Randy scraps them. He sometimes gives us leads on muscle cars that haven't been claimed and sometimes tells us about the police impounds. "If anyone's getting a Porche it should be me, Angie wouldn't know what to do with all that power." I can feel all those ponies thrusting at once and really wish I was bringing home a little 911.

We pull into the auction lot, mostly a mud pit in the winter and spring with a few weeds scattered here and there in the summer. Dad approaches the pay booth. Auctions used to be free, but the dollar became more important and the auction house decided that looking should cost a little bit, too.

"Three dollars," the man says, then points to a row of cars. Dad's paying for parking. Shit. I remember going to Mariner games where we had to walk a fuckin mile because Pops wouldn't pay a few bucks to park next to the Kingdome, but here he is at a field handing over cash for a little spot of mud. What Dad wouldn't do for his little Angel.

Dad parks the truck, the emergency break screeching when his boot hits the pedal then pulls a toothpick away from the truck visor. He twirls the toothpick then releases the dog seat belt with his thick fingers. "Come on buddy," he says to Yoyo and scoops him up.

I look up, curious to see what's up this week and see the usual clunkers; pintos, some nameless little Japanese cars and some huge-ass American-mades. We stroll down the rows, looking in windows, checking out tires, Dad eying the upholstery, always noticing when the leather is smooth.

"Hey Pops, there's an MG over there," I say, pointing to a white convertible.

We near the car, where the trunk is open. Boxes of shiny parts sit in the back. "Or maybe it's more of a parts car." The plastic window is in worse shape than Angie's with a nice Ducktape motif zigzagging across it.

Dad peers through the dishwater opaque plastic window. "She's going to need more than one to fix her heap."

"That's our Angie, always going the difficult route," I say, yanking the driver's door open and spotting a nice MG medallion gear shifter.

90

Dad turns and looks at me, takes his toothpick out and rumbles his bearish laugh. "You think she's difficult? She's still on training wheels while you're trying to be Mario Andretti."

"I'm just going for the gold." I climb into the car, letting Pops stand at the open door, inspecting the door panels. "You looking for drugs?"

"Never know what you can find in these things."

"Yeah, we don't want to bring Christine home and have Angie's car go all Stephen King freaky and shit." I sit back, imagining Angie in this car, her long legs touching the petals as the petals lock up, not responding and making her slam into a cement wall. "These little cars really do feel like a coffin," I say, jumping out of the seat feeling like I just released some sex offender on a kiddie school.

Dad tries to release the hood, but a chain connects the hood to the grill. "Guess someone else has a hood that pops up on the road," Dad says. "What do you think?"

I squat in front of the wire wheels that Angie marks off in her MG catalog of wishes. "These have the tires Ange likes," I say, my boot squishing into the mud.

"Maybe they won't work in her car. May not be interchangeable."

A fuckin rim attaches a tire to the car, big deal. But I don't want Dad thinking I'm an asshole.

"How much should we bid?"

"It's too small for the 'Humpty Dance,' so it's worth at least the cost of birth control."

Dad looks at me, his eyes beady and pissed, reminding me of crows swooping down to bombard my ass. Then he smiles.

"How much are the wheels she wants?"

"I think they were over a grand."

Pops places Yoyo in the driver's seat and takes a picture, the Kodak instantly reproducing the moment. Then he then walks away, his decision made.

Chapter 19- Angelina

October, 1991

"I don't understand why I'm not enough for him," Morgan says as she's driving me to the clinic. Her mouth barely lifts at the corners as she stares ahead at the red light, the windshield wipers making a hypnotic sweep.

"He's an ass!" Morgan's boyfriend always brings out swear words.

"I love him."

"But he asked you to go tanning! That's like asking a black guy to bleach his skin because you find it sexier."

"I'm pasty."

"Do you think tanning beds will burn less than the sun? Besides, he's a jerk for telling you to lose weight. You have the body most of us would kill for. You should ask him to attend a church that's in a different language and see how he likes it. And have your mom tell him she'd rather you date a white boy in front of his face. He needs to stick up for you. Caleb couldn't figure out why somebody more in your league hadn't snatched you up. I just want you to be with somebody who treats who better," I say. We're in front of the clinic where the boarding dogs are singing a chorus.

Morgan sighs. "I know you're right. I guess I'd rather go tanning than deal with it."

"No tanning!" I say, hopping out of her Camry. I hope Morgan throws the loser to the curb.

I walk into the clinic where the smell of rotten cheese knocks me over. My eyes follow the thudding from the corner where I see a cocker spaniel scratching his head. Ah, cocker ears. Poor babies; they have so many allergies. When you add heavy ears and moisture, their ears become the best bacteria and yeast houses around.

"Angelina, would you set up an ear swab?" Dr. Mike asks after the cocker is brought into the room.

I swab the ear goo and wipe a thin film across a slide. I grab the Bic lighter and find Steven. "Would you light this for me?" I ask. I'm a weenie, convinced the fire starter will roar to life like a dragon and burn me.

Steven applies the flame to the bottom of the slide, heat fixing it. The slide is then submerged into three different solutions, rinsed, and dried.

"Do you see the structures that look like footprints, those are yeast," Dr. Mike explains. "And those smaller rice-shaped structures are bacteria. So this dog has both yeast and a bacterial infection." Dr. Mike rarely swabs ears; this pup's swab is a testament to how painful and gross his ears are.

Later, Dr. Mike offers to drive me home.

"I'm meeting my best friend up the street for pizza."

Instead, I walk to the bus stop and catch the bus to Morgan's house. I hope she doesn't hate me for telling her that her boyfriend sucks.

Morgan lives about nine blocks down from the bus stop. Unfortunately, I have to walk by Lyndsey's house. I don't see Caleb's car, that's good. I don't see any obvious "Bianca prizes" on her lawn, but it's been six months, an adequate time frame for condom removal.

Bianca, my beautiful and unpredictable friend from the ritzy school, did *not* appreciate Caleb's abrupt departure from my life, as her own boyfriend had just messed up. When Bianca flew to Iowa to see her boyfriend, he dropped her off at the front door of the local mall while he went to park his car and he never came back. Imagine being out of state, in a town you didn't know, and being treated like an unwanted dog.

When Caleb began seeing Lyndsey again, Bianca made it her mission to "get even." She didn't know Caleb or Lyndsey, she wanted an outlet for her "boyfriends suck" rage, which they provided. When Bianca asked for Lyndsey's address, I thought a couple of eggs would spread across her lawn or something I would've giggled at but would never participate in. Instead, she sent a large quantity (34 separate cards) of Business Reply Mail to Lyndsey Walker. Business Reply Mail, the junk mail and advertisements for unwanted material in the Sunday paper in the coupon section. You know, a "Collector's Edition (fill in an actor's name here) Plate" for three easy payments of $19.95, c.o.d., or a must-have figurine. Yes, the c.o.d. thing is especially unwise, but they offer it. Who would send you something without payment first?

Reveling in her revenge, Bianca wrote Lyndsey's name and number in many men's rooms. I told her not to humiliate Lyndsey's parents, as Caleb thinks the world of them. She told me she'd already strewn undergarments and condoms all around their yard.

I continue walking until I reach Morgan's house. "We were hoping we'd see you tonight," Morgan's mom, Mary, says as she opens the door and steps aside.

"I couldn't stay away." I say, sinking into their plush couches. I sat here watching the Berlin wall come down, living through history and knowing I'd rather be with this family than anywhere else.

Morgan is sitting next to me eating my favorite meal—chicken salad with roasted almonds and Top Ramen noodles.

"Angelina, have you eaten yet? I have gobs of salad on the counter." Carol knows that even when I'm obsessing about weight issues, I can't turn down her creations.

"I didn't come over here for dinner."

"Does that mean you don't like my cooking?" Mary asks.

Morgan's dad, Rob, laughs, his tummy rolls moving up and down. He stands up. "I'll dish you up a bowl."

"So, Morgie, there's a group meeting at the school tonight in honor of Homecoming. Are you going?" I'm sure I'm breaking teenage code to have this conversation in front of her parents, but I can't keep them out of the loop.

"I'll think about it."

I eat a forkful of salad. It's perfect.

Morgan stands up and takes my plate when I finish. "Let me grab my keys and I'll drive you home. Unless you're going to tee-pee the school on foot."

"It's probably better to have a fast get-away. Thanks for the wonderful dinner," I say to Mary and Rob.

"Are you feeling any better?" I ask when we're driving back to my house.

"Um, yeah. I don't know why I can't be Michael's dream girl. I ignore so many of the obnoxious things he does."

"Why don't you guys take a break?"

"I told him I don't want to hang around somebody who tries to make me feel bad."

"Good. I can set you up with my previous blind dates," I joke.

Morgan looks at me for a moment and we both laugh. She met UpChuck and a few others.

"If I had anyone worthy, I'd offer him up to you right away."

"Like my brother?"

Morgan's brother and Caleb are close friends and roommates. After *Caleb and Angelina Chapter 2* went south, I had a few dates with her brother as well. I'd convinced myself I liked him and wasn't trying to get closer to Caleb, etc. I love him as he's such a part of Morgan's world, but it wasn't meant to be. He did enlighten me as to the many methods of gaining employment. He invented all kinds of jobs to pad his resume with the philosophy that anybody bothering to call an out-of-state previous employer wouldn't be worth working for. I know Mary and Rob would be embarrassed if they knew their son lied.

"I don't think I'll go out tonight," Morgan says.

"You're going to the game, right?"

"Of course. I need to see your blind date! But I have dance class very late, so I'll miss the first part of the game."

My house, the "brown turd" as Aaron calls it, looks quiet, but toilet paper is streaming all over my car. If the toilet paper is placed on a site that's easy to clean, then it's a sign of respect; if it's accompanied by eggs, not so much.

I walk up to the British beast, noticing there's something written on the windshield. "'92 Babe." That's not so bad. It could've said the b-t-h word.

Letting toilet paper go to my head, I know I've just won a high school Emmy.

I walk into the house and see my little man waiting for me, standing next to his dish, making me feel inconsiderate.

"Yoyo, do you want to come with me?" I buckle Yoyo's doggie seat belt. Since there is so much writing on the back window, I unzip it and let the cold breeze through.

I turn the key. The dreaded moment. My little chitty chitty bang bang (and yes it moves and chugs and sputters) starts up! Keith Sweat's "Make it Last Forever" sings through the radio. Yoyo's little tongue sneaks out and his eyes dance like he's smiling.

When I arrive at Seattle High, Vanessa's leaning against a car with about thirty other people and paper snow is everywhere. Toilet paper streams from lights, along the parking lot, from the roof of the school to the ground, every surface I can see is covered. Good old Seattle High is squeezably soft.

I let Yoyo out of the car and walk over to Troy, shaking my head when I see his poor banged up car. Even Oscar the Grouch would by-pass this doozy in favor of a straighter can. Everyone's painting their name on a door panel.

"What's the matter, Angelina? Do you think I won't be able to sell it with signatures?" Troy asks. Both doors are smashed in, the hood is chained down, and duck tape and bungee cords hold it together, who cares about a little paint?

Alright, it's silly to have reservations, but it feels *wrong*. Nonetheless, I sign my name on his car in purple paint.

"Your handwriting looks like calligraphy," a classmate says.

"Too bad I couldn't market it." Yes, it's true, I have beautiful handwriting. It's not something that would win me a talent portion of any beauty pageant, so I guess I'd better not submit my application.

Troy turns up his stereo and "Back to Life," a constant at every Seattle High dance, blares. Yoyo's in heaven, his eyes are sparkling and he's bouncing back and forth. I should take him with me more often.

The night ends pretty quickly when we hear sirens and see a police car across the field. Not wasting any time, we boogie to our cars to leave. I rebuckle Yoyo's seat belt and turn the key. The damn thing just clicks.

Chapter 20–Angelina

October, 1991

I turn the key again. Nothing. My heart, keeping up with the sirens in volume and rhythm has moved to my ears as I hear blood pumping.

Come on, car, please start! I turn the key and press the gas pedal again just as two police cars race through the parking lot, their lights dizzying.

"Put your hands on the steering wheel!"

Oh crap, oh crap, oh crap! I place my hands on the wheel as ordered, my hands shaking like a Parkinson's patient.

"Keep your hands on the steering wheel where I can see them!" The officer approaches slowly, my eyes drawn to his gun. His flashlight reaches my window piercing through the car. After sweeping the interior, the blinding light lands on my face. "Roll down your window!" he barks.

Blinking, I follow his orders.

"What are you doing here?" He clicks off the flashlight, my eyes still dazzling.

"I saw the toilet paper and wanted a closer look." I notice a second officer on the passenger's side and officers from the other car walking towards the gym.

"What's your name?"

"Angelina Hulgey."

His eyebrows arch as though he recognizes it. "I'd like to see your ID." I reach to Yoyo's side and fumble with my wallet. "Any relationship to Aaron or Randy Hulgey?" he asks, examining my driver's license.

"They're my brothers."

"What do you have in your car?" he asks, his stare boring into my eyes.

"Just my dog."

"Did you participate in the vandalism of school property?"

"No."

Tawnie K. Bailey

"You were driving by and thought you'd take a closer, huh? We received a call about vandalism and possible burglary. Did you see who did this?"

"I must have just missed them," I say.

"Didn't you hear our sirens?"

"I tried to leave but my car wouldn't start."

"I'm going to run your information and will be right back."

Oh shit. So far, I haven't lied—I didn't see anyone apply toilet paper....

"Alright Miss Hulgey, I need you to get out of the car, place your hands on the side while I search your vehicle." I climb out, sure I'm going to join my brothers and have a rap sheet. So much for all of my hard work.

Since the MG is tiny, it doesn't take him long.

"I'm going to talk to the principal and discuss your involvement here tonight. You'll be hearing from me soon."

Ugh. I don't want our principal to think I did this. I climb back in the car and turn the key. Nothing. I open the door again and lift the hood as the second officer leaves to check the grounds.

"Is it your battery?" the officer asks.

"Probably not. I poured Pepsi on the terminals last week and the alternator is new." As light illuminates the engine compartment, I remove the fuse box, looking for the usual suspects. Another blown fuse. Thank goodness! I have extras in the glove box. The stupid starter blows through these things like crazy. If this electrical system is any indication of how the English operate, I wouldn't be surprised if they still rely on kerosene lamps. Stupid shaking fingers! I replace the fuse and close the hood.

"This has happened before, I take it?" The officer looks amused.

"I should've bought a Honda."

"Don't you mean steal it?"

"Excuse me?"

"Your brothers, wouldn't they just steal one?"

"Maybe. I don't know what they do when they aren't home. I don't think Hondas are their thing. And I'm not my brothers."

He chuckles. "Be safe and stay out of trouble."

I turn the key and this time it starts.

Chapter 21–Angelina

October, 1991

It's Homecoming and date night with William. Morgan and I get off the bus and head into the law offices.

"Angelina, I'm working on a discovery. There's a bankruptcy for you to type and it's lick and stick time," says Mark's legal aid, Gail, a wild woman in her late-30s who's become my foster mom in the last year.

I groan. I've tried the office supply store's solution to this licking and sticking (a little device with water in a receptacle on a sponge), but the envelopes don't stick. I start by photocopying the usual letters out to clients and opposing counsel.

"I'm skipping dance class tonight for Homecoming," Morgan says while the copier chugs out my letters.

Then I fill in the bankruptcy paperwork. I hate the medical bankruptcies; most revolve around sick kids. Nobody should have to give up their future because their kids got sick.

Finishing up the bankruptcy, Mark's gregarious laughter fills the room as his footsteps near.

"Kristoph, Gail will give you a couple of forms. The sooner you fill them out and return them, the faster we can prepare your response." I look up briefly then jump back, the room becoming a giant kaleidoscope, swirling around and around.

Mr. Hughes looks over at my desk, his head jerking as his eyes grow round.

Gail notices the exchange. "Do you know our assistant, Angelina?"

Mr. Hughes pauses, shifts his weight then his gaze. "I do. Angelina, it's nice to see you. Have you worked here long?" Mr. Hughes asks, once again the professional he's supposed to be.

"A little over a year," I say.

Tawnie K. Bailey

His lips tighten. "I trust you're aware of confidentiality standards in this profession?" he asks, pushing his glasses up higher on his nose, but staring at me.

"Mr. Hughes," Mark says, resuming a more distant tone, "Angelina is a valuable member of our team. Do you need more time to consider our arrangements?"

"I'll complete the forms and get back to you," Mr. Hughes says, his loafers squeaking as he turns to leave.

Mark slowly closes Gail's office door, a door that like mine, never really closes.

The tension is thick enough to see. "What's that about?" Gail asks.

"He's my history teacher," I say, chuckling. What a small world.

Mark runs his left hand through his hair, his eyes calculating some risk before sitting down. "He's seeking representation."

"So I gathered," I say, wondering at the mystery. "What's up?"

"A former student's accusing him of sexual misconduct."

Oh boy.

"Does she have grounds?" Mark asks. "Off the record, Angelina."

"He has a reputation for sleeping with his TAs." Several weeks ago he asked if I had time to become his assistant and placed his hand on my shoulder. "I get that creepy vibe," I say.

"He married a previous student?" Mark asks.

I nod. "His teaching assistant before he divorced his first wife."

"He claims an obsessed former student's jealous of his marriage, so she filed the suit to get even."

A chuckle escapes and I shake my head. "Did he give a name?"

"I think we'd better bow out. Conflict of interests," Mark says, rising.

Gail scoots her chair closer to mine after Mark leaves. "Do you know her?"

"I think so. I think it's Caleb's girlfriend."

"Your Caleb?" Gail asks.

"Yeah. And as much as I can't stand Lyndsey, she wouldn't do this just to get even." But I still don't like her.

"I'm glad Mark's giving him the Ole Heave-Ho. We don't need Clarence Thomas walking through our halls."

Our history class watched the Judge Clarence Thomas trials and discussed the possibility that the judge sexually harassed his staffers and what consequences should ensue if these allegations were true. Now this teacher, who discussed at length virtues we should uphold, may be disciplined for his unvirtuous actions.

"Well, forget what you saw and heard today." Gail turns back towards her desk. "I have a deposit for you." Gail hands me two bank bags.

I grab my jacket, hoping the weather won't ruin the hairdo for my date tonight. I'm wearing black knee-high boots and tight black pants with a V-necked longer sweater and my leather jacket. I've done everything I can this week to avoid scratching my face. Just like every other girl, my hair is permed and Seattle rain can make it frizzy. Usually I lock my curls in with a curling iron and hairspray, so it looks more like large curls than a fresh perm but the weather has the power to destroy all of my hard work.

"If you want to head out straight from here, go for it," Gail says. "I hear Vanessa set you up on another blind date." She giggles. "Bow chickie bow wow."

"Did Morgan tell you I coerced her to come, too?" I ask.

Gail throws her hands up. "Chicken!"

"Maybe she'll find true love tonight and not me," I add. She knows I can't stand Morgan's boyfriend, Michael.

She laughs and sends me out of the door. "We'll want details next week." Maybe I shouldn't have told her about my date last year with the Date Singer. I heard Jonathan singing a duet of "Ebony and Ivory" with our football star and told Morgan I wanted somebody to sing to me like that. Apparently God has a sense of humor because later I went on a date with Jonathan and he sang everything; we were at dinner and literally every conversation was met with a show tune, or having my last word repeated in a medley. Dinner invoked some looks of awe from surrounding diners then some looks of "ahhhhh." Then he wanted to dance. Who dances at restaurants? I agreed if for no other reason than I didn't want to hear any more spontaneous musical chords. They continued and were accompanied by bursts of hot air in my ear. I don't know if he was so naive he didn't realize that blowing in a woman's ear was supposed to be subtle, almost a tickle, not feel like gusts of strong winds.

The night inspired a regular feature in our school newspaper, called "The Rules." The rules were general recommendations for guys trying to date us ladies. Jonathan is a truly good guy. Who knows, maybe he'll be famous or sign with Motown or even open for Keith Sweat someday. I'm sure I'll think he's the hottest guy alive, but for now the date is commonly used against me by my coworkers.

Morgan and I finish our bank transactions and head over to the Seattle Center, where our football games are held. We walk towards Seattle High's bleachers and spot Vanessa, our butterfly. When I dated Caleb, I listened to his friends but rarely added to their conversation, whereas Vanessa seemed to fit in readily. I think it's her self-confidence and her infectious laughter. I'll have to work on the laughter thing.

We walk down the stairs until we're standing adjacent to Vanessa. The rather hunky person sitting next to her stands up like a gentleman as Vanessa introduces us. "William?" I greet. I need to remember not to drool. "Are you ready for your blind date?"

"Vanessa doesn't think I have enough culture to hang out with your classmates," he says.

I raise my eyebrows. William and Jacob's school is "all white." My school, to steal a commercial quote, is a rainbow of fruity flavors.

"What do you think?"

"I can handle it," he says and smiles, his perfect teeth the center of the masterpiece of chiseled jaw, kind expression, bright blue eyes and dark brown hair.

Morgan jumps in. "So, William, what do you do for fun?"

He laughs. "Ah, group dating, huh? If I date one, I date you all?"

"No, we haven't said we'll let you date our friend yet. We'll see if you meet our standards first. Then we'll let you try to meet Angelina's," Vanessa says.

He looks over at me and smiles. Hmm. Can I picture us married with kids yet?

"Bring it on. I play baseball and guitar and I enjoy listening to music and hanging out with my friends." So not as intriguing as my date with Charlie. I need to keep an open mind, especially since William lives close by. And he is eye candy.

Seattle High is not known for its athletic prowess. Because of the poor performance and the location of our "home field" the attendance at our football games is pretty low. Losing is a tradition at Seattle High. Caleb's senior year, we once lost 96 to 6. Tonight's game is a little more populated. I scan the crowd and see the back of a familiar person. There is fried blonde hair and the back of a shirt that says "Can't touch this." The matching shorts say "Caleb's." At least the apostrophe is in the right place!

"Look what the cat dragged in," Morgan comments as her eyes lock onto the MC Hammer shirt. I don't say anything, as I wonder whether her lawsuit is real. It makes me wonder how many other girls go to school, put on a smile and pretend everything is alright.

Vanessa picks up our comments. "William, don't you know Lyndsey?"

"Lyndsey Walker? Yeah, I've known her family for several years."

Great, another contaminated male. I suppose he finds her to be beautiful and smart and sweet.

"Did you ever date?" I ask. I can't help it. Morgan nudges me.

"No. She isn't my style. She's used to being the center of her universe and wants to be the center of everyone else's. Look at her clothes."

Maybe he has potential! "So you play sports?" I ask William, who looks like he could be an Olympic star.

"I play them, but I'm not great at most of them. I do dabble in baseball a little."

"Dabble?"

"All right, I'm trying to sound humble. Vanessa said you can't stand arrogance." My face is turning red. "Baseball is my sport and I'm awesome at it. There. I said it."

"You don't have to be humble for me. If you've earned the title of greatness, I'll accept that." I'm smiling. And, yes, even I can tell I'm flirting.

"What do you want to be?" Morgan asks.

"I don't know. What a sad answer, isn't it? My parents own a financial management company, so I imagine I'll go to college for investing. I'm good at it, I just don't know if I'm passionate enough to make it my life."

"There's always baseball."

William laughs. "I'm a pretty awesome baseball player, but not delusional. What about you?" he asks Morgan.

"I'm reconsidering studying dance and biology at UW. I think I'll follow Angelina to WSU and figure it out."

That is the first I heard of this plan! "Morgan! That would be incredible!" I can't help my face from glowing at the prospect of having one of my dearest friends with me on the other side of the mountains. Too bad she's joking.

"You couldn't get in at UW?" William asks.

"I realize WSU doesn't have high standards," I joke "but I want to be a veterinarian, and it's the only vet school in the state."

"I suppose it's excusable then," he smiles.

The football game starts. Let me be the first to admit I don't understand football. I attend games to support our school and be with friends. Vanessa is paying more attention than I can ever remember to a football game. Ah, there's Jacob. He's doing pretty well but he is playing against my school's team, so that isn't hard.

***

I wake up exhausted. Sometimes I wish I didn't work so much. I know I'm a type A personality, but it doesn't mean I wouldn't like to change.

I smile, thinking about last night. William is a confident dancer and quite the flirt. He and Jacob grooved with most of my friends and me. At the end of the night, William walked me to Morgan's car, held my hand and gave me a single peck on the cheek. I'm not sure what to make of the whole night. If I wasn't so tired, I'd analyze every moment over and over, but I need to focus on getting ready for work.

Clients are waiting in their cars as I arrive; I'm not late! Why do I feel like I'm behind? I enter through the side door, turn on the lights and place my car keys and purse in Dr. Mike's office. I unlock the main door, open it and wave to the awaiting clients.

The day is very busy with vaccines and sick patients. I don't have time to converse with anyone beyond the scope of veterinary medicine. I'm mopping up the lobby when Dr. Mike reminds me of our meeting at the New Moon Cafe.

"Do you want to drive over there?" he asks.

"Parking can be tough. Let's walk. I got my little car fixed but it ended up costing a great deal more than the quote."

"Do you like it?" Dr. Mike asks. I have my back to him as I'm dumping the mop water and replacing the bucket in the closet.

"I've only driven it this week. And I haven't crashed it!"

Dr. Mike locks up the door to the clinic as I wait for him. He has his jacket with him, but not the usual paperwork.

We walk several blocks together. I look at the British automobile parts store where a Jaguar sits in the showroom. Now *that* is a car I'd like to own.

Approaching the cafe, I notice nobody from the clinic has parked in the lot. I wonder if they needed to run errands before the staff meeting.

"For two?" the hostess asks.

Dr. Mike answers "Yes."

I'm confused. We're supposed to be having a staff meeting, why would Dr. Mike say we should be seated for two?

The waitress seats us in a booth with bright red seats and stainless steel accents. "Weren't we supposed to have a staff meeting?"

"Nobody else could make it tonight, so I thought we could have dinner and relax." Of course you did.

Chapter 22–Angelina

October, 1991

Of course you thought we could come here and relax. As if I'm relaxed sitting across from my boss on a Saturday night. You've been a mentor and a friend, but I don't want to be naïve and keep dismissing your bizarre behavior.

The waitress takes our order. I order the French dip and Dr. Mike orders a seafood platter.

"Are you stressed?" I ask, not sure why he needs to relax.

Dr. Mike grabs for my folded hands and holds them in his rough surgeon mitts.

"Peggy found out she has breast cancer." Dr. Mike looks away, his demeanor serious.

"How advanced?"

"We won't know until the biopsy results come in."

"You should be with her, you could've canceled! A staff meeting isn't as important as your wife, especially since nobody else could make it."

"Her sister flew in last night, so I thought I'd give them some time together."

Wishing I'd mentioned our staff meeting to Steven, I pat Mike's hand then place my hands around my water. Maybe Dr. Mike didn't even tell anyone else about it? And I could've gone out with William tonight. He invited me to hang out, and I declined because of this stupid staff meeting. "Is there anything I can do? I don't know anyone who has cancer, so I can't even think of any support group or anything, but I'm sure there are dozens out there."

"No. I need to relax and not think about it for a while."

"Okay." I'm scrambling for something to talk about. "How's the business doing?"

"We're doing alright. What did you do for your birthday?"

"Mom and I went out to dinner on Sunday night to celebrate and my friends and I went out on Tuesday."

"Now you can vote?" Dr. Mike smiles.

"No, I turned seventeen. I'd get a credit card and move away from my family if I was eighteen."

Dr. Mike hesitates. "Do you need money?"

"Don't we all? My mom convinced the mechanic he could be sued for a breach of contract. I didn't want to upset this guy since there aren't many British auto mechanics out there but now my car works and I'm broke."

Dr. Mike pulls out his wallet. "Consider this my birthday present to you." He pulls out four $100 bills.

What, is that all? This is crazy. "Mike, I can't accept that. It isn't right." Just then our meals arrive. I smile at the waitress as the money sits on the table. I'm sure this looks bad: an older man sitting across the table from a teenager, holding her hand briefly and setting $400 on the table! And, no, Dr. Mike does not look like Richard Gere and I am not The Pretty Woman.

Dr. Mike takes a bite and makes a face. Does he have gas?

"Is it bad?" I ask.

"No, it's good, just not Salty's." Dr. Mike has his eyes half closed and has assumed that weird soft spoken voice I've only heard on rare occasions.

"I've never been there."

"We should go there to celebrate your birthday."

"I'm not a big seafood person. Besides, you should take your family out, not me." Please, please, please stop inviting me places! I am not imaginative enough to create new excuses!

Dr. Mike puts a quarter in the tabletop jukebox and picks an Elvis Song—"Love me Tender." Oh please. You are not Rico Suave. You're not going to sweep me off of my feet. I can keep telling myself that the staff meeting is a misunderstanding but I keep thinking about my conversation with Charlie. I am not stupid. Dr. Mike, who I considered a dear friend for some tough years of my life, is acting like an ass.

Dr. Mike told me long ago not to get married until after vet school. I wanted him to believe in my commitment to veterinary medicine and often joked about my bad dates with him, while I never told him about the gentlemen I enjoyed spending time with.

"What car would you like?"

I don't tell him about the cute little black Toyota MR2 with Momo wheels I looked at one day when my car wasn't working. "One that works! "

"Let me know if you need anything, a new car, whatever."

"Thanks, but my dad bought a little MG for a parts car, so between the two, I should have a functional car soon." Dr. Mike co-signed on a loan for Steven and Carrie's house and for another coworker's new car. I know he's generous, and maybe his intentions are pure. I don't want to be some dumb girl who thinks everyone is after her. I know I'm not drop dead anything, but he wouldn't do this with my mom here.

"How's your mom?"

"She witnessed a pretty brutal beating on her bus."

Dr. Mike shakes his head. "She's a beautiful and kind woman. She deserves to be treated better and to stay at home or go shopping."

I laugh. "I agree. She deserves the best but I don't think she'd be happy staying at home anymore. Every Friday for the last ten years she's made ten dozen cookies. She wraps them in Saran Wrap and gives them out to her passengers."

I finish eating my sandwich as Dr. Mike asks for the bill. He shoves the money towards me. "Go ahead and take it. Use it any way you want to."

I smile and shake my head. "I haven't earned it, but thank you for the offer."

"Are you ready to go?" Dr. Mike asks as he scoops up the money and puts it into his wallet.

"Yes."

"Are you going to drive home first or straight to the skating rink?"

"Isn't everyone busy?" I ask, confused.

"They're meeting us there."

"Oh." We leave the cozy little café, walk a few blocks back to the clinic and I approach my car. After pulling at the handle, the door creaks open—I can't lock the doors since the locks have broken keys stuck in them. I get in and turn the ignition. Keith Sweat blares out of the radio. I start the car and pull out of the driveway, wave to Dr. Mike and pull into a busy West Seattle street.

I drive home and let Yoyo out and pick up my skates. I arrive at the rink in time to see my coworkers waiting in line with Dr. Mike. I wave.

Steven waves. "We saved you a spot slow poke! Did you have to Fred Flintstone it to get here?"

"Haha, my car isn't that bad!" Okay, so the floorboards are rusted and have holes in them large enough for a foot to drop down, but carpeted floor mats cover them.

As we advance in the line, Dr. Mike pulls out a wad of cash and pays for us.

I enter through the double doors and enter a world that's as familiar as my bedroom. The carpeted floor follows the perimeter of the rink. The smell of carpet cleaner and nacho cheese combo comforts me. I spent three days a week here for years.

The clinic first skated together right after I started, and Dr. Mike joined us about a year ago. Dr. Mike wasn't steady on his feet initially and would hold my hand while his wheels rolled. Now everyone is good enough that we only hold hands on trio skate, where I whip two people across the sky blue floor.

I feel such freedom when I skate. It's like gliding and flying and just responding to the music. I have sharp instincts and luckily haven't broken any bones since junior high. My instructors told me I was the most graceful student they'd ever trained. I would've preferred to be the fastest back then, but grace and beauty are nice too.

I tighten up the laces and stand, my adrenaline high bubbling up as I approach the floor. I'd love to rent the rink all to myself and play my music all night long. I start the long strokes and quickly turn backwards. I see Dr. Mike approach the floor in between looking over my shoulder and looking ahead.

The rest of the crew follows his lead. We used to play tag and other games like follow the leader, but it's frowned upon—and I adore the owners of the rink.

"Fancy moves, Angelina," Steven teases.

"Yeah, yeah." I'm a bit of a show off when it comes to skating. It's the only sport where I don't feel totally awkward. We skate for the rest of the session with me intermittently helping Steven with his daughter or free skating. She's good enough now to skate without holding her dad's hands.

"I kissed my first boyfriend at this rink," I tell Steven during couple's skate.

"Oh yeah?"

"Sam in sixth grade." I remember kissing Sam's cheek and seeing the light blonde fuzz on his cheek and thinking about its softness. "We skated to Madonna's 'I'm Crazy for You.' An older girl asked if we were in love and I said yes. The funny thing is that even back then I knew it wasn't right to say it without meaning it. I didn't want to say no and hurt Sam's feelings but worried I said too much."

Seven laughs. "You were worried in the sixth grade?! Do you ever relax?"

I give him a funny look. "You know me. What do you think?"

"Nope."

"Exactly. I'm a little Miss Priss through and through."

"I didn't say that. You worry too much." Steven is trying to skate backwards but he keeps looking at the ground and I correct him. Your body follows your head, so if you look down, your weight is distributed wrong.

"Hey, how come you couldn't attend the staff meeting?"

"What?" Steven looks up suddenly and loses his balance. I steady him.

"I asked why you didn't show up at the New Moon for our staff meeting."

"I didn't know we were having a staff meeting."

Just what I thought. "I think it's a poor communication thing." I say, trying to change the subject.

"Did anyone else go?" Steven looks concerned.

"Nope."

"Angelina, that sucks. I'm sorry. I'll call you the next time I hear of a staff meeting."

"No, don't worry about it. I need to take care of this myself." I'm not sure what to make of this, but I'm angry.

It's my turn to couple's skate with Dr. Mike. Normally, I spin the guys around, but I can't even handle the thought of touching his hands. Instead, I instruct him how to skate backwards. I feel like shoving him backwards, but I restrain myself. I'd like to think I misunderstood something. Then, as the song ends a little boy asks if we're married. "Us? Not at all. He's my boss. He's way too old, is married and has a family. I'm just a young girl." Dr. Mike looks amused.

Why would a little kid confuse us for anything but friends? I hope Dr. Mike listened to what I said and wasn't confused himself. For the rest of the couple's skates, I stay at the far end of the rink and practice my jumps. I don't want something else I love to be tainted. I concentrate on skating and am back in my own world for the rest of the night.

I drive through White Center and see Dad's favorite tavern and his rusted grey truck. Dad doesn't usually drink on the weekends; he's usually just hung over. Mom thinks he's her prince charming and I think she was given the wrong story.

"Blame it on the Rain"—a big hit the first time I dated Caleb, sings out during the drive home. It played right after we broke up (Round 1). I thought it was so poetic, as if the rain was as likely of a cause to the end of our relationship as anything.

I pull into the driveway, turn off the car and open the front door. My fuzzy little man doesn't greet me. The house is quiet but lights are on in the entry, kitchen, living room and hallway.

"Hello?" I call out. I expect at least to see Yoyo come running. "Yoyooooo!" I walk into my room and peer under the bed. There's Yoyo, front legs flexed, his toes curled and his body shaking. High pitched whistles whimper out from his cave. I pull him out from under the bed and cradle him in my lap. "It's okay," I say to soothe him. This seizure lasts about a minute. Usually they last a minute or two and follow chaotic events. He blinks his eyes at me, moving his front leg in a stretch and sighs. I stroke his soft white curls and pull my hand along his ears. He fits so perfectly in my lap. He's been there through all of the big moments—my first kiss, my first love, the breakups, Dad's mistakes.

He stands up and shakes, his blue harness ringing his tags. I roughen up his head and stand up, realizing I've just created another bloody mound on the side of my face while sitting with Yoyo. I walk back into the kitchen and look around. There are empty milk jugs on the counter—nothing new there. After all, the recycling bin is a few feet away from the counter, so who can blame anyone for not trying to place the carton under the sink into the bin? At anyone else's house, it might look like someone left in a hurry. Here? Who knows?

I pick up the kitchen, place the empty cereal boxes into the garbage, stack the dirty dishes in the sink, that kind of thing. But "clean" requires a wet washcloth, chemicals, and scrubbing. I open up the cabinet under the sink and pull out some Windex. Alright, I realize Windex is supposed to be for windows. I'm hoping the strong chemical smell means it can break up the harmful germs running amuck in my house.

After the kitchen is as spotless as I can make it, I walk into my bathroom. Since it's the main bathroom, many-a-behind has sat on the same seat as me and my buns. The toilet seat receives the Windex treatment (okay, I use Raid when Lee's Herpes-Infested-Female comes over). I don't imagine anyone will want to see their face shine off of it, but at least it won't have any streaks.

It's pretty late. I take Yoyo out for a quick walk then notice the answering machine is blinking. I hit the play button. "Angelina, this is Mom. Aaron's in the hospital. He has a grinder lodged in his head."

Chapter 23–Angelina

October, 1991

"Wake up Sunshine! It's a glorious day outside." Mom does this rain or shine. It takes me a moment to remember Aaron has a grinder in his head.

"Is Aaron alright?" I sit up and yawn.

"Aaron tried to take a car apart using a grinder, you know the large disks with metal prongs? It got wrapped up in his hair, went into his scalp and bled like crazy. The fire department came over and tried to shave his hair off to assess the damage but decided to take him to the hospital first. We had an ambulance here, the fire department, you name it."

"But you said he's okay?"

"Yeah. The grinder wasn't deep, mostly superficial wounds. He lost some of his hair to a shaver, though."

Did I mention Aaron has longer hair than I do? I don't mention the smell anymore, since the last time I told Aaron to take a shower he stuck Yoyo under his armpit and Yoyo's little fluffy head smelled like a homeless man's sleeping bag. Yoyo didn't appreciate the bath he got thereafter, either.

"Oh, I'm sure he's mad! What are you doing awake now?"

"I couldn't sleep and my only daughter is at home."

Mom sounds euphoric. I smile at her. I used to want a little sister. Now I'm glad I don't have to share her. And I wouldn't want a sister to try and use my name if she got caught by the police. Randy and Lee have each other's social security numbers memorized. If either of them is in trouble, they often use the other one's info to try and avoid jail time. Aaron has given out Todd's info as well. He doesn't pass for a 15-year-old, but he tries to pull it off.

"Do you want to go to breakfast or something?" Mom loves to have bread pudding for breakfast. Anything called pudding shouldn't be eaten for breakfast.

"We could do that."

"Maybe I'll have some cottage cheese and fruit." We don't have any good fruit since our old refrigerator ruins anything tasty.

"Would you like to go shopping instead?" Now, I don't often pass up the opportunity to go shopping. I am a girl. But I also feel guilty.

"I don't have any money left after the mechanic."

"I went and refinanced one of the houses, and now I have money for taxes and for your trip to Greece."

"You went and borrowed more money?"

"It isn't really borrowing money. I got a much better rate, so I'll be saving money. Besides, I want to pay fifty percent of Greece now so when spring nears I'll have most of it paid for."

Mom's logic is beyond me, but I'm glad that she remembers her promise to send me to Greece this spring as a graduation present. "Let's go to breakfast, then."

We're seated at a small booth.

"Hi, Caroline!" our waitress greets. "Have you had a nice week?" Oh no, here it comes, the polite question that will be answered with honesty. I'm cringing inside as I know my mom will spill the happenings of the last seven days.

"Oh you know, Garrett's drunk again, Aaron keeps visiting the ER, Lee and Randy don't have jobs, I never see Angelina, and Todd doesn't like school."

"I'm sorry to hear that." The waitress smiles sadly. That's pretty tame for my mom. Fort the last fifteen years, my mom has shopped at the same grocery store, filling two shopping carts. In fact, food falls out of the carts on the way to the register most of the time. She places the food onto the conveyor belt and hunts through her purse for her checkbook or pen. She writes out the check as she and the checker talk. Inevitably there is a long line of people behind us (because it takes a long time to ring up that much food) who will then hear the tale of our life that week. Mom is generally flippant and casual about it, like "Garrett urinated on the carpet in our room again," and I am horrified.

We place our orders: bread pudding for Mom and side of cantaloupe and a banana crepe for me. "How was your date the other night?" my mom asks. It's funny because she never likes anyone I'm dating until we break up. Then, I never hear the end of it. Or rather, the next guy I date never hears the end of it. And she often calls them the wrong name. Oops!

"Pretty fun. William is attractive and interesting."

"Are you going out with him again?"

"Probably. Vanessa's dating his best friend."

"I remember when Sally and I dated friends. I think it made the guys seem so much better than they were."

"I don't think William has much baggage." Alright, I know I'm lying. I over analyze enough to know that I'm attracted to other people with chaotic and messy childhoods. But does my mom need to hear that? No.

"Weren't you dating some boy from Gig Harbor?"

"He doesn't live in Gig Harbor, but close. I didn't date him, Mom. It was a blind date. He's also pretty great, but he lives far away."

"And Caleb? Anything new with him?"

"I haven't dated him in a long time."

"I know, but I think you were happiest with him. Go after what you want, Angelina." I don't know how to respond. My mom knows me better than I think. She's loved her husband her entire adult life, and that couldn't be easy.

Chapter 24–Aaron

October, 1991

I stole from my mom last night. She slept in the recliner, her nose sucking in air all loud while my brain eased off a long week of fun. I felt awful and wanted to get something better so I didn't crash off of the shit. I went into Angelina's room looking for money since she sometimes stashes cash in her desk drawer, but no paper or baubles—and I needed it.

My head became heavy, the weight squishing me to the ground when I heard my mom's ring calling my name. "Here Aaron, here little Aaron. Your mom won't mind, she loves you." I have to laugh remembering it. I fuckin stole Mom's wedding ring off her finger while she slept.

***

Mom thinks I took her ring and I feel like shit. I hocked it and took off for a week and ended up back in the hospital. She sent me to rehab, but I walked out after the first day. Mom's all attached to it and shit, just because Dad gave it to her when he proposed. I'll buy her a new one. A better one. My brain just isn't letting me remember who I sold it to. I work with about a dozen pawn shops and a couple of 'my boys'. Nobody remembers me having it. So, I'm fucked.

The last time I stole from Mom and Dad, they changed the alarm codes on me. When I triggered the alarm, the police came and wouldn't do anything since I'm family—they called it a domestic matter and charged my mom $50 for a false alarm. Today I climbed onto the roof and onto the deck. The deck doesn't have much of a lock, and the alarm wasn't even activated. I walk into the kitchen. I'm so hungry. My stomach's a slowly churning pit, burning away everything I feed it. Before my diabetes diagnosis, my skin itched like I had fuckin ants running all over me. I yelled at Mom for buying cheap ass laundry soap. She switched soaps. Then I started drinking and pissing all the time and she shipped me off to the doctor. She's always taking me to the doctor and asking me what she can do to make my life better. I know she loves me. I hate myself for stealing from my mom, but when I'm in that moment, when I need to feel something else, I don't care about anything except that feeling.

I've done a lot of things I regret; my anger is a gun without a safety. I've beat up my little brother a lot. He's pretty short and can be an ass, but I'm a bigger one. I once hit my sister with a car, thinking for a moment she was the devil. Mom doesn't know. Angelina wasn't really hurt; as soon as I heard her yelling, I saw Angelina and not the dark thing that stole my eyes for a while. I turned off the car and got out, and called out to her. She turned around while she was walking up the back steps and told me to fuck off. Mom took her to the doctor a few days later because her ribs hurt. Angelina said it was from coughing too hard, and maybe it was; she was sick. I'm not going to hurt her again.

Chapter 25–Angelina

October, 1991

If bad breath could be visualized, a plume of death fog would be escaping from my mouth as I yawn. I take Yoyo out and return to bed. I pull the covers over my head and hope to fall into the abyss. Instead I stare up at my green covers. I wonder if this is what spelunkers feel, surrounded on all sides in darkness, feeling the weight of your own breath as it leaves your mouth and boomerangs back to you. It feels like I'm hiding.

Aaron and I used to hide together all the time, sometimes while playing with Todd, sometimes for "the real thing." When I was about four years old, as Dad was preparing to leave for work, he looked in his lunch box for his coconut Sno Ball snack.

"Caroline! Get in here!" His screaming woke me up. I could hear my mom as she went into the kitchen.

"Your God damned kids stole my coconut ball!" I couldn't hear what my mom said next, but heard the lunch box as it flew across the counter and hit the adjoining window and *crash*! The window broke and a few pieces of glass tinkled nearby.

Mom is soft spoken and gentle. I couldn't hear what she said, but it wasn't enough to calm my beast of a Dad. I heard his feet hit the steps on his way downstairs. Then I heard him yelling at my sleeping brothers.

I could hear Mom screaming back at Dad at this point, a rarity. Aaron snuck into my room and grabbed my hand from under my blankets. He didn't say a word. I followed his lead out of my room, down the hall and into the kitchen.

We snuck into the kitchen and crawled into our dark game cupboard on the backside of the kitchen peninsula. It smelled like plywood and barely fit the two of us.

"Angelina, I ate Dad's snack."

"Oh." Dad would discipline my older brothers until one confessed. I felt bad for him and worse for Lee and Randy. I could understand the appeal of the Sno Balls. We aren't given much junk food but Dad's lunch box contained tantalizing treats daily.

I could hear Mom crying. "Don't go into the little one's rooms! They are babies!" We're not babies, Aaron is in kindergarten.

"They need to be taught to respect me. You coddle them and train them to be pussies!" My mom is still crying.

My mom offered to go to 7-Eleven and buy him more goodies. Apparently he agreed because he quieted down and we heard Mom grab her purse and close the front door.

Aaron hummed "This Old Man" to distract me. Aaron then whispered to me. "Once upon a time a beautiful princess lived in a dark castle ... ." Aaron wove a safe little cocoon for me. He'd hold me and keep me safe and entertained. Dad never found us.

I continue to stare up at my sheets and sigh. I'm baggage. I don't want to lie here feeling sorry for myself. Aaron might send me Bounce Back—an audio cassette sent via request from the Church of Jesus Christ of Latter Day Saints. Whenever we heard the commercial, Aaron and I would call the 1800 number and request a tape in Lee's name. Then, we'd sing him the lyrics. This was during the time when we were required to wake Lee up. We placed Bac-O Bits in his bed, poured water on him, blasted his music. All these tortuous acts were condoned by Dad as he couldn't stand the perceived laziness in his oldest children. Depression is more likely than laziness, but I'm not a psychotherapist and these flights back in time make me ashamed of my participation.

I step over Yoyo to get into the kitchen when my little toe catches on the side of the fridge. The pain is so intense for such an unimportant structure! I used to consider myself brave, but clearly I'm not. I limp over the bathroom and sit down on the side of the tub. I remove my black sock and inspect the damage. This little piggy is all purple, but in alignment. Great! I am so annoyed with myself. I put my sock back on and cannot believe how painful a small appendage can be. Didn't my seventh grade Biology teacher insist we (humans, that is) were going to lose the little toe (due to evolution)? Tell my pain receptors that! They are very active!

Throbbing couples and dances with knife stabs when I walk. Wow, I'm a wimp. I walk out of the bathroom and into the living room. It's less of a walk and more of a slide to the side as the act of bending my foot makes the little bruised toe hit against the floor more.

It is absolutely stupid, but I know I cannot drive. One bruised baby toe and my independence is sucked away. I dial Vanessa's phone number.

"Hey Vanessa, I have a problem."

"Did you change your mind?"

"You're going to laugh. I stubbed my little toe on the fridge this morning and I'm having a hard time walking."

Vanessa laughs.

"I'm serious. It hurts to bend, and when I act like I'm depressing a pedal it hurts so badly I don't want to move. I don't want to crash my car because my baby toe is purple. William's meeting me at your house." Vanessa's high peeled laughter echoes through the phone.

"I'll be over in fifteen minutes or so."

She arrives and honks outside. After managing to slip on my boots, I limp and drag to her car. She's laughing and pointing.

"It's not that funny."

"I wish I could record your limp. It reminds me of a bad Halloween movie a few years ago."

"It's throbbing and everything." I'm feeling sorry for my body.

When we arrive at her house, we walk up the turn-of the-century mahogany stairs and into her room overlooking the Puget Sound. She turns on Enigma and breaks open a bin of licorice. "Have you ever eaten warm licorice?" She asks with a smile on her face. I take a bite and pull it through my teeth. It's a little tough.

"As in microwaved?"

"Not exactly."

"I do bite the ends of the licorice off and drink my hot water through it."

"I wonder what toasted licorice would taste like."

Tawnie K. Bailey

Uh oh. Not another experiment. A few weeks ago Vanessa decided she wanted to know how much liquid a Kotex pad could hold, so we poured cups of water onto it. It felt like a brick, but no spillage.

Vanessa closes her drapes and turns up Enigma. She lights a candle and chants. "Please oh fiery wonder, make this licorice taste even better." She holds the licorice over the flame. "Your turn."

I repeat her motion and laugh.

"Make a wish and eat the licorice."

"You first."

"I wish that Jake and I continue to have a great time together and that we eventually fall in love and spend lots of money together."

"Okay. Well, hmmm." I can't mention Caleb to Vanessa. She doesn't like how he treated me and would look at me as I look at my mom for staying with Dad. "I wish for a super amazing and attractive man to find me appealing, to fall for me and make me happy."

"Sure, ask for the moon while you're at it," Vanessa adds.

We eat our hot burning licorice. It's pretty gross—hot burnt wax. Vanessa blows out the candle as I walk into the bathroom and splash some water into my mouth. I don't know if I'll be able to enjoy the taste of anything today. The Red Vines company didn't think to label the licorice tub warning about the consequences of burnt licorice, but maybe they should. Wow, worse than a pizza burn—that feeling on the roof of your mouth as you bite into a yummy piece of delivery pizza expecting to taste the succulent tomato sauce only to have the roof of your mouth protest in pain as the tip of your tongue and roof mucosa slough off a bit, leaving you yearning for that expected pizza taste. Ahhhh. Big sigh.

My purple baby toe and burnt tongue are telling me I've made some pretty awesome choices today. Hopefully the day will improve.

Vanessa's doorbell rings as Jacob and William arrive at the same time. William's driving a Toyota 4Runner. This is *not* a car that would be seen long at our high school. It would be broken into, stolen, and stripped. Vanessa bought The Club after her Honda went with some thieves on a joy ride earlier this year.

"Hi," I say, surprised William is still as pleasing to my eyes. I stand away from the door jam.

"What have you guys been up to?" Jacob asks as he walks into Vanessa's kitchen.

"Experiments with food."

"Oh. Anything good?"

"Far from it," I add as I limp over to Vanessa's freezer, open it, reach for an ice cube and place it on the tip of my tongue.

"What happened to your giddy-up?" William asks.

"I hurt my baby toe."

"I'm sorry. Do you think you'll need a wheelchair?" Geez, he's a smart ass and I barely know him.

"No, that's why you're here."

William and I head towards his SUV, him walking, me trying not to limp, but hurting with every step.

"Do you want me to lift up your poor battered body and help you in?"

Of course not! I don't want anyone to know how heavy I am!

His mocking cavalier attitude changes when I grimace and take a step upwards. He steadies me with his arms.

"What did you do?" he asks before closing the passenger door.

"I tripped over my dog and caught my toe on the fridge."

"That stinks. Normally I would've said you should have stepped on the dog, but I know he's pretty important to you."

I smile. I'm not sure how to take that. I understand sarcasm and humor, but it's mixed in an unpredictable way.

William starts the car and hot airs blows towards me from the heater. I hold my hands out in front relishing the warmth.

William follows Jake's Toyota MR2 sports car along Vanessa's private street and into the heart of West Seattle. His cologne is wicked; it's trying to place me under a spell. I'm not sure if it's Eternity, but it's nice.

William turns on his stereo and "Bust a Move" is playing. I feel right at home, especially as William and I danced to this last weekend. William turns towards me and sings in a high pitched voice then winks.

I would love to be carefree with him, but I can't.

"Did you have a nice staff meeting last night?" William asks as he merges onto the freeway.

"The meeting was postponed and I wasn't told, so I ate dinner with the boss."

"Brown-noser."

I laugh. "Hardly. This guy's ego doesn't need any massaging. He just found out his wife has cancer. With her family in town, he wanted a breather before he went home."

"Hmm."

"What's that for?"

"Just sounds a little weird, some old dude taking out his hot teen-age employee and giving her this sad story about his wife."

What is it with guys thinking the worst? Maybe all guys think with their North Pole? "Thanks for saying that I'm hot. I wished I'd accepted your offer to hang out instead. What did you end up doing?"

"My mom bakes cookies for church, so I helped taste them. Then I went to the gym for a while. You should've called. I would've driven over to pick you up."

"Oh yeah, what would we have done?"

"Hmm, I could've taken your little dog for a walk with you or taken you to my gym and taught you how to swim, or gone out to a movie, or over to my house to watch TV."

"Lots of options, huh?"

"Sure, I'm a flexible guy."

I raise my eyebrows and smile.

"You know what I mean. I thought we had a great time at your dance the other night. I've never seen so many people with black hair in one location, but Seattle High's a pretty happening place to be. I'll have to show my friends some of the moves I saw."

"Are you making fun of me again?"

"Not at all."

"I'm just a nerdy white girl who doesn't know how to dance," I say, enjoying the heater's tender warm kisses on my face.

"Nerdy, huh?"

"Complete nerd."

"I think you were pretty sexy, and your moves weren't so bad, either."

I can't help but laugh. "You are such a liar, but thank you."

William pulls his SUV into the parking lot next to Jake. I open the door and step down as William runs to my side.

"What, you don't believe in chivalry?"

"It's a door. I can open it, but the gesture is wonderful."

Vanessa and Jake have their arms wrapped around each other. I don't know if Jake re-spritzed himself with cologne, but he sure smells strong (and I didn't smell it at Vanessa's house).

William pulls out his wallet as we approach the ticket line. I sneak up in front of him.

"Two, please for Father of the Bride," I say.

"That will be $14." I hand the clerk my twenty.

"What's that for? Are you some women's libber or something?"

"No, I want you to have a good time without the money coming into it."

"Angelina, my parents are loaded. I work for them. My grandfather paid for my college when my bike had training wheels. Let me pay the seven dollars to take you to a movie."

"I don't want to get ahead of myself, or anything, but maybe next time?"

"Maybe. Are you one of those girls that won't eat at the movies either?"

"I'm not in the habit of eating at the theater, but if I see something tempting, I'm not opposed to sampling a bit. What's your vice?" I ask.

"Skittles. I can't even remember when it started, but every time I go to the movies I need to have those little fruit candies."

I smile. So, he isn't perfect.

"How about you buy the Skittles and I'll buy the chocolate?"

"No go. You're my date, I'll buy you chocolate. What's your fancy?"

"Junior Mints, and maybe a Coke." They taste great, aren't hazardous to the breath ... . When I dated Caleb the first time, I worried so much about bad breath that I'd pop a cough drop in my mouth almost every time I saw him in the hallway. Can you imagine smelling mentho-lyptus every time you went to kiss somebody? No wonder we didn't date long that first time.

William purchases the chocolate mint morsels of goodness and hands me my drink. Jacob and Vanessa have the standard popcorn and soda. I like popcorn, but the smell turns me off. I sold popcorn at sporting events to save money for our class. Stupid class officer duties. The smell reminds me of wiping burnt butter off glass.

We walk sideways down the aisle to sit down. I slip my purse off my shoulder and turn to place it on the floor as William sits down. My purse strap catches the lid of the soda and as I'm trying to correct it, the soda slips out of my hands and lands on William's lap. The sound of ice and fluid hitting the ground doesn't compare to the sound of William's intake of breath.

"Oh Crap! I'm so sorry!" I apologize and try to wipe his wet pants off with my hand.

Vanessa laughs loudly.

"Her hands are on your pants and the movie hasn't even started yet!" Jacob says as Vanessa slips past us to go and retrieve some napkins.

Oh my God. I'm the girl who returns from the bathroom with her skirt tucked into her panties. He is going to be uncomfortable the whole night.

William smiles up at me. "Don't worry about it."

"How can I make this up to you?" I ask, my face lava-hot.

"You can blow it dry."

My eyes widen.

"Kidding!" he says. "Loosen up."

Vanessa returns with a wad of napkins. She hands several to William and a few to me. William wipes off his lap and his leg as my attention is focused on the floor where a puddle of soda and ice has accumulated around my purse. As I pick up the purse, soda drips off of the leather.

The movie starts and I'm enjoying it (minus my utter humiliation and the head-pounding smell of tree sap). But who wants to watch a movie starring a girl far more beautiful than you are? William moves his hand so it's resting next to mine—almost touching. He's good at this. What girl doesn't go crazy wondering if a guy is going to try and hold your hand? Maybe he doesn't like me. I just doused his leg and pants. Not the smoothest of moves for me.

Towards the end of the movie, his little finger is rubbing the side of mine. Who would think those little caresses could be so incredible? But they are. I still have my panties on, but that reminds me. I should write a manual for guys everywhere on what to do on first dates. I've been on a lot of them.

Jacob stretches. William stands up and offers his hand for me to get up. My little toe is killing me. I should've stayed home and worn a slipper all night. But then I would've wondered about William and if he was out having a great time while I moped at home. I half limp, half slide my foot across the floor holding William's hand as we walk towards the lobby. I probably look like the villain in the Halloween horror film "Shocker." William laughs as he points to my foot.

I look down. Trailing behind my black leather boot and injured foot is a napkin. As all movie napkins are thin and folded, the napkin has unfolded lengthwise and now looks like I'm trailing toilet paper behind me. Great. Just another memento to keep stashed in my brain. If only a spotlight would glow and showcase my foot so all of the movie patrons could participate!

"This isn't my night." I pick up my foot to remove the napkin, but it's so sticky it dissolves onto the sole. "I need to actually clean this. Would you excuse me?" I ask William.

"Sure."

I let go of his hand and limp towards the bathroom. Vanessa, William, and Jacob are all laughing at me.

I shake my head. I am a nerd. There's no way around it. I look up, about to enter the women's bathroom when I see Caleb and Lyndsey.

Yep, I'm on the Gong Show. Somebody please, hit the gong!

"Hi, Angelina," Lyndsey says, her hair reminding me of a bleached S.O.S. pad. Lyndsey has stepped out of her recent "Caleb's" fashion attire by wearing tight jeans and a sweatshirt.

Oh great; the one person in this world I truly dislike, with my prince. Nice. In my mind, she's flipping me off and licking Caleb's face. "Hi." I stop briefly on my slow escape route. Caleb has his black hair trimmed short with it blended so the top is a bit longer and gelled.

Tawnie K. Bailey

"You alright?" Caleb asks.

"A napkin became infatuated with my boot after I spilled Coke all over my date's lap."

Caleb raises his eyebrows as he smiles. It feels like it's just him and me all alone, as I skinny dip into his eyes. His face is so expressive. "Lucky lap," he says as Lyndsey gives him a dirty look.

I have to smile back. "So, nothing special. How about you?"

"Oh, we're doing great," Lyndsey says as she puts her arm around Caleb's waist.

Can I roll my eyes, vomit on her or do some other vile display? Bianca would say something obnoxious. I'm a wimp and just smile.

"Have a good time with that then," I say, wanting to crawl under a rock.

I slide my foot to the nearest restroom, just wanting the night to end. The line for chick toilets is five deep.

"Are you okay? I didn't mean to laugh at you," Vanessa says, meeting up with me inside.

"Don't worry about it. Of course this happens when I'm on a date with a hot guy." Plus Caleb and Ms. S.O.S. are here.

"William said he thinks you're great."

"Sure he did, poor guy probably looks like he had a wet dream during the movie."

Vanessa giggles. "He probably did. Couldn't we go to a movie with Sigourney Weaver as the star or some other brute of a woman?"

I finally have the sticky remnants off and we walk toward the restroom exit when I see Lyndsey waiting in line for an open stall.

"So, are you still sleeping around? Or do you only cheat when you two aren't doing great?" I ask the skank whose green eyes shoot darts into my face.

Vanessa grabs my arm and rushes us out of the restroom, giggling.

William holds his hand out for me. I smile at him and grab his hand. He then pulls me in for a hug. "Rough crowd."

"Geez. No kidding." Ah, his embrace is nice. I could get used to this. The cologne wraps itself gently around me as well. I know why the olfactory center is located so close to the memory center. It's a casual embrace, but in a different location, with a smaller crowd, who knows.

132

His arm lingers on my shoulders as I pull away. "Are you cold?" I ask thinking of his wet pants.

William laughs. "No, not too bad, but I think I'll turn the heater up in the truck."

We all walk (I limp) out of the door and to the vehicles and drive to every high school kid's favorite late night hang out—Denny's, where older women serve you, or ignore you.

I order hot water and Vanessa and I share a sundae. The guys buy breakfast meals. I've never been a fan of breakfast foods. Eating it at nighttime doesn't make eggs taste any better.

"What are you gals up to this week?"

"We have our egg babies for health class. Do they do that at your school?" Vanessa asks. "Or would it confuse the celibate crowd that may not know how babies are created?"

"Hey, just because our parents want us to go to college and not to a drug school doesn't mean we aren't well versed in how babies are created," Jacob says as he tickles Vanessa's sides.

"Our school gives us a bag of flour, so we realize babies are a heavy burden."

"That's actually funny," I say. He has such a different perspective than we do.

"What about you guys, what's your week like?"

"I need to put some hours in for my parents this week. They're talking about heading down to St. Thomas for Thanksgiving. They want me to pull more of my weight paying for vacations since they bought me the Toyota this summer," William says. Oh, the lessons our parents teach us.

"Yeah, I always seem to be working," I admit. "But I love it."

The rest of the evening goes by quickly. After the check has been paid I ask William if he would mind driving me home.

"Of course not. I know how to be a gentleman."

I smile. "That private school training isn't just a front?"

"I'm a good guy."

"We could use a little bit more of you around." William takes the initiative to scoop me up and carry me out to his truck.

"Goodnight Vanessa!" I yell back at her as they walk towards Jacob's car.

William half runs with me in his arms and gently sets me down while he fishes for his keys. The alarm turns off and he opens the door.

A small surprised scream escapes my mouth when he scoops me up again. He sets me down on the passenger seat. "Thank you."

He leans in, his face inches from mine, and wipes my hair away from my face. Wow. Maybe this one should write a how-to book on impressing a date.

"Anytime." Then he kisses the top of my forehead. He steps back, closes my door and circles around to his door.

"Where would you like to go?" he asks.

"I should get going home."

"Tell me how to get there."

I give him directions. He turns on the truck. "What music do you like?"

"R & B mostly, how about you?"

"Yeah, that's pretty good. I like a little bit of everything, Maxi Priest, Garth Brooks, U2, Boyz II Men and all kinds."

We talk about different bands and our favorite songs for a while. As we approach my house, I suggest we drive to a park a few blocks away so we can talk. He parks the Toyota and turns towards me. Did I mention Dr. Mike has a Toyota 4Runner, too? It isn't a brand new one like this is, but it's nice.

"Is this night going down in infamy?" I ask, still embarrassed.

"It's been pretty amusing."

"It wouldn't have been so bad if you were as nerdy as I am or if I didn't want to impress you."

"You were *trying* to impress me when you poured a cold drink down the front of my pants?"

"Of course. That's my way of trying to get you out of them." I pause, William's eyebrows taking a sudden lift-off while porno music plays somewhere in his head. "I'm joking, by the way. I hate I have to clarify that, but I do attend Seattle High, known for having its share of easily accessible women."

"Thanks for the clarification. Do you fit in at your school of easily accessibles?"

"You know, I do. I'm not sure why. My best friend's boyfriend called me 'easy' in the tenth grade. Maybe he labeled me accessible because he saw me in a swimming suit at the pool where I took lessons?" That's before the birth control pills and the subsequent shrinkage of the tah tahs once I stopped taking them.

"So, does that mean you are or are not available for physical relationships?"

"What are you referring to?"

"Are you interested in having sex?"

"Of course I'm interested. I just have to be in love with the guy."

"Oh."

"How about you?"

"Oh, I'm always interested. And, I don't have to be in love—especially not with a guy. Having sex and making love are very different."

"I see."

"But I can honor your noble intentions. I think that after dating me for a while you'll change your mind."

"Oh, and not want sex at all?" I'm joking, but I don't want him to become arrogant.

"Ha, ha. No, I think you'll come to realize God gave us the gift of desire, and there are ways of satisfying that desire with and without sex."

This conversation is getting weird. Is he talking oral sex? Who wants to rest their mouth where yeast infections and gonorrhea begin unless they are in love? I know, probably not a popular way to view things, but my brain can't think any other way right now. Or maybe he is talking about praying? Boy, am I out of touch with religious stuff.

"Hmm. We'll see."

"Does that mean you haven't had sex before?"

He is so direct. I don't know what to make of this. I'm used to flirting, not this open discussion. "That is indeed what it means," I say. "Since we're on the subject, have you partaken?"

"Of course."

Tawnie K. Bailey

"Good to know," I say as I nod my head. What else am I going to say? This is getting awkward.

"I should get you home. I wanted to let you know that despite the cold start to the night, I had a good time."

Cold start? Oh, the drink, the pants... I thought he's saying I'm an ice princess or something.

"I think we're going to have some fun together."

"Good, go home and dream of Kimberly Williams."

"Who?" He looks puzzled.

"From Father of the Bride?"

"That would be a great dream." He smiles "Hey, give me a hug."

I unbuckle my seat belt and reach across the seat and hug him. I again breathe in his cologne. Somebody knows his way around the Nordstrom cologne counter. I pull away a little and look at him. He is eye candy. He winks at me and kisses me on the tip of my nose.

I sit back, refasten my seat belt. That was weird, kind of intimate, kind of sensual. Do I want more? Um, yeah.

He starts the vehicle and drives the two short blocks to my house. I have him stop in front. There are two fewer cars than usual in front, making our house look not quite so trashy.

"Have a good night, William," I say as I open the door and hop down. I land on my owwie toe. Not a smart move. I hobble to the front door, open it, and turn and wave.

Okay, so not a bad way to spend the night. I did get to see Caleb, as if that encounter's the bright light in my night.

Hey, stop thinking about Caleb. He is with *her*. You were on a date with somebody that many a woman would chew off their arm to impress. But he isn't Caleb. He isn't even Charlie.

Chapter 26–Angelina

October, 1991

I'm groggy and tired. I didn't finish as many of my assignments as I planned, but I don't have to work today. I should cut down my hours. Maybe I should only work weekends at the clinic until I leave for college so I can have a little more fun with my friends. But I've followed my "route to vet school" plan. I've volunteered, I've worked at a vet and I've joined just about every activity in high school (minus sports). I can't go and sputter along the path now. Admission is highly competitive. Not only do they look at your college grades and activities, but high school as well, and I want to make sure that in eight years, I'm an unbelievable candidate.

I open the front door and see Aaron. "You have something in your room."

Usually that sentence is followed by my discovery of some unsavory item (dog or cat vomit). Maybe my cat vomited in my shoe again? I open my door. The door squeaks for a brief second and falls off of the hinges. On my pure white desk is a bouquet of red roses.

I open the card, "Happy Belated Birthday! Please don't tell anyone at the clinic about this. Love, Mike."

What? I hoped William sent them after our date, or maybe Caleb sent them because he felt bad, but Dr. Mike? Great.

I try not to think too much about the color of the roses. Dr. Mike may not know the significance of red representing love. But, I can't ignore the "don't tell anyone" comment. This requires immediate action. What should I do?

I'm getting rid of them. My grandma needs flowers. She's been in a nursing home for the last four years. Dad's mom enjoyed boyfriends, smoked cigarettes, and would come over to our house for birthdays. Yes, she's the one whose nose is going to grace my face in the coming years. Irene Hazel Hulgey is one tough Norwegian/German cookie. I remember looking forward to my grandma coming over for holidays and birthdays. She gave us five dollars each in a card, baked desserts and half of a block of her yummy processed cheese. I don't remember when exactly I stopped looking forward to her visits, but I dreaded her presence years before she stopped coming over.

She became widowed a year after Dad enlisted in the Navy. Apparently, Grandpa Hulgey drank like a fish (but do fish drink that much?), beat his only son and to top off his lists of faults, did not provide for his family. The drunken version of my father gets pretty hyped up about how his dad embarrassed him because they were so poor. My drunken Daddy doesn't seem to remember my sixth grade graduation. I know it's stupid to hold onto these moments of blunders and transgressions, but every important day is marked with memories of Dad drunk.

I wore a blue ball gown and walked down the aisle with the salutatorians Morgan and Angela during our sixth grade graduation. We gave our speeches and received our certificates. Afterwards a reception was held where Dad promptly made an ass of himself.

"Holy shit, I didn't know you went to school with so many niggers. No wonder you came in first in your class, there isn't much competition from anyone smart."

A few years ago, Grandma had a stroke and became paralyzed on her right side and unable to verbally communicate. While she went to live in a nursing home, her furniture, pots and pans, and everything she owned was split between my aunt's house and ours. My mom's dining room (aka, keeper of lots of paperwork, junky-armchairs-Dad-was-supposed-to-refinish, and an old organ that barely worked) was converted into a bedroom.

During the next several years, my brothers and I went through her drawers and boxes that filled every storage space in our house. She kept funny postcards, lots of yarn, items of my grandfather's, and more knick knacks than you can dream of. One of her dresser drawers contained a small box with thickened, yellowed, ribbed rubbers. I couldn't believe she'd save them! I knew grandma dated, after all, her husband (my dad's dad) died in 1962. But to keep them for the memories? I've never heard of reusing such an item, but she did grow up close to the depression….Then I took health class. Much to my amazement, those yellow crusties were not rubbers, (unless they were antiques), but were thimbles. How stupid/naive can a girl be? I wasn't sure if the thimbles were only supposed to go over a tip? And, I have never seen an erect "North Pole."

I start my little car and drive it over to my grandma's nursing home. I enter the back door and am overwhelmed by a distinct "old people" smell, kind of an aging newspaper odor mixed with urine. I take the elevator up to the third floor and walk in to Grandma Hulgey's.

"Grandma! I brought you flowers!"

She looks up and gives me a big smile and clasps her hands together. Since her stroke she hasn't been able to talk—she exclaims and gives curious and frustrated looks, but the communication is one-sided.

I try and visit every few weeks, but I don't enjoy performing; I didn't enjoy spending time with my grandma prior to her stroke and now it's even less enjoyable. I hate that I feel this way, but I do. Dad visits every six months or so; it's hard for me to blame him. I know it hurts him to see his mom so dependent, but this is his *mom*.

I leave the bouquet of roses with my grandma. Still feeling bizarre, I drive to Alki Beach with my favorite music blaring. I walk out to the sand as the sun is setting. Even though it's windy out, I sit down on the wet sand, letting the cold permeate through my jeans. I pull up my knees to my chest and wrap my arms around them.

I'm feeling sad for myself and wish my life was different. I wish that I mattered. What in the world is my boss doing sending me flowers and asking me not to tell anyone? Hello! How many red lights need to be blaring? He's driven me home a few times when my parents couldn't. Actually, he offers to drive me home all the time. He lives in the opposite direction; he drives on two separate interstates and across the floating bridge to get home, so his driving me home isn't "on his way." I've never admitted this to anyone, but whenever he drove me home he would reach over and grab for my hand. My face would get hot and my heart would pound and I'd hope he wasn't a creep. But he is. I love working at the vet clinic! I get to touch animals all day and connect with people; I have a family there and clients and patients I adore! How dare he make me feel dirty! That piece of shit!

I stare out at the water and feel the warm tears sliding down my cheeks. The clinic is my solace; a piece of my heart where I could shine, and now it's tainted. I wipe the tears away. I wish someone would wrap their arms around me right now—just to make me feel something else.

I take a big breath. I should go home and see Yoyo.

I'm still in a mood as I pull into the driveway. I open the front door and call for Yoyo. He greets me with his smile and woo.

It's a weeknight, I didn't have to work, and I've wasted a couple of hours. I need to study, my poor boy needs a walk, and I'm not in the mood to study. I pick up his leash and he dances around at my feet. We enter the night; the wind still slices through to my soul as we walk up the hill. I don't know how to get out of this funk.

I notice a house at the top of our hill I haven't paid attention to for years. The house used to be occupied by a family with four kids but the parents moved out and left their teen children behind. The brothers were known to use guns, the sisters known prostitutes. One night Randy rushed into the house screaming that the brothers had beat him with a crowbar.

As I stare in the night, the house is quiet, but the memories are loud. Most of the time I try and focus on the potential my brothers and I have, but I feel beaten down, pulled away from my dream of veterinary medicine and back into the chaos.

Chapter 27–Angelina

November, 1991

"Hi Charlie, this is Angelina. You know, the girl from Seattle," I say into the hum on the other line. I'm not sure why I'm doing this, but today I can't take wearing big-girl panties and figuring out life on my own.

"I am very aware of who you are."

"I've had a pretty cruddy day and wanted to talk to somebody who makes me happy. It was either call you or walk down to 7-Eleven and buy a Coca-Cola Slurpee, and well, I've drank so many of them lately that I may need to check myself into a twelve-step program."

"Ah, you're making my heart pitter patter. I make you happy."

"Maybe I should have gone to 7-Eleven instead," I say.

Charlie's voice grows serious. "What's wrong?"

"My boss sent me flowers today with a note asking me not to tell anyone at the clinic."

"I told you to follow your instincts."

"Yeah, I know."

"I'm sorry. The bastard. Has he asked for any special favors?"

"No. We were supposed to have a staff meeting last Saturday night at a restaurant, and conveniently, nobody else showed up."

"What did he say?"

"He gave me excuses."

"You should quit."

"I need his letter of recommendation for vet school. I'm not compromising my career or morals for a sleaze. I have to figure out a way of keeping the job and keeping him at bay."

"Any ideas?"

"Decrease my hours at the clinic. But I need to pay for my car, which broke down at the beach tonight."

"Let me guess, you were at the beach with a date."

I laugh. "You make me sound like a guy who's about to make the moves on a girl," I say.

"If the shoe fits...."

"I have been going on a few dates lately. How about you?"

"Me too. I'm actually dating someone."

Oh. I should be happy for him. How come my stomach just tightened up? "What's she like?"

"Her name is Summer and she's a year younger than I am," he says.

She sounds pretty. Nobody with warts on her nose is named Summer. "That's such a cheerful name. I think I'd be named 'Dour'."

Charlie laughs. "You are far from dour. You light up my world."

It's my turn to laugh now. "You're such a charmer. What are you doing this Sunday because I'd like to see my friend from across the water," I say.

"That sounds good to me. Let's meet at the coffee shop at two pm on Sunday."

"How will I know you when I see you?"

"I'll be the one falling in love with you." He laughs.

"And a smooth talker, too. You'd better watch out or someday I'll think you're serious."

"I'll be the one worshiping you from afar, then."

"Thanks for the advice. I'll see you at the Westlake coffee shop on Sunday."

William is working this weekend and I'm going to see my buddy, Charlie. I'm not sure how I feel about either of them. I'd like to transport Charlie to William's house, let him live a nice padded lifestyle, free of worries, and closer to me. And yet, that would force me to deal with my potential for leading him on. I still have this nagging sensation that the best is yet to come for Caleb and me. Maybe I'm the girl from *I Never Promised You a Rose Garden*, and I'm inventing this whole other world for myself, one where Caleb flirts because he wants to be with me, not because he flirts with everyone. And here I am, just like the sixth grader worried about saying I love you. I worry about things that haven't even happened yet. I haven't told Charlie I like him. I think about it, but I like him so much I don't want to be his Caleb; I don't want to feel like I'd ditch him when "something better" came along. It reminds me of a song that would play after skating on Love Line "The One Who Loves You" by Glenn Frey. I know it's 'easy listening.' I truly love Keith Sweat and R & B, but the easy listening songs have their place in my life, too. Maybe I'm not a freak? I mean, these songs make it onto infomercials at night, so they must be good.

Charlie matters; he feels like an extension of my dreams. I can picture myself married to him—which is bizarre, because up until this point, I would've been appalled if anyone brought up the 'married' word.

I've dreamed about my parents divorcing for years. I'd help my mom get on her feet, rebuild, and redefine her life. We could be a loving family but somewhere along the line, my brothers and I became so desperate to survive that we stopped taking care of each other.

Chapter 28–Angelina

November, 1991

"Why is a girl like you sitting down all alone in a coffee shop?" The voice brings an instant smile to my lips.

"Charlie!" It's been several months since our first and only encounter and he looks good. Very good. Because he's dating somebody else? Probably.

I stand up and wrap my arms around him, unable to control the impulse. I smile up at his mischievous heather eyes as the barista finishes another latte.

"What did I say about reading in front of me?" He points to the large book.

"You'll love this book!" We sit down in front of the window at the coffee shop and I describe the intricacies of *"The Witching Hour."*

"I won't tell you anymore. It's so well done I can't put it down, which is not good for me because I have a tendency to read all night long." I decide to change the subject and dive into a more important one. "Tell me about your girlfriend, Summer. Is she wonderful?"

"We get along pretty well. She's sweet, but rather quiet. She's shorter than you are and has long blonde hair." Why do the guys I like prefer blondes?

"Is she okay with you meeting me?"

"She has to be. You're my friend."

I smile at him. "Good." Yes, Charlie is handsome. He has full lips, a light natural tan and light eyes. His hair is short, curly and a blondish brown. He is considerably taller than I am, but not in an imposing way and he's wearing a sweatshirt and jeans.

We continue to talk for about an hour. "I bet the coffee shop would prefer we leave these seats to new customers," I suggest.

"You're not saying?" Charlie jokes.

"No, don't rush me and get ahead of yourself! I'm not ready for a fast food restaurant, yet!"

"We could go and walk around the Space Needle."

"It's a deal."

We take the escalators up to the monorail and ride it over to that saquatch, Weedle's place.

"So, are you still getting over Caleb?"

"Working on it. I keep seeing him everywhere lately. And now you're taken so I can't even fantasize about what we would be like together," I say in a teasing tone.

"Fantasies *are* better than the real thing."

"I wouldn't know. And maybe I'll never find out." I pretend to pout.

"Are you flirting with me?"

"I always flirt with people who aren't available. It's almost a trigger for me. I find out I can't have something and then the shirt gets ripped off—"

"Who said you can't have me?" Charlie says seriously. Then he smiles a big broad smile.

I punch him lightly then hug him. "You're just awesome. I'm glad I met Bianca so I could meet you. I want great things for you. If I ever win the lottery, I'll give you a large portion of my winnings, maybe buy us nicer cars."

"I bought a VW—not as fancy as your little car, but easier to fix."

"Assuming we're friends beyond today, maybe you could take me for a spin sometime."

"Huge. Assumption."

"Yeah, I know."

"Let's not risk it. Why don't I drive you home today, just in case?"

"That's way out of your way."

"I'd rather not go straight home. I'm thinking about driving out to Federal Way or Tacoma, and West Seattle's just a short detour so let me see where you live," Charlie says.

"Maybe you should drop me off at a friend's."

"It's too late, I've already heard the stories and I haven't ditched you for a girl with a better family." Yeah, I think he's referring to Caleb.

"Yet. Besides, we're not dating, so you couldn't ditch me, you'd have to be embarrassed for me instead."

"How about sad for you?" I look up at Charlie and see him. He should be my prince. I remember Caleb and I talking about books and authors and later about my dad when he compared my dad to a goblin from Dean Koontz' *"Twilight Eyes,"* one of my favorite books. The concept of seeing a person's soul as wretched and putrid and horrific captivates me. As much as I *hate* my dad sometimes, he's not all bad. If I had twilight eyes, I'm sure Charlie would glow in the most beautiful way.

I don't know how to respond. I feel tears coming, but I haven't cried in front of anyone in years. Instead, I give him a sad smile. "Me too. I'd be honored if you would drive me home, Charlie."

The rest of the afternoon goes by quickly; we stop at the shops, bypass the food court and buy some fudge then take the monorail back to Westlake Mall and walk to his car.

He unlocks my door first and opens it. I get in, lean over and unlock his door. "What colleges are you applying to?"

"Just WSU."

"Only one?" he asks.

"It's the only one I've ever wanted to go to—they have the only vet school in the state."

"It's so far away."

"That's a big part of the appeal. My brother's rusted out cars can't make it over there. Then again, maybe mine can't either. It's four years of undergraduate studies and four years of veterinary school."

"I'm thinking about going to a community college for the first year then transferring to UW."

"Will you be happy there? I mean, will a community college challenge you enough?" Charlie earned the highest SAT score of anyone I've ever met.

Speaking of the SAT, I didn't study for it at all. I thought those tests were supposed to evaluate your knowledge and if I studied, it wouldn't be an accurate account of what I know. Stupid me. I should have studied, I could've at least tried to get a scholarship based on my SAT scores then. Oh well.

"Are you prejudiced against community colleges?"

"No, I just don't want you to sell yourself short. I'm sure you're eligible for all kinds of scholarships. You should apply to WSU and we could live in the same dorm. Actually, I don't know too much about the housing at WSU. For all I know the dorms are same sex."

"I'm not sure what I want to do yet. Maybe I'll stick around here."

"Maybe you'll meet a Sugar Momma at the golf club who'll take you under her wing. Then you'll have a free ride to any university you want."

"I'd travel first."

"Where would you go?"

"Anywhere that isn't my house."

I laugh. I've had that feeling more times than I can count. "You should come with me to Greece," I say as I look at him and see so many possibilities.

His eyes brighten.

"My ninth grade Honors English and History teacher started making arrangements in 1988. She liked our class so much she wanted to take us on a class trip to Greece. "

"That is awesome!"

"Yeah, but I'm the only one in my class who's going. Most couldn't afford it. Vanessa wasn't allowed because a teacher thought she behaved in an "untoward" manner during a trip to Ashland a few years ago. The rest of the students are in the classes behind me."

"When?" he asks.

"Spring break."

"That would be amazing. I'd have to caddy like crazy and golf season is pretty much over now."

"So, when you said you worked today… ?"

"I did, there's a country club attached to the golf course, so other peon-type activities need to be completed, but I don't receive tips like I do when I caddy."

"Keep Greece in mind in case your parents run across a bunch of money." Greece with Charlie would be pretty cool…

"Yeah, okay."

"I'm sorry to have monopolized your time, I'm sure you want to get home, especially as you have a fairly long drive." I'm actually getting tired. "I could easily take the bus, you know."

"I want to see where you live. I love driving." Charlie starts his VW, its engine revs higher than the MG (okay, when my car won't start, any car revs higher than mine). Charlie turns the radio on when Sade finishes. "Oh baby you got what I neeeeed..." screeches out of the radio.

His car is noisy, as are most teenage cars—our mufflers aren't as functional, the seals are not sound, and Troy's car has bungees cords.

Troy was there the first time I saw a condom out of a package (I didn't tell him I'd thought my granny's thimbles were used condoms, I mean, who's that dumb? And for women everywhere, thank God I was wrong). We placed a condom on a banana, discussed the benefits of dental dams and couldn't get over the luscious descriptions of STDS as they related to food items. I won't go into detail, as I truly love cottage cheese and don't want my mind veering towards any visuals of cottage cheese looking like an STD secretion.

I shouldn't be thinking about health class while I'm sitting in the car with a boy. Alright, so maybe that's the intent of the course, to get you to think of your health class *while* you're sitting in a car with a boy.

"You're awfully quiet over there," Charlie says, as I haven't been giving him directions and have been lost in thoughts. Yes, lost, my brain's stream of information becomes pretty tangled.

"As are you. What are you doing after you drop me off?" I ask.

"Driving home."

"I'd invite you in, but then you wouldn't have anything left to come back for," I say as he turns up our block. I can see a fire truck in the road in front of our house and two ambulances with their lights on. The hippo jumps back onto my chest. There isn't any room on our street for two cars let alone these emergency vehicles. Charlie stops the car as there isn't anywhere to go.

"Is that... ?"

"Yeah. It's my house," I say.

"Why don't I park the car and walk you in?"

I'm trying to stay focused and not assume the worst.

Charlie parks his VW on the sidewalk a few houses down from mine. I get out of the car, my stomach a gymnastics match. There aren't police cars, so probably not a domestic disturbance. I can't think of good things with a fire truck and two ambulances in front of our house. Charlie places his hand at the small of my back as we approach the house and hear the radios squawking. The front door is open.

We walk in. Aaron is lying on a gurney and is moaning. An oxygen mask covers his mouth and nose while a medic tries to place an IV in his left arm. "Get me some fucking pain medicine!"

My mom's crying, a white noise background.

"What happened?" I ask. Anyone who can stomach their mom crying is a robot. There are people trying to calm Aaron down, hanging the IV bag, and one looks to be preparing the gurney for transport.

"It's the same car as last time," Mom says, her voice thick.

"What?"

"You know, when the wire brush thing embedded in his skull? His blow torch hit the gas tank and blew up."

Are you kidding me? Using a blow torch near the gas tank? Thank God it wasn't in the upper garage—our house would've blown up, too.

"I'm going with the ambulance team. I couldn't get a hold of your father. Would you stay at home and wait for Dad and Todd?"

"Of course." I look up at Charlie. There are radios cracking everywhere, Yoyo is on the deck barking like crazy and the house is a disaster; the carpets need to be cleaned, they have accumulated those set-for-life grey/brown tones. The nicotine brown walls close in. There are piles of papers on each of the coffee tables; the ashtrays are spilling cigarette ashes onto the veneer tops. There's a half-eaten TV dinner on the recliner. My discomfort and anxiety is palpable. I need something to clean. I hope Charlie doesn't need to use the restroom.

Mom leaves with Aaron, who has apparently been given some pretty strong pain killers.

"So, here we are-"

I'm exhausted now. We're standing in the living room where moments before there were numerous uniformed EMTs, firemen, Mom and Aaron.

"Here we are," he says. "That has a nice ring to it."

"What?" I shift my attention from the room and look up at Charlie.

"This time, it's us, and not just you dealing with this." His face doesn't show the horror most people would feel after coming into my house.

"Yeah, but it isn't the impression I'd like to leave you with."

"You don't have to protect me," he says.

"I'm protecting me."

"Don't build walls to keep me out."

"How else will I survive?" I say it half-jokingly, half serious.

"I'm your friend. I'm glad you aren't alone for this."

"Thank you."

"Do you want me to stay?" he asks.

"Charlie, you need to get home, I'll be okay."

"I'm staying with you. Where do you think your dad is?"

"I don't know. He doesn't usually drink on the weekends, but who knows."

"I'm not leaving you alone to deal with this."

"Charlie, it's okay, it's just another crappy ass day in the Hulgey household. I'll be fine. And, I'm sorry I swore. I try not to do that."

Charlie walks over and like a huge down comforter, encircles my body with his arms. I feel like crying, spilling my frustration and fears and the constant bleakness that pulls at my family.

"You'd better go or your mom will wonder what the holdup is," I say as I look up at him, still feeling his embrace.

"Who cares what she thinks," he says. I pull away then give him another hug and a squeeze. I collect myself.

"Charlie, if you'd like, you can stay. I enjoy your company too much to kick you out now, but I'll be okay."

"I'm sure you'll survive this, but I want to know you'll be better than that."

"Let's start over. Charlie, welcome to my house. It's a mess."

I open the door to the deck and let Yoyo in. Visibly upset, he continues barking. Charlie leans down to pet Yoyo, who runs behind me, wags his tail and chortles at him "Wooo wooo woooooo."

"And, this is Yoyo."

Charlie pushes the heap of clothes over to sit down on our previously-soft, but now crusty brown sofa. Yoyo runs out from be-

151

hind, jumps onto the couch and licks Charlie like he's the yummiest ice cream cone around.

"What do you think, buddy? Do you think I should stay and keep your lady company?" Charlie consults Yoyo. "What is that? No, I won't spend the night."

"Don't worry, Yoyo, Charlie has a girlfriend. Your position as the love of my life is secure." I smile up at Charlie.

"So, let's see your 'cave' as you call it," Charlie offers.

"It's down this hallway." I escort Charlie down the hall towards my room. As I turn and push the door to my room open, the front door opens.

"Hello?" I call out. There is no answer. I turn around and head towards the front door. I can hear something stumble against the entryway wall. Charlie follows behind me. "Hi, Dad."

"Hi, Ange." He's leaning against the wall, his hair all amiss, his eyes closed.

I'm peering out from behind the wall in the hallway and staring into the entryway. I hate to take support from the wall, but I'm used to hiding. With Dad's eyes barely open, I can pretend he doesn't see me. Charlie grabs my hand and squeezes it behind me. He then crosses the entryway into Dad's line of vision, into the living room and sits down on the couch. Shit. Dad's going to think Charlie was in my room.

Nope. Dad's taking a siesta on the wall next to the front door. I follow Charlie and sit down on the floor in front of the couch. Yoyo follows me and settles onto my lap. I look up at Charlie. He winks at me. I smile and roll my eyes upward. I can't imagine myself here with anyone else.

I hear something (clothing?) sliding and a stumble. I look over my shoulder and see Dad walk into the hallway. He is stumbling along and makes it to his room.

"He'll probably pass out now," I quietly say to Charlie. Instead, Dad re-emerges.

"Where is your mutthhher?" he slurs.

"She went in the ambulance with Aaron." I say.

"Oh." He turns around and walks back into his room and closes the door. Doesn't he even care? I just told him his son was in an ambulance!

"Charlie, I appreciate you waiting with me, but I'll be alright."

"I could sleep on your floor and make sure." Yep, he is superman.

"Maybe someday." I smile at him. Summer is a lucky girl.

Charlie gives me a strange look and asks "What's the smile for?"

"Summer is a lucky girl."

"Yeah, I agree." He then laughs and stands up. "How about this, we sit on your porch with Yoyo for a little bit longer to make sure your dad's sleeping, then I'll head home?"

It's after eight at night. "Only if you check on the ferry times and take the ferry home, instead."

"It's a deal." We walk over the telephone counter and I fish out a large phone book. There's a boat leaving tonight in about 90 minutes.

We sit on the porch steps and talk about my little car, my fingers finding a bit of peeling house paint.

"It is pretty cute," he concedes.

"Yeah, I look great in it waiting for tow trucks."

"Someone has to."

"It's been pretty amazing of you to stay here during this. I'm embarrassed you saw it," I say.

"You shouldn't be. This is something you have to deal with all of the time. You're the amazing one."

"Because I have such a grand family?" I'm smiling. I'm comfortable with him. I lean my head against his shoulder and breathe in his cologne. My neighbor pulls the ladder out, climbs it and after sitting atop the top step, twangs on his saw-turned guitar. I don't recognize a tune, but he is deeply absorbed in his concert. Charlie's eyebrows raise but he says nothing. "I'm convinced it's our water."

"How many people live here?" Charlie asks looking at the cars.

"It depends on the month. Currently, there are five of us: my parents, Todd, me and Aaron, but my older two brothers have open-refrigerator privileges."

Charlie shakes his head. "Are you sure that you don't want me to stay until you hear more about your brother?"

Tawnie K. Bailey

"No, Aaron will be alright. He's cussing, so he's feeling pretty normal."

"Then I'd better go."

"Thank you again, for sharing your Sunday with me and staying through the little turmoil." I still have my head on his shoulder. He puts his arm around me.

"Anytime." He stands and pulls me up, too.

"Goodnight, Charlie" I give him a big hug and hang on tight for a little while. He pulls away from me and gives me a wink.

"Goodnight." He walks to his car. I feel like running after him, (like in a black and white movie), and pulling him to me and kissing him, but I am not that girl. I have gone outside of my comfort zone numerous times tonight; allowing him to see my house was a big step for me.

Dad doesn't get up. I wait until midnight but still don't hear from my mom.

Todd knocks on the door, which is funny, because nobody ever knocks on my door. I used to tape notices on the door "requiring" knocking before entering. That's around the time I used gum to try and seal my door shut and tacks and rubber bands as a makeshift lock.

"Do you think he's okay?" Todd asks as he comes and sits on my bed.

"Yeah. When hasn't Aaron bounced back from injuries?"

"Hopefully the burns don't hurt too much," he says.

"I can't stand the thought of him hurting." I'm looking over at Todd. He spends most of his time at his friend's house up the block playing football and baseball. They're Mormons and treat him like he is a part of their family. Todd is small for his age. He sometimes yells at Mom saying that his small stature is her fault since she smoked during the pregnancy. If he's anything like Randy and Aaron, he'll be taller than the average kid—they're over 6 feet tall.

"Well, good night, Todd."

"Night." He turns off my light and leaves my room.

I roll over and turn on my fan. It's hard for me to fall asleep; a large part of me thinks Aaron gets what he deserves. Aaron courts danger. He repeatedly makes horrible decisions, and can be awful to

154

live with. He has been to rehab countless times, and yet he chooses this life on the edge.

***

The morning arrives before I'm ready for it. The alarm screams and Yoyo's tongue is ready to try and clean my face. I step into my parent's room and see that only Dad is sleeping. I need to take a shower and my parents' bathroom doesn't have a lock on the door. Mom and Dad's bathroom houses some bad memories, though.

One rare evening when Mom wore her beautiful swishing brown dress, Mom spritzed her White Shoulders perfume and buckled her high heels and kissed us good night, leaving Lee and Randy in charge of us little ones. Sometime during the night, Aaron and I went into Mom and Dad's bathroom where scissors were stored and Aaron cut his hair. I watched as his bangs dropped onto the floor and then we hacked away at my hair. When we showed Lee and Randy our masterpiece, their eyes popped out and they started swearing.

Surrounded by Dad's friends all night, Mom needed some Calgon before she saw me. When Dad's buddy, Dexter, tried to touch her bottom, Dad screamed at her and accused her of having an affair, just a mild prequel to his eruption at the sight of his only daughter. Aaron and I were sent to bed. Lee, Randy, and Mom were beaten. Lee's eyes regarded us as traitors. He wouldn't come out of his room and play with us. Aaron and I knew we were somehow to blame.

Dad has never done anything sexually inappropriate with me and I'm not worried about that. However, depending on his level of drunkenness, he might just walk straight into the bathroom, leaving me horribly exposed.

I have hidden most of my life. I hide my feelings and hide my pain. Exposure is terrifying.

Chapter 29–Aaron

November, 1991

When I close my eyes I see Randy and a spark. I hear a boom then nothing. The pain is ridiculous. This happens every time I fucking close my eyes. I feel the pain over and over again. I smell my body burning. I smell my hair burning. I think I hear myself screaming, but realize I can't hear anything at all.

I don't know if I can stand much more pain. I move in and out of knowing anything. On good days with diabetes I hurt. What I feel right now blows all of that pain away. I wasn't even wasted when we were cutting up cars, just helping Randy make a buck. I'd inject a bolt in the gas tank, then Randy would cut up the metal, but my timing sucked. I shot the bolt in right when he cut. Then I blew up. At first I thought Randy fuckin torched me on purpose, but now I wonder if God hates me.

I can't shake a strange dream after the boom. I can't hear or see anything. Then I'm spinning, but in slow motion. When my vision returns, my head aches from the colors, like someone threw up a Rainbow Brite. My hearing's still muted when I see Benji drinking from a light blue stream. Benji doesn't notice me and walks over to a man whose face is turned away from my view. I try to edge closer to hear and yet I can hear nothing; then silence is replaced as the shroud is lifted.

"Please let me trade places with him. Give me his pain and his sadness. I can be brave, he has endured so much."

I don't see the man's mouth move. I more feel than hear these words. They wrap around me and seem to whisper to my bones. "Benji, you have given him more than you know. He needs to choose his happiness."

"He doesn't think he deserves to be happy. I'm tired, but I can be strong for him."

"You are allowed to rest. I am watching over him. I will lead him home if the pain is too great."

I feel like turning away. I walked in while someone is praying. As I turn, I feel a voice echoing in my soul. "You are loved and deserve to be happy. Go and forgive. Then choose to live."

I've been told I'm lucky to be alive, yet again. I have burns to my face, but they aren't too bad, I guess. The doctors are worried because my blood sugar has been bouncing all over the place. And they're worried I'll get a secondary infection. But I think I saw God or Jesus and I think He was talking to an angel. And, unless I'm really fucked up right now on morphine or something, I think God gave me another chance to change my life.

Chapter 30–Angelina

November, 1991

Aaron just arrived home after 13 days. What hair remained from the grinder was singed and burned off by the gas tank explosion, including his eyebrows. I'm worried because he's been quieter than usual.

William met me at the law offices today and brought me flowers and I don't feel like I have to take an emergency outing to see grandma!

I need to work on my paper for my writing class, but I can't concentrate, my mind inventing worse scenes with my brother burning alive and screaming; I need to check on Aaron. I walk downstairs and knock on his door. The drapes are drawn, making it pretty dark. Aaron is sleeping on his side while Benji's lying next to him, watching me. I walk over to his bed and look down. The light from the hallway sneaks into the room. I can't make out the exact burn marks, but his head is bare. I kneel down and place my hand on his forehead. He doesn't wake up, but I can feel his body move a little under my hand. He doesn't feel especially warm. I sit and stare at my big brother. If only I could hide him in cupboards and keep him safe. I kiss his forehead, stand up, and leave.

I waste so much energy trying to merge chaos with normalcy. I need to finish my homework, do some laundry, and walk my pup.

Yoyo jumps on the bed and I rub his shoulders after we take our stroll. His deep brown eyes close. Sometimes when I look into them, it feels like I can touch his soul. "Yoyo, what do you think? What do I want to teach my children? I want them to have animals. Can you imagine how awful it would be to have a baby and find out it's allergic to dogs or cats?"

I struggle through the paper. I've written a lot down, but it doesn't seem to flow very well. I need a break. I could drink more hot water or eat… I head into the kitchen and see what's for dinner. Oh, TV-dinner time.

The phone rings just as the oven timer buzzes.

"I'm fulfilling my promise to call you," William says as I peel the cover off the instant meal.

"Be still my heart." I'm sarcastic, but smiling.

"Oh yes, you and every other female who has ever been graced by one of my calls," he says.

"There must be a lot of still hearts."

"You'll never know."

"Thank you for the flowers. They're incredible."

"I needed an excuse to come and see you."

"You need excuses?" I ask.

"I ditched a club fundraiser to see if your limp was gone."

"And?"

"And, I was so captivated by your smile that I forgot to look at your foot," he says.

"The limp is much better, thanks." And I forgot to look at your pants to see if they were dry.

***

This paper sucks. I don't know what I want to teach a child. I haven't ever thought about kids—except how to prevent one. I've watched enough after school specials on teen pregnancy to know that being a teenage mom isn't something I'm prepared for. Noise brings out my cleaning regiments and my sorting behaviors. Maybe Martha Stewart is a relative of mine? I'm a misfit in my family. Maybe I'm adopted. I'd want to know my other family. I'd find my mom; she wouldn't be as nice as Mom, but who can be? She'd be stricter and less forgiving, and she would be a cleaner. My dad? He would be anal retentive and freak if I didn't achieve perfect scores on every subject. Maybe he'd like badminton or some other silly sport. I'd be even prissier and more judgmental. Maybe I wouldn't know animals. Or, maybe Aaron wouldn't have been hiding with me and he would've been hurt worse. Who knows? I should think about other more mind-blowing possibilities, like, what if I'd been born with blonde hair or blue eyes? Einstein, you have nothing on me.

A Promise

Dear Baby,

The world may be cruel to you. The world can be unforgiving. I promise no easy roads. I promise the truth.

I hope my truths remain on paper and never greet you and torment your life. I can't foresee the future, and I introduce them only to ensure they remain in the past. I offer you my hopes and beliefs which have continuously restored my desire to exist. I offer these so you may know my heart and more than my pain.

I promise you will know animals. Craving warmth and love as a child, I found wonderful, gentle creatures whose fur and presence absorbed my tears. My pets helped me laugh, and run, and smile. Their love was unconditional and they needed me. I then decided to become a veterinarian. As a veterinarian, I could give a voice to the creatures who have nowhere to turn when their caregivers prove incompetent. I transferred onto animals my need to help my family escape my father's undeserved punishment. I couldn't help my family's wounds. I could only watch as they grew deeper and deeper. I believe every little face deserves dignity. I'll be there when the suffering are in need. My father never answered our pleas for approval—his ears were closed to everyone but his drunken friends. I promise you will be heard. I promise you will never meet my father.

You will never have to look into your father's face with hatred, fear, or pain. I will not let you go through that. My mother never had the strength to protect us from such torment. You will find only pride and affection beaming from your father's eyes.

Your father... I know not who he will be, for I, too am a child. In fact, you are just a dream for me, a hope for my future. I hope I meet somebody amazing, we will fall in love, get married and create you. As for your father, I know he will respect me and care as those are the minimum requirements. I hope you will have the dignity to know and recognize the difference between a man's love and a man's lust. It is often deceiving, but necessary to know. Love grows deeper and stronger, while lust grows old and fades. Love is honest and based on the soul. Body and soul are different. The body can be killed and destroyed. The soul's remains never die but live within the hearts of loved ones. You will always live in my heart; you are loved with everything that I am.

I hope you know God. I used to. I hope you can believe and rely on someone or something other than yourself. I do believe in God: a kind, loving God exists. Whose God? That, I leave to you. I hope your God doesn't want you to experience miseries for strength. My God... I am not sure. I don't know why God would make me watch my father beat my family. I don't know why He would let their cries echo in my dreams. I need for a heaven to exist, but my God has taught me not to expect goodness. I hope your God is different.

I believe in justice. I know circumstances do not always appear just. Eventually, however, the scale will tip to the correct side again. I wholly believe any wrongs will have serious repercussions. I cannot find it in myself to believe abusers, thieves, and murderers receive the same rewards of freedom as I do. Do not give up hope in our system. Our country was formed by such aspirations.

Aspire to be your best. Education is the tool of opportunity. If I hadn't tried hard to succeed in school, I'm positive I, too, would've fallen into my father's low expectations—I wouldn't have thought I was worth anything if my accomplishments were not above expectations. I remember when I was valedictorian of my 6th grade class. Education gave me an opportunity to shine. Hard work is necessary for betterment. I tried, constantly, to overcome my situation. I still have not "overcome" it, but am farther away from my childhood memories. Education unlocks doors and helps me know that I don't need to settle. My mother, when she decided to leave my father, felt trapped—she could "do" nothing—she had only a high school diploma. My mother is still trapped. I promise you your freedom.

With this freedom, I give you new traditions. My family "heirlooms" are alcoholism, abuse, and thorough unhappiness. We will start our own traditions based on love, understanding, and respect.

With animals by your side, parents to tuck you in and support you, a God to guide, a justice system to protect, and an education to open *doors, I give you high self-esteem. That is the greatest gift I can offer; it will allow you to struggle through the difficult times. I promise you the tools for happiness. You are the architect. Draw your blue prints, plan your future and build your dreams. Promise me you'll try.*

My voice is pretty heavy for a letter to a baby. I wrote it after another bad day at work, can you tell? Last week my stupid car broke down at work. It's getting to be fairly routine—the exact mechanism of failure is different, but the broken down part is the same and I keep pouring money into British Auto Nation. Lately when I hit a bump, my car turns off; if I wiggle a certain wire, the car restarts. This is after discovering that the Brits placed the wire to the fuel pump in the trunk. A metal cage normally surrounds this wire so any trunk items won't dislodge the wire, but my car didn't have one, so I'd hit a bump, and the fuel pump wouldn't work.

Dr. Mike offered to drive me home but I told him Steven had already offered. No big deal. Then Dr. Mike asked if we could go out to dinner 'to talk.' I wasn't prepared with a lie and told him my mom wouldn't approve of me going to dinner with him.

Today's payday. Normally, Dr. Mike finishes up the accounting and hands me cash, which I stuff in my pocket, embarrassed. I love what I do and think money sort of devalues that. When I pulled the money out of my pocket, I found only half of what I expected. Then Steven called and asked what I did to piss off Dr. Mike because his pay dropped. I'm not sure how to handle this. I should confront the doctor and tell him to go F—- himself, but I can't.

"Charlie's on the telephone," Todd says at the door.

"I thought I'd check up on you and make sure you're staying out of trouble."

"You know me, I'm not trouble." I say, smiling.

"So you say, but I'm sure you have left an awful lot of broken hearts out there," Charlie teases.

"You're greatly misinformed."

"Nope, I have the inside scoop," he says.

"Maybe I broke hearts in the third grade when boys were chasing me."

"There you go."

"Oh, are they seeking your counsel?" I joke.

"They're sick with heart ache," Charlie says.

"Good thing I never kissed them back. Otherwise, we might be dealing with a suicide-watch or something. I did, however sing to a boy in the third grade."

"You floozy."

"I'd just watched Grease the movie and chased a boy with the blondest and thickest hair I'd ever seen. I sang 'I need a man ... .'"

"You were ready for a man in the third grade, huh?"

"Some of us are gifted, but his rejection repressed my social growth for the next nine years."

"That explains a lot. Are you normal now?"

I laugh "I wouldn't say that. I don't exactly attract the cream of the crop."

"Come on, what about Mr. Wonderful, Caleb?"

"Oh, maybe I attract him for a delirious moment or two, but then I'm left for Lyndsey."

"What if they aren't dating?" Charlie asks me in a conspiratorial tone.

"I saw them last week at the movies, they were pretty together." And, I'm seeing somebody who is pretty great so far....

"Yeah, but they're always fighting and arguing, dating one minute, not the next." Charlie has taken on an amusing sing-song-voice.

"All passionate emotions. I inspire contentment." I pretend to sigh.

"Geez, give yourself some credit. I know of plenty a male who has been interested and shot down."

I'm laughing. "I don't shoot down, and you don't know any of my friends." How can Charlie always make me smile?

"I'm shocked you don't consider me your friend."

"Oh, Mr. I'm-Seeing-Some-Blonde-Chickie, you should talk. Just as I start falling for you, you become hard to get a hold of, off seeing your girlfriend. What else am I supposed to do but pine over an ex and date some new guy?"

"Well, if you ever seriously start falling for me, tell me. I'd break up with any blonde to have my dream girl."

"You're so great, Charlie. If you ever move closer to Seattle, let me know."

After more bantering we hang up and I finish my calculus problems. We finally started learning the shortcuts to derivatives. It's crazy to learn the long way at all, but whatever. I'm sure there are greater math minds that understand the 'why'.

Yoyo and I have our date with the Chuck Woolery in a little while. I turn off the light and crawl under the covers. What do I do about Dr. Mike? Should I ask him for a W2 so I know how much money I make? I don't know.

The phone rings.

"Hi, sexy. I hope I'm not calling too late."

I'm all cuddled up and get to hear William. What could be better? Can he hear my smile? Does he know I've been thinking about him? "I just crawled into bed and pulled the covers up."

"Don't say anymore. I don't want to picture you in your bed."

I giggle. "Good. I don't want you to have impure thoughts."

He is silent.

"Are you still there?" I ask.

"Yeah. I was starting to have impure thoughts."

"Did you pray instead?" I hope I didn't just offend him. He does attend a religious school. People who value God so much are weak and need a crutch. I hope I'm wrong, but I'm too bitter to have a relationship with God right now. People who are super religious are hiding something. Our youth group's pastor admitted to molesting little boys. Kids whose parents attended church were snobby and tried to make other kids feel inferior and that is definitely not what I believe in.

"I'm just praying to see your bed for myself."

"Maybe someday, but not this weekend. You want to go to a hockey game, huh?" I ask.

"That's one idea."

"How about a play?" Some guys are not into plays. I felt lucky Caleb enjoyed them as much as I did.

"Are you trying to bring me culture?" he asks.

Tawnie K. Bailey

"Somebody has to."

"Yeah, and somebody has to teach you the finer points of a great American sport."

"Isn't hockey a Canadian sport?" I ask.

"No. All great sports are American."

"Like rugby?"

"Alright, so you want to see a play, huh?"

I laugh. He gave up easily. "Yep. Are you up for it?"

"I wouldn't say I'm up, but give me time."

"Now now, my private-school boy, behave yourself. That is way too much information for my little innocent ears."

"So, I'm 'your' private school boy, huh?"

"Oh, that's a bit presumptuous of me, isn't it? Sorry. I'd prefer to see the play and would love for you to accompany me to it."

"I can manage that. You want to double with Vanessa and Jacob?"

"Sure, would you care if a couple of other friends went, too?"

"No, whatever you think. Why don't I let you do the leg-work. I'll plan on spending Saturday evening with you and your posse."

"You're going to clear your schedule for me?" I can't help yawning.

"Yep." Wow, that's nice.

"Hmm, I'm starting to like you a little." My voice is getting a bit softer as I'm snuggling under the covers with my eyes closed. I like hearing his voice while sleep tries to lure me in.

"Just a little?" he asks in a flirtatious tone.

"Hmm, yep, just a little bit more every time I talk to you." It's true. If I wasn't so tired, I probably wouldn't admit this to him, but my guard is down.

"You pretty much worship me then?" He laughs. He is cocky.

"Do you need another cold soda spilled on your lap?" I ask, yawning again.

"Oh, do you have plans for my lap?"

I laugh. "My plans don't include anything like that. But maybe someday." My eyes are closed. Yoyo is snoring softly next to my head.

"Most performance theaters don't allow beverages, so I think I'll be safe."

"That's what you think," I add before drifting off to sleep.

166

Chapter 31–Angelina

November, 1991

Morgan and I are getting ready to leave the attorney's office to meet William for dinner as Gail hands me my check. "I'm sure you'll have a great time. Maybe Mark and I'll stop by the Keg and see what your guy is like," Gail says with a sparkle in her eyes.

"Be my guest. He's easy on the eyes, and his family has a lot of money."

"He sounds like a keeper."

I laugh. "I don't know him well enough to know."

Morgan walks in smiling.

"Have a great weekend, Gail!" Morgan and I say in unison.

"Mark, you want to go to the Keg for some appetizers?" I hear Gail ask.

We head back downstairs, out of the lobby and onto the busy street.

"Have you been thinking less about Caleb since you've been dating William?"

"It's exciting to have those early feelings again. You know, when you're not sure if he likes you, if you aren't sure exactly what your feelings are, but you think maybe you'd like to kiss him."

We arrive at the restaurant. The lighting is dimmed and there are real table cloths on the tables. William stands up as we approach. I should wipe the drool off my face before he notices. He's wearing a dark blue V-necked sweater with a white undershirt and jeans.

I walk over and kiss his cheek. "Do you remember Morgan from Homecoming?"

"I never forget a beautiful face. Are you going to join us for the play later, too?" He asks as he puts his arm around my shoulders.

"I am. But don't worry about me tagging along all night. My boyfriend's meeting us there."

"Vanessa and Jacob are meeting us at the theater," I add.

Tawnie K. Bailey

"Are you going to fight over me?" He asks, his eyes laughing.

I laugh. "You don't know us very well. We'll be friends forever. No guy is worth losing Morgan over. So, if she wanted you, I'd bow out," I say as I look up at him.

William arches his eyebrows.

"Don't worry, it isn't going to happen." Morgan laughs. She's so easy going. I wish I could be more like her.

The waitress takes our drink order and returns with appetizers. "I think you have the wrong table. We haven't ordered anything yet," I say as I look at the breaded calamari and potato skins.

"It's from the table across the way. It's for the gentleman." I look up and see Mark and Gail a few tables over. Gail is licking her straw seductively and waving at William. William's eyes grow larger. I spit out my drink and burst out laughing as Mark joins in with a rather feminine wave. Mark is homosexual, but he isn't feminine.

William leans towards me. "Do you mind if I kiss your cheek? Those guys are giving me the creeps." Morgan is trying not to laugh either but can't hold it in and bursts out laughing.

"William, that's my boss and the paralegal I work for. They're here to check you out. "

"Oh." William takes a drink and licks his lips seductively towards their table. Then winks at them.

"What, I don't get a kiss now?" I joke.

"No, the moment's lost." William says, winking.

I get up and grab William's hand and head over to their table.

"Mark, Gail, I'd like you to meet William." They also have calamari and potato skin appetizers. They must have phoned in the appetizer order; I've never had service so speedy before!

"Hi! I hope we didn't disrupt your appetite with our flirting. I'm acting out my daughter's worst nightmare," Gail says.

"No. But thank you for the appetizers." William is quite the gentleman.

"We wanted to see who brought our Angie flowers."

"Hopefully I'm the only one bringing her flowers. I'm trying to persuade her to sleep with me, you see."

Mark is shocked and laughs. Gail laughs and cries "Oh no, oh no!"

I'm not sure what she's talking about, but Mark looks concerned. He bends his head towards Gail when laughter roars out of him.

William's eyebrows are furrowed as Gail lifts up her head with tears streaming down her face. Gail then pulls a piece of calamari out of her nose. I laugh and can hear Morgan from a few feet away with her higher pitched laughter.

"Are you going to eat that?" Mark asks as he pretends to reach for the calamari with his fork. Gail is laughing so hard she's begun to snort.

William smiles. "I'm kidding about sleeping with Angelina. Sorry to have ruined some of your calamari."

Gail's eyes are still glistening. "It's nice to meet you, William."

We return to our seats and order dinner. I can't help but slop part of the sour cream from the baked potato skins onto my dress. The rest of dinner is rather uneventful.

We meet Michael, Vanessa and Jacob at the play. William's hand warms my shoulder, while his breath on my neck gives me chills. We're waiting in line for tickets when I hear a high pitched sound, like an injured cat.

I turn around and see Bianca.

"William? Oh my God, and Angie! It's been forever!" Bianca squeals.

I smile. What a small world we live in. "Bianca! How are you?" I hug her. She looks exactly the same.

"I'm doing great! I didn't know you drove this direction anymore, Angie. And William, what are you doing over here?"

William looks at me, his eyes are sparkling. "I attended high school with Bianca in the ninth grade, then we moved and my parents enrolled me in O'Dea." That explains things, except the sparkle. I wonder if he has "critters." Yeah, well, no investigating for me. I am in health class.

"Are you two dating?" she asks.

"This is our third date, so we're still getting to know each other," William says. I wonder what a third date with Bianca would entail.

"That's awesome. Angelina, he's a good man." Bianca turns and looks William up and down. "I should have held on tight to you. Look how big your muscles are now!"

Tawnie K. Bailey

Most guys would be a little embarrassed by the noise and attention, but William just shrugs.

"Bianca, are you here with friends? You can sit with us if you'd like," I offer even though I notice the looks Vanessa's giving me.

"No, I have a date myself. We'll be hanging out in the back row in case we don't like the play much." Mmmhmm. "Oh, William, are you going to South America with your parents?"

"Probably. You?"

"Yeah. My parents have that same place in Brazil—they didn't want to sell it so they use it more as a timeshare thing between the two of them."

"We still have our place, too. We're going down this Christmas."

"Maybe I'll see you," she says then saunters to the last row.

The play is humorous. Luckily I'm not sitting next to Jacob—I can't handle the thought of smelling Fahrenheit again. I need to talk to Vanessa about buying him better cologne, even Dad's Old Spice'd be better!

After the intermission, when the lights go down, William again lightly caresses my pinky with his finger. Why won't he hold my hand already? Or, maybe slip his arm around me? The dating dance is very delicate, and he is well practiced and smells incredible.

After the play, William walks me to his truck.

"Thank you for giving Morgan a ride here," I say.

"Of course. You were to handle the details, I'm just supposed to show up, remember. Whatever you want, it's all you."

"Whatever I want, huh?" I tease as he climbs into his truck.

"Yep."

"Is that the past tense?"

"No, would you like to go to the beach? Denny's? Home? Whatever or wherever you want, I'm your chauffeur."

"Hmmm. Let's go back to the park by my house."

"Alright. Hey, I brought some R & B music with me this time."

William's 4Runner is loaded. It even has a multiple CD player. He turns on the stereo and OPP comes on. "Get down with OPP—Yeah you know me!"

170

He drives over to the park by my house and keeps the Toyota running with the heater blowing. Such a nice guy.

"What other plans do you have for the night?" he asks.

"I thought I'd let the night play out and see what happens."

"Not a bad idea."

"Yeah, especially after I dumped soda on you last time. And, to-night wasn't for the weak. You got hit on by my coworkers and got to witness a calamari's journey through Gail's nose."

"Definitely not an average date for me," he says.

"What's an average date like?" Is it black tie? Do you go to church? Do volunteer work? I know, I'm making his life into a cliché and that's not my style.

"Well, she is gorgeous and she fawns over my every word. She knows I'm brilliant and she can't wait to be with me. So, she peels off her clothes…." I roll my eyes. I'm sitting with my knee on the seat facing him.

"Oh, yeah, then this is not an average date, for sure." I smile.

"There's still time…." His eyebrows go up and down. I'm sure that if he had a mustache he'd be twirling it.

"Not that much time!" I laugh. "Are you at least having an ok time?" I ask, a bit more serious.

"At least 'OK'." He smiles.

"Good."

"So, you like me?" William asks.

What about the dating dance?

"Something like that," I reply.

"What exactly?"

"You can't ask a girl a question like that."

"Why not?"

"Because! We're insecure; we never tell a guy how we feel first! What if I like you for a friend and you have stronger feelings, or worse, what if I like you more than you like me and you just want your ego stroked?"

"Is that what you think?" He looks serious, maybe even a little concerned.

"I don't have any idea what you think," I say.

"Would you like to know?"

What? A guy is going to tell me how he feels? For real? Just like that? Maybe I should call Oprah! "I don't know," I say.

He looks startled. "Why?"

"Best case scenario you may be a bit interested, but there are so many factors to dissuade you."

"Oh yeah?"

"Yup." I nod.

"Well Angelina, I do like you, and that is not the best case scenario. It's the current truth. Where it'll go, I don't have a clue. There isn't anyone I'd rather be with. I'm not a Boy Scout, but I'd like to get to know you better."

"That sounds good to me."

"Would you mind if I called you more or assumed that you'd like to spend more time with me, too?"

"That would be lovely."

"Lovely? Really?" I can tell William's laughing at me.

"Yep, my vocabulary is weird." I've inherited some of my mom's annoying habits. She calls Dad 'My love' and 'Dahhhling' and adopts a 1930s voice when she says these words. I don't know if she realizes nobody talks like that anymore (if they ever did outside of the movies). And I say 'yellowlovely.'

"Alright, Ms. Angel. I should be getting you home."

"Do you have a curfew?"

"No, but I need to get home before I think of other things that we can do together."

"Like volunteer at a soup kitchen?" I tease.

He smiles and asks "Do you have a curfew?"

I shake my head.

"Does that mean you could sleep at my house and not get into trouble?"

"That's a loaded question. I could spend the night with a friend and would be expected to call my mom. Now, whether I'd get in 'trouble' if I spent the night with you is a different question."

"Ah." He is looking at me with laughter in his eyes.

"Besides, wouldn't your parents object to having a girl spend the night with you at your house?"

"They don't encourage it, but they know I'm responsible."

"Hmm." I don't know what to say. Mom would never allow me to have a guy spend the night even if he slept on the floor with my bedroom door wide open. "So, it sounds like I wouldn't be the first, then, huh?" I'm not sure what to make of him. He vacillates between a gentleman and a leech. Okay, I'm a prude. I don't care if I'm not the first, but I want it to matter. Aand I wouldn't want to be the twentieth.

"Not the first. Does that bother you?" He has a serious look on his face.

"I don't know, William. That is so far out from where I think we are that I can't really think about it."

"Alright. But I can't help thinking about it." He gives me a huge smile.

"Oh, you mean dreaming about it. I should get going home, though. I have to be at work in the morning." I smile and lightly tap his shoulder. He turns on the Toyota and backs out of the parking lot and drives me home. When he turns off the Toyota, I hear the sliding of his jeans against the leather as he turns and looks at me. Ah the moment of 'truth.' The incredibly awkward moment of most dates. I hope my breath isn't bad.

William leans over. "May I walk you to the door?"

"Sure." I start to ask if I should wait for him to open my door, when he jumps out of the truck and is at my side of the truck super-fast.

"Oh, my hero." I say in a falsetto voice as he opens the door.

He reaches up for me. "Shut up and kiss me." He says with a huge smile—a different approach to the wooing, for sure. I'm standing over him in his truck and lean toward his face and kiss him as he lifts me down. Mmmm. He is a gentle kisser and that cologne… What a great combination. His lips barely touch my lips at first. He pulls away and smiles down at me.

"What?" I ask. Yes, every insecurity I have comes flooding forward. Before I can identify which insecurity to focus on, he pulls me closer to him, leans down and kisses me again. This time he applies a little more pressure and I match it. His hands are wrapped around my back. We're standing next to his truck in the middle of the road. Mmmm.

I pull away and look back up at him. He strokes my hair and takes a few curls between his fingers.

"I should let you go," he says grabbing my hands and swinging them.

"Thank you for a great night." I stand on my tippy toes and kiss him lightly one last time. He walks me to the door. I don't want the night to end. Being responsible sucks sometimes!

"Would you like to spend some time with me tomorrow?" Um yeah!

"I work until five-ish." I give him a sad smile.

"Tsk, tsk. Would you like to hang out at my house tomorrow night? Maybe watch a movie or something?" His eyes are smiling at me. I like this guy. My heart is beating faster, and it isn't because I'm trying to end the date quickly, the usual "grand finale" of a date night.

"Sure."

"Call me after you get off of work."

"Okay." We're still holding hands. He's looking intently at me. It's kind of seductive, kind of disarming, kind of uncomfortable.

He looks at the door to our house. Above it is a plaque with "Hulgeys" etched into the wood.

"Is that your last name?" He looks astonished.

"At least for now. Most guys I date are required to divulge their last names before I agree to go out with them, you know, a prerequisite to see if it's worth my time."

"How do you pronounce it?"

I say my last name. Hull (as in the covering of a nut) then a hard G and EEE. William laughs.

"You haven't asked me my last name, yet."

"Maybe you're not in the running," I joke. "What's your last name?"

"Koviac."

"Hmmm, Angelina Calliah Koviac, has a nice sound to it." I'm joking and would never be so girl-like in front of a guy.

174

"Angelina Calliah, huh?" William plays with a curl again.

"Yeah, don't ask." I can hear Yoyo on the other side of the door scratching and whining.

"Goodnight, Angel." William winks at me and turns around.

"'Night." I turn to the door, open it and wave.

Yoyo's at the door wiggling for me. After taking him out, I get ready for bed. Yoyo follows my every move. "What a night! Did you miss me? I enjoyed a yummy dinner, saw a great play and got to kiss a very hot boy."

Yoyo looks at me with his soft eyes. I lie down and cuddle with him. William likes me! Is it better to be the less attractive person of the couple? I wonder if William's ex-girlfriends are model worthy.

Chapter 32–Aaron

November, 1991

"Hurry the fuck up, Jimmy! Frankie's outside already," I yell. We're at Finney's place again, looking for the old timer's stash of pain meds. The hunch back leaves a couple of his pills on the counter and hides extra in his avocado Westinghouse. The first time we found the hidey-hole Frankie left his liquid yellow calling card in the oven. It doesn't smell like it's been cleaned since. But Oxycontin is pretty good shit—that's why we return.

This is our final stop for the night. We've already jacked some pills from a house a few blocks away. We took a dozen and left the rest, then grabbed a handful of change out of the pink piggy bank. Figure if the owners don't notice, we can always come back.

Tonight I'm looking for Finney's gold coin collection. I know it's here somewhere, his grandson told me about it in jail a few months ago.

I feel like a pair of skivvies that haven't been changed in weeks, it's so dark and skanky in here. Angie would freak and start cleaning. She'd probably hyperventilate.

I'm in Finney's den. We try not to enter rooms without windows so we can see red and blue lights coming. I have a buddy who likes to dabble with gold coins. We used to have a TV console like this, where you could slide a covering over the TV screen. I walk over to the book shelf and pull out a few books then replace them. I don't want Old Man Finney to know we were here; we want him to think he misplaced his items, you know, senility, so we can jack this one again.

I've already looked in the stereo—it too, looks like our old stereo—a huge clunky piece of furniture. I've looked in the bar area, in the decanters, next to the recliner. Fuck! I'm looking out over by the fireplace when I notice the little picture. Ah. I bet he has a safe back there. I walk over, flip the picture to its side, and …" There it is. Just a hole in the wall with gold coins stuck in firm plastic sheaths. No need to even worry about cracking a safe. Tonight is my lucky night.

I drop the gold in my backpack and head out. As I'm leaving through the sliding glass door, I hear something to my side. I look over and see Old Man Finney.

"Who is that? Get out of my house!"

The old fucker can move. I'm out of the house before he can reach me. I run out of the back yard and to the car.

"Stay away from here you little shits!" he screams. He's standing right behind our car with a baseball bat. He takes a swing. Frankie puts the car in reverse and hits the pedal!

I hear a loud scream/moan. Frankie then thrusts the stick into first and peels away. I turn around and see Mr. Finney crumple to the ground.

"Frankie, Stop!" I yell. Oh my God! Oh My God! Fuck! We really hurt this dude.

Frankie continues driving as fast as he can. My heart is pounding. This night wasn't supposed to go down this way. Frankie continues driving as fast as he can until we hit Westwood Village. Then, he pulls in and sits in the car.

"That was awesome, man!" Frankie says. I hit him in the side of his face.

"What's that for?"

"Why'd you have to hit him? He's a helpless old dude with a base-ball bat. What the fuck do you think he could do to us? This isn't our car. Who the fuck cares if he got the plates?"

"He wanted to hit you with the bat."

"My ass was already in the car, you dumbfuck. Drive over to the pay phone."

Frankie does what he's told, never using his noggin. I climb out of the car and walk to the pay phone and dial 9-1-1, my fingers stuttering like a scared little girl.

"I want to report an injury to an old man on Trenton Street in White Center." I say as soon as the dispatcher comes on. I repeat it and hang up before she can ask me any other questions or trace the call. The moon spot-lights my every move.

I walk to the window of the car. "Frankie, you'd better wipe this clean and hope that geezer doesn't die." I grab the sack of pills sitting on the front seat and walk away from the car. Jimmy climbs out of the seat and lopes up to me.

"Such a dumbfuck." He says quietly. We walk through the night. I wish I could be in school or in bed—anywhere but here. I chose this. I'm such a fucking idiot. My mom would rather have a bus fall on her than find out I hurt someone. I open the bottle and take a pill—my first in a long time. I don't want to think about this shit anymore. I keep taking pills until I don't see Old Man Finney's face crumbling in my mind. I was given a second chance and I've blown it.

Chapter 33–Angelina

November, 1991

The alarm wakes me up from a great dream where Caleb's asking me out on a date. I had a great night with William and still dream about Caleb. Ugh. This teenage stuff stinks.

I sit with the car idling for a few minutes before I back out of the driveway. Sometimes the car doesn't turn off after I remove the key from the ignition, but never the other way around! "I'll Give All My Love to You" sings out from the radio. Who would not love to hear that message over and over again? I definitely need someone. Please come running!

I arrive at the clinic. Dr. Mike looks different somehow. Oh, he's dyed his hair. He's a few years younger than my mom. Did I mention that?

"Hey, Angie, been on any fun dates lately?" Steven teases.

"Just last night. And I'm going out again tonight." I'm sure my face is beaming.

"Ooh. Don't tell Dr. Mike. He might dock our pay again."

Don't remind me. I walk back the reception area and see the most gorgeous German shepherd I've ever seen. Since I brought Yoyo home, I've changed my opinion on shepherds. I used to think they were beautiful and regal and brave. Since then, most I encounter are fear biters.

I walk around the counter and kneel down. This boy wags his tail, places his ears back and wiggles. He looks like an adult and acts like a puppy.

"Where did you get this beautiful boy from?" I ask as I crouch down and pet his neck.

"We adopted him from the shelter at ten weeks," his owner replies.

"Wow." He's absorbing the attention like he's meant for it.

"Yeah, he is everything we always wanted in a dog," his people admit. I think about my own little man, Yoyo. He is everything I need in a dog.

***

At four thirty in the afternoon, I'm in the surgery room recovering a cat from neutering surgery when I'm called up front.

I walk up front with the groggy little cat and see William standing in the lobby, his leather jacket open. Wow. His blue eyes are shining.

"Hi! What are you doing here?" I walk up to him and wink. The kitty is fairly large, so my hands are full.

"I wanted to see my favorite girl. Now that I know where you live and your last name, there isn't anywhere you can go to get away from me."

"Are you Sting?" He said I'm his favorite girl!

William just smiles and winks back. Steven clears his throat behind me at the reception desk.

"William, I'd like to introduce you to a dear friend of mine, Steven."

William walks up to Steven and shakes his hand. "It's great to meet you." William says.

"Likewise. We enjoy meeting Angie's other dear friends."

"Oh, I don't know if I'm a dear friend, yet, but she likes me well enough to kiss me."

What? Does he always try and shock people?

"Good for you." Steven says.

I'm not sure Steven appreciates William's sense of humor. I see Dr. Mike has stopped in the hallway and is watching this exchange. "William, this is my boss, Dr. Mike." Mr. Normal-and-Great, meet Mr. Bizarre.

"Hello." William says and shakes Dr. Mike's hand. My patient is starting to wiggle, so I walk him to his cage and close the door.

When I return up front, William and Dr. Mike are talking.

"Angelina is special to me. I haven't known her for very long, but I know I love having her in my life."

Dr. Mike nods. "Everyone loves having her in their life." How sweet.

"Ahh, you guys are going to make my head swell." I say, trying to change the subject. "William, I need to help clean the clinic, so it'll be at least another thirty minutes until I'll be ready."

"Hey, that's okay. Would you like me to wait outside?" William asks.

"If you'd like you can wait here or check out West Seattle and rent a movie, or something."

"My parents bought some new movies, so I thought we could check those out or go and pick one together."

I quickly finish mopping the surgery suite when Steven walks into the room.

"Angie, remember what I said about bad dates?"

"I only remember you laughing about my bad dates."

He's serious. "We were talking about college rapists, bad dates...?"

"Not really."

"If somebody touches you, even if it's after, scratch their face. Dig those nails in. Everybody will take notice if their face has large scratches down it."

"Geez, Steven. Did William say something that made you think he's scary?" I ask.

"No. But I'd tell my little sister the same thing before any date."

"You're a mood booster," I say. "We've been on three dates now, and last night he asked to me if I wanted to make it a more regular thing." I pick up the exam room chair and place it on the exam table.

"As in going steady?" he jokes.

"Nobody under fifty calls it that."

"Ooooooohh, Angie's got a boyfriend."

I'm smiling. "I think we're about two steps more casual. You'd classify it as 'I'm seeing him.'"

"Same thing. Remember, scratch his face," he says before patting my back.

I finish up the sweeping and say goodbye to everyone.

"Would you follow me home so I can drop off my car and take my dog out for a walk?" And, I'd like to change my clothes.

"Sure." William walks me over to my car. Keith Sweat sings out when I start the little British mobile.

"Who's that?" William asks.

I pretend to look indignant. "Umm, the greatest singer ever, Keith Sweat."

"Oh, I've heard of him." William leans into the door and whispers "That sounds like baby-making music." I'm sure I'm blushing. He kisses my cheek and tries to close the door, it bounces back making him lift the door a bit to engage the latch.

Our house sits on a hill and appears to be incredibly large. I suppose it is big—five bedrooms, three baths. But it's not impressive. It's brown and sad. The peeling paint just hints at the sorrow that's been fostered in its residence. I remember gardening and Dad paying us five cents for each slug we killed, but I didn't know how to ride a tricycle, so certainly the upkeep is overdue. Mom mows the grass a few times each summer, but in between, the grass grows waist-high, which wouldn't be a problem if we lived at Walnut Grove with Little House on the Prairie. I however, live in Seattle, certainly not a prairie. I try to keep weeds out of the front yard, but it's primarily a rockery with a large cracked cement driveway. Where the landscape ends, my brothers' and father's junk cars begin. It's bad enough to have people drive by, but inside is worse.

I can hear Yoyo barking from the driveway. I open the door and he comes running. He heads straight for me then barks at William.

"Who is this?" William asks as he looks down at Yoyo.

"This is the love of my life," I gush.

"All that love is packaged into a teeny weenie little dog?"

"Yeah." Yoyo is super excited. "Do you mind if we walk him before we leave?"

"Not at all."

"I'll be right back." I open the front door and grab Yoyo's leash off of the counter. The three of us head out into the night. My serenading neighbor is absent. William reaches for and takes my hand.

"What are your parents like?" I ask William.

"We're your typical type A personality household. I'm the only child, so their expectations are high. They love each other but don't always appreciate each other."

Hmm. "How are they with your dates?"

"They like the girls with good families; they seem to think those girls are more goal-oriented."

That sucks! I have a crappy family but I'm a good 'catch.'

"What about you?" We're still walking up the hill. One street lamp is supposed to illuminate the entire block—it falls very short but finds easily finds its way into my room at night.

I don't know how to answer this. "My family is... interesting. You can see my parents aren't made of money. My dad is a truck driver and my mom is a bus driver." I wonder if that changes things for William. A rose by any other name... ?

"My mom isn't impressed with my dates," he says. "So, they'll be pleasantly surprised when they meet you tonight."

"We'll see."

"They were glad we moved away from Bianca."

"Bianca has affluent parents."

"Affluent, yes, but she's run wild for years. Our parents were good friends and even bought timeshares together. When her parents divorced, they stopped keeping her in check. My mom hated how she manipulated her parents. So I liked having her around."

"You liked having her around because it drove your mom crazy?"

"Yeah, I had a little bit of a rebellious stage and Bianca embodied everything my mom didn't want for me."

Hmm. "She may change her definition after she meets me. My family sucks. My older three brothers are addicts, my dad is an alcoholic, we are not religious, and my family doesn't know how to keep anything clean. We are the picture of white trash." There, I said it, so Mr. Perfect Family, Perfect Relationship with God, Perfect Body and Nice Too, there are all my cards, my vulnerabilities laid out before you. Go ahead, take my self-esteem and step all over it.

William stops walking and turns and looks at me. I can't read his expression as it's so dark. "Good thing I'm not dating your family, isn't it?" He touches the side of my face, then kisses the top of my head and pulls me in for a hug.

I pick up Yoyo when we reach my house. He looks up at me and kisses my nose. "Have a good night, Yoyo, I'll see you later." I kiss his head and place him in the house.

"William, I'd like to change my clothes. Do you want to come in?"

"Do you want me to?" Wow, what an awesome question.

"It's pretty embarrassing."

"How about I wait for you out here?" William asks.

"It's cold out here, how about you wait in your truck?"

"Alright."

I hurry into the house and change out of my veterinary-tainted clothing, spray a little Obsession on my tummy and neck and feed Yoyo before getting back into William's truck.

We make the long drive over to the Eastside and arrive at a beautiful house with a circular drive. William turns off the Toyota and turns to me. "Are you ready for this?"

"Lead the way."

"Not so fast. Please let me open your door for you. My dad will be upset with himself for raising a thug if he sees you getting out without my assistance."

"Okay, I'll humor you." William hops out and opens my door.

I roll my eyes as he offers me his arm and we walk into the house. The doorway has a double door with glass inlays. The entrance is wide and bright with a chandelier hanging overhead.

William again reaches for my hand and walks me towards a room to the left of the entrance, my boots clicking on the marble tile. Several couches and a nice little nook next to the window help create a homey feel while a big screen television dominates one wall. My mom also bought a big screen television a few years ago because it's too large for my brother to carry away.

"What's your pleasure?" William asks as he walks up to a cherry built-in. He opens a door and pulls out a drawer with VCR tapes. "We have dramas, some light comedy, and romance."

I should force him to endure romance. I have to smile at the pure torture of it. Then again, William cried at Father of the Bride.

"How does Pretty Woman sound?" he asks.

He wants to watch the romantic flick? "Sounds good."

"We haven't talked about food yet, and I know I stole you away before you ate, so don't say you aren't hungry."

"I picked the movie, you pick the food," I suggest. He holds his hand out for me as he walks towards another room.

"I've been craving pizza like crazy, but I could whip up something out of the fridge." Hmm. William in the kitchen wearing nothing but an apron …

"Are you talented in the cooking arena?" I ask.

"I can hold my own." I raise my eyebrows. William looks at me and we both start laughing. Angelina, stop thinking those things!

"Let's order the pizza, and maybe do a dinner another night, assuming I'm not being too presumptuous."

"Too presumptuous?" He looks confused. He walks over to a cabinet and pulls out a large phone book.

"That there'll be another night." He's opened the book and looks up.

"You'd better stop. I don't want you putting yourself down. I told you I really enjoy being with you." William looks way too serious.

"Oh, I'm not putting myself down, just referring to whether I'll still like you," I say.

"That has yet to be seen, then, doesn't it?" He walks over, towering above me and teases, "Would you like me if I did this?" Then he lifts my chin gently, leans down and kisses me. I could easily get pulled into a little hungrier kiss.

"Mmm, maybe," I say and kiss him back. The kiss doesn't last too long since we're in his parent's house and I haven't met them yet. "Would you hurry up and order the pizza already?"

"Geez, girl. You must be hungry." William laughs and turns away toward the phone book.

"Hi, William!" A woman's voice calls behind me. I turn and see a woman my mom's age with shoulder-length brown hair and bright blue eyes enter the kitchen. She's Cindy Crawford-fit, but her laugh lines suggest she wasn't a teen mom.

"Mom, this is Angelina."

William's mom approaches me. "Hello. I'm Paula. So, you're the blind date, huh?"

I'm surprised William told his mom about me. "I *am* the blind date."

"Looks like he got lucky," she says with a smile.

"Not yet, Mom. Angel won't sleep with anyone unless she's in love with them," William interjects. I can feel my cheeks burn.

"Does he always do that?" I ask.

Paula laughs. "He tries to shock me. Good for you, Angelina. And good for you too, William. We don't need to worry about grandchildren."

"See, I told you. My parents just want me to be responsible." Again I blush. I didn't realize our private conversations were going to be relayed to his parents.

"What are you guys doing tonight?" Paula asks.

"A little kissing, a little hugging …" William says.

"Would you stop?" I ask, getting annoyed. Both William and Paula laugh.

"I'm joking. We're going to watch a movie in the family room and order pizza."

"Your dad and I are going for a walk and then to the gym."

"You don't want to watch a movie with us?" William asks.

"We might catch up with you after the gym, but don't wait for us."

William orders the pizza—half pepperoni and black olive for me and half meat lover's for him.

"Would you like a tour of our house?"

"Sure." He shows me his parent's office, the bathrooms, a sitting room and saves his room for last.

"And this is the crème de la crème." He says in front of his door.

"Oh yeah?"

"Yeah, I should charge admission fees for it. But for you, it's free. This time." He opens the door. I don't hear porn music. His queen-sized bed is covered by a black comforter. A desk with a telephone and computer sits in the corner. Next to his desk is a bulletin board with girls' pictures on it.

"Ooh. Ahh." I mock.

"Just wait. You'll understand the power this room has."

I roll my eyes and smile. "Are these previous conquests?" I ask.

William, who's still holding my hand, looks at the photos. "Some of them." Then he laughs again.

William grabs a blanket off of his bed; then we head back towards the family room. Once the pizza arrives, my blue eyed waiter carries the dish of heaven and glasses of water into the room and pops the movie into the player.

He kicks his shoes off and places his feet on the glass coffee table. I too, take off my boots and sit with my legs curled to the side and wrap the blanket around me. I'm sitting fairly close to William as we eat the Italian delight. William's parents return after the movie ends.

"I understand that vet school is harder to get into than medical school," William's mom says.

Why do people say that? Do they want me to feel better in case I don't get in? Are they trying to tell me to give up now and not bother trying? "That's what the school counselors all say."

"William will attend the University of Washington, assuming he doesn't do something stupid to make his grades plummet," she says giving me the 'I know you stole the last cupcake' look.

Am I the 'something stupid'?

We sit and talk for about thirty minutes until his parents decide to head to bed.

"Are you working tomorrow?" I ask.

"I am. You?" William asks. He's running his hands through my hair when he leans forward and scoops me into his lap.

"Not me. Do you need to drive me home so you get enough sleep?" I ask.

"Mmm, no," he replies. He's still playing with my hair, looking at me with a soft smile on his face.

Mmm. I could easily let myself fall into this. I'm so comfortable. Normally I worry about how heavy I am when I sit on a lap, but I'm tired and it feels so nice. His eyes are the most beautiful blue I've ever seen. The edges are a dark blue and lighten towards the center where they're speckled with white. His thick brownish-black hair calls my fingers, just begging to be touched.

"You're good at this." I smile and look at him.

"Just wait to see what else I'm good at."

I continue to smile. Are you always so aggressive with your flirting? "Why do you even like me?" I ask.

"Well, you're a very pretty girl who's smart, knows what she wants, has this smile that makes me want to see it all the time, and you aren't like anyone I've ever dated." I think of my family and agree I'm probably not like anyone he's dated before.

"What, you don't date pretty and smart?" I ask. "You normally date plain old knock-out gorgeous?"

"No, I don't normally date plain people, but as for gorgeous, I've dated a few of those, too." Then he laughs. "I have fun when I'm with you. You haven't asked me to go shopping at some ridiculous Nordstrom event. I'm fascinated."

I laugh. "So, anybody not attending the girl's exclusive school would be novel for you?"

"No. I attended school with Bianca too, remember? But I'm enchanted."

I laugh. "You're a dork," I say as I lean up and kiss him all around his mouth, his laughing eye watching me. Then I kiss his lips lightly and he reciprocates. The kisses are soft but enticing. I let out a soft moan. I lean my forehead against his and stare at him. "That is addictive."

"I agree." William says. "You could spend the night here. And, I'm not talking about anything more than sleeping. You could sleep here on the couch, in the guest room, or in my room."

"Is the distance between my house and yours going to be a problem?" I ask.

"No, I want to go to sleep knowing you're here."

"So you can come in and convince me to be a naughty girl?"

"As great as that sounds, no. I want you to come to me. But not until you're ready. I want us to be amazing. When the time is right, I want you to have no regrets."

"We've been on three dates and every time we talk about sex. Isn't that weird?" I ask.

"That's the way I am." Oh. "Let me enjoy kissing you for a while more." I don't need too much more convincing.

"Alright, unless you want me to carry you off to my room, I'd better drive you home," William whispers as he stops kissing me for a moment.

I scoot off of his lap. I could so easily stay here. I mean sex must be pretty amazing for everyone to do it all of the time, right? Maybe I'm missing out on a large part of the teenage life?

William drives me home just after the witching hour. Dad's sitting on the reclining chair with Yoyo on his lap. Yoyo is sleeping upside down in the crook of Dad's arm.

"Hey, Dad." I'm surprised to see him. Yoyo's eyes open, he wiggles to right himself, jumps off of the recliner, shakes his body and runs over to me.

"Did you have a nice time?" Wow, a normal father-daughter conversation. I pick up Yoyo and rub his shoulders.

"Yeah. William surprised me at work. After dropping off my car we went and watched a movie at his house."

"Was the movie good?"

I want to laugh. Almost. Is he really interested? Does he think I'm lying? "We watched Pretty Woman."

"What's William's story?" Dad asks, sitting in his worn brown recliner and faded blue bathrobe.

"He attends a private school. He's an only child and lives on the Eastside."

"I'm glad you came home safely. If you ever need me, just call." He stands up, pulls his robe tighter and winks at me. "Night, Sis."

Now that's weird. Dad waited up for me. Huh. I grab Yoyo's leash and take him outside. Should I go to 7-Eleven? No, I should avoid the Kit Kat and Slurpee. It would be so much easier to hate Dad if he was all bad, but he isn't. He's a hard worker and commonly works overtime to ensure we have food and clothing; he paid off our large house in twelve years. When he smiles, it lights up my world. I've seen pictures from his younger years and he looked like a movie-star.

For as much as Dad's been gruff, when our family dog chased a motorcycle a bit too efficiently and died, Dad cried and brought us

191

home a hound pup the following week. When it expelled spaghetti worms, he returned her and adopted a shelter pup.

Mom's shrink, who's spent all of five seconds with me, thinks I want to become a vet because I don't like people. I know that when people open up the door to the clinic, we have something in common, that no matter what their life is like, we share a love of animals. I share this connection with Dad.

I'm surprised that Every Girl's Dream Boat (aka William) didn't slam his truck door and drive away when I revealed what my life's like. I wonder if Dad was as great with Mom when he saw her house.

Chapter 34–Angelina

December 10, 1991
Dear Charlie,

I hope all is well with you. My brother returned from the hospital minus his hair (on head including eyebrows, and eyelashes) but ripe with attitude and a new found adoration for morphine and other opiates. His career as a rockin' heavy metal singer will have to wait for his hair to grow or for him to get fitted for a wig.

I can't thank you enough for waiting with me that night. It meant more than you will ever know.

But alas, my dating travesties have temporarily abated. I've enjoyed a few dates with a gentleman. We'll see how long it takes before one of us realizes that I am Angelina, enchantress of outcasts and repellant of all others.

Please do not be apologetic for living a few hours from me. It is what it is. We are young and at least until our cars work, trapped by the worlds our parents created for us. Don't worry, it won't be for long. I'm truly grateful you are in my life.

As Always,
Angelina

Christmas is only a few weeks away and I'm still dating William. I haven't dated many people beyond six to eight weeks, and we've passed that threshold. I don't have much experience with boyfriend gift giving. I could call Bianca, she'd know what a guy would like. No, that was a wedding gift. Hmmm. I'll have to think on this one.

"Ok, Angie, you need to focus. Tell me why Christmas is your favorite holiday," Todd says, pencil poised.

"Can't you just make something up?"

"No, I'm getting graded on this. Mr. Wilson wants this to be about holiday traditions."

"Aaron and I walked to Pay 'n Save and scoped the aisles for gifts every year: a duck napkin holder/ salt and pepper shaker combo for

Mom, a little bear holding a flag saying "No smoking, please" for Dad believing all he needed was that bear, a two liter of Pepsi and a toothbrush for Lee, some Icy Hot for Randy, and a matchbox car for you."

"And then Aaron would spend extra money on you and remind you of his generosity whenever he wanted something."

"Pretty much."

"Christmas Eve, we'd turn on the Christmas tree lights and place our stockings on the fireplace. I'd run and grab my pillow, hoping my speed would encourage Santa. Then I'd skip downstairs to Randy and Lee's room where all five of us would zip our sleeping bags together—"

"See you can do this without me. Write about whatever you want to. Write about the new holiday tradition of getting wasted and landing in jail. Or better yet, make something up. Talk about serving dinner at a soup kitchen and meeting a poor family, whatever you want," I say.

"What are you giving William for Christmas?" Todd asks, grabbing his notes and sliding off my bed.

"He has just about everything he wants. He's become a coffee drinker, so I suppose I could buy him the latest rage, an espresso maker, but that doesn't sound like a girlfriend gift."

"I think he'd like sex," Todd says with a grin. I throw my pillow at him as he skirts out of my room. I could buy lingerie and model it for him, but I'm not that bold, and don't know if I'm ready for what follows.

Chapter 35–Angelina

December, 1991

"Would you like your presents before you go or after you return?" I ask William.

"Mmm. Well, if it's the present I'm hoping for, then anytime, but not at Vanessa's house," he says, his teeth taking little nips on my neck.

"But we have it all planned out. I'll run down to Vanny's basement to get the dessert out of their freezer, you'll follow and then you'll do me against the washing machine."

He stops snuggling and bursts out laughing.

"'Do you,' huh?"

"Isn't that what they call it?"

"Maybe some, but I like you way more than that," he says, brushing a curl away from my face, his breath not quite a tickle.

"Oh come on, you two! No mushy stuff at my house!" Vanessa says, walking into her family room with Jacob and her mom's ceramic bowl full of popcorn.

"We were just trying to figure out when we're going to get together again," I say, scooting off William's lap.

"Let's watch some TV before talking about your coaches turning into pumpkins again," Vanny says, clicking on Star Search.

Jacob groans. "Do we have to watch this again?"

Vanessa jabs Jacob. "Shhh. There's supposed to be a local on tonight."

"Wanna go downstairs for the dessert and the freezer action?" William whispers.

"Angie! Look! It's him! Date Singer!"

I turn away from Williams' neck and see My Worst Date Ever standing next to Ed McMahon.

"Who's this guy?" William teases.

I grab the clicker and turn the volume up. "A date from a few years back," I say.

"And now he's a superstar," William says.

Ed McMahon has his arm on Jonathan's shoulder before Jonathan starts his song. "See what happens when you date me," I say.

"Or when you don't," Vanessa says. "It was only *one* date."

Jonathan begins his jazz song, the amazing range and fullness seducing my ears. You wouldn't know he's a "white guy" by listening to the soul pour out of him. His looks suggest he'd be very attractive to any normal girl (you know, as would Tom Cruise) and to top off his "good guy qualities," he's religious. This was a turn off for me back then and William's religious tendencies are something I'm still getting used to. I've looked at religion as a crutch for so long that when William invited me to church last weekend, I almost laughed. I realize my outlook is a defect in me, but that's where I'm at right now.

And look at my Date Singer now, reaching for his dreams. He'll probably sing on Broadway and I'll have to fly to New York for super expensive tickets. I'll think he's the hottest guy alive and I'll have to show him our dance photo to remind him who I am. And he'll deserve all the recognition.

"Are you lusting after him?" William asks. "Because we could leave the room and let you be alone with the TV."

"I don't even need to see if he wins," I say.

"I do," Vanessa says dropping a blank VHS tape into the recorder.

"I have huge projects due in two classes on Wednesday and finals all week," William says, grabbing my hand and pulling me up.

"I could take the bus downtown after school and meet you...." I say, my fingers rubbing his hand.

"Angie, you don't want Paula down your throat if her little boy doesn't do well this semester," Jacob jokes. William pulls me close as Jacob and Vanessa move outside for their private goodbyes.

"When our plane lands, the first stop will be at your house, I won't even go home first," William whispers, so close to my ear my spine shivers.

I laugh. "Are you going to make your parents wait at the park while you drive over to my house?" I'm quiet and add "It's going to be a long ten days."

"We'll figure out something better next semester. When I come home you'll have me all to yourself until school starts up again." William and his family are vacationing in South America for Christmas and New Year's and won't be back until January third.

"We should build a tunnel from your house to mine," I say, joking, hugging him and not wanting to let him go.

"I'm sorry to tell you, babe, but your geology skills stink."

"My brothers made a tunnel between our backyard and their friend's yard across the alleyway. Aaron and I crawled so far into the tunnel we couldn't see light anymore."

"Ooh, more Angie Family Magic Moments," William says, looking amused, his finger whispering spirals down my cheek.

"Are you making fun of me?" I ask, rising onto my toes to kiss him again.

"No! I love hearing about your brothers. It's like comparing my Canada to your Africa. Nobody should be an only child. What happened in the tunnel?"

"The tunnel collapsed with Lee's friend in it a few weeks into the excavation, and we hatched the ploy to upset Mrs. Smith. She lived across the alleyway from the tunnel. My brothers said Mrs. Smith cooked hamsters up and served them as hamster cookies. I thought the witch in Hansel and Gretel lived up the block because Mrs. Smith offered us cookies."

"Really?" William is laughing, his arms wrapped around my back. "Hamster cookies?"

"To keep Mrs. Smith quiet after she found out about the tunnel, my brothers rigged up a bicycle to a microphone and a siren. They asked Aaron and me to serenade Mrs. Smith with a song they'd created years before. The siren rang out as Lee's heavy friend peddled the bike. We were hidden by trees, when all of a sudden, I looked up and saw Mr. Smith's brilliant red face."

"I can't believe you'd do that!"

"He marched us home and lined us up along our fence. Mr. Smith called my dad out and told him about the cruelty our family handed down to his. My dad threatened to take the Oldsmobile away from Lee and the rest of us picked up trash from the back alley."

"So if I built this huge tunnel, would I see you more often?"

"It would need to have an express way. But you could see me every day."

"Sign me up. Girl, if we had a tunnel, I'd steal you away, convert you into a Husky, and we'd travel the world together."

"All for a tunnel, huh?"

"No, just to hear you talk about hamster cookies," he says, against my ear, reminding me what I've been missing these last two weeks. We talk every day, but it isn't the same as seeing him. Last time we were together I wanted to stay the night—not necessarily *with* him, but at his house. We watched a movie and I fell asleep within the first twenty minutes or so. He kissed my cheek to wake me. "Hey, you missed the rest of the movie. Do you want to stay sleeping and forget I woke you, or would you like me to drive you all of the way home?" he'd asked when my eyes could barely stay open. It would've been so easy to fall asleep there. William's parents went to bed before we'd even started the movie. I decided to make the trek home. I felt awful. He could barely keep his eyes open and having him drive all the way to my house and turn around to make the journey back didn't seem safe. Now we only go out on Friday and Saturday nights. As the weather has gotten colder, Vanessa's mom has kiboshed any after-dark visits out of West Seattle.

"I want you to study hard for your finals." I say, pretending to move away from him. "I don't date dummies."

"Ditto," he says, pulling me to him, my body touching more parts of his than Mom would ever want to know about. I kiss him again, the soft texture mixed with pressure the perfect cocktail.

"Goodnight, William," I say just as Jacob's car honks.

"Goodnight Angelina Calliah," he says, kissing me faster this time. This isn't a fairy tale romance where I meet an amazing person and everything falls into place; I would never fall in love after one dance or after an itty bitty kiss, and God knows they don't make a size eight glass slipper, but I'm changing my mind about his Christmas present.

Chapter 36–Aaron

December, 1991

I walk into the visitor's area and notice the dude right away. Although his suit jacket is sitting next to him on the table, he looks relaxed, his long torso dwarfing the table.

"Aaron, look at you," Dr. Shawn says, standing up and offering his hand while I wait for the jailer to unlock the handcuffs.

"I didn't know you do house-calls," I say, glad to see anyone who isn't wearing orange or a gun.

"I got a little worried after your mom cancelled your last few appointments. But this is off the clock. More of a personal mission."

"*You* need to see a shrink, waiving $150," I say.

He just shrugs. As if money isn't a big deal.

"Mom likes it when I go to jail. Says she knows I'm safe and getting my insulin."

"You're really not the picture of responsible, are you?"

"Plus I'm not raiding her fridge all the time. It saves Mom lots of cash not to feed me. Maybe that's why she won't ever bail me out."

"Does she post bail for Randy or Lee?"

"Nah. She thinks we deserve it."

"What have you been doing here? Have you thought about our last conversation?"

"Shit. All we can do while we're here is think or watch TV. Skinny little dude a few cells away plays his guitar once in a while."

"Have you thought about your dad."

"Yeah. I guess he does have a problem handling emotions. But he's a man."

"You know that isn't what we were talking about. And don't pull that 'men don't show emotion crap.'"

"When our cat died a long time ago, I ran in the house freakin and Dad went outside and took his body off the street. After ten minutes of us kids crying Dad got all pissed and told us to shut up or he'd give us something to cry about. Is that what you're talking about?"

"Yeah. I have some theories and I want you to listen to them. I think your dad is autistic. Do you know what that is?"

"Them's fightin words. My dad ain't no fuckin Rain Man."

"Your dad isn't like Rain Man. He's a highly functioning autistic. That means they can function in the real world, have jobs, have families, but still don't relate well to what the world and people want from them as far as emotions go."

Whatever.

"Your Dad didn't talk until Kindergarten."

"So you think Dad has some genetic disorder? And that's what makes him a dick sometimes?" Maybe he's handicapped in the whole emotions department?

"It makes sense based on all or our conversations. Also, your mom said he witnessed some horrible moments in the Navy. So there might be a touch of post-traumatic stress syndrome."

"Fuck. Are you trying to make me forgive him after you spent years trying to convince me it wasn't my fault?"

"No. I want you to try and let it go. To consider that life isn't black or white. To think maybe your dad did the best that he could."

I don't know what to say. I'm out of cigs and need a smoke.

"So, get yourself cleaned up. Use the resources they have here. Take classes, get your GED. Just figure it out before it's too late and you die."

Dr. Shawn stands and holds out his hand, helping me up. Then his big arms wrap around me.

"You're smart, Aaron. You're more than capable of beating drugs. I'll make sure to send the autism book to you."

The guard returns and slaps the cuffs back on.

My dad, handicapped? He's great with money. He's a fuckin cheap skate, so we never see the money, but we have food and clothes.

People with genetic disorders are handicapped, right? If God takes away something important, doesn't he try and leave you happier? Maybe Dad can't do any better, and here we are pissed at him and having high expectations and shit. It makes me think about my dream with God. Maybe I should try to forgive.

Chapter 37–Angelina

December, 1991

"Merry Christmas, Angel!" William's voice cuts across the phone into my drab vacation.

"You just made my night."

"That should've made your year," he says laughing.

"Good thing I like you so much."

"Oh yeah, how much do you like me?"

"More than kickball," I say.

"Not ready to say it, huh?"

"I just don't know if I like you more than chocolate, ok?"

"So what's my favorite girl doing?"

"Sitting on my bed."

"I can't believe I haven't seen your bed yet. We need to change that."

"I'll describe it to you." I cough and try for a 1-900-Porn voice. "I have the same twin bed Santa brought before I could read, except Aaron swung on the canopy and broke it right after it came down the chimney. I also have the same white dresser with light blue, pink and yellow handles." I resume my normal voice. "Are you excited, yet?"

"Mmm, tell me more."

"There isn't really more to tell."

"What are you wearing?"

"William. Tell me about South America."

"It's gorgeous and I've gotten hooked on coconut water. We'll be in Rio de Jenairo for New Year's. Now, tell me what you're wearing."

"The Cliff's notes version, huh. Well, I've been invited to a New Year's Eve party."

"Are Vanessa and Jacob going?"

"They didn't mention it when we went bowling."

"I don't want you to go if they aren't there."

"Why?"

"Because there are creeps out there and I don't want any of them to get their hands on you."

"I can take care of myself."

"What would your mom say?"

What do you care what my mom thinks? "My mom would freak if she thought alcohol might be involved."

"I don't think you should go."

"I'll take that under advisement."

"It kills you to even think about doing what I want, doesn't it?"

"I'm not sure why the request is being made. I make pretty good choices. I don't know if your ego is getting involved."

"My ego?"

"More of a 'you're mine' type thing."

"I know you're not mine. I worry about you and miss you like crazy, Angelina. We should've gotten your passport, so you could be here with me."

"I miss you, too. This vacation stinks: Morgan's in Pullman visiting her family, Vanessa has the flu and I've been working full time to pad my bank account." At least the boys are having fun: Aaron's in jail for who-knows-this-time, Dad is in jail for "falling asleep" with his truck running—not quite a DWI, and Lee's in for previous warrants.

"I'm sorry. When I get back we'll have a few days before class starts up again. We can go roller skating, go see a show, put on our own show ... ."

"Are you trying to butter me up?"

"I always want to be in your good graces. You can tell me about Troy's New Year's party..."

1992 is going to be a great year! I have a boyfriend, I'm going to Greece, I'll be graduating and then off to college. I resolve to exercise more and eat less, be nicer to people I don't like (Lyndsey), and resolve to stop scratching my body. Oh, and I promise to tell my brothers how much they mean to me.

Chapter 38–Aaron

January, 1992

I'm sitting on this stupid bed trying to do homework. Yeah, I know. I dropped out of school a few years ago even though Mom and Dad offered to buy me a new car if I went to class and graduated. I don't even have enough credits to be in Todd's graduating class. Can you imagine if they let me back into high school? Parents would see me and take their little darling pussy-ass-boys out of school! But it's too late, now. Mom's now pushing me to get my GED. Maybe I can hold out…maybe a new truck for a GED?

Nah, I'm not doing that kind of homework. I'm here in rehab. Again. My sixth. My dad's insurance paid for the first one, and my mom's savings account has financed three or four more. Now, the tax-payers of Washington are giving me this little vacation from jail.

I've been to this rehab before, too. In fact, Mom, Angie, Todd, and I were here in 1988 visiting my dad. It's still super smoky as all drug and alcohol places are; they can't have you giving up everything at once because they know your mind'll reject sobriety if you have to give up nicotine. But it's nice enough. They feed us five times a day—which is awesome because I'm hungry all of the fuckin time. I have to go to the nurse here and have my blood sugar tested every few hours and they give me insulin twice a day. They don't want me having needles or any of the other freaks seeing my syringes. The nurse here thinks maybe they can regulate my sugars better if they know what the levels are throughout the day. The nurse is a pretty cute little number; she reminds me of Angie's friend, Morgan. I can't stand the fucking needles, but I'll do it for her.

So the homework—same old shit, different locale. I should teach rehab. I know all about the twelve steps and the fuckin family roles in addiction and shit. I'm sure Randy, Lee, Angie, and Todd could tell you all about them, too. My mom's taken us to all kinds of wacky help groups. Right after Dad beat me up, some shrink left us in a room with nerf bats. Of course we beat the hell out of each other. Except for Angelina, whose prissy ass sat in a chair with her arms wrapped around her because she needed to work on a project for school, seventh grade—high nerd-time for baby sister. The shrink watched us through her little fake-mirror and decided we were all in "crisis" or some other crazy-ass diagnostic "locale." The shrink said if my mom didn't get a restraining order she'd have CPS come out since we were all such violent people. Fuck. What kid wouldn't use a nerf bat on his brother?

Then Mom tried to get us to go to alanon. It's a nice thought. I mean, we are all fucked up. Even Angie. And we know it, but who wants to hear somebody your Mom's age coddle you when they don't have a fucking clue who you are? We're tough. And maybe that's why I'm here. I didn't think I'd be an alchy. Everyone said we'd become little Garretts. There was no fuckin way I was going to do that to my mom. And here I am.

The latest counselor—who reminds me of our fuckin little-boy-molesting bible camp counselor—has a new "tool." He wants us to start writing. Yeah, nothing new. Everyone has you write crap. He wants me to write to my family as if I'd died. He even asked Mom to mail him a picture of me when I got sick and shit. She took a picture while waiting for the ambulance one time when I danced with unconsciousness. She thought she'd never see me again. So, last night at group, little "queer boy" shows me this picture where I'm all crumpled up and shit on the floor. I'm in the fetal position and look like I weigh maybe a hundred pounds. Fuck. I can't believe my mom took that picture. Dad used to black out after drinking and not remember hitting anyone so she took pictures of the bruises. And they've come in handy for restraining orders. But I'm surprised she had film in the camera.

So, in addition to sending our little good bye letters, we have to write a description of each of our family members and see how they fit into the classic roles: the addict, enabler, hero, scapegoat, lost child and the clown. Do I get a cookie if I get this right?

I know I need a better attitude. For all the dumbfucks out there, I am the addict. I'm the one who "thinks the world revolves around me." My mom would tell you I've always been that way. Before I became the addict, I played the clown then the scapegoat. Bozo when I made fun of Randy for getting into trouble and Lee for not having the balls to nail me when I flung underwear on his head. Then I got into trouble—I stole shit, stayed out late, got into fights, all of it. Randy, the fallguy and scapegoat, got into trouble and challenged Dad, willing to take him on. He got the worst of it, I think. Lee is the lost child—he's quiet and tries to stay under the radar. Todd is a little bit of the lost child mostly because he is smart enough to stay the hell away from the house after school. We all fucking know Angie is the little hero and my mom is the enabler. That label pisses Mom off. Or at least she gets hurt when she hears it. Mom's placed more legal restrictions on Dad than anyone in her family thought she should. Grandma told her she should stay and love her husband until death. We all love Dad, we just hope he'll change. And here I am, causing my family pain and they're all hoping I change.

Chapter 39–Angelina

January, 1992

I've been watching him for some time, not sure if the curly hair belongs to my friend, or if like a mirage, my mind created him. "Charlie!" I yell, returning the gas nozzle to its receptacle.

Just as he's climbing into a Honda, he turns around and I see the grey-green eyes. "Angelina!"

"What are you doing in Seattle?"

"I'm looking at a car for my sister then I'm going to pick up Summer from the airport."

"Where's Summer?"

"She flew down to Portland for the day."

"Do you want to go find a coffee shop?" I ask, knowing gas stations aren't the best conversation sites.

"You want to come and look at the car with me? I need to meet the people in a half hour."

"Why don't you follow me to my house, and we'll figure it out there, alright?"

Once we arrive in front of the Hulgey homestead, I park the car and climb into Summer's Honda.

"So, do you want to go car hunting with me?" Charlie asks.

"Ordinarily I'd do anything with you, but William's coming home today and I want to get everything ready for his surprise."

"There you go saying you'd like to do anything with me and in the next breath you're talking about your boyfriend."

"He's been in South America for most of Christmas break. Who would've thought I'd like a boy enough to miss him?"

"He must be pretty perfect; I don't think you'd settle for anything less."

"He has faults, but his are more annoying than deal breakers. He enjoys making me uncomfortable by implying we're very physical to everyone—my bosses, his mom…"

"Want me to punch him?"

"No, I like him. He's just a bit too confident sometimes. He also says he isn't 'better' than poor people, but joked about giving a homeless man his half eaten cheeseburger. He said if people beg they should be happy to receive our crumbs. That pissed me off. But faults and all, I can't wait to see him tonight. I just filled the gas tank, added oil and anti-freeze."

"I'll drive you to the airport."

"I'd rather surprise him at his house. If I drive, I won't worry about him falling asleep at the wheel when it's time for me to go home. Why isn't your sister with you?"

"It's kind of a surprise for her. If I like it, I'm going to have Summer drive her car home and I'll drive my sister's new car home. Mom doesn't get up to take my sister to school anymore, so she's been riding in early with me. This semester I've got a crazy schedule. Besides, she needs her independence."

"Charlie, you are such an amazing person."

"I have my moments," he says and smiles. "I'd better move it if I want to see the little VW Bug."

I lean over, hug him and kiss his cheek. "Go be Superman for your sister."

I walk back into the house after Charlie leaves. I've been trying to keep my fingers away from my face by placing glue over my fingertips. If I can't feel any bumps I won't try and smooth away mounds. I bought a new black slinky dress (it's long, but clings where it should) and I have my hair up. I packed my toothbrush and a change of clothes, just in case.

William's Christmas gifts are in the car. I hate moments where time seems to stand still. I'm ready to jump out of my skin when the phone rings.

"Hi Angel! I'm home!" William's voice sings into my ear.

"Who is this?" I joke.

"Ahh, you're breaking my heart, girl. I can't wait to see you and you're breaking my heart."

I laugh. "I can't wait to see you, either."

"I have to help my dad with a few things, but will leave here in an hour or so."

"I'll see you then." I haven't driven this far before. Maybe my little car will finally help me escape.

I turn the key and start my wonder car. I back up and head down the street, then take Boeing Hill, as driving down hills helps to cool the engine. I'm constantly trying to avoid looking at the semis that always veer towards my lane. I'm glad I remembered the deodorant. No music is playing; my whole body is rigid and focused on traveling to see William. Why did I think I could do this?

I finally exit the freeway and turn down the now familiar roads near the Koviac house. I pull into the circular drive, thankful to see William's 4Runner. I was worried I'd finally make it to his house and find he'd left already.

The door opens. William, wearing his letterman jacket, looks excited to see me. I forgot how nice he is to look at; his body fills the entire doorway. "Did you drive here?" He asks, looking over my shoulder.

"I did."

"You shouldn't have risked driving your car over here."

"You're not worth it?" I joke.

He turns towards me, picks me up and hugs me tightly. "God knows I'm worth it. I am sooo glad you are here," he whispers into my hair. I get chills down my spine; he takes a breath in and moans slightly.

"What?" I ask as I smile up to him.

"I'm glad you're here."

"Me too." He is still hugging me tightly. I could get used to this. I start to pull away, and he hugs me closer. I relax and enjoy.

"Mmm, let's go catch up." He murmurs and pulls me in to the house. He holds my hand, smiling at me with a mischievous look.

We walk into the entry way, my boots clicking on the marble tile. I see William's mom in the kitchen talking on the phone. Looking up, she smiles and waves in my direction. I wave back and follow William towards his room.

"We shouldn't go straight to your room," I chide.

"Why not? I haven't seen you in such a long time. I don't want to have to share you just yet."

"Let's go and be civilized," I tell him, half joking, but wanting to be convinced otherwise.

"You drive me crazy, do you know that?" he complains into my ear. "Besides, she's talking to a client, so she won't be off of the phone for a long time."

His whispers are enticing. "You win," I whisper back, and follow him to his room. It hasn't changed much since the last time I visited. Luggage is sitting open on the ground. I pick up a pair of his boxers that are sitting on the top.

"Is this what you wear?" I have a large smile on my face and am holding them out to him. He's climbed onto his bed, patting the comforter beside him.

"No tighty-whities for me," he says. I crawl onto the bed and snuggle next to him.

"Maybe someday, if you're lucky, you'll get to see what I wear."

He raises his eyebrows and smiles a less-than-innocent smile. We kiss. I breathe in his cologne, which he has mastered, not too strong, just enough to draw me in. Wow. This could get dangerous. I pull away a bit and stare at him. Of course I've thought about having sex with William. I don't know how anyone who's ever dated him wouldn't think about sex. He and Caleb exude sexiness. I trace the side of his face with my fingers and follow the line of his jaw to his neck and chest. I kiss his lips again, slower. We stop kissing for a moment and I lean my forehead against his. "I missed you."

I don't want to stop kissing him, but I *really* need to use the restroom; my nerves are frayed from driving and now I feel like my bladder is going to burst. Leave it to me to ruin a nice moment with a potty break.

I kiss him gently on the mouth and whisper, "William, may I use your restroom?"

He gives me a crazy look. "Of course, you don't have to ask."

I use the facilities and feel so much better! I walk back into his room and am about to resume my position on his bed cuddled up beside him when I again notice his luggage. There are condoms in his luggage. Did he bring them back home for us? Did he pack them for his trip?

I climb back to his side a little confused. He's taken off his jacket and is lying down looking at me. Then I notice the other side of his neck. I rise onto my arms, still on my stomach. He has a hickey. A hickey! What the hell?!

"What's wrong?" William asks, noticing the change in my demeanor.

"William, have you been seeing somebody else?" I ask, feeling like this is a déjà vu—same storyline different characters.

"No. Why?"

"What's on your neck?" I ask. If he was a girl, I could imagine a curling iron causing that mark, but William is not at all feminine and his hair is short.

He slaps his neck as if an insect's crawling on him. "What?"

"Go and look in the mirror." I sit up and move to the end of the bed.

He stands up, looks perplexed then looks in the mirror.

"Is that a hickey?" I am so stupid. I should have seen this coming.

He looks at me and nods then looks down. His previously flirtatious attitude has been replaced with somber quietness. I take a deep breath and shake my head.

"Angel, I'm sorry."

I don't say anything. He walks up to the bed where I'm sitting and squats in front of me, placing his arms on the bed on either side of me. "I was on vacation, and I was drinking and met up with some friends," he says quietly.

"And you made out with somebody?" I ask, fearing there are worse things coming.

"And everybody was sniffing coke and having a great time." He pauses. "I tried it, too." He looks disgusted with himself.

"You took cocaine?" I'm shocked and disgusted. I'm still sitting on his bed and feel like getting out of here but bricks weigh me down.

"Yeah." He pauses. "Things got all crazy after that."

I look down at the black comforter I'm sitting on. "Did you have sex with her?" I ask, knowing the answer without looking at him. I look back up at him. He nods. My heart drops to the floor. Every hope for us crashes down. I feel tears coming to my eyes and know I can't have anything more with William.

"Angelina, I was out of my mind with drugs. I didn't do it on purpose; I didn't do it to hurt you. I've never waited this long for sex. I was, *and am*, happy to wait for you."

I'm shaking my head. "Don't imply any of this is my fault for having you wait." I can feel the tears slipping down.

"I didn't mean it that way, I just lost control. I will never do drugs again. I do not want anyone but you." He wipes my tears away, but they keep coming. I close my eyes so I don't have to see him watch me cry. I wonder if he would've told me if his neck and his luggage weren't telling his tales for him. I'm alone again. "Angelina, please talk to me," he says quietly, stroking the side of my face.

I open my eyes and look away. I stare at the wall, not seeing anything. I then turn back towards him. "I can't be with you." I'm angry and dazed and sad. I let myself get close to him.

I stand up.

He stands up and blocks my way to the door with his body, not in an imposing way, just to delay me.

"Please stay. I'm so sorry. I don't want you to leave like this."

We were just kissing and cuddling and now I'm crying. What a difference a few minutes can make.

"Why would you ever take drugs?" I ask as I wipe my nose with the back of my hand. I have only cried in front of my dog and brothers.

"It was a stupid, stupid moment. My friends were doing it, and I thought it wasn't a big deal. I'm so sorry; it's a huge deal." William is looking right at me, still blocking the door. "Angel, I love you."

"You don't get to say that." I whisper, moving closer to the door. I touch his side, motioning for him to move over. I just need to leave.

He moves to the side, but tries to hold my hand as I walk by. I shake my head and walk towards the door. I can hear William's mom talking as I walk by the kitchen area. I don't look in, but walk directly to the door. Opening the door, I'm met with the frigid air. I see my breath hanging in the air, mocking me.

I open the door of the MG and sit down, trying to gather my thoughts. The tears have stopped, leaving an ache in their place. I buckle and start the car. The heater hasn't been blowing hot air for a few weeks now and I can't even turn the stupid dial mechanism. The windshield and plastic rear window are frosted over—I wipe the inside off with my sleeve and unzip the rear window so I can see out. I'm naked being far from home with my stupid car.

I turn on the radio. The Williams Brothers' "I Can't Cry Hard Enough" is playing. How appropriate. I never noticed the band's name before. I drive to West Seattle. All kinds of thoughts are running through my mind. I'm mad at myself for liking him so much. I'm embarrassed he was willing to cheat on me. I'm embarrassed he wanted to see another girl's body and be with her and that my guy didn't care enough to stay true to me.

Chapter 40–Aaron

January, 1992

Dear Todd,

You're a great little brother. I know I led you to some scary places on our bikes and let you meet some people no little brother should meet. I was an asshole to you a lot of the time. I shouldn't have hit you when we were kids, or jumped off the top bunk to body slam you. You got the belt more than you deserved just because you wouldn't rat on me, and I'm sorry. Todd, you'll grow taller and won't be small enough to get stuck in lockers pretty soon. I should've set a good example for you and I fucked that up, didn't I? You've been my best friend and watched out for me and I led you astray. Please stay away from drugs and alcohol. I know you will grow into a great man. Please take care of Mom and Angie for me.

Love Ya,

Aaron

Dear Randy,

After the car blew up, I said you did it on purpose, but I know you didn't. You tried to teach me to be tough, so maybe I wouldn't get hurt. I know that when you'd hit me after I was mean to Angie you were trying to teach me to be a better man than Dad.

We've been on some amazing money making adventures. I bet that if we'd grown up with a different Dad, you would've shown me how to do Tai Kwan Do and we could have done body building together or something. I know you did the best you could for me. I love you.

Dear Lee,

You were the greatest big brother. I remember your collection of architecture magazines where you'd talk about the glass houses you'd build and how you'd want us to come and live with you. You put up with us little shits for so many years. Thank you for loving us enough to play with us; thank you for making paper Mache puppets, for playing Star Wars and dollhouse with us. Thank you for rigging up go carts out of rusted barrels, adding carpet and a steering wheel and helping us race other neighborhood go carts. Thank you for letting us feel like we were worth your time.

Love ya

Dear Angie,

I luv ya, sis. Do you know what a pain in the ass it is to have you as a little sister? All of my friends have been asking about you since the sixth grade. You've always been beautiful. Your nose isn't big and your hips aren't huge—why do you think my friends think you're fine? It's the one thing I could say that'd crush you. I'm sorry you believed it. Do you remember when I broke my arm and slept on the cot in your room? We'd tell stories and "Guess what I'm thinkin." Think of me when I helped you after you were stung by the bee. I wish I could've taken better care of you. I was mad the day Dad beat me up because you weren't hit, but I didn't want him to touch you. Please believe that I never wanted you to get hurt. Next to Mom, I love you more than any other woman in the world. I'll miss you.

Love,
Aaron

Dear Dad,

You fucked up. I'm dead and you can't even yell at me for it. I've been so mad at you for most of my life. You were supposed to be the best thing ever and you fucked up. I loved you like nothing else in this world and you let me down. You let us all down. I wanted to forgive you and sometimes I think I did. My doc thinks you did the best you could. And maybe that's true. At some point in my life I stopped blaming you. This was all me. Please do me the honor of going back to rehab. You can start your retirement off right— maybe take Mom on vacation, work on your cars, actually be happy.

Aaron

Dear Mom,

I'm sorry I broke your heart. You've been the best Mom I could have asked for. And I know I've been a huge pain in the ass. You've done every- thing in your power to make sure I'm safe and healthy. This was all out of your control. I used your love and hurt you with it more than I should have. I

216

don't know where I'm going to, but I've talked with God a lot more lately and I think I'm going to a pretty nice place after all. Whenever anything dumb happens to you, know it was me playing with you. I need to apologize for putting Todd's weight gain powder in your tea, it was the only way I could convince you sugar free soda was better for you. I love you Mom. I always will.

    Love,

    Aaron

Chapter 41–Angelina

January, 1992

Our room is dark but the street light sneaks in like a mouse, lighting up my race track. Unable to sleep and unable to ignore that pull, my knees pump while my toes squish into the carpet, my hair bounces off my face and I try to steady my breathing so Mom doesn't hear.

Yoyo barks, piercing my trance and making my eyes bulge like a Pekinese. "Shhh." I pant while bending over, my hands resting on my knees. I wipe my forehead with the bottom of my T-shirt as Yoyo wiggles over to me.

"Do you have to go potty?" I ask.

He barks again and runs to the front door, knowing the night is waiting for us. He loves to walk when the moon is up, and aside from the cold, I like how the darkness wraps around me. Sometimes his ears perk or his nose twitches and he growls or barks. Then he wiggles back and I laugh at him. I think he practices being brave.

"Oh buddy, it's late. We shouldn't go walking in the middle of the night," I say, still catching my breath.

He whines again and guilt wins out. Poor dog. I'm sure he'd rather smell and feel the wind than go on a wee wee pad again.

"Alright," I say, grabbing a jacket. "We can't go far."

We walk into the night, Yoyo's nose pulling us down the hill and around the corner, his breath a little rabbit that jumps out then runs away.

I've had a hard time sleeping lately, my mind whirling around "what might have been." While Yoyo sniffs and digs at the embankment, I sit on the grass, the crunch of the frozen blades the only other sound. I pull my knees to my chest, not noticing the cold whipping my legs.

Yoyo kisses my hand just as a stereo's bass booms louder and a car approaches.

"Hey girl!" a voice yells just as the bass ends. I don't recognize the car, but the voice resonates in my heart. Of course I'd see Caleb when I'm all sweaty.

"You ok?" he calls, his arm draped across the steering wheel. He sits and watches me then turns off his car.

My pulse quickens.

"Angelina," Caleb says, his strut almost a limp, now invading Yoyo's territory.

Yoyo's body is rigid, ready to fight. A growl rises from his chest, if he was a bull, he'd be puffing air out his nose.

"It's ok, buddy," I say, resting my hand on his head.

"What are you doing sitting in the dark?" Caleb asks, kneeling down in front of me filling my vision with a white v-neck stretched across his marble chest.

"Dreaming of you," I say then laugh. "Insomnia." And crazies. And this horrible need to run every night after my Love Connection routine.

"Anything I can do?" he asks, raising his black eyebrows.

"You have a cure?" My fingers, seeking a job, are pulling blades of grass.

"I wish. I used to work out when I couldn't sleep, but the gym isn't a 24 hour gig anymore," he says, moving to sit closer.

My smile at the sound of his voice is all but an admission. I brush sweat-laden hair behind my ear then look down, focusing on the frozen blades.

Yoyo walks between us then asks to be picked up.

"Did you buy a new car?" I ask.

"Yeah, my dad helped." Caleb moved out and wasn't talking to his Dad before *Angelina and Caleb Chapter Two.*

"What is it?" I ask, not recognizing the car's lines.

"An '88 Audi. I don't have to worry about driving it on the freeway."

Ah, but do you know the routes to the movies and work that don't require left turns?

220

"My dad went and bought a rusted MG parts car at an auction, but hasn't been able to do anything with it. He was pissed when he had to buy different sized sockets and hasn't touched it since."

"You said it's a little convertible?"

"Yeah, it's pretty fun when it runs. So far, I've bought a new master cylinder, clutch, fuel filter, fuel pump, fuses (dozens), ignition switch, battery, alternator, brake pads and rotors, glove box and lock, and various other small necessities."

Caleb's eyebrows furrow. "Now what's keeping you awake? Talk to me," he says, his eyes insistent.

"Boy stuff. But I don't want to talk to my 'dream boat' about boy stuff." My face only manages a soft smile while turning to look at The-Boy-Who-Doesn't-Love-Me.

"Well, tell that other guy his ship has sailed. I'll take him down if he hurts you."

I feel my eyes fill up but don't want him to see. "You're too late, my friend."

He leans in and wipes the hair away from my eyes. "I'm sorry. We suck."

His eyes are soft enough to jump into. "Yeah, and now you're madly in love. So you really do suck."

He laughs then stands up. "Let's get you and your short-shorts home."

I look down, suddenly aware of my night clothes, then let Caleb pull me up. My hug tightens around Yoyo as I shift my weight.

"Since when do you leave the house without layers and layers of clothes?"

"Yoyo asked to go outside during my bedroom run."

He opens the passenger door for us, "If only all girls would treat us boys so well."

"If only all you boys deserved it." I climb in, Yoyo's body moving against my hummingbird chest as my legs slide against the leather seat.

Obsession cologne follows Caleb into the car, romancing me. He turns up the heater, making the Vanillaroma tree dance near the windshield.

Tawnie K. Bailey

After driving up our hill, he parks the car and turns towards me, "I meant what I said before. I'm sorry about last time."

My eyes are watching his, "I meant what I said earlier, too."

"Remind me." He stares at me his dark eyes softening. I could jump right into them and be happy forever.

I look down at Yoyo, still rubbing his ears. "You're my dream boat." I turn back to Caleb and scrunch up my nose. "And you love someone else, so you suck." Tell me I'm wrong and love me.

He gives me that slow blink that used to set my sex notions stirring, then holds out his hand.

If only he knew how much I want the hand that reaches to touch. I kiss Yoyo's head again and feel for the door's handle. "Night Caleb."

"Night my princess."

222

Chapter 42–Aaron

February, 1992

It's a big day. Girls smell pretty and boys just might get some. Dad says every man worth anything would know not to screw up a girl's Valentine's Day. I tried calling the only woman I've ever loved to see if she'd send me some smokes, but she's out driving a bus while I'm stuck in this shit hole.

My doc wrote out a prescription for frequent high protein meals, so I've got my own can of peanuts and a "get out of mind probing free" card that lets me visit the cafeteria whenever I'm bored. The clashing of trays is sweet music—not quite Metallica, but it's better than the fuckin Greensleaves they have piped all over this joint. It's group therapy time here at the Addict Ranch and I couldn't handle the old dudes crying all the time about people they've hurt, so I took a little jaunt over to the slop house to be away from all the other freaks.

"You up for sharin' some chow with me?"

I look up, and just like Cupid shooting up my heart, I see Pop staring down at me, twirling his toothpick between his teeth.

I stand up unable to contain myself and I wrap my arms around his chest, Dad's Old Spice a welcome aroma. "You sure smell pretty," I say stepping back and looking at my old man wearing his good jeans for me.

Dad looks down then smirks. "I call it forgiveness in a bottle."

"Does it work?"

"Not as much as I need it to."

"What are you doing driving all the way over to see me when you could be getting some Valentine's Day action?" I ask, sitting down at the long lunch table.

He sits across from me and slides a pack of Winston's across the table.

Cigarettes are candy in this joint, keeping me as happy as I can be while I'm in this freakish twelve-step program.

"And coming to see me, is that so Mom'll give it up?" I ask, hitting the cigarettes on the table then opening the pack.

"I just wanted to see if they're treating you right."

"Shit, they hired us hookers for the Valentine's holiday."

Dad's tobacco-stained teeth give a rare appearance with a true smile.

"How's everybody?" It sucks I have to ask. This is my first non-doctor visitor ever. Every time I go to rehab there's family weekend and I'm solo.

"Same-old, same-old." Dad looks around then picks at his teeth with the pick. "They haven't changed much here."

"It's the same as when Crocodile Dundee played in the auditorium and I made lines out of sweet-n-low for the residents to drool over."

"What?"

"When me, Todd, Angie, and Mom came and saw you here."

Dad nods his head.

"Did ya get the girls anything for Valentine's Day?"

"Yoyo's hair got chopped and made all pretty for Angie. When I got home some pansy-ass with a fancy rig showed up at our house for your sister. He put a card and a flower under her windshield wiper."

"You show him a gun?" I ask.

"No. But he had this guilty-ass look about him," Dad says, once again twirling the toothpick. "Mom says Angie's been upset about something, so I figured this kid's to blame."

"Did he look all ethnic and shit?" I ask. I wonder if Angie's finally snatched her buddy, Caleb.

Dad stops twirling his toothpick, his stained fingers taking it out of his mouth, his eyes getting all beady. "Ethnic? Angie dates chocolates?"

"No, there's a half-spic dude she's liked for years."

"Mexican?" Dad's eyes are still buggin' out.

"Fuck, I don't know. Cuban? Columbian? Mexican? I didn't get a geography lesson from the guy."

224

"Nah, this kid's white bread. I told him if he hurt your sister he'd better drive something faster than a truck because I'd hunt him down. Then some flowers showed up for her."

"Same guy?

"Your mom said it must be some new guy named Mike."

"What did you get for Mom?"

Dad's lips move into a sly line as he smiles and raises his eyebrows. "A promise to come and see you."

Chapter 43–Angelina

March 1, 1992
Dear Charlie,

Destiny called and said I'm not supposed to enjoy the company of a boyfriend for any major holiday. So, alas, William and I are no longer dating. Apparently the appeal of South American women and cocaine were too much for him to resist. I enjoyed Valentine's Day as a single girl in Seattle at least until I came home and saw flowers from William and my boss. My advice to you, my dear friend, is to make sure Summer knows how incredible she is and come enjoy Greece with me in a few weeks. And no, I won't accost you (unless you want me to) or tempt you with drugs. I want to have a friend travel with me to paradise, is that too much to ask? Can't you find a Sugar Momma to sponsor your trip?

On a more serious note, life at the Hulgey house is pretty much unchanged. I'm just biding my time until I take flight to Pullman this fall.

I hope you and yours are doing well. Please don't forget about me.

As Always,
Angelina

Mom and I leave for WSU in about an hour. I received my acceptance letter a few weeks ago, which isn't mind blowing given my grades and their low requirements for admission, but my body is dancing, my nerves firing with glee and my dreams are just a few months away. I'm hoping to talk to students, ask questions that wouldn't be answered in campus hand books, and visit the dorms to see if there is any way around the "no pets policy."

I need a distraction from the loneliness that's made my mind crazy and my legs flee since I left William's house. He's called multiple times at home and at work. My fingers dialed six of his digits before my brain took over, but what kind of a loser calls the boy who cheated on her? Charlie called last month to wish me a happy Valentine's Day but he's happy and still dating that "season." I received a bouquet of roses from a previous blind date of mine, Chuck (aka UpChuck). I called to thank him for the gesture and he still had nothing to say. I also received flowers from Dr. Mike, but I don't want to think about that.

"I'll be in the car," I call into Mom's dark room after packing the Monte Carlo with Diet Sprite, water bottles and licorice. I'm trying not to pressure her, but I want to see as much of Pullman as I can and the sooner we leave the sooner I can see my future.

As I step off the mist-covered porch, my boot slides off a broken muddy tile and my thigh slams against the driveway's cracked cement creating a nice diaper-squish of mud on my jeans.

I stand, annoyed and a little sore. Stupid porch light still doesn't work and the sun's sleeping in, not wanting to spring forward just yet. The mud pile, shaped a little like Africa is already soaking into my skin.

"Are you alright?" calls a male voice from behind Mom's car.

Shit. I can't stand fast enough, unsure who's awake and watching me.

"Angelina, it's Charlie," he says, his voice now familiar as he steps into view.

"What are you doing here?" I ask, scrambling over to hug him. "Did one of the boys tell you we're heading to Pullman today?"

"One of the boys? Oh your brothers. No. I didn't know."

"Do you wanna come in?" I ask, unable to read Charlie, his voice losing some luster and the sky not yet awake enough to illuminate his face.

"I went for a drive and thought I'd come and see you," he says, his voice cracking.

"You decided to go for a drive at three am?" I ask. I don't think the ferries run much, if at all in the middle of the night, and the drive hasn't gotten any shorter. Charlie must've left two or more hours ago.

"After that a little." His body's rigid, ready to shatter with a little pressure.

"What's going on?" I ask.

"My mom showed up tonight."

"Your mom?" So? I don't understand what's wrong. "Was she exceptionally bitchy?" I know she thinks I'm a slut. Did she show up at Summer's?

228

"My *mom*, Angelina. The biological."

"Oh my God, Charlie." My hand flies to my mouth. The sudden return of the drug addict birth mom is not good.

I grab him and hug him tight, hoping my body can chisel away his armor. I pull away, cupping the sides of his face with my hands. "Charlie, you are a great person. Don't you believe anything else."

"I've got her curly hair," he says, his eyes distant.

"What did she want? And why now?"

"She thought it was my eighteenth birthday, when I'd be man enough to understand why she gave me up. Also, she thought I'm inheriting some money or something." His voice is dripping with venom.

"What?"

"She even got the day wrong. My birthday is next month. My crazy grandma-turned-mom told Biological that we were all getting money so Biological showed up to cash in. I guess Biological calls her Mommy Dearest on mother's day every year and she's never even asked to talk to me."

"Charlie, I'm sorry."

"I can't believe Dad let her in the house. Mom was tossing back the beer, slinging curse words and throwing bottles at Biological. I grabbed a couple of clothes and took off. Mom's screeches about Hell and damnation and her bastard grandson followed me out the door."

What I wouldn't do to torture those women, pluck out their fingernails then scrape them over their eyes. I'm sure Aaron could come up with something better, something that would hurt them, make their souls burn. "Come with me to Pullman. We're leaving in a few minutes."

"What about your mom?"

As if on cue, Mom walks onto the porch, the sun just sneaking up. "Oh. Who is this?"

"Mom, this is Charlie. He planned on following us to Pullman, but his car's acting up. Do you mind if he comes along?" I ask inventing lies as easily as Aaron steals.

Mom sighs, then looks at Charlie's face. "I suppose. Have you eaten breakfast?" she asks, always the caretaker.

Tawnie K. Bailey

"I'm not very hungry." Charlie looks anxious. "I'd be happy to give you gas money, Mrs. Hulgey." Charlie says.

I frown, "Save your money. We might make you spring for some junk food if you hog all the licorice, otherwise, we've got this adventure covered."

"Grab your things, I'll be warming up the car," Mom says.

Charlie shoots me a look of disbelief then disappears behind Dad's truck.

"What's going on?" Mom asks.

"Charlie's mom is too drunk to take him to Pullman today and he knew we were going."

Mom says nothing, maybe understanding Charlie's demons more than she'd like.

***

We arrive in the land of crimson and grey. I'd always heard that my dreams were in Pullman, but I didn't know they're surrounded by wheat fields. Nothing but wheat fields.

We drive down Main Street and along Grand Avenue, encountering five stop lights during the entire tour of the city and make our way to the campus visitor's center and purchase a parking pass, having been warned of parking nazzis. I grab Charlie's hand, suddenly nervous and needing the contact. Our first stop is at Wilmer-Davis Hall, a women's dorm near the campus bookstore that boasts a basement cafeteria. It's close to the frat and sorority houses, as if that would woo me. The students have old wooden bunk beds and little floor space. The draughty rooms hold little appeal for this cold-blooded girl.

Stephenson Hall, the newest dorm cluster, grabs my attention. The co-ed halls are brighter and the corner rooms provide just enough elbow room that I won't consider murdering my roommate the first night. Mom agrees with my choice, but drills Charlie, as if he planned to join our tour just to live a floor away from me. Too bad Charlie has his sights set on community college.

And now Saturday Night Live has ended and airplanes are taking off all around me. Or at least lying in bed next to me, rattling my brain. Mom's snoring and kicking have blown apart any notions that sleep will bless my night. While my feet continue to seek a chilly spot in the

230

sheets, I flip the pillow for a cool refuge from the noise and see my friend a few feet away.

The tropical island decor bounces off the bed, transporting Charlie straight to a bad episode of Miami Vice as the motel drapes barely dilute the outside light. Our eyes meet just as Mom's blowhorn erupts and we laugh.

I try to scold him with my eyes but Charlie lifts the covers and pats the bed next to him.

Clark Kent is turning into quite the Superman. And I need rescuing. I can feel my eyes dancing, my body wanting to accept his invite. I slip out from the shared queen bed over to Charlie's.

"Hi," he whispers as I crawl under the covers and tent them around us, the thin, low-percale sheets our only protection from the outside world.

"Are you trying to get me in trouble?" I ask.

"Just saving you from the mommy monster," he says, his eyes dancing.

I stifle a giggle and roll towards his chest, cuddling in, forgetting there's a girl back home who loves my friend. "I'm glad you decided to look at WSU with us, even if this trip is just for a short escape." My arms are wrapped around him, appreciating his recent devotion to the gym. "Are you ok?"

"I've never been better." He pulls me closer, Irish Spring his weapon. "I've dreamed of having you in bed with me for a long time, but not with your mom in the room," he says into my hair, the whisper causing chills down my back.

I pull back and stare into a face I've memorized. His faded temple scar testifies against his family. My heart screams out, yelling at my brain to go back to bed. His hands rub my shoulders as we watch each other. I wait, not sure who's driving.

"Are you tired?" he asks.

I shake my head, not trusting myself to answer while Mom's snores provide our song.

His chest moves the tropical tent. "I can't do this," he says.

My heart stops.

"I can't lie with you and think about you and wonder." His hands are smoothing my hair while his eyes pull off my mask. "Wonder what would happen if I kissed you, if I pulled you tight and never let you go," he says.

I want time to hold still so I can hear his words linger in the air.

"I wonder if you taste as sweet as your Slurpees, and if you'll forget about me when you leave for college. I wonder if you'll ever let me love you." His fingers caress my cheeks.

I drink in his words and run my finger gently over his scars, hoping to erase them, my master destroyers trying to soothe instead of damage. I lean in and Charlie sucks in his breath, his chest rising gently. I pull closer, watching his eyes, smiling before I kiss him. I'm bungee jumping into new territory, scared of heights, wanting so much to let go.

His kiss is tender, almost a question then becomes deeper, his lips mastering every touch. My friend, a fellow broken one, is pulling me into his dreams. His lips linger next to mine, his breath a warm whisper whose secrets are gifts I have yet to unwrap.

Charlie sighs, then kisses my cheek. "I know I'm not your dream man. I know someone else has your heart and when you're ready to let him go, I'll be first in line."

"Charlie? How could you possibly think that right now?" Do I suck at kissing? Am I some rigid ice princess?

"Shh. Just pretend I didn't just pour out my dignity. Pretend we were just talking about a book or you were telling me about your last date with Caleb."

I watch this incredible man retreat. I pull close to him again and kiss his cheek, unsure how to make him mine again. "I wasn't thinking about anyone but you."

He's quiet, a book without a cover.

"Summer's a lucky girl."

Charlie snorts, breaking the mood. "Because her boyfriend is lying in bed with you?" He looks away, no longer very happy I'm beside him.

"Because it's you," I say, the weight of the air a mountain on my chest. I pull the sheet down.

"And it's you," he says rolling over, the shroud a thick wall of silence between us.

Here I am, lying in bed with Charlie moments after I finally decided to kiss a boy worthy of my affections a few feet away from Mom, in the city I've dreamed of since I played with Strawberry Shortcake. Charlie's feeling bad and I'm confused and Mom is still sleeping.

Just then Charlie rolls over, yanks the sheet back over my head and pulls up my Coug t-shirt, "I want to see your abs," he says, exposing my belly button and a world of nerves. He leans down blows on my stomach, my laughter too loud to control.

"Angelina Calliah, thank you for letting me experience a little bit of fantasy. I'm sorry that I got all somber on you. I shouldn't have kissed you while I'm dating Summer. I want you to know that nothing else will happen in this bed tonight. Sweet dreams."

"What is going on?" Mom hisses, tearing down the sheet and revealing my shorts and t-shirt.

Every little piece of me is smashed to the ground like a piece of dog poop.

"What are you doing in his bed?"

I stand up, my shorts forming a wedgie I don't dare fix. "It isn't what you think."

"I can't believe you would do this, Angelina Calliah! Playing house with a boy while we're on a trip together? Is that a hickey on your thigh?" Mom's hands are shaking.

What? I look down seeing the African bruise I acquired on the porch.

"How convenient that Charlie showed up at our house this morning." She stands next to me, her fury painted all over her face.

"Mrs. Hulgey, we weren't doing anything to disrespect you," Charlie says, sitting up, his bedhead pushing his curls every which way.

"Getting my daughter in your bed is not respectful," Mom says, storming into the bathroom and slamming the door. I inherited Mom's trigger-sensitive bladder that requires a potty stop as soon as my eyelids lift.

"I'm sorry," Charlie says, getting up.

The toilet flushes. "Where are you going?" Mom asks, walking back in and noticing Charlie's pulling a sweatshirt over his head.

Charlie's eyes widen. "To sleep in the car."

"You're not going to up and leave my daughter like this." Mom's standing between the two beds looking likely a momma bear waving her paws around.

Oh my God. "Really, Mom? You accuse us of messing around and then you're mad he might be leaving me, as if it's a Wham Bam Thank You kind of thing? We kissed—big deal!" I sit down on the shared queen bed, grateful the bedspread didn't puff with dust when I sat, and give Charlie a small smile.

"You were laughing under the covers with a boy!"

I take a breath. I can't believe we're having this conversation, especially in front of Charlie. "We were trying to talk after SNL but couldn't hear each other over your snores," I say.

"This trip is about your future, not about sex." Mom's anger is replaced by exhaustion.

"There was no sex. Charlie has a girlfriend. I promise not to laugh or enjoy another moment on our trip, ok?" Charlie remains seated on his side of the bed.

"That is not what I'm saying, Angelina, and you know it."

"Ok, ok. I'm sorry. I love you and I'm sorry I used bad judgment. Now can we go to bed?"

Mom returns to her side and turns on Showtime where Patrick Swayze is helping Demi Moore create pottery on "Ghost." I roll away from the TV towards Charlie, watch him and mouth "Hi."

He smiles, a haunted look pulling at the corners of his eyes. His face looks like he's struggling, not sure where he belongs. I wink and continue to watch but sleep pulls me away.

Sometime later, a feather rubs my cheek and my eyes spring open to see Charlie standing above me, rubbing my forehead with his hand, tears escaping from his eyes.

I sit up, Patrick and Demi reuniting on the TV. Charlie walks back over to his bed and sits up, his back against the rattan headboard. I know I shouldn't do it, but I climb out of bed over to Charlie, the queen bed squeaking. I rest my head against his shoulder and hold his hand.

"Charlie, I never want you to hurt. You need to know how incredible you are no matter what happens with your family, with me and with your girlfriend."

His hand squeezes mine.

"I'm honored your car drove to my house this morning and that you came with us to see where my life will be. Whenever I'm sad I'll imagine you sleeping in Stephenson Hall keeping me sane." I grab our intertwined hands, kiss his palm, then climb back into bed with Mom, who's back to snoring.

Chapter 44–Angelina

March, 1992

She Smiles

She lies there, smothering me. Bitterness permeates from my skin to her lower layers; but still the smile lingers on. Her paint glistens in the sunshine, beaming of happiness. Her surface appears smooth and polished. Her smile is straight and brilliant. Her smile is painted on. She is known at the masquerade of life as Angelina, for others see no disguise. But she is not me. She is, instead my mask, my many layers of artificial character, whose presence shields me from the pain of intimacy.

My mother introduced me to my mask at a young age. My mother showed me how to sand out the lines and creases of an imperfect mask and present the world with an image of beauty and happiness. My mother appeared gorgeous, a woman who had all the world going for her—never a woman whose life was battered and crumbled by her husband—never a woman who was psychologically tortured and physically abused for years. My mother took great pains to continue attending luncheons and dinners after a night of hell with my father. I, too, learned such etiquette. In the third grade, for the father-daughter tea, I presented my class with a father who was "away on a business trip" and couldn't make it. I neglected to tell them this trip was to a bar and that he simply forgot about me. I kept hoping my father would walk in the door to the cafeteria, sober—hoping he would come and sit in the empty seat beside me, smile, and ask for some tea. There I sat, alone, mask in place smiling away and pretending to have a good time. If I pretended, maybe it would come true. If I pretended, no one would ask me questions I could not answer. If I pretended, I could believe my daddy loved me.

Throughout the years, I added more paint to my mask. I now appear to be self-confident, fairly attractive, and intelligent. My artistry gains me respect. With this respect, I feel a little better about myself. This little morsel doesn't last long, as I then believe the respect is based on my mask, and not on me. *If people knew who existed behind my mask, they would shudder and withdraw, as those who've seen me unveiled, immediately walk away, leaving me exposed and vulnerable to pain. Those people have seen who I really am. I'm not self-confident. How can I be self-confident after growing up walking on eggshells, trying not to agitate my father, trying not to make my mother's life any more difficult, trying to please everyone and pleasing no one? I don't like myself much. How can I like someone whose own father only cared enough to yell? But this, too, is hidden, as I apply another layer of paint.*

Layer upon layer is added because I do not want anyone to know how desperately I need to depend on someone. Everyone I have ever trusted has let me down. I fear that with this knowledge, people would look for reasons why others deserted me and, finding them, do the same. I fear I deserve my disappointments. My mask keeps my history from the public eye and does not allow my own poor self-image to bias anyone against me.

These layers were easily plastered until I reached high school, and relationships with friends grew more intimate. For some reason, high school was the breeding ground of vulnerability. Here, I learned masks can be removed and happiness found with a few special people. The removal of the mask is scary, but Morgan and Vanessa, people who have erased their masks with me, have made it easier throughout the years. They listen to me and do not judge me. They cannot, however, give me the security I seek. I need male approval—something I've never had. I've been given doses of it from my brothers, but they couldn't compensate for my lack of self-esteem when theirs was nonexistent.

My mask crumbled when I met Caleb. He made me remember life's hardships, but made it seem right to be vulnerable and to trust him. Caleb's childhood was worse than mine and he came out of it a survivor. Unlike anyone else, he gave me hope. He did not pretend hardships didn't exist in his presence; he did not promise he could protect me from life's wrongs. While fooling the world into believing that he was as confident as they came, Caleb was honest and defenseless with me. Caleb was gentle and wanted to hear, not erase my experience. Because of my deep respect for him, I respect myself. I knew Caleb wouldn't date anyone that was awful. I knew Caleb would not spend time with anyone out of pity and would not pretend to have a great time with me. For these reasons, my self-esteem grew, and my outer mask reflected much of my inner self.

When our relationship ended, it wasn't on bad terms, but my mask reappeared. My mask hides tears and guilt. Guilt manifests from hurting my brothers. We were a team and now we're separate. My mask hides self-loathing and memories.

Many forces drive me to continue; my expectations of hope, my need to make people feel envious—the need for them to believe they lost something special. I go on because of Caleb. He showed me life offers genuine smiles and laughter and that tears are to be shared. My mask lets in the wind and the rain, but also artificial sunshine. This sunshine, people's respect for the mask, is not as desirable as the rays of true acceptance and affection, but can be warming. If I hadn't believed a chance existed for my father to walk into that cafeteria sober, if I hadn't believed he could be compassionate, I would've killed him long ago. My mask hides these murderous feelings and instead presents a civilized human being. I go on because I owe it to my mother. My mother has watched her high school sweetheart turn into her heartache. My mother has watched as her three oldest children, my brothers, fell into the trap of drugs. My mask hides the pain of watching my brothers, whom I looked up to for guidance and who were the loves in my life, slowly kill themselves because of a lifetime of emotional and verbal abuse from my father. My mask hides my anger at the world for letting my father do this to us.

My mask is like an eggshell. It keeps the surface looking clean and keeps the rotten decay from the consumer's eye. My mask is used to protect me from the judgment of others. My mask hides my insecurities so others will not feed off them. If I'm vulnerable, I am open for attack. I have been preyed on enough by those who "love" me, and I could not withstand more pain.

She lies there, smothering me. Bitterness permeates from my skin to her lower layers; but still, the smile lingers on.

Tawnie K. Bailey

I couldn't have written this essay at the beginning of the year. I wasn't ready to give my fear of exposure a permanent reality on paper. And maybe this is like burning love letters, getting the emotion out and keeping it away from my heart. Caleb and Charlie have helped me heal. Caleb represents everything I want. Charlie represents everything I need.

Chapter 45–Aaron

March, 1992

I've been in rehab for seven fucking weeks, now. The judge reviewed my caseworker's recommendations and decided I needed to be here for two extra months. I've never heard of a three month rehab program. Lucky me. So, I'm out having a smoke, pissed off that this shit isn't over yet. I have days where I think that I can change and others where I just want a hit.

"Why are you here?" a smoky voice asks.

I turn and see a tall brunette, just opening the door to my unofficial smoking site, interrupting the night's silence.

I snicker. "For being an upstanding citizen, why else?"

She lights a cigarette and takes a drag. "Maybe you're here because you were forced to," she says blowing smoke out.

"Fuck. Nobody makes me do anything. You?"

"Blackmailed by my parents."

I laugh. "What did they bribe you with?" There's nothing my parents could say or buy that would convince me to go to rehab.

"My parents threatened to cut me off and sell their vacation house," she says and flicks the end of her death stick.

"Oh, you're a little rich girl."

"Something like that."

"What's your poison?" I ask. She looks like a coke chick, her boots probably cost more than a week of Mom's salary.

"Cocaine sometimes, nothing most of the time."

"Nothing?"

"My parents think I only do what I do because of drugs. Most of the time, I just do what I want. They're pissed because I got a friend's kid in trouble."

"Did you sell to a little kid?"

Tawnie K. Bailey

She takes a long drag and looks at me then blows out the smoke all seductively and shit. "I don't sell anything. He wanted it and I provided it."

"Are you still talking about cocaine?"

"Maybe."

She's pretty hot in a Wynona Ryder kind of way. "Or a piece of ass?"

"I'm the best piece of ass there is," she says, turning towards me. When her eyes meet mine, she winks and my boy starts to act up.

"I'm sure you are." I laugh at her moxee.

"What's your name? And don't tell me it's whatever I want it to be."

"That's too 'Pretty Woman' for me. What's your name, Mr. preppy-haircut?"

I blow smoke out. "Fuck. I used to have long hair, but the fire department shaved it all off. I should've done it sooner. The Po-Po didn't recognize me. Or maybe I should have bleached it blonde."

She looks me up and down, making me want to twirl around for her. "Blonde wouldn't go with your black eyebrows."

At least she didn't say unibrow. Angie plucked my eyebrows for my catholic schoolboy days. "Now I look like the son my mom always wanted."

"What's your name, Boy Scout?"

I chuckle, wanting to have a little fun with this minx. "What do you want it to be?"

"I once knew a Boy Scout named Travis," she says.

"What should I call you?" Girls that look like this are usually called "Heather" or "Jennifer", but she acts more like a "Cinnamon."

"Hmm. How about Angel?"

"Are you an Aerosmith fan?" I ask, hoping she isn't into New Kids on the Block.

"No, it reminds me of a girl I know."

I chuckle, thinking how funny it would be to call this girl Angel while little prissy Sis is at home. "My sister's name is Angelina, and you are nothing like her."

242

Her brown eyes bug out like a crack-addicted Iguana. "Where are you from?" she asks.

"West Seattle."

"Oh my God! Is your sister Angelina Hulgey?"

"How do you know her?" I ask, looking up towards the moon.

"I went to school with her last year."

"I didn't know my nerdy little sister knew girls like you."

"I'm here because of her," she says, pulling her hair behind her ear.

What the fuck? "My sister?" Now I'm getting mad.

"Yeah. I stayed at our vacation home when I met up with her boyfriend. We were all at a party and one thing led to another..."

"What does that have to do with my sister?"

"She dumped her boyfriend and he told his parents he took cocaine with me. Our parents are friends and my mom freaked." She blows more smoke, then looks at me. "William's mom didn't want her son around a culture that fosters drug use so she talked about selling their timeshare. My mom and dad had an intervention for me. I haven't seen them in the same room together for years and there they were all cozy and supportive because Angie dumped her boyfriend."

"You screwed my sister's boyfriend?" Fuck. "Maybe I should call you Scank."

"I didn't sleep with him. He had sex with a local, but it was my cocaine." She sighs. "And I probably would've slept with him." She looks over at me, her face slack. She squishes her cigarette butt into the can.

"I liked you better before you fucked over my sister."

"So did I."

Chapter 46–Angelina

March, 1992

"Hey, beautiful!" I look up and my heart begins to giddyup. Charlie's nemesis is talking to me, his strut more subtle than a few years ago.

I unclasp Yoyo's leash from the drainpipe next to 7-Eleven. "Caleb! Can you believe I leave for Greece tomorrow?" He's standing right in front of me, naturally tanned, with thick black wavy hair. His subtle curls are probably missed by most people. His eyes are deep chocolate and don't hint at his mom's red hair and fair skin. Ahh. Caleb. I sound like a soap opera. I suppose some goofy music could be playing overhead, instead the hum of the sign plays my love song. I'm treating myself to a Coca-Cola Slurpee.

"Greece?" His eyes light up. "Wow!" Caleb's eyes dig deep into my body, reminding me why I fell for him.

"Do you want to come? We might be able to 'off' one of the guys I'm going with; you could steal his passport and tickets, try to pass for an underclassman?" I'm smiling up at him, my heart going crazy.

His chuckle is rich, almost a baritone. "My mom might miss me when I'm taken to jail for murder."

"I promise it'd be worth it." I'm trying to flirt, but know I'm dive-bombing.

"You'll have to tell me all about it when you get back." He kisses my cheek, a patient older jock appeasing a young geek who's got a crush. "It's great to see you."

I can't be expected to have an intelligent conversation with the man of my dreams, can I? I take a drink from my Slurpee, then motion for him to come closer. His eyes dance. I stand on my tip-toes and kiss his lips, the cold sweet liquid merging with his mouth. "That's a Slurpee kiss," I say.

"I couldn't quite feel that," he says, his eyes matching his Desi Arnas smile.

Tawnie K. Bailey

I smile while my lips curve around the straw. I take another drink and kiss his lips again, the cola and ice making me throw some inhibition away. He returns the kiss and I forget about the glaring 7-Eleven lights and traffic sounds.

"Do they have Slurpees in Greece?" he asks.

"I'm sure any country as amazing as Greece has Slurpees."

"And all I'd have to do is kill some kid?" he asks.

"Or hide in my luggage."

"Tempting."

"Which part?"

"All of it. What happens if I can't make it to Greece?"

"It would be a shame to keep Slurpee kisses from the world. It's like Christopher Columbus keeping his trinkets from the Native Americans."

"They'll never know what hit them, Angelina," he says. "Too bad I never learned how to share."

"Neither have I." I wink and pick up Yoyo. "Night, Caleb."

'I kissed Caleb, I kissed Caleb' is singing out in my head. If I could skip home and not look like an idiot I would.

We arrive home, and no, Caleb does not come running to me, darn song (You know, Keith Sweat's "I'll Give All my Love to You." Duh). The house is quiet and Dad's truck isn't here.

I feel like calling Charlie and telling him I have a crush on him and that I wish he didn't live so far away. And I feel like calling Caleb and telling him he should dump Lyndsey and fall in love with me. Maybe I could finally be *that* girl—a girl who goes after what she wants without worrying about making a mistake.

I open the Samsonite luggage and stare. I need to leave room for gifts. When my parents went to Mexico, Dad's strict mother watched us. Aaron and I missed my mom like crazy and needed Mom to know what Grandma forced us to eat. We smooshed up whatever food we were given in between the pages of a moldy book. I remember pressing a piece of bologna up against the pages and stomping on the book to close it. When Mom returned, we presented our masterpiece. The book smelled of mildew and rotten food. I wonder if Mom would like a food book from Greece? A little souvlaki, a little moussaka, some olives… I'd probably have to mail it to make it through customs.

I place the curling iron complete with the European adaptor and the rest of my toiletries in the suitcase. I include the extra duffel bag for gifts and my address book for post cards. And I add the condom Vanessa gave me as a joke, just in case I decide love doesn't matter. I add the journal Morgan gave me for Christmas; my teacher has urged us to try and write in it every night, saying it will help us remember our trip—as if I'd ever forget this. I write my first entry: 'Night before trip: gave Caleb a Slurpee kiss. I don't think he minded.'

Unlike Vanessa, I'm not a traveler. Ear infections plagued my first and only flight when Mom took us to Disneyland. I now have Dimetapp, Mom's medicine of choice for kids with earaches.

Yoyo, who's been resting on my foot, jumps up and barks like crazy. Yoyo runs to the bedroom door and backs away growling. Dad pushes the door open, growling back at Yoyo. Then he laughs. Yoyo stops barking, tucks his tail and runs up to Dad's feet. I'm four feet away from my dad, sitting on the ground and I can smell the alcohol.

"Hey Ange, watcha doin'?" Dad is not a conversationalist; he rarely talks to anyone, including Mom. I don't know what he did to woo Mom while they dated, but it wasn't oratory in nature.

"I'm packing."

"Come here."

"Why?" I'm still sitting but have averted my eyes to the floor trying to look like I'm super busy—too busy to get involved with whatever his drunken self has decided is important.

"I said come here!" His voice has gone from jovial drunk to pissed off. I look up, his eyes are slits, but not because of relaxation.

I stand up and walk to my door, where Dad's head is still peering into my room. He should have at least knocked. He fixes his eyes on me.

"Did you know I never went anywhere until I joined the Navy?"

"No."

"My old man didn't bother paying the bills let alone paying for us kids to have luxuries." Dad has a little spittle at the corner of his mouth and he's leaning on my door. I wonder what will happen when he leans harder on it. The door has been broken since Todd rammed my tricycle into it fourteen years ago, stripping the door and jamb. Dad tries to fix it every once in a while with putty and things, but mostly it stays ajar, or, if I actually close it, I have to lift up on the handle and the screws come out.

"I'm sorry," I say. I've heard this so many times that I'm impartial to the information, but scared of the delivery.

"I said come here." I'm now an inch from his face. "Now, you, you make me proud. I want you to know that, Sis. Here," he says, handing me a $100 bill.

"Thanks," I murmur. Please go to bed and leave me alone.

"Huh?!" he barks.

"I said thank you Dad."

"Now, don't ever say I don't do anything for you. Not like my dad."

I take the money, but can feel my anger bubble up to the surface and spit out of my mouth. "You can keep your money. I'd rather have nothing than take your drunken offerings." I feel my hand trembling as I crumple up the bill and throw it at him.

"You think you're better than me, don't you?" he shouts.

"No but I'd be happier if you weren't a drunk or if you were gone."

"That isn't going to happen, now is it?" he says, his metamorphosis to Dean Koontz' goblin almost complete. He looks absolutely disgusted in me. "Keep the fucking money, you bitch," he says, throwing the money back into the room as he turns around.

Dad has never called me a bad name before. He's called my mom all kinds of names, but not me. Although I felt calm while he yelled, the adrenaline's left me idling like a lawn mower, ready to take off.

I hear him slam into the wall and swear, his belt buckle scratching the wall as he walks toward the living room and away from his bedroom. I take a deep breath and try to focus on packing my things. The tape pops on my stereo as the first side comes to an end, leaving my room quiet.

I feel jittery and nauseous and need to clean something. I walk into the kitchen bypassing the living room and see Dad teeter as he attempts to stand. I walk into the unusually tidy kitchen and look for some rags under the sink. The front door opens and Todd walks into the house. I'm still searching for cleaning supplies—maybe a little Lysol and water to wash down my walls?

"What are you doing?" Todd screams in the living room. I jump up and hit my head on the cupboard. "You fucking drunk! What are you doing pissing on the floor? You dumbass!" Todd continues to yell.

I rush to the living room just as Dad rams Todd up against the wall. His arm is against Todd's throat, Dad's eyes bloodshot and popped out. "Don't you ever fucking swear at me," Dad hisses. Todd is staring up at him, not backing down. I can't tell if Todd can breathe, as Dad's arm is pressing into him. Then, Dad grabs the front of Todd's shirt and lifts him off the ground. "Do you wanna piece of me?"

Oh my God. I walk back into the kitchen and grab a knife—a long knife. I will not let you ruin another one. You don't get to hurt us anymore! I'm at the telephone counter clutching the knife, ready to turn the corner and plunge it deep into his stomach. All that is refined and good and pure is ebbing out of me as I see the cause of our pain standing there, hurtling his brute force against my little brother.

"Leave him alone!" I scream. Todd is quiet, just staring, his face purple-red.

"Stay out of this!" Dad yells back, the vein in his neck and forehead bulging.

"I'm calling the police!" I still have the knife, but I haven't shown it to him yet, the wall between the kitchen and the living room hiding the weapon. I know that if he sees it, things will never be the same. Then he puts Todd down.

Dad looks again at Todd and spits on him. Then he walks into his bedroom and slams the door. I drop the knife.

"That mother fucker tried to choke me!" Todd cries. His voice is strange, sort of hoarse, very scratchy. Todd is crying and mad. When I look at Todd, I see Aaron crying when he was first hit in the eighth grade, I see Randy screaming when the neighbors attacked him. I see Randy's head being beaten into the floor.

"I am so sorry, Todd." I rush into the room crying. I couldn't protect him. I have always been protected by my older brothers and

Tawnie K. Bailey

I couldn't protect Todd. I wimped out. I should've killed my dad. I should have given our family some peace. And now, my little brother has choking marks on his neck and wounds that will never be erased. Todd looks at me with tears streaming down his face. He says nothing but walks out of the house and slams the door. There is a huge pool of urine on the floor.

I pick up Yoyo and leave the house. "Todd!" I call, my eyes unable to make out any details. I can't see him or hear him as I walk over to my car to leave. To finally leave. I put the key in the ignition and it won't start. I hit the steering wheel, the horn doesn't even sound. I pick up Yoyo again and close the door to the car. I am crying as hard as I can remember crying. I'm walking down the hill in the dark crying. We have nobody to help us. My brothers are ruined. They don't believe in themselves, they don't have goals, they don't have jobs. They are constantly looking for approval from Dad and he hurts them over and over again.

I walk down the hill, cross the street and walk towards the park a few blocks away. I sink into the grass and hold onto my little dog. Gut wrenching sobs escape from me. I can't believe this. I'm supposed to be leaving for the time of my life tomorrow.

I remember the first time Aaron was beaten. We'd been fighting and we woke Dad up. Dad ran across the living room, picked Aaron up like a ragdoll and slammed him into the fireplace. Afterwards, Aaron looked at me like I was a traitor and asked why Dad didn't hit me. My brothers have always made me feel like I belonged. When the whole world was unaware of what went on in our house, I belonged with them. And now, once again, I'm alone.

Worn out by my sorrow and by the day, I gather up my little dog who's been shaking on my lap and walk home. I skip the living room and forego cleaning my walls and head straight to bed, turn on the fan and pull the covers up over my head. I should have called the police. Maybe this time it would've been different.

Chapter 47–Aaron

March, 1992

I've seen the cokehead in most of my group sessions. This chick's hard to miss, with her high heels, tight ass and bouncy jugs. She wears the same fuzzy sweaters Mom and Angie like, but wears them better than the Hulgey girls. She twitches her foot like a well-dressed hooker waiting to get paid or hangs her head back in her chair and stairs at the ceiling. One of the counselors pulled her outside to talk and when she returned she sat up all straight and prim, then swore and made fun of one of the other groupie's issues, pointing out that the other addict chose to take the first hit and then wasn't man enough to find a better hobby. I'm sure if shock therapy was allowed the counselors would've gladly strapped her down and wired her head with some juice. But these recovering addicts-turned-counselors are far more civilized.

"I didn't do it on purpose, you know," she says, plopping down next to me on the couch and folding her leg underneath her. She makes me think we're in Nordstrom's and less like Kmart.

"Ridicule another junkie?"

"No, I did that. These freaks just want to whine about how tough addiction is. They need to grow a pair and admit they wanted it and need to change. No, I didn't mean to hurt Angie. I saw her and William together and thought they were a good match."

"So you thought you'd break them up?" I ask. Her eyes are extra large, the outer rim a deep brown and the center tan.

"I was just in a mood and wanted to get high. When I saw William was in town, I got all giddy. He can be such a momma's boy and I wanted to see if I could break him."

This chic is a lot like me, doing things just to see what'll happen. "And he broke."

"Yeah, but not the first day. He called your sister and talked about how great they were. What guy ever talks about how great his girl is?

Tawnie K. Bailey

Then he said he couldn't drink after the first of the year because he didn't want to fail a drug test."

"How noble." I would've hired someone to take a piss for me. Pretty easy shit, you'd think Angie'd date smarter dudes.

"The next night we decided to hit some local clubs and things got a little wild. Before too long we were all snorting."

"And Angie's boyfriend met up with a hooker?"

"No, she's just a local kid who makes some money from the club owners showing Americans how to have a good time. I was too busy with this dude to pay attention to William. The next day when I came by he was freaking out, pacing, swearing, doing totally un-William things."

"So you never did him?"

"He got a handjob when I felt frisky in seventh grade, but he moved away right after."

"And now you're here spending time with me at Addicts-R-Us."

"Lucky me," she says. She places her hand on my knee then laughs. "My parents would love the irony. Me ending up here with you. I'm not even an addict, I just wanted to have access to vacations."

"Addicts deny. That's what we do."

"Even you?"

"Shit, girl. They should have a punch card at these places for me. There's no point denying it."

"So what's your problem?" She asks, switching her legs around.

"I like it too much. What's your problem?"

Her right leg swings back and forth while she looks around, almost like she's looking for somebody's paper to cheat off of. "I'm bored."

"Do something different." It's so easy when you say it to someone else.

"And maybe I want attention," she says, looking up from her eyelashes in that 'I want you' way.

"Ah. Now we're getting down to the shrink shit. I've had one for years."

"Me too. Therapy's a status symbol. All my mom's rich friends had weekly shrink sessions, so I had them, too. Then my mom and dad got divorced and she remarried right away."

"Not quite the Cleavers?"

"Not unless step-daddy Cleaver rapes the Beav."

"Fuck. I'm sorry."

"He got out of jail a few months ago and was ordered to stay at least a hundred yards from me. So Mom sent me to live with my dad while she invited step-daddy to come back home."

"What a fuckin bitch. You choose your kids first. What did your dad do?"

"My dad's in Europe most of the time. His house is my crash pad and I mostly do whatever I want to. He freaked when I got taken in for panhandling. Then William's parents called my parents about their little boy and my ass landed in the Big Rock Candy Mountain Rehab Center."

"I don't see any peppermint trees here."

"You know what I mean. Everything is just perfect here for their little girl. I can just stick a little smile on my face and this place will just fix me."

"You're not really into drugs then?"

"Nah. It's just something to do. Most of the time I go to school and think about what to do next."

"What do you want to do?"

"I don't know. Maybe travel. Maybe go to college. I was always jealous that Angie knew what she wanted."

"She's known since we were little."

"How about you, Aaron. What do you want to do?"

"No clue. I don't want to make my mom sad anymore. And I don't want to feel like shit. My shrink thinks I'm trying to off myself."

"Are you?"

"Not today. Not yet. But sometimes, everything sucks so much."

Bianca says nothing, but leans into me and hugs me. "Angie doesn't know how good she's got it."

Chapter 48–Angelina

March, 1992

I wake up early. I'm too nervous to eat so I walk downstairs to see if Todd is awake. I don't know why I still expect to see Aaron and Todd's old bunk bed converted into a fort, but I do.

Todd turns over and looks at me.

I walk in and sit on the floor next to his bed. "I'm sorry I didn't do more last night. I should've called the police." When we were little, we looked after each other. I don't know when that changed. We're so busy trying to survive that we have nothing left to give to each other.

He's quiet. I can see his hazel eyes are troubled, his wavy hair is short but tousled. He sighs. "You got him off of me. You know how mad Dad got the last time the police came. You did as much as you could. Angelina, just go and have fun. Don't think about this place."

"I love you." I stand up and leave the room.

We leave for the airport a few hours later. Nothing has been said about Todd or the urine on the floor.

***

Dear Charlie,

I'm here in Paradise and am having the time of my life staring at the gorgeous men (and taking their pictures)! I want to remember Greece just the way I see it!

We've visited museums, the Acropolis, and the Parthenon. Our tour guide has more knowledge than teeth, but crooked black teeth aren't a rarity here, so if you ever decide to stop brushing, this is the place to live.

Olympia has been my favorite site so far. The Temple of Zeus must have been massive. The drums of the columns are monster-truck-tire sized, and are lying on their sides. The Greeks are continuing to dig this site as it was covered with more than 50 feet of dirt. They've found slave quarters next to the ruins. It reminds me of my joint quest with Aaron to unearth the miniature Noah's Ark.

And, I ran like a slight breeze down the field where the first Olympic Games were held. Yes, I said field, it isn't very impressive; it doesn't even hold a candle to the silly field across the street from our high school.

Then I went to a discotheque where I let loose. Not literally, just on the dance floor. Oh, and I kissed a Greek God. I could barely understand him, but it could've been such a fun little fairy tale, I meet a man in Greece, we dance, we talk, we write to each other, fall in love … . But no. I only kissed a hot guy.

Oh, and I burnt my bangs. Off. I brought a converter, but apparently it didn't work and my hair dissolved onto the melting curling iron. Let's just say that my room smelled like a bad day at beauty school! Six weeks for fried stubby bangs to grow until prom.

Tomorrow we embark on museums and sight-seeing adventures (read more pictures of beautiful men).

I'm planning on quitting my job at the clinic (long story) to be FREE from the mentor turned betrayer. I hope you are doing well. I imagine Summer has discovered that you're an amazing catch and is keeping you all to herself (since I haven't heard from you in a while).

Take Care!

Angelina

I'm still in paradise, and I can't shake my family. Like my mood, the turquoise water has transformed into brown swells with dragon-like ferocity. Yesterday I could forget and lose myself in the museums. Today, I can't forget how helpless I was, not able to keep my little brother safe. Yep, even in paradise, they follow me.

We're on a small ferry going from one Greek island to another with Gypsies packed all around us. Normally, Greek men are amazing to look and masterful in their cologne choices, but when all of the smells converge in a small space, even with the air dilution, I want to run. Like traveling carnivals, I thought Gypsies were tall tales told to spark your imagination, to make tamborines jangle in your brain like a belly dancer. Our tour guide warned us of Gypsy pick pockets sitting close and brushing against brightly-clothed tourists, so they must be real.

"You American?" yells a girl sitting to my right. We're some of the lucky few to have landed seats on the open deck. She's all but covered by a hooded robe, her dark bangs whipping in front of her. I think she's a Gypsy, but she isn't wearing any of their hallmark dangly earrings.

I nod. Since arriving in Greece, I've been saying I'm Canadian because of the loose-American-persona, but I don't want to lie today. "You have a beautiful country," I shout, competing with the snapping blue and white flag.

"Today wind isn't so kind," she says with a thick accent. She smiles, lifting up the corners of her green eyes and pulling her heavy blanket tighter around her shoulders. The ferry is slow to navigate through the swells, the open boat a prisoner to the wind. My only relief from the biting weather is from the beautiful tall bodies looming all around me, their voices thick in a language that's foreign and isolating. I look around for any of my classmates or my teacher, and catch a hint of the bright clothing only Americans wear. My stomach is turning like a broken washing machine, churning but never righting itself. I close my eyes, but the darkness and roaring of the water urges my breakfast to join the wind. Just as I open my eyes, a large wave smashes against the side of the boat and soaks the shoes of all aboard, the sound of shock a universal language.

I look over at the beautiful Gypsy, a nervous smile playing at my lips. She smiles back and scoots closer to me as I shiver in my jeans and sweatshirt. Our pedestrian ferry rolls with the sea like a little sailboat on the ocean. The roar of the boat battles the roar of the water, both heavy-metal contenders. Several passengers point to the side.

I can't see well and stand briefly, my eyes widen as a gargantuan rock presses in. Just like my little car driving parallel to semis, our boat is pulled toward the mineral mountain. I hope this is stronger than my rusted car.

"Boat goes this way every day!" my seat mate yells as if reading my mind. "They come close, never hit."

I smile again, thankful for the comfort as the sides of the ferry roll upward with the swells. I lower my head and prop up the bowling ball that's taken over my head with my hand, beads of sweat tickling my forehead like I'm a Pepto-Bismol commercial.

Tawnie K. Bailey

Voices rise. "Hold!" my seat mate yells as bodies push toward us, hands searching for something solid to grasp just as a large wave again hits the ferry, the scream of the boat now as loud as her passengers. The ship's metal fingertips scrape against the rock chalkboard in deafening tones, my hands hold tight as people around us lurch and fall with the impact. My head slams into the huge metal post behind me. I'm spinning and sliding, my head on fire, the smoke somewhere in my head not allowing me to see well.

I hear Todd somewhere calling for me but can't see him. People right themselves, freeing my chest to suck in air. Water is rushing over the deck, the railing on the right crumpled. I finally stand, the deck tilting and rush forward following the flock of panicked Greeks trying to escape this rickety Titanic, but slip. I need to find Todd. The waves continue to crash and throw our bodies around, voices muffled by the torrential water.

Todd pulls me toward the mammoth ship-smasher. I can't push against the herd who's trying to make it to the stairs.

"Toddie!" I try and yell, but only a whisper escapes.

I can't see anyone near the rock, but plunge toward it, hoping to see my brother. My shoe slides and I fall against the deck, my lips tasting the salt water. I look up and realize I'm alone near the crash site.

Dark colors stampede toward the stairs. I struggle to stand and make it to the back of the herd. The stairs are an hourglass and I'm a big speck of sand. I hold onto the slick metal rail waiting for the funnel to expand. I can see life boats filling and jackets thrown around on the deck below. A few rafts are in the water already, but there are so many people left on this little ship. Our ferry rocks again and I throw up all over the deck, my face sticky with sweat.

I finally make it down the stairs just as another lifeboat is lowered into the water. My legs are cement, and I can't lift their weight over the edge of the boat when my body is lifted into the vessel by someone murmuring soft words to me. "Thank you." The words are the most difficult I can manage. I look up and see Charlie. Charlie came to Greece? He's smiling at me while helping other women into my boat. "Charlie! Get in!" I say, using all of my energy. Don't die, don't be the hero. Please oh please, just come with me. I need you.

258

His eyes are greyer than usual, but as kind as ever. "Choose happiness," he says, then pats my hand and walks away, now invisible among the bodies.

I try to stand, but fall backwards. Charlie needs to make it through this. "Charlie!" I call, my voice hollow.

My left hand is gently squeezed. I look over, noticing others in the boat for the first time. I can't recognize many faces, the colors swirling together. I'm sure at least a few of my classmates are here based on the colors alone. I try to stand again, but my Gypsy friend grabs my right hand. "Let him go," she says.

My breath comes in short spurts. For a moment, my vision is clear when a young girl is helped into the boat by a dark, slightly curly haired man, with a familiar physique. Just as he lets go of the little girl's waist, I smell his Eternity, my eyes filling when I realize my Caleb is trying to help us to safety. I stare as his large biceps contract lowering our boat into the water. He looks at me and winks. "Caleb!" I yell. I can't leave both Charlie and Caleb behind. "Jump in the boat," I try to say, my voice now a whisper. I'm thrown backwards, our raft hitting the water. I can't see Caleb or Charlie any more. "I love you!" I try and scream, not sure any noise has left my mouth.

The lifeboats are no match for the waves, water soaks what remains of our dry clothes. I turn away from the ferry, wondering if I should've left the bigger vessel for this yellow, blow up imitation. When a motor starts up and we make some headway through the dark swells, I lie back, letting the world turn like a ballerina en pointe.

***

We arrived back at shore somehow. Fairies or flying monkeys may have picked us up and flown us to land for as much as I remember. But I'm here, my head is killing me, and I haven't thrown up for a while now. The back of my head is caked with blood, which means that with my perm, it probably looks like a dog matt.

"You better?" my Gypsy friend asks. We're sitting next to a dock, waiting for our turn with the emergency personnel.

I smile, realizing those tamborines were indeed jangling in my brain for a while. "Thank you for looking after me."

She smiles. "Friends watch over."

I squeeze her hands then hug her tight. So far there are a few injuries, but nobody is missing and the ferry didn't sink. The site of impact was fairly close to the harbor so the ferry took on water but limped its way to the dock once the passenger load reduced. Rumor has it that the Greeks exceeded the boat's capacity. Maybe I should've run a few miles last night, lost a little weight and reduced my part.

I can't get away from the feeling that Charlie and Caleb helped save me and I left them behind. And I am so not ready to do that. I know I just bonked my head and hallucinated. But maybe this bloody dog matt is my wake-up call.

***

"We're home!" I feel my shoulders shake.

The white porch tiles are still broken and are a dingy brown. My car sits in the driveway with Dad's truck, Mom's car, grandma's old Dodge Dart, and a rusted little Mustang. The rockery is overgrown with weeds, moss is clinging to the cement adjacent to the house and I'm glad to be here. Maybe my head bump's worse than I thought.

I open the door that houses our chaos. Yoyo is talking to me and jumping up and down and turning in circles. I pick him up and he licks my face as fast as he can. Dragging my luggage into the entrance way, I see Dad sitting on the recliner in his bathrobe while Todd plays a video game.

"Hey, Sis," Todd says, looking up briefly from the game and smiling at me.

I drag the too-heavy suitcase to my room. Too bad I couldn't pack a Greek man with me who would pop out of my luggage, carry it into my room, unpack and maybe even fluff up my pillows. I sit on my bed and drink in the scenery: pink walls, man posters, old pictures (Caleb, William, and a few other brief romances), my desk and Tandy 1000 computer.

"Lots of people called while you were gone," Todd says while standing at the doorway. "I wrote some of them down this time." He hands me a paper towel with names on it: Charlie (!), Troy, Vanessa, and Morgan.

"I feel so special."

"I think Caleb also called. I know it was a guy," Todd offers. "I told him you were in Greece on vacation."

I unpack the suitcase and lay out the painted shell windchimes, handpainted pottery, worry beads, and other gifts. I'm exhausted but want to talk to Vanessa and Morgan.

"Morgan, I wish you were there with me. The men were so handsome and flirtatious. I also have a really awful haircut in the back of my head and short bangs."

"Like the girl on Sixteen Candles?"

"I hope not. I hit my head while we were on a ferry and needed stitches. I got a bit loopy and thought I was dying."

"Did a Greek man come and save your life?"

I tell her about my strange fantasy before I see my mom hovering and end the call.

Mom wants me to go grocery shopping with her. Ugh. Grocery shopping was the highlight of the week when we chose the candy bars (one per kid per week) and one extra box of cereal (in addition to the Raisin Bran and Frosted Flakes—which aren't my favorites) back in the day. We'd look for the cereal with the best free candy. Mom would choose one kiddo to shop with her, and rarely, she'd go by herself. I hid in the back of her Escort on more than one occasion, just wanting to be with my mom.

We're at the produce section when I look up and see the freaky man who lied about his age. Yup the one who followed me home a few times in his cute little Honda.

Larry is a fitting name, just like Jack Tripper's slimy friend in Three's Company. "I got a promotion at Boeing," he says.

You're still a slug. "Oh, good for you," I say, looking at other produce. I'd rather pluck nose hairs than talk to him.

"Are you doing anything tonight?"

"I just returned from vacation and have a lot of things to take care of. I'll be in touch if anything changes or if I want to go out with you," I say. There. That's as rude as I can muster.

Mom rounds the aisle and looks at us. "Are you ready, Angie?" she asks.

"Just talking with an acquaintance," I say giving a polite smile.

Tawnie K. Bailey

"Oh, come on, I'm more than that, aren't I?" Larry asks.

"You know, I don't know you very well, but I know you lied to me. I don't like liars. You're too old for me and too immature for me. Have a nice day," I say and walk away.

Mom lifts her eyebrows and says nothing for a while as we walk down the next aisle.

"Who's that?" she asks, perusing the coffee.

"Just some guy who used to drive by when I walked home."

"Call Caleb," she says, changing the subject.

"Since when do you like Caleb?" Mom hasn't liked anyone I've dated.

"You light up when you talk to him."

I hope he can't see it, too. We move on to the cookie aisle and I pick out the usual. I may as well have 'loser' light up in big letters on my forehead as I don't need to eat more cookies.

We finish the grocery shopping and head to the line, just in time to see Larry.

Once again, he approaches me. "I'm sorry if I offended you. I didn't think age was a big deal."

"The age thing doesn't matter except that you lied about it, so I don't trust you. End of story." I walk to another check-out line.

The checker, a short Hispanic woman quietly asks, "Do you know him?" and nods her head towards Larry.

"Not really," I answer in a quiet voice.

"Good. He's bad news. He comes into the store drunk all of the time."

Oh goody, just what I need to attract!

We drive back home where we stash the groceries. I grab an apple and head back to my room. It should be a fairly nice day tomorrow, so maybe I'll wear shorts. I hate my calves. Have I said that before? There isn't one body part I like, other than I have a tiny waist. My calves are muscular. I blame their size on running around our playground in 4th grade during every recess, but I think it's genetic. How rude. Maybe that's why people inherit money from dead relatives, to make up for their poor genetic donations. Yeah, I'll need to save a lot of money for my kids.

262

I return a few phone calls and leave messages for Troy and Charlie. I'm still lying on my back when I drift off to sleep. I wake up several hours later and realize I haven't washed any clothes. After visiting our dungeon, this Cinderella wants to talk to a prince and I call Caleb.

I dial the number, impressed that I'm not shaking too much for my fingers to push the right numbers. Sitting on my bed (where all important phone calls are made), I pull the covers around me.

"Hello?" A super sexy deep voice answers. It's him!

"Caleb, this is Angie. Hey, my younger brother said you called. Or rather, he thinks it was you." I'm trying to be calm, but feel all giddy. At least I'm not a boy going through puberty having my voice crack mid-word (think of the Brady Bunch, poor Peter), but I still feel awkward.

"I didn't, but I'm glad your brother got it wrong." Caleb could make lots of money reading books on tape, or reading junk mail, for that matter.

"Oh." Did you just say you're glad Todd got it wrong? I smile a little.

"You're back from the land of temples and olives?" Caleb asks.

"Barely. The turquoise water tried to woo me into staying. The people were super friendly and gorgeous and flirtatious and the ruins were everything I dreamed of." Caleb and I share a love for history, debate, and books. He would've loved Greece, too.

"I wish I could've gone."

"Our ferry hit a rock and took on water. I hit my head and was helped into a life raft by someone who looked a lot like you."

"You were in a boat crash?"

"I thought I was going to die." Then you and another friend appeared and saved me.

He's quiet. "I'm glad you didn't."

"I have a lot of things I want to experience before I die."

"Like…"

"I want to fall in love. And learn how to swim. And all of the things in between."

"You should show me your pictures sometime. Unless you're still seeing the guy from movie night."

"Movie night?" What's he talking about?

"When you were limping."

"We stopped dating after New Year's. He was a pretty great guy, and then he wasn't. And I never would've kissed you if I was seeing someone."

"Ahhh." Caleb elongates the word. "Was he the reason you were exercising instead of sleeping?"

"One of them. How about you? Are you seeing anyone?" This is the moment. Watch him tell me about the model he's dating, or the pre-med student.

"I've just started dating again. I didn't want a rebound or anything, so nothing serious. I don't need that head ache." I picture him with a gorgeous blonde on his arm and I'm instantly jealous. "I've thought about calling you a few times, but figured you hated me," Caleb says.

You should have called. "Maybe I should," I say.

"You dated Morgan's brother for a little bit…."

"Just long enough to know it wasn't a good idea."

"What else is going on with you? Weren't you working for the vet and an accountant or something?"

"An attorney. And I should quit working at the vet."

"I thought you loved that job."

"It's a long story."

"I've got all night. Why do you want to quit your dream job?" Caleb sounds concerned.

I relay how I'd started, the progression in duties, how my pay worked, and discuss a few of the bizarre behaviors.

"Quit."

"I love that job. He's just a big butt pimple I have to deal with." I sigh. "You aren't the only one who's said I should leave, though." I think of Charlie and his wise advice.

We talk about slimy guys, his parents a bit more, my parents, Morgan and Vanessa, and of course, Yoyo.

"Does he know how lucky he is?"

"Who?"

"Yoyo," Caleb adds. "He's pampered and gets to sleep with you," he says.

I laugh. "When he's naughty he sleeps on the floor," I say, smiling.

"But he's your everything."

You had that option.

"I'm sure there are many people who'd like to try out for that position," Caleb adds.

Are you flirting with me? "Most guys attracted to me are lacking something major. If he's good looking, then his personality sucks or if his parents are rich he feels entitled, or he thinks I'm going to sleep with him and I don't want to settle."

"You shouldn't have to." He sounds serious. "You're a pretty perfect package."

"Gee thanks," I joke. Okay, my smile is huge.

"Accept the compliment nicely. Someday, I'm going to get it through your brain that you deserve great things."

"Everybody deserves great things," I say.

"Angelina Calliah Hulgey. I am serious."

He remembers my name! "I didn't call to manipulate you into giving me compliments." But you can keep them coming. Why don't you ask me out while you're at it?

"I definitely don't think *you're* a manipulator. Lyndsey lied to me repeatedly. She'd only come clean after I'd find out the truth from somebody else."

"I don't understand what you see in her." Here I go, speaking the truth. Dummy.

He's quiet, every second my heart stopping.

"I loved her."

Enough said.

"And her parents are amazing. They're supportive, helped me get my job, and talked me through a lot of big decisions. It's too bad their daughter's a spoiled brat."

I would've said a different 'b' word, but that isn't lady-like. So, that's the appeal—love and family. I don't have the family, and he's not in love with me.

"But I'm over it. I've been living my life without her for months and it feels good. We fight so much when we're together I'm miserable."

"Passion is a strong emotion," I say. I know; I'm sweet. Sweet is boring.

"Mmm. Yeah, but testing for STDs after she cheated with the Thunderbird Hockey team turned passion to disgust."

So the rumors were true? "I never liked her much."

Caleb laughs. "I'm sure the feeling is mutual. She knows you and I have a strong connection."

"Yeah, I think you're pretty groovy," I say. "Not as good as Yoyo, but I suppose if you had tickets to a great play, I wouldn't turn you down."

"I'll work on that," he says.

"Filling Yoyo's footsteps?"

"Getting tickets to a play. I haven't been on a date with anyone who appreciates the finer things in a long time. As for Yoyo, and filling his footsteps, some of us can only dream of being so important in your life."

"Maybe you're already that important?" I say, then laugh before ending the call.

I wish I could keep talking to him, but my eyes are heavy and my contacts haven't been the same since Athens' pollution coated them. I don't have the extra money right now for new violet eyes.

Before I turn off the light, Dad startles me and swings open the door. "What are you doing awake?" His dark eyebrows contort into an ugly check mark.

"I couldn't sleep and was talking on the phone." I didn't even know Dad was still home.

"Do you pay the phone bills? No. How the fuck am I supposed to know if I'm getting called into work if you're on the phone?"

Uhhh. "I'm sorry. I didn't know you were waiting for a call."

"You'd better be sorry. From now on I want you to ask permission to use the phone," he says, his finger pointing into the room like a lightning rod.

What?! Do you know I could've died while I was in Greece? My life is not going to be about this shit anymore. I choose my own happiness. "That is nice and all, but if we're talking about wants, I want a Dad who doesn't get drunk and beat up my mom or my brothers." My

266

face is hot and my heart is beating super-fast. I usually just listen and sneak off to my room.

"What did you say to me?" He looks at me the way he looks at the boys before he hits them.

"I said sorry. And by the way, you can't tell me what to do. I don't smoke. I don't drink. I don't do drugs! I have a 3.82, and I have two jobs. I am a great kid and that has nothing to do with you!" I don't know how my night has swirled into this mess. I'm surprised Dad doesn't rush in and thump me.

Instead he laughs. "You're stout." What the hell does that mean?

I get out of bed. I don't know what my body is doing. Please don't do something stupid, Angelina! I walk up to the doorway where Dad continues to smirk. I'm close to his face when I whisper, "And by the way, any good Dad would've fixed his daughter's door a long time ago." I know I'm challenging him, egging him on.

He laughs, "Touche little girl." Then he rubs my hair and turns around.

Chapter 49–Aaron

March, 1992

Tomorrow I get to leave good ole 12-step behind. We have the typical "Graduation Ceremony" where we all get medals and shit but this time I'm taking a better treasure home. And today is the typical "Don't forget what can happen if you stray" assembly and our exit interviews. Hopefully they'll decide I've made the leap.

"Hey Baby," Bianca says, moving her cute rear before she sits in the theater seats.

"Hi beautiful," I whisper, hoping the rehab counselors don't give me a talking to. We're not supposed to hook up right after rehab, and if they don't think I'm serious about changing my ways, they may talk to the judge again and have me spend more time here.

She bats her lashes. "Are you excited?"

"Shit yeah. I can't wait to live again." I grab her hand and kiss it. She makes me want to be a better man.

"You sure your mom will like me?"

"Why wouldn't she?"

"I hurt her daughter."

"She doesn't know that. She'll just be glad you have front teeth and no swastica tattoos on your face."

Bianca hits my arm. "I suppose she'd be glad to know I'm not a blow up doll, then too."

"Exactly. Although blow up dolls can't get pregnant. Doc says I may not be able to shoot bullets for very long, so if you want a kid with me, we'll have to get working on it." I say, laughing.

"I don't need to be a mom, so you can keep your bullet for somebody else."

"I don't want anyone else. I'm choosing my own happiness, remember." I say, making fun of her mantra.

"We'll see. Now be quiet, we have some people who want to talk to us and remind us to be good," Bianca whispers, then grabs my hand.

The lights dim, the center's signal to shut up. The director takes center stage with a few visitors, all of them against drunk driving. The first speaker is an innocent dude, looking all preppy with his leather jacket and sweater. When he starts talking, Bianca jabs me in my rib.

"Oh my God! I know him."

"So, you've known of lot of boys. And men," I say with a smile.

"Aaron, I'm serious. That's...I can't remember his name. Angie and I went on a double date and that's her date." Her face is animated, her body leaning towards mine.

I look back at the speaker, and listen to his words.

"It's a small fuckin world," I say.

"We should talk to him. Maybe it's a sign."

"Like STOP."

"No, from God. My parents always want me to go back to church. Maybe this is God's way of saying I should help bring this guy and Angelina back together. Or maybe he's just a reminder that I shouldn't forget why I'm here."

I look over at the girl who's made my balls sing even without touching them and smile. "Maybe."

***

We walk up to the stage, where a few of the criers are crying and talking with the speakers. The speakers are varied this time—the high school kid, the old lady whose daughter died and the biker who killed his wife on the back of his hog.

The kid watches us approach, his eyes moving from Bianca to me, almost as though he knows who we are.

"Are you a friend of Travis?" Bianca asks, breaking the barrier between freaks and speakers.

"I am," he says. I can almost see his hamster wheel spinning in his head.

"Merry Fuckin Christmas," I say, walking over and shaking his hand. "I hear you know my sister, Angie."

The kid's body jumps back a bit. I could see Angie going for this guy. She likes the muscle-bound brainy dudes, and it looks like he hits the gym a little.

270

Bianca smiles, her eyes singing. "Look at you! I wish I could be that leather coat wrapped all over your hard body," she says, then laughs.

I laugh, too. Bianca knows just how to make your skivvys get all tight.

His eyes widen and he ignores Bianca. "I'm Charlie. I met you last fall when you blew up a car and were on a gurney."

"Shit, I don't remember much about those days. Are you treating my sister alright? My pops came and visited last month and said some dude dropped off some flowers for her."

"We're just friends."

"So you wouldn't want to see her panties?" I ask, joking.

"My girlfriend wouldn't want me to see her panties, but thanks for asking."

"So, do you think Angie'll be attending our graduation ceremonies tomorrow?" Bianca asks.

"I haven't talked to her since we visited the WSU campus," Charlie says.

"Well, if you see her, would you tell her I love her?" I ask.

"Aren't you done tomorrow?" Charlie asks.

"Aaron might have to go back to jail," Bianca says. "Unless King County thinks it's too expensive to treat his diabetes in jail."

"It's cheaper to send me here than to keep me in the hospital," I say.

"What'll you do if you get out tomorrow?"

"I'm gonna get me a scholarship," I say, trying to quote "The Breakfast Club." Charlie raises his eyebrows. "I'm kiddin man, I'm gonna change my life."

"No taking down gas tanks?" Charlie asks.

"No running down old men, no breaking into houses. I'm going straight."

"But not boring," Bianca says.

"I'm never boring."

Charlie looks like he wants to say something.

"Just say it, dude. It looks like you're holding something back. I know I've been a shitty brother. Did my sister tell you I hit her with a car once? That I stole her cash?"

Tawnie K. Bailey

"I'm worried about her."

I feel my jaw tighten. "What's going on with my sister?"

"Never mind. She wouldn't want you guys to know."

Bianca grabs my hand and squeezes it. Oh, he's probably talking about that William kid.

"Angelina's boss at the clinic has been making suggestive comments and she's scared he won't write her a letter for vet school if she quits."

"What?" I see my director turn and walk towards us. I must have used my 'outside Aaron' voice.

"Is everything alright?" Mr. Director asks.

"Oh, yeah. This kid just knows my sister and said she's having some problems, that's all."

"Her problems are not your problems, Aaron," Mr. Director adds.

"I know," I say. Our director smiles and walks towards another group.

I look over at Bianca, her face looking like her kitten just got crushed. "You ok baby?" I ask.

"Men are creeps."

"How do you know this?" I ask Charlie. "Angie's worked for the French Fry for a long time."

"He's sly. He makes her think it's his culture, but he's offered to give her a bath, he sent her flowers, and it's bothered her enough she's thinking about quitting. Your sister is fairly private, but she's scared of him."

Bianca shakes her head and I see tears in her eyes.

"Little French Freak." Bianca's hands wrap around mine and she unclenches my fist.

"He's going to find out what happens when you mess with a Hulgey."

Bianca just stares at me.

"I'm not talking about landing in jail again. But this dude's gotta know."

"And I need to make things right for her," Bianca says. I squeeze her hand and then rest my arm on her thin shoulders.

Charlie smiles. "The doctor needs to pay."

Chapter 50–Angelina

May, 1992

I'm quitting my job at the vet clinic today. I've been thinking about this day for months. I should work more hours to save for prom, college, that kind of thing. But I'm done. I used to be excited to walk through the door of the clinic and I've been dreading it. One night I agreed to meet Dr. Mike at The Keg, and when he showed up wearing youthful clothing and placed his arm around my shoulder while we were waiting near the hostess, I wanted to run. A client recognized him and stopped over to say hi, then she looked at me. I wanted to crawl under a rock. That's as close to a tramp as I'm going to get. And I dreamed Dr. Mike raped me last night. I don't have control of my family and my car works at random moments, but I'm not going to sit back and let this man make me feel this way anymore. So, I've decided to quit. Today, I am going to quit.

This is the day I change my life. I feel empowered and like a wuss at the same time. I'm scared most of the evening and very uncomfortable when I'm in the same room with Dr. Mike. A kitten is abandoned in a taped box behind the clinic at lunch time. Dr. Mike's treating it for fleas and dehydration and plans on keeping it as the clinic cat.

I walk into his office. "Mike, can I talk to you?"

He looks up briefly from the calculator. I can hear the tape advancing. "Sure, give me a minute, okay?"

"Alright." I've finished mopping and cleaning. Steven is still here taking care of the dishes a few rooms away. I ease down onto the chair.

"Do you want to go somewhere else?" Mike asks quietly as he walks towards me. His voice has changed to his "I think I'm sexy" crap, and his eyelids are lowered.

"No. I have a friend expecting me to study with her tonight." Why such lies, Angelina?

"Oh, maybe we can do it tomorrow night then." He says, his voice returning to normal, his eyes brightening. He sits down in the chair adjacent to me.

"I'm moving." All day I've been thinking about what I'd tell him, and that's the best I could come up with.

"What?" He looks shocked as his head lurches backward with the news. "Where are you going?"

"I'm moving in with a friend. Her parents know our family issues and have offered to let me stay with them." I take a breath. "They live in Kent and work in West Seattle, so I'll ride in with them during the day then ride back to their house in the evening—at least until I leave for college." I take another breath and finally say the words I've been thinking about for months, "I need to give you my two weeks' notice."

"What? I wasn't expecting this. I can't believe I'm going to lose you. What am I going to do without you? Nobody else understands me." We're both quiet. "Maybe we can go to dinner tomorrow night and talk?"

"I can't. I have a date." Where did that come from?

"How about tonight?" His eyebrows are up, his mole still there.

I shake my head. "I need to study and have so much to do before I move out. I just can't go." I'm not moving anywhere. No such luck for me.

"We'll figure it out over the next few weeks, then."

I smile. I can't believe how well this is going. I am free! I stand up. I'm sweaty, my face feels clammy. I can still hear Steven clattering the dishes in the background. I told him about Dr. Mike a few months ago. He wasn't surprised.

I stand up and lean in to hug him briefly. He turns and kisses my cheek, leaving me with my own scarlet letter. My legs feel like Jell-O. I walk into the "food room" where the meals are prepared and dishes cleaned. I'm trying to fight back tears.

"I did it." I say quietly to Steven. I give him a hug and he pats my back.

"Good for you, Angie." I turn around and head towards the front door.

"Good night, Mike!" I call.

"Night!" He says, counting up the receipts.

I open the door feeling like a bird let out of a cage. I'm free. I open Chitty Chitty's car door. It doesn't fall off, a great sign. The key goes into the ignition, turns, and my little Bang Bang turns on! I pull out of the parking lot, making sure not to hit the telephone pole, and enter the West Seattle streets. I should head home, but I turn around and head towards Alki Beach. I feel so liberated and grown up. Okay, so I lied, but it's done. I can stop hating myself for allowing my boss to treat me like a slut. I turn on my radio and pop in Gerald Levert's "Baby Hold on to Me." I cruise Alki and allow myself to cry. I let go of my admiration for a mentor. I let go of my need to impress a veterinarian. I let go of my safety net.

***

May 20, 1992
Dear Charlie,

I've been trying to get a hold of you for weeks; I can't believe you've abandoned all telephone communications with the girl who introduced you to Anne Rice. Convenient you call back when I'm not home. Maybe you've read some of Anne's racier books and think I'm a slut? Or maybe the horrors of my family have finally repulsed the last of "the good guys." Your latest letter depicted a busy boy with a girlfriend, scholarships, cruises, prom planning, etc. Well, I'll have you know that I drive by a McDonald's almost every day. Way to manipulate me into thinking about you!

I have taken your advice, oh-wise-one, and officially gave my notice to my weirdo boss. I expect my summer will be fraught with long walks with Yoyo, beach parties, Slurpees, and all kinds of wondrous things that have suffered because of my long hours. Maybe I'll take up dancing or gum chewing? I hope your caddy career doesn't monopolize every moment this summer as I'd like to see you before I move to Eastern Washington; I'd be willing to trek over to see you, but the last time my car drove more than a few miles, the night didn't end so well for me.

Waiting for our lives to begin,
Angelina

I hear Vanessa honking and I grab my overnight bag and pillow; Jacob's having a party at his place tonight. Mom thinks I'm staying with Vanessa. What she doesn't know won't break her heart.

I climb into her car and we drive over to the Eastside. Jacob's house sits on an embankment overlooking Lake Washington. Vanessa knocks and enters without waiting for anyone to answer. The glass front door illuminates the foyer.

"Hello!" Vanessa calls.

"Out here!" I hear a male voice.

Vanessa guides me through the house and into the kitchen. From the grandiose kitchen, a large bank of windows show a dozen or so people mingling outside.

Vanessa walks out to the patio where she's greeted by Jacob. "Hey, there's my beautiful one," Jacob greets. Vanessa walks over to him, places her arm around him and kisses his cheek as he disengages himself from his buddies. "Angie! It's good to see you! I've missed having you around to keep my buddy in check," he says.

"Is William coming tonight?" I ask. I'm equally curious, nervous, and excited.

"He might stop by for a bit. Is that alright with you?" Jacob asks quietly. He actually looks concerned.

I smile. "I wouldn't be here otherwise."

"Let me introduce you to some of our other friends."

Jacob makes the introductions. I've heard of a few, met a couple more at the Homecoming game, and think I recognize one girl from William's pinup board. I'm out of my element and feel like I'm zooming straight back to my geekness.

I don't usually drink, but decide to have a go with my good old friend, the peach cooler. Yep, I met her at my brother's house then revisited her for New Year's this year. I'm not driving home, and I'm a pretty good kid. I open the cooler and take a drink. It isn't nearly as yummy as a Coca-Cola Slurpee, but the peach flavor coats my tongue and with every subsequent drink, the flavor lessons and becomes a little bit less important. It's been a gorgeous day and is now a gorgeous evening.

I sit down on the edge of the patio and play with the bottle cap, making lines in the bark when I feel hands cover my eyes. I smell that heavenly scent and so want to lean back towards the hands and relax. "Hi." I say as I look up. I wasn't going for a "languid" sound, but I think it came out that way—the way Dr. Mike lowers his voice gives me grossness chills—again, inventing new words. William uncovers my eyes. He looks so—wow. The tan makes his blue eyes see more vivid.

"Are you having a good time?" he asks.

"Umm, mostly." I feel pretty shy and am out of my comfort zone. The last time I saw William, I felt so betrayed and humiliated. Surely I can't forget that just because he looks nice and I'm lonely, can I?

"Is there anything I can do to improve that?" he asks sincerely.

Like leave? No, I don't want that. I don't know what to say. I wanted William to be my dream guy, and he'll never be that, now. I shake my head and smile sadly.

He leans over and kisses the top of my head. He can be so tender. He sits down next to me and we both stare out over the lake.

"I'm glad you came," he says.

My heart dances a little as I turn and look at him.

"I want you back in my life, Angel."

Is he trying to ram the nail deeper into the wound? "You must say that to all of the girls," I say, trying to lighten the mood.

"I'm serious. I told Jacob to make sure you came tonight."

"Why? Haven't you felt free?" I joke.

"No, you weren't a ball and chain. During baseball I thought how great it would've been to see you in the bleachers cheering for me."

"Now, that just proves you never really knew me. As a dedicated former class officer for Seattle High's class of 1992, I'd never cheer for the opposing team at a game—even if their short stop's hot."

"I see."

"Yup, so it'll just have to remain a fantasy. Like so many of your thoughts about me."

Vanessa walks over. "William. How are you? Have you cheated on anyone recently? Besides my best friend, that is."

"Angel and I are just catching up." William says, ignoring Vanessa's question.

"She's way over you, buddy."

I know I have a small smile on my face watching their exchange—okay, maybe I'm smiling because of the peach cooler, too.

Speaking of peach coolers, Jacob walks towards us with another cooler in his hand and offers me the pale drink. William's eyebrows lift but he doesn't say anything as I accept the alcohol. He knows I rarely drink.

"Guess what," I say raising my bottle in a toast. "I gave my notice at the clinic so I'll get to play a bit more this summer."

"Can I play, too?" William asks.

Jacob walks over to greet another guest and motions for Vanessa to join him. "No you can't play," she adds before walking off.

"You quit a job, huh?" William asks. He is still sitting beside me on the steps. The sun is hitting his face and making him squint a little.

"Very necessary." My hand curls like an elephant trunk, offering to hold William's hand. He grabs it and I lean my head on his shoulder. He smells incredible. "William, you have to know I can never date you again," I say quietly. "I promised myself a long time ago I'd never let somebody I care about treat me that way."

He's probably seeing somebody. His 'I want you back in my life' probably means something different than what I'm making it out to be.

William's quiet. My head's still resting on his shoulder.

"I'm sorry." William says.

"Me too." I take another drink from the cooler. I can barely tell what flavor it is—my tongue is so coated.

William stands up, takes my hand and pulls me up, too. I realize as I stand that I'm a bit tipsy, which is probably why I'm craving another tropical drink. Such a girlie-drink, and I shouldn't partake. I know my family's history.

"Can I get you anything to eat?" William asks. Does he notice I'm uncoordinated?

"No thank you." I know I'm consuming a lot of calories in the form of alcohol and don't want to add to any potential tummy fat. Alright, now that doesn't make sense. I'm smarter than that. If I don't eat, I'll get drunk, and I don't want that. "Actually, I think I'll get something to eat," I add.

William smiles, "Good girl."

He holds my hand and walks me over to a table with fruit and snacks sitting out buffet-style. "Is this spody?" I ask, having heard of the fruit soaked in all kinds of liquor.

William laughs. "No, it's just fruit. Taste it. Spody is left in a big bowl where it floats in the alcohol, it isn't disguised."

"Oh." What do I know?

I use a toothpick with pretty tags at the end to grab some pineapple and cantaloupe, then add grapes to my little plate. William adds cheese and a roll as well.

"Thank you." I say.

"Of course. You need to eat more." He's staying pretty close to me. I know these are his friends, too. I wonder if they know who I am? Or if he even told anyone there was a "me." If so, did he tell them he cheated on me? Do they know he tried cocaine? "I tried calling you a few months ago during spring break, but your little brother said you were in Greece. How was your vacation?"

Ah, so that's who called. 'Caleb and William' don't sound anything alike. I wonder how Todd got their names mixed up. I take another drink of the cooler. "Amazing. Better than I ever expected. I even kissed a Greek guy who told me he wanted to become an American citizen so he could fly planes." I take a bite of the cheese—I think it's Havarti—mmmm, I could get used to eating this mild yummy goodness.

"Was he a good kisser?" He's staring at me, his super blue eyes smiling and burrowing holes through my walls.

"Um, I don't remember, I just enjoyed kissing somebody." I'm smiling at him as I take another drink. I can tell I'm getting tipsy. How much alcohol is in this thing? I'm sure there's a lot of sugar, but not sure about the other. "Why do you care?" I ask and hit him lightly.

"I don't like hearing you kissed someone," he says.

I laugh. "I didn't like hearing you had sex with someone." I'm smiling and trying to keep things light between us.

"Point taken."

"And I almost died on a ferry boat, which isn't ideal for hairdos with the matted blood and all, but the bad boys love my scar."

"Are you kidding me?"

"No. I think it made the news."

"Oh my God!" William pulls me close, his arms and chest seducing my body with memories of us.

"No biggie, I'm here."

"I could've lost you."

"You already did," I say, then giggle. "But maybe I should've hit my head earlier. So what did you call me about?" I take another drink.

"I was going to invite you to prom," he says, pulling me tighter and kissing the top of my head.

"Oh." Wow. You were still thinking about me up until a month ago? "Who did you take?"

"Bianca." My eyes bulge.

William laughs. "I'm joking. I took an old friend from the girl's school. We dated a few years ago but definitely aren't good for each other."

"Is she here tonight?" I look across the patio at the beautiful girls.

"Nah, we aren't that good of buddies."

I laugh. "Oh, William, you are just…"

"Just the greatest? Just the one you've always dreamed of…?" Ah, now there's the guy I know.

"No, just…."

"Aren't you going to finish that statement?"

"Nope. Now you'll never know how I feel." I'm smiling at him.

The music picks up, and I'm feeling more playful, so I grab William's hand and decide Vanessa, William and I should dance. "Celebrate Good Times" is singing out of the patio speakers. Alright, so this isn't like me, but I'm about to graduate and will probably never see William again.

I drink two more coolers. I don't want to get drunk, but maybe I am. The night is fun, and I watch William with his boys. It sounds like he had a great baseball season and will be attending UW on a baseball scholarship (as if he needs the financial assistance). The scholarship is a testament to his skills however.

As the night progresses, Vanessa becomes tipsy and playful. She sends everyone to bed at one since Jacob's drunk and horny. I claim the leather couch near the restroom then change into my pink baby doll pjs and paisley pink silk robe.

William crawls over to the base of the couch.

"Angelina!" he whispers loudly.

I lean over the couch and look into his face and start to laugh.

He is looking up at me with puppy-dog eyes.

"What are you doing?" he whispers loudly.

"I'm trying to sleep," I whisper back.

"Oh. Will you come down and play with me?"

I'm still feeling tipsy and carefree. I roll off of the couch and tackle him. He catches my uncoordinated descent.

"Mmmm," he jokes.

I'm lying on top of him and laughing when I start kissing him. It feels so good to be with him.

After a few minutes, the kissing intensifies. I'm stroking his face and his shoulders when I pull away slightly.

"Mmm, I've missed you," he says.

"I've missed you too." I hover over him, kissing him and wanting him. His hands move from my lower back to the front of my waist making me shudder.

"We could still be great," he murmurs between kisses.

I open my eyes and stop kissing him. "We shouldn't do this."

"It feels pretty good to me," he says, his eyes smiling.

I chuckle and sigh again. "That doesn't mean it's right." I roll away and sit up. "We should go our separate ways."

"Don't say that. I love you." William is still lying on the floor, his arm reached out towards me.

"I'm leaving for college in a few months and as much as I adore you, I don't trust my heart to you anymore." He doesn't say anything as I lean back over and kiss his lips again. "I could've loved you." This is as close to saying the all-important three little words as I've ever come. I climb back onto the couch as the price for what I desire is too steep. I used to become so angry with Mom for not leaving Dad and now I understand the appeal of staying. "Good night, William."

I hear him whisper under his breath, "Fuck."

Chapter 51–Aaron

May, 1992

I've been out on work release cleaning up good old fuckin Pac Highway after spending a few weeks in jail post Addict Ranch. I'm a work release virgin; when I go to jail, I spend most of my time seeing doctors. Don't get me wrong, I'd rather be in the hospital than in jail, but it's a bit screwy. My probation officer wanted to know if I'd spend a few days doing some work in exchange for cutting down my stay at the county jail. I was getting two injections of insulin every day, my glucose monitored daily and I thought, what the hell. I feel good. I could use some sunshine, so I agreed.

I'm a hemorrhoid for the county, and they repay me with great medical care—a system bound to fail, a system I love. If I could figure out a way to magnify that defect, I would. I'm always looking for a buck.

I'm sittin on the side of the highway with my stupid glow in the dark shirt, not feeling too hot. My guard was told I need to take it easy because my sugars run low with most activities, so he's cut me some slack. I'd rather be sitting in a cell than sitting out here feeling like I need to puke, but I look like a vampire, my skin all pasty and shit. I have a date with my girl tomorrow and need to look more alive.

I look up, the sun blinding me. There she is, a combination of panther and kitten and she drives me wild. Today she's wearing black eye make-up, jangling bracelets, and a huge shirt; she looks like she's trying to be all goth and shit, but I can tell she's soft underneath.

"Hey, are you okay?" Bianca asks.

"I'm alright." I shield my eyes to see her better.

"You look funny in those bright colors." She has a crooked smile on her face. She's been visiting me on the highway for the last three days, the guards cutting me some slack and appreciating the view of my girl in skin tight jeans.

"You look funny in those dark colors," I say, thinking I'd rather see her au naturale.

"What are you in for?" she asks, playing dumb.

"Life." I laugh.

"So, they have you out here picking up trash?" She has her left leg crossed behind her right, looking all coy and shit. "Why do you get to sit on your ass while everyone else works?" Damn she's smoking hot.

"The county is worried I'll keel over and die on them. Then they'll have to answer to my mom."

She snorts. "A bitch, huh?"

"Nah, she's a nag, but she's doing what she knows how to do. What are you doing today?"

"Looking for company," she says, turning her Lexus car keys around her fingers. She's all serious and shit. Bianca's been bored waiting for me to get sprung from jail. She had enough credits to graduate last semester, before her "medical condition" landed her in rehab.

"You can get fucking hurt doing things like that. Tomorrow we can be boring together."

"Are you still thinking about taking Dr. Dick out?" she asks.

"Of course."

"Then I have some shopping to do," she says, a smile spreading across her face and her manner all giddy as if I just said we're going to Disneyland.

Chapter 52–Angelina

June, 1992

"Angelina, are you ready for graduation, yet?" the voice smiles across the phone.

"Charlie! It's been so long." I say, cutting up a Golden Delicious and exposing a seed.

"I received your postcard from Greece a while ago."

"I wish you were with me," I say.

"I've been busy applying for scholarships and playing the studious son."

"Did you make off with lots of money?" I ask.

"I did pretty well. I'm sure you did great."

"We had our awards ceremony last week," I say, my teeth sliding on the skin before sinking into the apple's soft center. "I received Student of the Year for all of Seattle Schools from the Rotary Club. It isn't much money, but the plaque's pretty cool. And English Student of the Year, presented by my writing teacher—the greatest honor for me of the night, and a few other scholarships—not much moolah, but oh well." My self-esteem has been largely based on my academic prowess, so I enjoyed the recognition for years of hard work. "How was prom with Summer?" I ask, picking a piece of apple skin out of teeth.

"As lame as any school dance."

"Did you dance?"

"I never dance at those things. We did the usual couple thing-dinner, show up at the dance for pictures, hotel room…"

"You got a hotel room?"

"Yeah. Summer's sister let us use her credit card."

"Oh." I can't help my voice dropping and my heart sinking. My Charlie has done the deed. "I almost got back together with my ex a few weeks ago, but my brain took over."

"Good brain."

"Good brain, sad body," I say.

"Maybe you shouldn't tell me things like this."

"You're the one who got a hotel room. I don't have a boyfriend and just wanted to feel wanted again."

"You've always got your boss, Pepe Le Pew."

"Charlie! Did you really say that? You're hitting below the belt," I say.

"Never on purpose." His tone grows serious. "I'm sorry. You're always wanted."

"I'll forgive you this time." We end the call when his wicked witch of a mom tells Charlie he'd better not be talking on the phone with a girl. I don't tell Charlie that during a weak moment, I thought I saw him on my Greek ferry boat or that I sent Caleb a graduation announcement. Commencement is this Wednesday. Commencement—'the start.' I hope my new start is incredible.

***

Mom went shopping with me for "the" prom dress. It's a floor length black gown with a tight beaded bodice with flouncy things and a slit at the side. I feel guilty; it's so expensive. Mom wanted me to have the dress of my dreams since she shared and scrimped for her high school necessities. Having done enough sit ups for many Love Connection episodes, I looked as good as possible without plastic surgery.

"Tell me about prom," Mom says, as I walk through the door after my weekend away. Yoyo jumps off Dad's lap and runs to see me.

"Troy picked me up for prom and I felt beautiful." Mom was working so she didn't get to see me. Nobody was home to take pictures or capture the moment, but we went to Vanessa's house and had photos taken there.

"What's he like?"

"Funny, sweet, and nice to look at. We held hands when we were walking down the street, but I've known him since elementary school, so no sparks. After the dance, we went to Vanessa's house, where we spent the night in a spare bedroom."

Mom's eyes bug out. "I didn't know any of that was going on."

"We slept on the floor and held hands for a while, but no romance. The next day we went to Vanessa's family's cabin, and got into a water fright." The water smells like sulfur, so it's hard to even think romantic thoughts around someone who smells like rotten eggs.

"Overall a good time?"

"Definitely. And thank you again for buying the most perfect dress ever."

"There's a list of people who called for you," she says, handing over a paper. I look down and see Caleb and Charlie called!

Mom's smiling. "Call him," she says.

I call Charlie, but the boy is never home. Just like eating chocolate chip mint ice cream and saving all of the chocolate chips on the side so I have one great moment of pure pleasure, I dial Caleb's number.

Morgan's brother answers the phone. After I ask for Caleb, I hear "Caleb, your dream girl is on the phone," in the background.

"Angelllliiiiina," he elongates the word. "Where were you when I needed you?"

"When would you need me?" I ask.

"I called on Friday night to see if you'd go to a play with me."

Really? Of course I missed my chance.

"I ended up taking my brother, but he wouldn't give me a good-night kiss."

"What makes you think I would?" I ask laughing.

"I was hoping for another Slurpee kiss."

"That was given during a moment of delirium. I was on my way to hot nude beaches and wasn't thinking straight."

"I wish your brains weren't so sexy, I'd tell you to embrace those crazy feelings."

"Are your flirting with me?"

"I'm trying."

"It's about time," I say.

He chuckles. "I received your graduation invitation; I'd love to go, but I have to work."

"Tsk, tsk. You're going to miss out on the event of a lifetime. I have a bench of geeks coming to watch."

"Oh yeah?"

"Yep, they'll send out some message through their geek radios telling everyone their queen bee's leaving the nest."

Tawnie K. Bailey

"Where do I fit into that equation?"

Are you kidding? Front and center, baby! "You were a little too popular in high school for my group."

"I wasn't voted class officer," he says.

Ah, yes, but when I ran unopposed the next year, a write-in (my prom date, Troy) beat me. "Well then, welcome to Nerd World," I say. "What are you doing this weekend?"

"Hopefully spending time with you. My brother's birthday is this weekend. It's going to be a pretty casual, but my mom will be there and I'd love it if you'd come with me."

I'm *not* working. "Casual as in no prom dress?" Through the various Caleb dating episodes, I've only met Caleb's father, who told me Caleb ate a slug as a little kid.

"Not this time. Maybe I'll be able to send you a secret message on your graduation night with my geek-o-matic head gear," he teases.

"Are you making fun of me? I used to wear head gear, you know."

He laughs. "No, I didn't know. I'm sure you were cute."

"I'm a geek, through and through."

"With a great body and personality, who cares that you're super intelligent."

"I sound like Wonder Woman. Do you think it's my underoos or my long red boots?"

"What are you doing making me think of long red boots and your panties when I have to leave for work? I'll send you something great for your graduation."

"Oh, just send yourself. In fact, why wait? Come on over right now and see me."

"Right now?" he asks.

"Unless you're scared." Thata girl! What do you have to lose?

He laughs. "What happened to my little Angelina?"

"What do you mean?"

"I begged you to let down your walls and tell me how you felt."

"What if you didn't like me as much as I wanted you to?"

"And now?"

"Now you'd be crazy not to like me."

"I've always liked you. It was "Just One of Them Thangs.""

"Are you trying to drive me wild by quoting Keith Sweat songs? I'm not going to take off my panties and swing them over my head at your brother's party even if you quote Keith Sweat, Mister. So get those ideas out of your head."

His deep laughter fills the phone. "Where have you been Angelina Calliah and why have I been too stupid to call?"

"I've been busy working out my kinks," I say, wanting to replay his words.

"I like you and your kinks. I'll call you on Wednesday. Happy Graduation."

I hang up and want to do a happy dance, shake my bootie and race around the house, but I shouldn't get all giddy. Our little bantering doesn't mean he wants to date me or anything. He's a flirt; it's in his nature.

Chapter 53—Aaron

June, 1992

"May I help you?" Steven asks Bianca, ignoring me. I don't blame him. My lusty lady traded in her low cuts for straight lines and heels and is classing up the bleached waiting room.

"I just adopted this little ferret, Frosty, and I want to make sure it's healthy," Bianca says, pulling my albino ferret out of her Gucci bag.

Steven's met me a few times when I came to the clinic to pick Angie up, but I'm incognito. Bianca plucked my eyebrows, shaved my face, squirt some smell pretty shit on me, then trimmed my mop with real scissors, not a blowtorch, making me her little polo boy. If only Mom could see what I do for my girls.

We're called into an exam room and I almost blow my disguise, needing to shift my boys around. Bianca catches my eyes then winks. Frosty is weighed and then sodomized with a thermometer. When Dr. French Fuck's assistant leaves, I look for a good stash site. They don't have an obvious heating duct system, but have those ceiling squares, perfect for a drop. I climb on the chair and lift up a ceiling tile and drop a piece of Pounce. Frosty's been in retirement for about eight months and his nose is twitching back and forth like crazy, wanting the kitty treat prize.

"Don't get all excited," Bianca says, sensing my mood. "This is your last criminal act." She grabs my ass just as Dr. Mike enters the room.

I want to punch the fucker right in the balls and spit on him, but I promised to behave myself.

"Where did you get him from?" Dr. Mike asks.

"A little girl in front of Kmart gave him and another ferret away this morning," Bianca says.

"Have you owned a ferret before?" he asks.

"My boyfriend has," she says, looking back at me and smiling.

"They're a handful," Dr. Mike says.

"So is my boyfriend," Bianca says then laughs.

Frosty doesn't bite his doc during the exam and I don't pound the French fucker's head. I borrow Frosty to scope out the bathroom while Bianca walks to the counter. I push a panel up and lift Frosty to the hole, the dime bag held in his front teeth. Frosty needs to find the kitty treat and drop his baggie. Frosty's deep brown eyes meet me, practically begging for his second Pounce. It's been a pretty slick system for motels. He retrieved the goods and took the money through the heating ducts and other tight ass spaces.

The coke's planted, enough to get the good doc in some big bad DEA trouble if they get a tip. Now it's time to mess with his mind.

Chapter 54–Angelina

June, 1992

This is my curtain call at the clinic and I feel like someone just told me Santa doesn't exist. Dr. Mike and Steven coordinated a surprise going-away party, complete with yummy Napoleons and visitations with some of my favorite clients. When the Gentrys arrived wearing wigs and presenting a stuffed Garfield cat they "found" next to their house, I wanted to rescind my notice and stay here forever. Dr. Mike and the rest of the staff pitched in for a word processor that even has cursive fonts. Its presence in the passenger seat suggests a sophistication I hope to live up to.

Steven left right after the party to pick up his dad and I've been waiting for Dr. Mike to finish the books so I can grab my paycheck and run.

I walk towards his office. His door, like a snake's den is open. Dr. Mike looks up, his black eyebrows reminding me of Gargamel. He points to the other side of his desk and motions for me to enter his office. "Make sure you send me your address for school, let me know you're doing okay."

I smile and enter the doorway while Mike's daughters stare at me from the family photo. "I haven't received my dorm assignment yet, but I'll let you know when I do." Liar.

"Don't forget about us."

"How could I?" I ask.

"I'll need to remember how great you are for your recommendation letter." He stands up, his body closing in on mine. Like a tidal wave about to sweep me away, the blood rushes in my ears, the sweat beading on my face like ocean mist. He wraps his arms around my upper body in a hug then turns to kiss me. I twist just in time for him to miss my lips and instead kiss my cheek. Like a mongoose with lightning speed, his hands are around my stomach and he's trying to kiss me again. My heart pounds as I pull away from him. He holds me tighter and tries to kiss me, pushing me against the desk, my thigh ramming into the side.

Give me a break! You fucking jerk! I push him away again, this time with all of my force. "You are *not* allowed to touch me!" I hiss. I continue to stare into Dr. Mike's eyes and wish that looks could kill.

Dr. Mike's eyes pop out and his head juts out. "I didn't mean to…," he starts.

I'm shaking and don't know how to finish without blowing my recommendation. "I've been devoted to this clinic and you just treated me like trash," I say as tears well up. "Go home to your kids and pray nobody ever touches them like that. Then pray I don't call your wife." I pause, wiping my face. "And when you're asked to write me a recommendation letter, you'd better remember just how great I am."

Chapter 55—Aaron

June, 1992

I've been watching the fucker all day, trying to decide if breaking into his truck when the sun's shooting down and burning my neck is bold or just stupid, the wind just a sliver of relief. Charlie offered to park his VW behind the 4Runner to give me a little bit of privacy since this clinic is on a fairly busy road, but Doctor Dickhead parked around back, between a tree and a dumpster and I don't want the kid to go down the vandalism road. The apple tree's provided a little bit of lunch and cover, but I don't need much time with these foreign cars. I already slipped the slim Jim down the window seal and practiced my craft, these dumb latex gloves worse than a rubber when it comes to tactile pleasure.

I open the door, imagining the Pink Panther theme song, and sneak into the driver's seat, the hot air hitting me like a wall. The grey upholstery has no ass-shaped wear marks and a New Kids on the Block poster sits on the back seat. I have a few choice photos to place in the passenger's visor. I don't know if his wife even sits in this thing, but I thought the pictures of tits I swiped from Randy would do, especially if she's like any chick I know always trying to check her hair. I grab the unwound "personalized" rubbers and stash them. They've been lined with globs of mayonnaise and a dash of tuna juice, well just because. Figure if he doesn't find the one under the driver's mat, or the one in the glove box, or the one under the passenger's seat soon, at least his rig'll smell like rotting fish.

I could siphon his gas, maybe take off the tires, but I'm trying to be a better man. Bianca offered to make a pass at the good doc just for some photo ops, but I don't want my lady to feel like a slut for anybody. I've offered to take down her fake daddy, maybe let one of my friends rough him up, but we're moving away from the shit that brought us together.

Last weekend, Charlie ditched his girlfriend for the night and followed Napoleon home from work. Dude's mom freaked on him when he got home, writing down the mileage on his car and shit. Charlie's taken pictures of the clinic, Dr. Mike's license plate, and the dumpster out back. I gotta hand it to the preppy teacher-pleaser, he's got balls.

Bianca's been calling Misses Dickhead for the last few weeks, hanging up sometimes, clearing her throat sometimes and even leaving a message telling Mike to call her. I expect they'll be changing their number soon, probably ditching the phone book, too. Hoping for just a little marital strife to make things a little more exciting for Dr. Mike, maybe he'll think before he touches.

Now for the piece de resistance...I unfold the note, making sure my glove doesn't smudge the letters, and scatter a couple of Charlie's photos. "Keep your penis in your pants. I know where you live." I leave the note face up on the driver's seat and survey my work. Not too bad, definitely tamer than the Aaron-of-old. I lock the Toyota and walk towards the alleyway. But what if the dude tried to touch Angie?

The slim Jim burns my hand, saying, "He deserves it, Aaron." I take the metal out of the duffel bag and start carving up the back of the 4Runner, the paint peeling off like butter. "I'm married but touch little girls" digs in nice bold letters across the back.

The sky shouts its approval, showering the afternoon with liquid gold, my work here done. I drop the slim Jim back into the duffle bag and walk through the alleyway towards California Avenue, the pebbles kicking up from my Nikes. A million bricks have fallen off my head. I've been a caged lion, pacing, miserable and pissed off for years and now the walls been blown away. I walk faster, no demons chasing me, and feel the ground push up against my feet. I haven't felt my toes since my sugars choked off the capillaries and left me with two dull flappers, but I can feel my toes now and I start to jog. I'm free.

***

The door jingles, warning the owners a former thug has entered. The place smells like a cross between blue-haired old women and Mom's White Shoulders.

"Are you looking for anything in particular?" the shop keeper asks, trimming a stem.

"Yeah. I want something to make some girls feel special." I say, not knowing anything about flowers.

"Girls, huh?" she asks, looking up at me quickly. "You're a good looking kid. Don't break their hearts."

The blowtorch and haircut's paid off. "My sister and my girlfriend are graduating."

"That's a big day."

"Yeah, I've been a shit to my sister and I want her to know I'm proud of her." Fuck. Why did I just swear? You can cut the hair and stick me in expensive clothes and I'm still an unimpressive asshole.

"Do you know what flowers she likes?"

I think about Dr. Mike's flowers. "I want something exotic for both of them, they're pretty amazing women."

The shopkeeper smiles warmly. "How about these Stargazer Lillies?" she asks pointing me to some big and bright flowers.

"My sister would love the colors."

She then carries over a combination of purple and white curled and elegant flowers, reminding me Bianca missed her prom.

"These are Calla Lillies."

"Perfect. Can you wrap them up?"

She wraps each of the bouquets in different layers of paper. I can't wait to see my ladies. Angie doesn't know I'm seeing Bianca. We've decided to surprise little sis after her graduation tonight. Then we're off to meet Bianca's dad who's flown in from Europe. He gave her the credit card telling her she'd better not wear her "freak" clothes. He wants to talk about Bianca's future. Bianca applied to college before her free fall from grace. Maybe Bianca's cut off, maybe he's looked into my past and wants me gone. I don't know. All I can say is that the girl is amazing. She makes me want to remember everything I used to want to forget.

"Thanks," I say, paying the lady.

I'm king of the universe, the sun smiling down on me while the wind applauses. I'm six months clean, dating a beautiful lady, and I just made sure women everywhere will have a little less to worry about from a certain French Fuck.

***

Tawnie K. Bailey

"I'm glad you're home, Aaron. Are you riding with us to Angie's graduation?" Mom asks as soon as my foot enters the house.

"Nah. I'll meet you there," I say, dropping the duffle bag with flowers on the floor and opening the fridge. Not much to raid. I grab the milk and take a swig, the cool liquid my beer substitute.

"What were you up to?

I wait, my mouth too full to answer, then belch. "Taking care of some business."

She walks into the kitchen. "Don't drink out of the gallon! Are you twelve?"

"I didn't dirty up any dishes."

"You haven't been up to the reservoir or anything have you?"

"Smell my breath. Look at my eyes. I'm clean, Mom. I'll piss in a cup if you want to." I grab the duffle bag, pissed Mom's giving me the third degree.

"Have you checked your glucose lately?"

Shit. No wonder I'm feeling all freaky. I've been checking my sugars every two hours for the last few months, eating almonds and dates when the sugars are too low, injecting a shorter-acting insulin when they're high. And I've been gone all afternoon, not even feeding the beast.

I dial Bianca's number. "Hey, Babe. Are you all dolled up for our reveal tonight?"

"Maybe. Did you enjoy your outing?" she asks.

"Immensely. Poor dude's gonna get egged on the way to the body shop."

"Body shop?"

"I carved a little note on the back of his Toyota warning others he likes to touch little girls."

"His wife will probably see it before then."

"You think he'll drive it home first?"

"I called her a few minutes ago and told her I've been having an affair with her hubby since I met him at the New Moon. Told her he was crying about her cancer and needed support because he couldn't divorce her until her treatment was finished."

I forgot about the staff meeting date night. Charlie must have taken notes whenever Angie called, cuz he gave us some detailed accounts of the shit Dr. Mike said. "Kind of sucks to mess with a woman who has cancer."

"Sucks more to have a shitty husband while you have cancer," she says. "Told her we did a little coke before our dates and that he stashed it in the ceiling."

"Shit, girl. Remind me to never stop loving you."

Bianca laughs. "So you love me, huh?"

"More than cockroaches love food."

Bianca laughs. "Are you reciting wedding vows?"

"Nah, Babe. I love you like nothing in this world. Now would you get your cute fanny over here?"

"I'm on my way," she says then hangs up.

I check my levels, my fingers numb to the pain. The "50" reading so different from the too-high-to-read levels I courted just months ago.

"You okay?" Mom asks, looking up while sorting through the mail on the counter.

"I need a little peanut butter or something," I say. "Where's Angie?"

"She's getting ready with Morgan and Vanessa."

Huh. Angie doesn't usually have friends over but I do recognize her fuck-me music.

"You have some mail," Mom says, plopping it down in front of me. Washington State Board for Community and Technical Colleges wrote me a letter. I wonder if they're going to give me a scholarship. I open the mail, expecting some dumbass to say I've qualified to apply for a grant to their college. Mom says Angie gets those offers daily. Maybe the prison informed them that I took some classes.

I unfold the letter.

June 1, 1992
Dear Mr. Aaron Hugley,
It is with great pride that I inform you of that you passed all five tests needed to earn your GED.

Tawnie K. Bailey

"What the fuck?" I look around for the devil laughing his ass off while I believe his joke.

"What is it?" Mom asks, grabbing the paper. Her eyes bulge like she's just found out she's preggo. "Garrett, get in here!" Mom screams.

The lazy-boy footrest slams down and Dad rushes in, his super-power-laser eyes just slits burning me to the ground.

"Look!" Mom says, tears streaming down her face.

Dad pulls the paper from her shaking hands. He looks up, his face as emotional as a Mr. Yuk sticker. The low rumble of his chuckle begins, and his smile causes the cigarette-lined skin to soften. "Good job, kid," He says, slapping my arm. Then, the brute pulls me in and wraps his arms around me, his rumble turning into a full deep laugh. "I'm proud of you. Maybe you should've gone shopping with Sissy for a graduation dress."

I pull away. "My new duds aren't good enough for you?" I say looking at the current Bianca-required wear for meeting her dad.

"You look unbelievable. We're so proud of you!" Mom says, hugging me.

"I'll have to put off retiring if I have to pay for two college kids," Dad says.

"Don't tell Angie, yet. Let this be her day," I say, spotting Bianca's Lexus in the driveway. I wave and pull Angelina's flowers out of the duffle bag. "Will you give this to her? I'm going to head out and see my lady."

"Why don't you have her come in so we can meet her?" Mom asks, looking at the window.

"You can meet her at the arena. I'm gonna run," I say, kissing my mom's cheek and walking out of the door, my footsteps stronger than I can ever remember.

I open Bianca's door, her face as beautiful as the Systine Chapel, so many nuances of light and intellect.

"You look happy," she says, leaning over to kiss me.

"If you bought me a '68 Chevelle all tricked out and shiny, it wouldn't compare to how I feel right now." I say, rubbing my finger on the side of her face.

"You choosing happiness?" she asks.

"She chose me," I say, clicking the seatbelt.

Chapter 56—Angelina

June, 1992

Nordstrom met Mom's credit card earlier this week for my Senior Brunch halter dress. It has a tight bodice and straps that criss-cross in the back and reveals more skin than I'm used to. I've used all of my anti-pick techniques—thimbles, Elmer's glue and gloves and don't have any marks that can't be covered by Clinique.

Today was our last day of classes, also known as Senior Skip Day. We were supposed to have morning classes, then Senior Brunch and rehearsal.

Morgan and I walked over to Seattle High, the last walk through the halls that fostered so many of my dreams. I remember walking into the building with Morgan our freshman year, sensing the possibilities.

I didn't expect to see many Class of 1992 students on Senior Skip Day, but everyone from my honors class showed up. With our dreams close enough to touch, I turned in my last writing assignment.

Swimming without a Suit
An ocean of words, anger, humiliation and tears crashed around me. I was alone among them. The beach offered little solace as the waters' echoes called to me. I tried crossing the haunting depths of emotions several times, but with each attempt, I almost drowned. Coughing, grasping for life, I'd pull myself back onto the beach. As my sides pounded from the struggle, I promised never to leave again.
I couldn't keep the promise, for the companionship we shared kept calling to me. Thanks for pulling me in.

I was so excited and jealous when the year wrapped up for previous classes but now, I don't want it to end. I've been looking forward to leaving for college for as long as I remember and now it hurts to leave the people I depended on to get me through the days.

I receive Prettiest Smile in the senior polls, surprising me. I guess my yuck-mouth and yellow teeth paid off.

When I arrived home, a dozen red roses are waiting for me, freaking me out that Dr. Mike was dumber than I thought.

"I wish I could be there, Slurpees in hand. Love, Caleb." I feel like I could race down the road and up again a million times and still have energy left.

Dad is home and sober, which is the first time I can remember sobriety and Dad merging for an important date. He's even sporting his Old Spice, reserved for special occasions, and a fresh shave, just for me.

Morgan and Vanessa just arrived. We don our graduation gowns and fix our hair together. I can only remember one other time I was this happy—the day Dad and I brought home Yoyo.

Mom takes pictures as our excitement grows then carries in beautiful flowers whose colors match my dress and hands me mail as I'm fixing a curl.

My Dearest Angelina,

Happy Graduation! Congratulations on ending one part of your life and starting a whole new chapter. I'm sorry I cannot attend your celebration as I have my graduation ceremony that same day.

I had a fun time at prom, but knew things were about to end with Summer and me. So, alas, I am a "free agent" for the entire summer and beyond. Maybe someday I'll convince you I am worthy of your affections.

As for me, I plan on sticking around the house and attending college over here. My dad hasn't been feeling well and needs me to help out a bit more for a while. I know, it isn't as exciting as your big adventure, but I hope to change that for our sophomore year. Maybe, I, too, will become a Coug.

I have long believed that you are an incredible writer. Thus, I am enclosing a blank book for you to write your story in. You'll sell a large number of books and captivate the hearts and minds of anyone with a soul.

Thank you for agreeing to go on a blind date with me all of those months ago. You have brought a new and finer dimension to my life.

Lots of Love,
Charlie

***

We arrive at the arena, the bright blue gowns a dancing sea.

I grab Troy, who's already in his line waiting for the Pomp and Circumstance cue. "Are you ready to escort me back from the stage?" I ask.

He whistles and looks me up and down. "You bet, girl. And by the way, you are looking fine. All eyes are going to be on my lucky ass for holding your arm."

"You're quite the stud, yourself. Can you believe we're really here? It feels like I just tore your coat pocket on the playground."

"The one I had to ducktape? You still owe me for that." Just as Vanessa rounds the corner from the lady's bathroom, Troy asks quietly, "Did you like Caleb's surprise?"

My stomach drops, wondering if Troy sent the flowers instead. "You know about it?"

"He's been acting like a little girl, super excited you asked him out."

"Mr. Rico Suave?" Really? Can I just do a happy dance now?

"The one and only. Said your kisses are like magic."

"Oh give me a break." I hit Troy in the arm. Boys don't kiss and tell.

"Seriously. He's digging you."

"Have any advice?" I ask, worried that maybe this little dream won't come true.

"No, baby. He's the one who needs the advice. We're in our prime," Troy says, practicing an exaggerated strut. Then he kisses my cheek. "Just go be Angelina. Happiness will follow you anywhere."

I hug Troy just as our vice principal waves me to the other line.

The music begins and my heart dances. I want to race into to the arena doing cartwheels and backflips. I manage to walk through the doors, my heels barely touching the ground, and see my rag tag family sitting right by the railing. I never expected to have them together and sober on any day, let alone one that symbolizes my beginning. I can't stop smiling.

Author's Note

She Smiles began as a way of thanking my brothers for building a world where our imaginations could shine. That's when a memoir blossomed into fiction and I was able to give my brother a happy ending, kiss more boys than I ever did (and make them say some incredible things), and create a foe that was easy to dislike and take him down. Any semblance to real characters should be looked upon as coincidental (and maybe a compliment) for my intention was only to tell a story.

In a time where teenagers feel even more alone and less understood, I hope Angelina's story will show that vulnerability is universal and can be found in front of every mirror. I'd like to thank my editors Jennifer McCord, Gabriela Lessa, and Becky Levine. I'd like to thank Kristin Contino, friend and author of *The Cameo* whose editing skills and insight helped with the most difficult revisions. Thank you to Kristen Marshall for reading the raw version and still encouraging me to continue. To my niece, Alyssa Bailey, who surrendered her beach vacation to fall into the world of Angelina. Thank you to my husband, Jeff, for loving me like no other and for supporting all my dreams. And finally, to my daughters Sydney and Lyla, who have filled in all my 'empty spaces.' I have been blessed beyond reason.

Made in the USA
Charleston, SC
16 March 2013